"Perhaps your memories are fading, but even the youngest witch knows of Bram's Oath and the hiding of the Book of Origins," said Dame Mala slowly, her eyes glittering. "It was said that Astaroth himself coveted the book, that he had devoted long study to acquiring the secrets that would permit him to use it. Bram took the perilous thing and hid it beyond the Demon's reach."

"That's impossible," scoffed Miss Kraken. "That book was destroyed thousands of years ago."

"It was not destroyed," whispered the witch. "Over five hundred years ago, the witches took it from its resting place and left a false relic in its stead. Word of the ruse, however, seeped out into the world and our treasure eventually attracted interested parties. Astaroth's messengers sought us in the mountains; great rewards were promised should we surrender the book. We considered their offers, but Bram came, too, and it was his proposal that we accepted."

"And what was Bram's offer?" asked Ms. Richter.

The witch met Ms. Richter's gaze and narrowed her eyes.

"That any child of your people blessed by the Old Magic should be surrendered to the care and keeping of the witches. Two such children sit here before me and yet I claim only the young Sorcerer, David Menlo."

THE TAPESTRY · BOOK 2

THE SECOND SIEGE

WRITTEN AND ILLUSTRATED BY

HENRY H. NEFF

A YEARLING BOOK

Grateful acknowledgment is made to the following for permission to reprint previously published material:
"You Can't Be Mine (And Someone Else's, Too)." Words and Music by J. C. Johnson and Chick Webb. © 1938. U.S. Rights Administered by the Songwriters Guild of America. All Rights Reserved. Used by Permission of the Songwriters Guild of America. Exclusive Worldwide Print Rights Administered by Alfred Publishing Co., Inc. All Rights Reserved. Used by Permission of Alfred Publishing Co., Inc.

Yearling and the jumping horse design are registered trademarks of Random House, Inc.

Visit us on the Web! randomhouse.com/kids

Educators and librarians, for a variety of teaching tools, visit us at RHTeachersLibrarians.com

The Library of Congress has cataloged the hardcover edition of this work as follows:
Neff, Henry H.
The second siege / written and illustrated by Henry H. Neff.
p. cm. — (Tapestry ; bk. 2)
Summary: Twelve-year-old Max and his allies risk much as they seek to acquire the Book of Origins, an artifact of unimaginable power, in hopes of halting the ancient evil that is bringing the world to its knees.
ISBN 978-0-375-83896-5 (trade) — ISBN 978-0-375-93896-2 (lib. bdg.) — ISBN 978-0-375-89236-3 (ebook)
[1. Magic—Fiction. 2. Demonology—Fiction. 3. Books and reading—Fiction. 4. Witches—Fiction. 5. Schools—Fiction.] I. Title.
PZ7.N388Sec 2008 [Fic]—dc22 2007050658

ISBN 978-0-375-83897-2 (pbk.)

Printed in the United States of America

10 9 8 7 6 5 4

First Yearling Edition

In memory of
David Peter Gogolak
1971–2008

CONTENTS

THE
SECOND SIEGE

ROWAN ACADEMY

~ 1 ~
THE WITCH

Deep within a tangled corner of Rowan's Sanctuary, Max McDaniels crouched beneath a canopy of sagging pines. It had been ten minutes since he had spied a dark shape slinking among the gray foothills far below, and Max knew his pursuer would now be close. He unsheathed his knife, using the blade's coat of phosphoroil to study the crude map he'd scrawled before setting out. The target was still far away. At this rate, he would never make it—this opponent was much faster than the others.

Shaking off the unpleasant realities, Max concentrated instead on the illusion he had created. The phantasm was a perfect replica of Max, down to its wavy black hair and the sharp, dark features that peered cautiously from a high perch in a nearby tree. He had taken care to mark the surrounding terrain with subtle signs of passage, knowing that a trained eye would spot them.

The shrill cry of a bird shattered the pre-dawn stillness.

Something was coming.

Max's pulse quickened. He scanned the switchback below for any sign of his pursuer, but there was only the smell of damp earth and the low sigh of the wind as it blew tatters of mist across the mountain.

While the sky brightened to a thin wash of blue, Max watched and waited, still as a stone among the roots and nettles. Just when he had decided to abandon his position, a flicker of motion caught his eye.

One of the trees was creeping up the mountainside.

At least he had thought the shape was a tree—one of several bent and broken saplings clinging precariously to the slope's dry soil. Slowly, however, the silhouette straightened and began to thread its way up through the sparse wood. It crept toward Max's double, as dark and shrouded as a specter. When the figure was some twenty feet away, Max realized why he had been unable to shake the pursuer.

It was Cooper.

The Agent's scarred and ruined face looked like a fractured mask of weathered bone. His pale skin was camouflaged with dirt; his telltale shoots of blond hair were tucked beneath a black skullcap. Reaching the base of the tree on which Max's double was perched, he drew a thin knife from a sheath on his forearm. Its blade gleamed with phosphoroil.

Cooper began climbing the tree with the fluid ease of a spider.

While the Agent climbed, Max's pupils slowly dilated.

Terrible energies filled his wiry form, making his fingers twitch and tremble.

Max sprang from his hiding place.

Cooper's head cocked at the sound as Max hurtled toward him with his knife.

Max's weapon struck home, but instead of meeting flesh and bone, it passed through the figure to thud against the tree in a spray of bark. Cooper's conjured decoy dissolved in a billow of black smoke and Max realized he'd been duped.

Max whipped his head around and spied the real Cooper darting out from a nearby thicket. The Agent closed the distance in five long strides. Shifting his knife to his left hand, Max swung himself up into the tree as Cooper's blade whistled past his ribs.

Cooper seized Max's wrist in a grip of iron. "You're caught," he hissed.

With a terrible wrench, Max pulled himself free and sliced his own knife across Cooper's shoulder, leaving a bright line of phosphoroil on the black fabric. Cooper gave a grunt of surprise. Slashing the Agent again, Max leapt clear of the tree.

In one fluid movement, Max landed and bolted up the path, veering right at the fork and dashing up the steep trail he had marked on the map. Cooper trotted after him, apparently unconcerned that Max was increasing his lead with a burst of Amplified speed. Ignoring Cooper for the moment, Max focused his attention on the coppery summit as he raced up the mountain, climbing steadily above the timberline.

It was ten minutes of hard running before Max spied a small white pennant fluttering from a distant peak of jagged rock. He fixed its position in his memory and grinned in spite of himself. Another ten minutes at this pace and he would be victorious.

As he ran on, however, his breathing was reduced to shallow

gasps and then to agonizing, frantic swallows as the air became
unbearably thin. A quick glance behind revealed that Cooper
had closed to a hundred yards and was running as evenly as ever.
Max spat on the path and increased his pace, coughing as he
climbed.

The pennant was tantalizingly close, but the pain and dizziness became overwhelming. Tiny motes of light swam before
Max's eyes; his mouth felt as if it were full of hot sand. Stumbling over a rock, he spilled onto the ground, scraping his knee
and dropping his knife. He scrambled to his feet just as a blurred
shape came into view.

Cooper stood ten feet away, his sturdy black boot planted
squarely on the hilt of Max's knife.

The Agent's eyes were locked on Max. His chest rose and
fell in long, slow breaths as he flicked a cold glance at the red
patch on Max's uniform. The patch was a target, positioned directly over Max's heart. A successful strike there signified a kill
and would bring the exercise to an abrupt finish.

"Do you submit?" came Cooper's clipped Cockney accent.

Max paused a moment, crouched in a defensive posture
while he considered Cooper's offer.

The very instant Max made his decision, the Agent reacted
so swiftly, it was as though he had read Max's mind. Before Max
had even moved, Cooper flicked his wrist and sent the thin
black knife darting toward the patch on Max's chest.

The knife's flight was straight, swift, and unerring. In a blur,
Max batted the weapon aside, registering a sting of pain as its
blunted edge sliced his palm. Leaping forward, Max caught
Cooper with a sharp kick to the knee that forced the tall man
backward. Max extended his fingers and his knife flew obedi-
ently into his hand. He pressed the attack in a blinding array of
subtle feints and blurred strikes.

Rage churned within Max. *How dare they send Cooper!* Cooper was not another student; he was a solitary killer who hunted the Enemy at the behest of his superiors. Today, he'd been sent to hunt Max—a move undoubtedly calculated to humble Max after a string of easy victories. Max pressed his attack at a wild, reckless pace. He would take the Agent's patch as a trophy and pluck the pennant at his leisure.

Unlike Max's previous opponents, however, Cooper was not cowed by Max's uncanny speed and aggressiveness. The Agent had overcome his initial surprise and recovered his knife. The two now danced back and forth, Cooper a disorienting mirage of steel and smoke as he began to gather a cloak of shadows about himself. Soon, Max had to squint to see him at all: an ink-black silhouette against a backdrop of charcoal gray. Under such circumstances, it was difficult to gauge in which hand Cooper held his weapon, or even if a strike was coming. As the darkness deepened, the knife's glowing point became a sort of will-o'-the-wisp, bobbing and treacherous as it disappeared periodically only to stab forward with exquisite speed and accuracy. Max tried to anticipate the attacks, but there was no pattern to them; he was forced to rely wholly on his reflexes.

There was a rush of air behind him. Max parried the thrust, seeking to catch the slim blade in his guard, but Cooper retreated, and Max's counterattack met empty air. He seethed. Again came the knife—three stabs, faster than a boxer's jab at Max's chest. Max knocked Cooper's hand aside and managed a pair of desperate slashes before the Agent slipped beyond his reach.

"Show yourself!" Max spat in frustration.

There was no answer. The darkness swirled about him, thick as pea soup.

Finally, Cooper made a mistake. Max heard a sudden shuffling behind him. Turning, he saw a flash of phosphoroil arcing low and wide toward his midsection. Swift as a serpent, Max stabbed downward and caught the blade within his parrying guard. Cooper stopped a moment—off balance and close enough so that Max could see a tantalizing glimpse of the Agent's target patch. Max grinned and went for the kill.

As he stabbed, however, he felt the Agent's weight shift, and Cooper's hand locked onto his elbow. Using Max's momentum, Cooper sent him flying while the Agent slipped out of harm's reach, as smooth and fluid as an eel. Landing hard on his backside, Max felt a sudden point of pressure on his chest. Cooper's voice dispelled the silence.

"Stop."

The command was delivered with calm, taut finality.

The unnatural darkness subsided into wisps on the wind. By the time it had gone, Max saw that Cooper had backed away to a distance of some twenty feet. For a few quiet moments, he merely watched Max. Apparently satisfied the fight was over, the Agent tapped a small receiver in his ear.

"This is Cooper," he said, his eyes still locked on Max. "I'm with him now. We're finished . . . outcome as expected."

Max watched as Cooper listened patiently to someone on the other end. Then the Agent switched off the receiver and turned to Max.

"We're to head back," he muttered.

Max got to his feet and craned his neck at the white pennant fluttering above them.

"Leave it be," said Cooper. "I've won."

Max followed the man's casual gesture to the red patch on Max's chest. A bright smear of phosphoroil was glowing at the center.

"Are you sure?" asked Max, glowering at the Agent before succumbing to a series of dry, hacking coughs.

Cooper glanced down at his own chest, where a glowing stab of phosphoroil was burned into the blood-red patch like a brand. A dozen phosphorescent scars laced the Agent's chest and arms.

The Agent surveyed Max's handiwork with a grim expression. He tapped his ear receiver.

"Retraction. Outcome unexpected. Both parties eliminated."

Cooper removed the receiver.

"Who was that?" asked Max.

"Director Richter," said Cooper. "We need to be back by noon."

Max groaned, but Cooper would have none of it.

"You should be happy to run," growled the Agent while Max retied his shoes. "Your conditioning is very poor."

"No one else gets chased up here by Agents," muttered Max, feeling drained and snappish.

"You're exhausting your options," replied Cooper stoically. "The older students complained. They refuse to train with you— they think the results are hurting their placement applications. It will be Agents or Mystics from now on."

Max thought of the terrified Sixth Year he had tracked earlier in the week and how the boy had stormed out of the Sanctuary following his rapid defeat.

"I promise I won't get them so fast," Max said with a mischievous grin. "I'll let them do better."

Cooper scowled at him.

"You'll do nothing of the sort. You've plenty to work on. Pleased with your little yellow dot, are you?"

"A little," Max admitted, reddening and studying his shoe tops.

Cooper counted off Max's errors in a flat, clipped staccato.

"I could have approached your hiding place from any direction. A basic birdcall let me get within thirty feet of you. Your decoys were crude and childish—"

"I get it," said Max quietly, feeling his face burn.

"No," said Cooper, stooping to look him squarely in the eye. "You don't. If this had been for real, there'd be no yellow dot on my chest. You'd be crossing the river before you ever even saw me."

Max said nothing.

"One more thing," said Cooper, sheathing his knife and turning his taut, scarecrow face toward Max. "Your self-control is atrocious—your emotions give away your intentions. A well-trained opponent will know what you're planning even before you do. Fatal flaw."

Max scowled and swallowed his response while Cooper turned and broke into a trot.

By the time they reached the Sanctuary clearing, the sun was already high above the eastern dunes. The clearing's tall grasses waved and rippled in the breeze, accented here and there by splashes of wildflowers and jutting pillars of sun-bleached rock. In the distance, dozens of small figures fidgeted nervously in the blue shadows of the Warming Lodge.

"Can we watch the First Years?" asked Max, tugging at his black shirt, which was slick with sweat.

Cooper shook his head just as Nolan, Head of Grounds, led YaYa out onto the porch. Max grinned as the First Years backed away in a sudden stampede. He had been in their shoes just a year ago, terrified at the sight of that rhino-sized shaggy black lioness now settling herself onto the porch.

Nolan waved as they approached.

"Heard you two would be comin' this way. Everybody still in one piece?" he inquired in his mellow drawl, his bright blue eyes twinkling with good humor. He smacked his thick leather gloves, scattering stray bits of hay.

Cooper merely nodded, seemingly oblivious to the stares and whispers of the students.

"My oh my," muttered Nolan, taking a long, curious look at the yellow dot on Cooper's patch. "Everyone, this is Cooper and Max McDaniels. Max is a Second Year—"

Nolan blinked suddenly; his smile faded.

"Now that I think of it," he continued, "some of you have met Max before."

Several gasps of recognition swept through the students. A few had indeed seen Max before; last spring he had rescued them from a terrible fate in the crypt of Marley Augur. Max gave a little wave, anxious now to keep moving.

"Director's waiting," explained Cooper, ushering Max along.

"I know," said Nolan soberly. "Glad you're here for this, Cooper. Don't let her get too close to our boy, eh?"

Cooper nodded but kept them walking briskly away. Max held off on his questions until they closed the Sanctuary's thick, mossy door behind them.

"What's Nolan talking about?" he asked cautiously. "Who isn't supposed to get close to me?"

Cooper's gaze followed the flight of a bright red butterfly while Old Tom chimed eleven.

"A witch," he murmured. "She arrived before dawn."

Mum was decidedly underwhelmed by the prospect of a witch. The squatty, gray-skinned hag gave a dismissive snort when Max told her, thrusting her taloned fingers deep within a turkey to extract its innards with a ferocious heave.

"*That's* what Mum does to witches!" she said impressively, brandishing the organs in her fist and flinging them into a pot.

Bob sighed from a nearby table, where he diced carrots with slow precision.

"The Director thinks this is important," Bob rumbled in his baritone.

"Oh, 'the Director thinks this is important,' " sneered Mum, mocking the huge Russian ogre's accent while seizing the unfortunate turkey. She planted the bird on her head and snapped up a nearby broom, waving it under the ogre's nose. "Is big, strong Bob afraid of witches?" she cackled. "Do they make him want to hide? Do they make him want to *tinkle*?"

Mum began to dance in little circles, the turkey wobbling drunkenly as she twirled the broom like a majorette.

"Tinkle, tinkle, tinkle, tinkle . . ."

Max finished his toast and nodded to his roommate, David Menlo, who stood in the kitchen doorway calmly surveying the scene. Mum sniffed the air and stopped abruptly. She shrieked and spun about to face David in wide-eyed horror. The hag had been terrified of the small blond boy ever since her failed attempt to subdue and eat him the previous Halloween.

"Hi, Mum," said David.

"Hello," mumbled Mum, her crocodile eye darting wildly about the archway above David.

"Mum, you have a turkey on your head."

"Thank you," muttered the hag, removing the battered bird and placing it gingerly on a roasting rack. "Please excuse me—"

Mum bolted for her cupboard, letting the broom clatter to the floor. Squeezing her bulk inside, she slammed the door behind her. A glazed sugar bowl tottered from its shelf and smashed in a spray of shards and sugar on the tiles.

"Sorry," said David, stooping to help Bob sweep up the mess.

"It is not you," whispered the ogre, rolling his eyes. "Mum

has been awful—worse than usual. I think her letters are to blame. She reads them over and over."

The ogre pointed a long, knotted finger at a small stack of airmail letters sitting near Mum's cutting board. Max picked one up and glanced at its blocky printing:

MS. BEA SHROPE
ROWAN ACADEMY
U.S.A.

"Who's Bea Shrope?" asked Max. He wrinkled his nose at the envelope, which smelled of cabbage.

A bloodcurdling shriek sounded from the cupboard. The small yellow door flew open, and Mum rocketed out to snatch the letter from Max's hand and sweep the rest against her bosom.

"Nobody! Bea Shrope is *nobody*! She doesn't exist!" Mum panted, clutching the letters and backing her ample bottom back into the cupboard. *"Go find your witch and stay out of Mum's business!"* she thundered, slamming the door a final time.

"Well, that was fun," said David, "but Cooper's waiting for us. You were supposed to shower, by the way."

"I was hungry," Max protested, his gaze lingering on a plate of crispy bacon. David merely hummed and strolled up the Manse's winding steps.

"What?" said Max, following after his roommate. *"You* stay up half the night with Cooper after you, and with nothing to eat!"

Cooper stood waiting in the foyer. He escorted the two boys to the Manse's top floor, taking an unfamiliar hallway and hurrying them past gilded portraits and a series of African masks until they arrived at a dark door of polished wood.

"The witch is just inside," Cooper said quietly. "She is not permitted within ten feet of you. She's aware of this. I will take the chair closest to her—the two of you are to sit by the Director."

"Cooper," piped up David, "this sounds dangerous. Are you sure we should go in there?"

To Max it appeared that Cooper's hard features softened for just a moment. The Agent knelt down and looked David in the eye.

"It'll be all right," he said with calm assurance. "Nothing will happen to you, eh?"

Cooper patted David on the shoulder before revealing a wavy-bladed knife of rusty, reddish metal. Max had never seen it before. The weapon exuded an unwholesome aura; its discolored blade suggested a particularly loathsome history. Max's instinct was to step away from the knife, but David looked positively green and wobbly.

"It'll be fine, David," whispered Max, steadying his roommate.

David smiled weakly, but he took a second glance at the knife as Cooper slipped it into his sleeve.

"Let's see what the old witch wants," said Cooper, rapping softly on the door.

The door swung inward and Cooper led the boys into a dark, windowless room arched with carved beams and lit only by oil lamps that cast a warm, golden glow over the room's occupants. Director Richter was seated at the head of a granite table engraved with the Rowan seal and set with crystal goblets and a decanter of red wine. Miss Kraken, Rowan's hunched and snappish head of Mystics, sat on her right. Max said hello to them but focused quickly on the strange, wizened thing studying him from the far end of the table.

"Boys," said Ms. Richter, "excuse the low light; it is on

account of our guest, who is more comfortable in such surroundings. I'd like to introduce Dame Mala."

The witch smiled and bowed her head low in greeting. In the dim setting, her skin initially appeared scarred, like Cooper's, but Max soon realized he was looking not at scars but at tattoos. Every visible inch of her body—her face, her ears, the tops of her fingers—was marked with small hieroglyphs and symbols arranged in neat little patterns and shapes before they disappeared into the folds of her plain black robes. Her braided white hair was as thin as corn silk and her sagging face had an air of polite expectancy as she took a small sip of wine. Pale green eyes glanced at Cooper as he claimed the seat next to her, lingering longest on his sleeve. The smile never left her face, however, and her interest returned quickly to Max and David as they took seats alongside Ms. Richter.

"Dame Mala is one of our distant kin from the East," explained Ms. Richter, brushing a stray strand of silver hair from her brow. "It has been several centuries since we've had contact with the witches, but they are old friends and we are honored by their visit."

The witch raised her glass in gratitude.

"Yes," said Ms. Richter, offering a tight smile in return. "You see, students, Dame Mala's arrival this morning was most unexpected. Apparently, during his travels, our own Peter Varga visited the witches to enlist their aid in finding the children who were kidnapped last year. He mentioned the two of you and . . . our guest arrived on our doorstep, to our great surprise and delight. Perhaps now that you are here she will share the broader purpose of her visit."

Dame Mala beamed, revealing small yellowed teeth that had been filed to points. Beads and necklaces of semiprecious stones clicked and clacked as she stood and bowed low before them.

"You are very gracious, Director," she said in a throaty tenor. "And I, in turn, extend greetings on behalf of my sisters to honor our kindred who crossed the sea long ago. It is only fitting that the young should be the sparks to rekindle old friendships and bridge the differences between us. We have waited a long time to see these two."

"Ms. Richter . . . ," whispered Max.

The Director held up a finger to silence him. The witch turned quickly from Ms. Richter to fix her piercing green eyes on Max.

"Which of the Blessed Children is this?" she asked.

"Dame Mala, this is Max McDaniels. He is—"

"The Hound," breathed the witch, widening her eyes and leaning forward. Cooper shifted slightly in his seat. "Forgive me, for only now do my old eyes see the light upon his brow. *Rath dé ort, Cúchulain. Saol fada chugat.*"

Max fidgeted uncomfortably as the witch touched her forehead briefly to the table and took her seat once again. She made a hasty sign before continuing.

"Now that Astaroth walks upon this earth, the great School of Rowan will have dire need of its Hound. To honor our past allegiance, my sisters have instructed me to press only half our rights. The Hound of Rowan may stay with you. The witches demand only the young Sorcerer, so gifted in our arts."

"What in heaven's name *are* you talking about?" interrupted Miss Kraken sharply, glaring at Dame Mala. "Who are the witches to show up on our doorstep and demand anything, much less one of our *students*, for God's sake?"

"Annika," said Ms. Richter with a warning tone.

Miss Kraken bristled to the point of bursting, but swallowed another comment. Dame Mala appeared confused.

"Have I said something that displeases you?" the witch asked, her eyes darting from face to face.

"Dame Mala," said Ms. Richter, "forgive our ignorance, but what exactly are you demanding? Surely you do not mean to leave this school with David Menlo. . . ."

The witch nodded and smiled at David, who gave a funny gurgle and slumped low in his chair.

"What on earth would convince you that we would permit such a thing?" asked Ms. Richter calmly.

"It is our right," said Dame Mala, her smile dissolving into a look of angry indignation.

David was speechless, slumping lower until only his eyes were visible above the table's rim.

"Ms. Richter," hissed Max, "you're not going to send David away with . . . with this witch, are you?"

"Of course not," said Ms. Richter with a sharp glance. "On what basis would the witches possibly make such an absurd claim?"

Dame Mala frowned as she traced the top edge of the Rowan seal with a sharp-nailed finger.

"There is nothing absurd about our claim," said Dame Mala slowly, her eyes glittering, "and we have waited nearly four hundred years to make it. Perhaps your memories are fading, but even the youngest witch knows of Bram's Oath and the hiding of the Book of Origins."

"The Book of Origins," repeated Ms. Richter, appearing to search her memory. "You're referring to the Book of Thoth?"

"Indeed," confirmed the witch. "It was said that Astaroth himself coveted the book, that he had devoted long study to acquiring the secrets that would permit him to use it. Bram took the perilous thing and hid it beyond the Demon's reach."

Ms. Richter frowned and glanced at Miss Kraken.

"That's impossible," scoffed Miss Kraken with a definitive shake of her head. "That book was destroyed thousands of years ago."

"It was *not* destroyed," whispered the witch. "Over five hundred years ago, the witches took it from Prince Neferkaptah's resting place and left a false relic in its stead. We sought in vain to divine its secrets. Word of the ruse, however, seeped out into the world and our treasure eventually attracted interested parties. Astaroth's messengers sought us in the mountains; great rewards were promised should we surrender the book or give information regarding its true whereabouts. We considered their offers—after all, they were generous, and the book had proven beyond our understanding. But Bram came, too, and it was his proposal that we accepted."

Max thought of Elias Bram, the last Ascendant who had fallen during the Siege of Solas, buying time so that a few survivors might escape aboard the *Kestrel*. While Bram was revered at Rowan, something about Dame Mala's tone made Max's spirits sink. He looked at David, whose eyes had taken on the detached, glassy look they often did when he was thinking deeply.

"And what was Bram's offer?" asked Ms. Richter, her voice very soft and serious.

The witch met Ms. Richter's gaze and narrowed her eyes, tapping the table for emphasis.

"That *any* child of your people blessed by the Old Magic should be surrendered to the care and keeping of the witches. Three we may claim and thus it is written. Two such children sit here before me and yet I claim only the young Sorcerer. If I may say, Director, you should be grateful for our generosity. We recognize that you did not strike this accord and that it must grieve you to bid farewell to so bright a pupil. Thus, at this time, we take only one as a token of our respect. . . . I urge you not to make us reconsider."

"Ms. Richter," whispered Max, incredulous at the long pause that followed, "you're not actually considering this, are you? You're not going to let her take David away!"

Ms. Richter glanced sharply at Max before returning her attention to Dame Mala.

"Of course not," she said. "Many proofs would have to be submitted before we would attribute even a grain of truth to this claim, much less honor it. I know nothing of such a pact—do you, Annika?"

"I've come across nothing remotely resembling this in all my years of access to the Archives," said Miss Kraken proudly. "The very idea that Bram would bargain away children is preposterous—it violates everything he stood for! Trading children for books? Nonsense! Where *is* this Book of Origins for which we supposedly mortgaged our future?"

"We do not know," said Dame Mala with cool reserve. "The fate of the book was Bram's concern, not ours. Our concern is payment and the fulfillment of our contract."

"If we refuse?" asked Ms. Richter.

"You will not," replied Dame Mala. "To refuse is to ensure the fall of Rowan. Astaroth is *here,* Director Richter—Rowan's efforts and vigilance failed us all and the very heavens point to the Demon's return. Rowan will need all of her old allies to survive the coming storm. Now is not the time for foolish pride."

Ms. Richter stood and folded her arms.

"I do not think it is foolish pride, Dame Mala, to remind you that the survival of your sisterhood has been secured by the very efforts and vigilance you critique. Through our charity, the witches have been hidden from the cities and machines and are permitted to live with the modern age at bay. These courtesies can be discontinued. Should the witches threaten Rowan or its interests, I can promise an outcome so swift and severe that it will shock even the greatest pessimists among you."

The witch's face darkened. She opened her mouth and shut it again, glancing briefly at Cooper, who sat unmoving and returned her gaze with unflinching calm. A small clock ticked off long seconds. The room became unbearably still; the threat of violence hung suspended in the air.

"It is regrettable that you should speak thus in front of these young ones," said Dame Mala at last, clasping her hands together and exhaling deeply. "I am well aware there are many men and many weapons at your disposal, Director. We do not flatter ourselves that the witches could wage open war with Rowan; indeed, that is the last thing we would wish. It is *you* who speak in threats; I speak only of honor and agreements. Be warned, Director, that to deny our righteous claim is to violate the terms of Bram's Oath and thus bring a curse upon yourselves that would be the ruin of this school and all who dwell here. The pact is bound in Old Magic—signed in Bram's own blood and utterly irrefutable."

"If it's written in Bram's blood, you must have the document," said Ms. Richter coldly. "I wish to see it and whoever truly speaks for the witches. It is not you, Dame Mala—you've merely been sent to deliver a message, and your task is now finished. It's time you returned home."

Dame Mala drained the rest of her wine and rose to her feet.

"You are my hostess and you have asked me to leave. I will go. But my sisters will come, Director, and they will bring all the proofs you require. And when they depart, these Blessed Children—*both* of these children—will go with them."

"Not while I'm Director," said Ms. Richter quietly, motioning for Cooper to escort the old woman out. The witch paused in the doorway; her fearsome visage might have been plucked from the carven masks that lined the hall outside. She gave Ms. Richter a secret, knowing smile.

"Directors are replaceable, Ms. Richter, as your predecessor knows all too well. You should know that Peter Varga is not the only son of Rowan to cross the mountains and seek our aid." She turned to Max and David. "Look for us in one month's time, children. A new home awaits you."

With a parting bow the witch was gone.

~ 2 ~

MILD-MANNERED MR. SIKES

Max and David conversed in quiet voices, seated opposite each other on the lower level of their magnificent room. Beyond the glass-domed ceiling, the sky deepened to indigo, revealing a brilliant field of stars. Periodically, constellations appeared among the heavens, their faint contours composed of slender golden threads that soon faded away. David watched the Great Bear wink out of sight and dipped his head to scribble several notes in a worn leather journal he'd taken to carrying over the summer.

"We won't have to live with the witches," Max concluded, squinting at David's small, practically illegible writing. "Ms. Richter won't permit it—you saw how angry she got."

"I don't think it's her decision to make," said David softly, with a shake of his head. A casual flick of his fingers ignited several candles and an oil lamp. "That witch wasn't lying. I think it's likely they have some sort of legitimate claim."

"So what?" scoffed Max. "You can't just sign away someone's life hundreds of years before they're even born! That's not fair."

David raised an eyebrow and smiled.

"I don't think 'fair' factors into it. The very idea that people should have a say over where and how they live is a fairly new one. Elias Bram must have been desperate to make that deal, though. That Book of Thoth or Origins or whatever it's called must be important—"

A loud, impatient knock sounded at the door.

"Hold that thought," said Max, trudging up the stairs to see who it was. Max's father, Scott McDaniels, stood panting outside, his plump frame leaning against the doorway. Normally cheery and bright-eyed, Mr. McDaniels' round features were now pale and curdling with concern.

"I came as soon as I heard," he croaked, pausing to kiss Max on top of the head before squeezing past into the room. "Been apple picking for tomorrow's desserts. Is David here?"

"Down here, Mr. McDaniels," called David from below.

"Good, good," said Mr. McDaniels, closing the door behind him and ushering Max below to where they joined David at the table. "What is all this baloney about a witch and promises? Ms. Richter told me something, but it all sounded like gobbledygook. She was joking, right?"

"She's not joking, Dad," said Max. "The witch said that there was some agreement made a long time ago—that David and I are supposed to go live with them."

"That can't be right," said Mr. McDaniels, worrying away his fingernails. "Ms. Richter said they live far away—in the

Himalayas or someplace! How would those witches even know who you are, much less where to find you?"

Max winced.

"They heard about us from Peter—he visited them last year and mentioned us. I think the fact that he was in contact with them may be why he was in trouble to begin with."

"*Peter's* responsible?" asked Mr. McDaniels. Originally known to Max as "Ronin," Peter Varga was an outcast Agent who had rescued Max on more than one occasion. His spine broken by Marley Augur's hideous hammer, Peter had been rehabilitating at Rowan and was often kept company by Mr. McDaniels, who pushed him along in a wheelchair so he could look out over the Atlantic.

"Well," said Max quickly, "I don't know if he's *responsible*. I mean, he didn't make the oath."

"But he's the reason that witch knew to come here and look for you!" fumed Max's father, his initial shock quickly turning to anger.

"Don't get upset, Mr. McDaniels," said David meekly. "If Ms. Richter didn't know about Bram's Oath, I think it's safe to say Peter didn't, either. Besides, Max isn't going to have to go anywhere."

"He's not?" asked Mr. McDaniels, the purple draining from his face. "How do you know?"

"Because I'll be difficult," said David simply. "If someone has to go, it'll be me. If they want me to cooperate, they'll have to let Max stay here."

Mr. McDaniels blinked twice and took a long, quivering breath while he fumbled through his apron's pocket for a handkerchief.

"David," said Max, dumbfounded by his roommate's offer, "there's no way—"

Max was drowned out by an enormous honk as Mr. McDaniels blew his nose. David was suddenly swept up and crushed against Mr. McDaniels's padded side, his pale face disappearing into an enormous tartan armpit.

"David Menlo," cried Mr. McDaniels, rocking the small boy back and forth, "I don't know what to say! That's so very good of you—ridiculous, but I'll never forget it as long as I live!"

"Grrrglpppp!" came David's muffled voice.

"Say again?" asked Mr. McDaniels, wiping his round, teary cheeks with the back of his hand.

"Dad, I don't think he can breathe," said Max, pointing to David's hand, which flopped about like a fish in a vain attempt to free his head.

"Oh," said Mr. McDaniels, releasing David at once. "Sorry."

"That's okay," said David with a weak laugh. "Just a *little* tight."

"Nobody's going off alone to live with any witches," said Mr. McDaniels, gripping both boys fiercely by the shoulder. "The three of us are a package deal—it's all or none, or else there'll be hell to pay!"

"I wonder what it'd be like living with the witches," mused Max in an effort to lighten the mood. He went to his bookcase to retrieve his *Rowan Compendium of Known Enemies*. "Probably lots of newts and black cats and gingerbread houses. Bet they don't have anything like the Course—Richter said they're afraid of machines."

He scrolled through the index but failed to find anything between *werewolf* and *wraith*.

"You won't find them in there," said David. "I don't think Rowan technically classifies the witches as enemies—just something to be avoided. And I don't think they're like witches from fairy tales. Did you see those markings on her face?"

"You should have seen her, Dad," Max said as he put the book away. "She looked like a headhunter!"

"Those markings were spells," said David, ignoring Max's sarcasm. "Weird spells—primitive—tattooed right into her skin. They're some kind of protection. . . . I think the witches are frightened of something."

Just then someone else rapped at the door, the knock as loud and impatient as before.

"Open the bleedin' door, you bogtrotters! I'm back for me edgemacation!" bellowed a loud voice with a thick Irish accent.

Max grinned and bounded away up the stairs.

There, in the hallway, stood Connor Lynch, Max and David's best friend. Fresh from Dublin, Connor was sporting a wild crown of chestnut curls that framed a pink-cheeked face so flush with good humor he might have been the Ghost of Christmas Present. He handed Max a battered set of golf clubs.

"Look after these like a good lad, eh?" he said, clapping Max on the shoulder as he dragged his enormous duffel in behind him.

"Hey, Connor," said Max, closing the door while Connor hurried downstairs to hurl hellos at David and Mr. McDaniels. "Don't you want to drop your stuff in your room?"

"Nah," called up Connor, settling into one of the lower level's cozy nooks and rummaging through his duffel like a badger. "My fine roommates are already gushing about how they spent their summer vacations milking yaks or building latrines or knitting booties for underprivileged kittens. Insufferable weenies," he concluded with a sad shake of his head. "I was hoping to crash here for a bit until—"

More knocks sounded at the door. Max heard giggling outside.

"Until the girls get here!" crowed Connor, retrieving a shiny bag from his duffel and tossing it to Mr. McDaniels, who caught it with a snort of pleasant surprise. David looked unsettled by the sudden prospect of more visitors, much less girls. He sniffed his armpit before quickly changing shirts behind the door of his armoire.

Max stood aside as Cynthia Gilley, Sarah Amankwe, and Lucia Cavallo streamed into the room in a swarming chorus of greetings and hugs. Within minutes, the six classmates and Mr. McDaniels were huddled downstairs and enjoying an impromptu party fueled by Connor's bags of Bedford Bros. Colossal Cookies, a new product introduced by one of Mr. McDaniels's former clients.

"Whatcha think?" Connor asked Mr. McDaniels as Max's father closed his eyes and sampled a thick, ridged cookie as if it were a canapé. "I saw 'em at the airport and thought of you."

Mr. McDaniels signaled for a moment of quiet while he thoughtfully chewed the cookie.

"That's a quality product," he said at length, giving the bag a brisk nod of approval. "Two jabs of light and flaky with an uppercut of chocolate. I should give the head honchos over there a call—suggest a slogan or two."

"Dad," said Max, shaking his head at his obsessively loyal father. "They're not your client anymore. Those cookies could taste like mothballs and you'd say they were great."

"Oh no," said Mr. McDaniels, smiling as he patted his enormous stomach. "You can lie to a man's face, but you can't lie to his belly, son. The belly *knows*. Remember that."

"Is that supposed to be some pearl of wisdom?" asked Max, burying his head as the others burst into laughter. Mr. McDaniels just gave a contented smile and passed along the bag.

"Enough of cookies!" snapped Lucia, a no-nonsense Italian beauty whose flashing eyes and indifference to Connor's charms had left the Irish boy smitten. "Out with it, you two!" she said, snapping her fingers at Max and David. "What is happening here?"

"What Lucia *means*," said Cynthia, swatting away Lucia's hand as she snatched up another cookie, "is that since the two of you were here over the summer, you must know what's going on." The ample-bottomed English girl bit into her cookie and fixed David with an expectant, maternal stare.

"With what?" asked David.

"Oh, like the fact that the charming little gatehouse has been replaced with a fortress," said Sarah, looking regal and splendid in a scarlet wrap from her native Nigeria.

"Whose walls are fifty feet high," said Lucia.

"And covered with thorns," added Cynthia.

"And crawling with Agents," finished Sarah.

"Mystics, too," chimed in Connor. "I saw them peering down at me from the windows. Two blinky old codgers! Gave me the creeps . . ."

"David knows more about it," said Max. "He's been helping Ms. Richter."

"Well, they haven't let me help with the design," said David, sounding a bit peeved. "They just use me for the grunt work— raising the walls and stuff."

"*You* raised the walls?" asked Sarah, wide-eyed. "They must be twenty feet thick!"

David nodded and nibbled a cookie. Ever since his arrival at Rowan, Max's roommate had exhibited a freakishly intuitive grasp of Mystics.

"Now that Astaroth's free, Ms. Richter thinks we need stronger defenses. Of all the banished demons, Astaroth was re-puted to have been the greatest scholar and Sorcerer," said David with a shrug.

"But isn't Rowan already hidden away from outsiders?" asked Cynthia, sitting up with a look of real concern. "Even if he's free, no outsider—not even Astaroth—should be able to find us here. Isn't that right?"

"That's the way it's *supposed* to work," said David, frowning, "but I have my doubts."

"What do you mean?" asked Max, glancing at Sarah, who looked frightened.

"How did that witch find Rowan?" asked David, his pale eyes boring into Max. "Of course Ms. Richter was shocked by what Dame Mala wanted, but couldn't you tell how surprised she was that a witch was even here?"

"Maybe they should let you run this place, David," said Scott McDaniels with a grunt as he waved off the circling bag. "You'd have my vote."

"Please don't even joke about that, Mr. McDaniels," said David quietly, reaching for another cookie. "I'm afraid Rowan has another traitor, or else we're not as hidden as we'd like to think."

Connor raised his hand in sarcastic schoolboy fashion.

"And just who are these witches?" he asked.

"That's my cue," said Mr. McDaniels, brushing crumbs from his hands and pushing back from his chair. "I'll let you kids catch up on all that. I've had enough of witches for one day. Besides, I told Bob I'd set up the ol' Beefmeister 2000 in the kitchen. Got quite a feast in store for tomorrow—lots of grilled meats on the menu. Save your appetites!"

The group said good-bye to Mr. McDaniels, who lumbered up the stairs like a sleepy bear. Max stretched and flicked on the lights, transforming the dark room into a two-tiered circle of golden wood crowned now by a sky of midnight blue. While the constellations twinkled above, Max and David shared the tale of

Dame Mala's visit, interrupted periodically by Connor's incredulous questions until he was finally shushed by Lucia. When Max described Dame Mala's parting promise that the witches would return, Lucia crumpled the empty bag of cookies and uttered a string of what sounded to be some choice Italian phrases.

"Do you actually think you'd have to go away?" asked Sarah, looking hard at Max.

"David thinks there's probably something to their claim," said Max, avoiding her gaze and shrugging. "It's hard to believe it could happen, though."

"There's no way, mate," said Connor. "That's like—that's like *slavery*! Things like that can't happen anymore."

"We'll see," said David, glancing at Max. "There's no point in anybody worrying about it right now, though. Please don't tell everyone—they think I'm weird enough."

"Done," said Connor, "but I heard some Sixth Years gossiping in the foyer about how they saw Cooper marching some woman out the gate. That must have been your witch, eh?"

Max nodded.

"They're bound to blabber," said Connor. "But we can take care of that if you like." He grinned and burrowed in his duffel once again, retrieving a slim book of red leather and a small bag of black felt. He placed them on the table with a triumphant gleam in his eye.

"What's that?" asked Cynthia, hovering close to peer at the book's unmarked cover.

"*That,* Cynthia my dear, is how we're going to keep Max and David's secret safe!" crowed Connor, untying the felt bag's drawstring and spilling six small stones onto the table. "It's also why I had my best summer ever—don't know how I ever got along without it!"

"What's it do?" asked Max, pulling his seat closer.

"What *doesn't* it do is the real question," cackled Connor, arranging the stones in a rough circle. Each of the stones had a slightly different shape and color, and Connor appeared very particular about which went where. "This one's the best by far," he said eagerly, motioning them closer as he opened the book and thumbed through several pages.

> When chores do stack to sap my strength
> And wee small wants do plague my heart,
> I call upon a friend so true, a friend who grants
>   my soul's delight.
> Upon this eve I summon you, the mild-mannered
>   Mr. Sikes.

The stones began to glow, flickering to life as reluctantly as an old lightbulb. There was the distant sound of a clock chime and a sudden flash of light. A moment later, Max found himself blinking at an elfin creature no taller than a candle.

The tiny being stood within the circle of stones, dressed neatly in a banker's suit and radiating an air of polite reserve. It had curling silver hair, bluish skin, an imposing Roman nose, and the attentive yellow eyes of a cat. Pivoting on a well-polished shoe, it took a long look at each of them. When its gaze reached Connor, the creature bowed low and spoke in a voice as smooth and flowing as a ribbon of silk.

"With proper stones and incantations Master Lynch does call and Mr. Sikes does answer. What ails the young gentleman? How may Mr. Sikes be of service?"

Max peered closer as the little figure held its pose like an obedient doll. Glancing at David, Max saw his roommate lean back, his expression wary.

"Nice to see you, Mr. Sikes," said Connor conversationally.

"I've got a little favor to ask, but first I'd like you to meet my friends and, er, maybe whip up a round of lemonades?"

"Mr. Sikes is pleased to meet the master's friends," said the creature, clasping its hands and bowing low to Cynthia, who nodded back in slack-jawed astonishment. "Iced lemonades may be found before you."

Max looked down and saw a tall glass of lemonade resting on a coaster at his right hand.

"Bottoms up!" said Connor, raising his glass in a cheerful toast.

"Stop!" exclaimed David, reaching for Connor's hand and almost knocking the glass onto the table. "Nobody touch those drinks."

"Easy, Davie," said Connor. "It's all right! Mr. Sikes has brought me loads of lemonades before, isn't that right?"

"The master does enjoy his lemonade," said the little being, smoothing his pocket square.

David ignored Connor and looked skeptically at the creature.

"Who are you, Mr. Sikes?" asked David, his voice quiet and serious.

"I am the summoned servant of Master Lynch," said the creature simply.

"*What* are you, Mr. Sikes?" asked Max.

"Max," said Connor, shooting an angry glance, "don't be rude!"

"Mr. Sikes takes no offense," said the creature smoothly. "Mr. Sikes is but a humble imp and begs pardon if he has insulted Master Lynch's friend."

"See?" said Connor. "He's an imp. Happy, Max?"

Max shrugged, but David clucked his tongue impatiently and looked at Connor.

"Do you know what an imp is?" he asked.

"Yes, I do," said Connor proudly. "He's a capital little fellow who comes when you call and gets what you ask. Why are you being such a pain? I called Mr. Sikes for you guys and now you've got the cheek to talk to me like I'm three years old! And— What are you doing now?"

"Mr. Sikes knows," said David calmly, using his finger to trace a faintly shimmering circle of light around the stones. "This circle will ensure Mr. Sikes stays right where he is. An imp is a *demon*, Connor."

Connor scoffed in disbelief and looked to Max and the girls for support. Mr. Sikes smiled and shrugged apologetically.

"The young man speaks the truth, I'm sorry to say. Technically, imps *are* demons."

"Really?" asked Connor, wrinkling his nose and leaning close to peer at Mr. Sikes, who bore the inspection with a patient smile.

"Yes, it's true," said Mr. Sikes, "but I have to differ with the young gentleman, who seems to believe I pose some sort of danger. There are many kinds of demons, my friends, and we are just as varied in our types and temperaments as humans. Do monstrous and horrible demons exist? Of course. Are there also monstrous and horrible humans? I daresay yes again. Would you recoil from a garden lizard simply because its distant cousin is the crocodile? Some demons exist to destroy; Mr. Sikes exists to serve."

"Those are good points," said Connor, nodding. "Davie, even you have to admit that those are some very good points the little guy's making."

David nodded, but his frown remained.

"Is that your only shape?" asked David.

"I beg pardon?" asked the imp.

"Can the harmless lizard *become* a crocodile? I've read that imps are shape-shifters."

"Of course I can take alternative forms," said Mr. Sikes, "but I hardly think the two available to me are cause for alarm."

"What are they?" asked Lucia, scooting forward with interest.

Mr. Sikes smiled at her and cleared his throat.

"For my first act, I give you . . . the terrifying field mouse!"

With a snap of his fingers, there was an audible pop and Mr. Sikes disappeared, replaced by a gray mouse with a pink tail that poked its nose along the edges of David's glowing perimeter. The mouse stood on its hind legs to look at them, its whiskers aquiver. A moment later there was another pop and the mouse was transformed into a small gypsy moth, hovering on a pair of tiny wings. The moth fluttered up, rising in tight little spirals.

Zbbbt!

A sudden jolt of blue electricity zapped the moth, making Max jump. The moth fell like a stone to writhe on the tabletop.

"Oh!" cried Cynthia. "He's hurt!"

"He hit the barrier," said David, folding his arms. "That's why it's there."

"That's uncalled for, David," fumed Connor. "He'd better be okay."

Max saw Lucia glare at David; even Sarah shot David a glance before returning to the moth with a concerned expression. Reduced to one functioning wing, the moth now fluttered about in a shaky little circle. Max watched the moth carefully; Mr. Sikes seemed very clever and Max knew it might just be a ploy to gain their sympathy. Still, he had to admit that the tip of its wing was badly singed and the moth's flutters seemed sporadic and distressed.

Pop!

Mr. Sikes reappeared, his face contorted in anguish as he clutched his arm. Against his better judgment, Max felt a pang of compassion for the small creature.

"I'm so sorry," cried Lucia.

"Are you hurt?" asked Sarah, reaching her hand out to the little imp. Mr. Sikes reached out his left arm to take her hand, but then he glanced at the nearby barrier and recoiled.

"I'll be all right," he gasped through gritted teeth. "It was my fault to begin with. The young master drew a circle for all to see." The imp gave a sheepish smile. "I'm afraid I was showing off and got my comeuppance. I'll be all right—don't worry about me."

David rolled his eyes.

"What's that for?" asked Connor, his eyes flashing. "Are you saying you *didn't* hurt him?"

"No," said David quietly. "I'm saying I think you should say good-bye to Mr. Sikes, scatter those stones, and burn that book."

Connor looked in disbelief at David and gave a short laugh.

"You're kidding, right?" he said. "Didn't you steal a forbidden grimoire last year—one that even Ms. Richter won't touch?"

David paused a moment before nodding.

"And," continued Connor, "don't you go wandering around the campus at all hours—even down paths we've all been told are off-limits?"

David blinked at Connor and gave another hesitant nod.

"And now you've got the nerve to tell me that I can't manage an *imp*?" exclaimed Connor. "Why, because I'm not David Menlo, Sorcerer supreme? How arrogant are you, mate?"

"Connor!" said Sarah. "That's enough."

David's face turned beet red.

"I just . . ." David choked off the sentence and bowed his

head, pushing away from the table. He scampered upstairs, closing the door quietly behind him.

"So much for the party," said Connor, looking guilty and miserable.

"We should go after David," said Cynthia. "He was just trying to be helpful."

"You're a kind girl," said Mr. Sikes, turning his luminous eyes on Cynthia. "And I agree with you wholeheartedly. Many have been led to believe the worst of imps, and I can't fault your friend for believing the stories."

"Maybe I was a little harsh," Connor admitted. "I'll go find him."

"No," said Max, stirring the melting cubes in his lemonade, "just let him be."

Connor nodded. "I'll catch up with him tomorrow, then. Oh! Mr. Sikes, I almost forgot the original reason I summoned you tonight—but I guess you're probably not feeling up to it anymore."

Mr. Sikes's ears twitched and the imp promptly smoothed his pearl-gray suit.

"If it's within my power, I'd be honored to fulfill Master Lynch's request."

"Excellent," said Connor, grinning at Max. "Can you make people forget things?"

"Of course," said Mr. Sikes, affecting a little bow. "There would be little need for imps if their services were restricted to lemonade. I can do what you ask, Master Lynch, but . . ." The imp hesitated.

"What?" asked Connor. "What do you need?"

"Their names, for a start," said the demon, rubbing his injured arm. "And, of course, I can't be bound within a circle. Mr. Sikes needs to visit them when they sleep, you see."

"Connor," said Sarah with a disapproving tone, "this is not a good idea."

Max was inclined to agree. He did not like the idea of a demon—*any* demon—flitting about campus on secret errands. Connor, however, merely ignored Sarah and kept his attention focused on the impeccably tailored creature removing a singed thread from his suit jacket.

"What if they see you?" asked Connor, ignoring Sarah.

"They won't," said Mr. Sikes reassuringly.

"And they won't be hurt at all?" asked Connor. "No side effects or anything like that?"

"Never in life," promised the imp.

Old Tom chimed seven o'clock, and Max felt his stomach growl.

There was another knock at the door.

"That's probably David," said Max, glancing at the key sitting on his roommate's dresser. He climbed the stairs and opened the door only to find Cooper looming outside. Max had never seen Cooper in the dormitory wings and guessed that his unexpected presence accounted for the empty hallway and its uncharacteristic silence.

"Hi, Cooper!" Max shouted, for the benefit of those downstairs.

Cooper gave Max a quizzical glance but said nothing as he stepped past Max to examine the room and its celestial ceiling. Max heard the frantic whispers of his classmates down below.

"Who else is here?" asked the Agent, eyeing the staircase to the lower level.

"Nobody," said Max defensively. "I mean, nobody who shouldn't be here. I mean, er, Connor, Cynthia, Sarah, and Lucia."

"Dinner's getting cold downstairs," Cooper murmured. "They'll need to hurry if they want to eat."

"What?" asked Max. "They have to go?"

"No," said Cooper. "You do. Grab a sweater."

Max hesitated.

"And where do I have to go?"

"The Director's decided that you and David are to be Acclimated," said Cooper. "We have to be there before midnight."

"Maybe I should talk to Ms. Richter," said Max, not at all liking the sound of Acclimation.

"The Director's been in meetings ever since that witch left. She's not to be disturbed."

"But I haven't slept in, like, twenty-four hours," pleaded Max.

"You can sleep in the car," muttered Cooper unsympathetically. "Where's David?"

"I don't know," said Max quickly, very anxious that Cooper should not learn anything of Mr. Sikes. "He left a little while ago."

Cooper frowned.

"We need to find him—now."

"Guys," called Max, "I've got to go somewhere with Cooper."

The girls shuffled upstairs, murmuring good-byes as they filed quickly past Cooper. Connor came last, hefting his duffel and holding the small felt bag of stones.

"Hey, Max," he said. "That thing is all taken care of—I wouldn't worry about it."

"Er, thanks," said Max, secretly horrified that Connor had sent Mr. Sikes on his errands.

Connor disappeared into his room across the hall, and Max trotted back downstairs to snatch a pair of sweatshirts. All evidence of Mr. Sikes's visit had vanished—the lemonades, coasters, and glowing circle were nowhere to be found.

As it turned out, David was easy to track down; Cooper and Max stumbled upon him as soon as they walked out the front door of the Manse. David sat at the edge of the drive's circular fountain, dragging his hand through the gurgling water and gazing out at a sky of fading yellows and oranges that signaled the end of the day. He accepted Cooper's command without comment and tucked the sweatshirt Max had brought for him under his arm as Cooper pulled a long black sedan round to the fountain.

Once inside the car, there was little talking as Cooper deflected Max's questions and David sat quietly gazing out the window. The sedan wound past clipped lawns and tended gardens until it reached the darkening woods, easing under a newly constructed archway that tunneled through the massive walls of swirling granite that David had drawn from the earth. Great gates of iron swung outward, and the car was bathed in the sudden glare of powerful spotlights. Cooper accelerated, leaving Rowan far behind as they joined the broader road and sped up the rocky coast.

Since Cooper refused to answer any questions, Max had resolved to sleep throughout the ride. He was still half dozing when he felt the car ease to a stop. The engine was shut off, and Max heard Cooper exit the car, his footsteps crunching on gravel. Max's door opened and he was unceremoniously plucked from the warm leather seat, his feet set down on the gravel, where he yawned and blinked at a stand of sparse-needled pines. A moment later, Cooper set David down beside him.

"Where are we?" asked Max.

Cooper ignored his question and glanced at his watch.

"No time for questions," he said. "The instructions are simple. You two are to follow that path down to the beach. Once there, you'll wait and offer your assistance to anyone who happens by. You are not to use Mystics or light any sort of fire. Understood?"

"Yeah, but—" began Max, but Cooper was already climbing back into the car. The engine hummed to life and he reversed up a long, twisting drive of patchy gravel.

Max and David were left alone, gazing at a worn, sandy path that wound past a long-abandoned cottage whose roof was warped and sagging. The cottage's windows were broken and dark; weeds grew in tall clumps about it.

"I guess we go down to the beach," said Max, passing the cottage on his right.

David followed, giving the cottage a generous berth as the two hurried down a crude staircase of sun-bleached boards half submerged beneath pebbly sand. Max's hair whipped about as he stepped over a low dune and down to a broad expanse of beach.

The waves retreated to leave a gleaming swath of sand beneath a dead white moon. The two boys walked closer to the water, hugging their sweatshirts around them. They leaned against a great black rock crusted over with barnacles and absorbed the sounds and sights of the wind and sea. Nothing, not even a gull or insect, seemed to inhabit the stretch of beach. After almost an hour of silent vigil, Max grew impatient.

"Want to have a look around?" he asked David, pushing away from the rock.

His roommate shook his head, clutching his sweatshirt with his eyes riveted on the distant cottage, now silhouetted against the moonlit clouds. David's teeth chattered from the cold.

"You sure?" asked Max. "Walking will keep you warm."

"I'm okay," muttered David, blowing on his hands. "Why don't you just stay here?"

" 'Cause I'm bored and freezing," said Max, stamping his feet. "I won't go far. Give a holler if you see anything, okay?"

David nodded and scrunched into a warmth-seeking ball once again. Max ducked around the rock and walked farther up the beach, scanning about and stopping periodically to watch the tide fill in his footprints. Plucking up a sharp rock, he skimmed it far out over the waves. He was still watching the glassy swells when a high-pitched cry sent a shiver down Max's spine.

The cry had come from David.

Max turned and ran up the beach, spraying sand in his wake. He found his roommate sitting bolt upright against the rock, staring straight ahead. Turning, Max saw light streaming from the cabin's windows, giving it the appearance of a mad jack-o'-lantern on the hillside.

"When did the lights go on?" hissed Max.

David said nothing but pointed straight ahead, positively dumbstruck with terror.

Max forced his attention from the cottage to the gleaming stretch of beach before him.

Something was coming at them—a faint light bobbing across the sand.

Max's breath turned to mist as cold crept up his toes and tunneled deep. A rising wave of fear almost made him gag. He heard David's lunch splash on the sand. But as the light bobbed closer, Max saw that it was only a bonneted woman, clutching a basket and carrying a lantern before her.

"It's just an old woman," Max muttered.

"Look closer!" hissed David.

Max blinked and caught his breath. On closer inspection, he saw the woman was faintly translucent. Moon-dappled waves gleamed through her old-fashioned nightgown and robe as she came to a stop some twenty feet from them.

The ghost shone her lantern at them with calm curiosity.

"Say something," hissed David, kicking lamely at Max's foot.

"Er . . . hello, ma'am," ventured Max, giving a hesitant wave and remembering Cooper's instructions. "Can we help you with anything?"

"Hmmm," said the ghost, her voice crackling with age. "Maybe you can. I'm trying to find my husband, you see. Silly me can't sleep till he's all home in his bed. Would you help me look for him?"

"Of course," said Max politely. He reached down to pull David up, but the small boy made a gurgling noise and waved Max away. "C'mon," whispered Max, tugging at David's sleeve. "It's not so bad, is it?"

David peeped once again at the waiting ghost and scowled at Max before clambering to his feet. The ghost thanked them kindly and adjusted the basket on her arm before continuing along the beach with the boys in her shimmering wake. David was silent and stopped periodically to spit up, but Max was determined to conquer his fear.

"Er, what's your husband look like?" he asked as the ghost walked several feet ahead of them.

"Oh, he's about your height," she replied distractedly, "and he'll be wearing the blue coat I made him last winter."

The ghost stopped to inspect a dark shape at the water's edge, but it turned out only to be an old oar and a shaggy clump of seaweed. She sighed and veered away from the water to search the hollows of some low dunes sprinkled with tall grass. After another ten minutes of fruitless searching, Max felt his nausea subside, only to be replaced by impatience as the ghost plodded on in a meandering path.

"Should we call out his name?" suggested Max.

The ghost stopped and flashed the lantern on his face.

"Why in good heavens would we do that?" she whispered, irritation flashing on her pale features. David nearly fainted.

"No reason," said Max, putting up his hands defensively. "I just thought, you know, if we called out his name, he might hear us and—"

"Well, of course he'd hear us!" hissed the woman. "Think I want to wake him, do you?"

"What do you mean, wake him?" Max was confused. "Is he nearby?" he asked, ignoring David's furious gestures to be quiet.

"Oh, I *know* he is," muttered the woman.

The ghost began to laugh, and David withdrew behind Max. As she laughed, her girlish giggling gradually dropped in pitch until it became a hoarse titter. The lantern's light shook on the boys' faces while the ghost fumbled about in her basket. Reaching inside, the ghost took hold of something that seemed rather heavy. She thrust it forward at them.

It was a man's head, its pale features clenched in silent shock.

Max shrieked. David leapt straight into the air, covering his eyes and flailing his limbs about in a sort of muscular spasm before collapsing on the sand.

"Where's the rest of you, love?" asked the ghost, now addressing the grisly thing. She succumbed to another fit of laughter and flicked playfully at its nose. "C'mon and give your Mary a hint!"

The head's eyes suddenly blinked and swiveled to look at her.

"Think I'll ever let you rest, you miserable woman?" it shrieked. "Ha! Keep searching, you murdering trollop. . . ."

A spectral squabble erupted. Max took the opportunity to pull his petrified roommate to his feet. Once set in motion, David took off like a rocket. Max had never seen his friend run so fast, his little legs churning up the sand as he raced screaming back up the beach. The two left the bickering ghosts far behind and dashed past the eerie cottage.

The car had returned and was waiting on the weedy drive. The boys made a beeline toward it, flinging open the back door and diving inside. The engine roared to life as Cooper glanced back at them with a look of private amusement.

~ 3 ~

AUNTIE MUM

Hours later, Max yawned between bites of cereal, hunching over a table in the Manse's vaulted dining hall while morning sun peeped through the stained-glass windows. The breakfast crowd was thinning, with First Years off to bond with their charges, mystic creatures that had been entrusted to them. The older students milled about in little clusters, comparing course schedules and marveling over the campus's summer transformation. Across the table, Cynthia failed to shoo Connor away as the Irish boy poked methodically at David's meager arm.

"He's sleeping!" hissed Cynthia, resorting to a pinch.

"I can see he's sleeping," replied Connor, undeterred. "But he's about to plop into his oatmeal."

Max slid David's bowl of oatmeal safely out of harm's way while his roommate continued snoring, his mouth agape.

"Reckon you'll be sleeping all day, too," moped Connor, glancing at Max as Lucia and Sarah sat down to join them.

"Nope," said Max, finishing his oatmeal and stealing a bite of David's. "I'm scheduled to do a Course scenario with a couple of Agents."

Connor nearly dropped his spoon at the mention of Rowan's high-tech and rigorous training simulator.

"You're doing scenarios with *Agents*?" he asked. "*Real* Agents? That's the coolest thing I've ever heard! What level?"

"Six, I think," said Max, wiping his mouth.

"Our boy is doing Level Six scenarios with Agents, my dear!" said Connor, wiping away a fake tear and taking the opportunity to squeeze Lucia, who scowled and squirmed out of his grasp. While Connor turned and crowed to a nearby table of Fifth Years, Sarah narrowed her eyes and cleared her throat.

"What do they want from you?" she asked pointedly.

"What do you mean?" asked Max, feeling suddenly self-conscious under the combined stares of the three girls.

"Let's start with Acclimation," said Sarah, folding her arms in the same imposing manner as Miss Boon, their Mystics instructor. "What's that all about?"

"Oh," said Max. "We're not really supposed to talk about it."

"There!" she said, snapping her fingers and leaning forward. "That's *exactly* what I mean! They've got you doing things— dangerous things!—and then they get you to keep quiet about them."

"I don't think Acclimation's actually dangerous," Max assured her. "Supposedly it works better if you don't know what to expect—that's why I can't talk about it. Everyone goes through it by the end of Sixth Year—"

"So why do they have you and David doing it now?" interrupted Cynthia. "We're just Second Years, if they haven't noticed."

"I don't know," said Max, shrugging. "They think we're ready for it, I guess."

"Ready for what, exactly?" asked Sarah. "You're *thirteen*, Max!"

"What does that have to do with it?" he snapped. "Why don't you ask the Sixth Years who trained against me over the summer? I whipped all of them!"

Max found that he'd been speaking louder than he had intended. A number of Sixth Years glanced over from a table underneath the stained-glass windows. Among them was the last student Max had literally chased out of the Sanctuary. The older boy gave Max a sour stare.

"Max," said Sarah in a pleading voice, "this is what I mean—they're using you! They're manipulating you—*sharpening* you like a weapon! Did your father know about Acclimation?"

"No," said Max warily. "Not that I know of."

"So, they've got you hunting down students, training with Agents, and keeping things from your friends and father. Does that sound okay to you?"

"Nobody's using me, Sarah," muttered Max, standing up from the table and stalking off toward the kitchens. Pushing through the swinging doors, he made a beeline for a nearby sink, splashing cold water on his face. From the next room, he heard the sounds of music and singing. His father's enthusiastic crooning was unmistakable, as was Bob's rumbling baritone, but the third voice was unfamiliar—a woman, whose deep and playful singing almost managed to rescue the jazzy number.

Peering into the next room, Max saw his father bent beneath an exhaust fan stirring a monster-sized pot of what smelled like tomato sauce while Bob slid meatballs off a cutting board to plop into the sauce with a gurgle. A third person—Max thought it must be Mum—capered between them, mincing some leaves of oregano as she sang along with Ella Fitzgerald, whose vibrant voice issued from an old radio.

Secondhand love I can't see
It's good for some but not for me
Oh, you can't be mine and someone else's, too
No, you can't be mine and someone else's, too

Upon second glance, Max saw that the third singer did indeed resemble Mum but was bigger by a foot in every direction. Five feet tall with patchy gray skin, this hag boasted a belly so taut and swollen she was reduced to wearing her apron like a smock, its untied strings wagging at her sides as she shook her formidable bottom in time to the music. Adding the oregano to the sauce, she clapped her hands as the song came to a close.

"Ah, that's the good stuff," said the hag. "Ella was brimmin' with soul, she was! Oi! Bob, you handsome devil, put this old girl to work—what's next on the menu for the young lovelies? Soufflé? Or how 'bout I whip up my triple chocolate layer cake?"

"You can make soufflé?" asked Bob, impressed. "Mum tries, but she peeks too soon."

"*I do not!*" cried Mum's voice, screeching from a side pantry. A potato came hurtling from beyond Max's view to thud dully against Bob's chest. The ogre sighed and reached for a clove of garlic, spying Max in the process.

"Max," croaked the ogre as another song crackled from the radio, "come in and taste the sauce."

Max's father spooned some of the bubbling red sauce onto a small slice of sourdough and Max nibbled at it. It was far and away the best sauce Max had ever tasted: rich with tomatoes and a dash of wine, and deliciously peppery.

"That's good," he concluded, his stomach rumbling once again. "That's, like, *incredibly* good!"

"Hooray, hooray!" The enormous hag clapped. "You've got good taste, my boy—no doubt a gentleman and scholar, too."

"Max," said Mr. McDaniels, "I'd like you to meet Mum's sister, Bellagrog—she arrived this morning. Bellagrog, this is my son, Max."

The hag's little red eyes peered intently at Max before she scuttled forward to seize him by both hands. Like Mum, her grip was soft and clammy but tight as a vise.

"Bellagrog Shrope at your service, my love—but call me Auntie Mum!" she crowed, looking him up and down. "Well, you're a handsome lad, ain't ya?"

"Thank you, ma'am," said Max, trying unsuccessfully to wriggle out of her grip. "It's nice to meet you."

The hag patted Max's hand as she glanced sideways at Mr. McDaniels.

"Father and son as good-lookin' a pair as I've set eyes on this past age," she said. "And, eh, where's the missus, if I might be so bold?"

Max looked with interest at his father to see how he would answer. Bryn McDaniels had been missing for more than three years and Mr. McDaniels refused to acknowledge that she was probably dead. Mr. McDaniels cleared his throat.

"Can't find her," he said with a sad shrug and a crooked smile. "If you see her, you be sure to let me know."

"Not on your life!" said Bellagrog with a bawdy laugh,

smacking Mr. McDaniels on the behind with a wooden spoon. "You're on the market again, honey."

Max grinned as Mr. McDaniels flushed pink and managed a chuckle.

Mum came hurtling out of the side pantry, looking panicked.

Hurrying over, Mum wedged herself between Mr. McDaniels and Bellagrog, standing on her tiptoes in a futile attempt to look the larger hag in the eye.

"You've had a long trip, Bel," panted Mum. "Very long, and you must be tired. Take a nap in my cupboard, why don't you?"

"Aren't you a sweet one, Bea?" said Bellagrog, pinching Mum's cheek. "I don't reckon I could fit, love. Imagine this great big place, and you're holed up in a little cupboard! Bwahaha-haha! I wish Nan were still alive to see it!"

"What's wrong with my cupboard?" sniffed Mum, sinking back on her heels.

"Nothing, Bea," chortled Bellagrog. "Fits your personality, it does. Had no idea my baby sis was livin' so high this side of the pond or I'd have looked her up a long time ago!"

"So you had no trouble finding Rowan?" asked Max, mindful of David's concerns.

"Nah," said Bellagrog with a dismissive wave. "Jumped ship in Boston and made my way up. Had to nose around the woods a bit, but I found the place sure as Sunday."

"What brought you here?" asked Bob as he rummaged through a freezer.

"Things gettin' awful bleak out in the wild, Bob," said the hag with a sober nod. "Right smart of you to get out when you did! Humans just don't let their wee ones wander about and play the way they used to, and, well . . . a girl's got to eat!"

The bloated hag gnashed her teeth and gave a mischievous

chuckle. Mr. McDaniels turned green and placed a protective arm around Max, causing the hag to roar with laughter.

"Aw, a good father you are, Scott, but not to worry, love. I know these young ones ain't for eating. Wouldn't dream of insulting me hosts! I'll catch my dinner in that cute little town outside the gates—lots of tourists, by the looks of it!"

Mr. McDaniels groaned. ·

"Perhaps we can have a second sniffing ceremony," volunteered Bob. "I'll ask the Director."

"What the blazes is a 'sniffing ceremony'?" asked Bellagrog, glancing at Mum.

"It's so we . . . don't *bother* anyone here," mumbled Mum, failing to meet her sister's eye.

"And you do this, do you?" asked Bellagrog.

"Yes," said Mum meekly.

"Should be ashamed of yourself, you should!" scolded Bellagrog, wagging a sharp, stubby finger under Mum's nose. "Imagine a Shrope submittin' to something like that!"

"If you want to stay, you'll have to do it, too," said Mum quietly.

"Pshaw!" said Bellagrog, stalking away to shake the radio, which now issued only static. She squinted at the dial and adjusted it, but no stations came through. "Well," she said, "that's it for Ella, I guess. So, Bob, how 'bout I get cracking on those soufflés?"

"That would be very nice," said Bob, directing Bellagrog to a refrigerator stocked with eggs, milk, and cream. Bellagrog immediately set to laying out bowls and pans, whisks and spoons in an efficient array.

"But I can make a soufflé," protested Mum, tilting a tear-streaked face up toward Bob.

"I know," said Bob gently. "But I need you on the roasts. Nothing's more important than the main course, Mum."

"Yes," said Mum, practically shouting in the direction of her sister. "The main course is terribly important! Much more vital than dessert! Children *never* forget a good roast!"

Mum snatched up a cleaver and shambled off into the meat locker, her cheeks pink with pleasure. Max took advantage of the momentary quiet.

"Dad," he said, "I want to tell you something that I did last night, so you hear it from me and not anyone else."

Mr. McDaniels nodded quizzically and reduced the level of flame on the range.

"Would you like me to go?" asked Bob.

"No," said Max. "It's not a big secret or anything—I just wanted to tell my dad that I got Acclimated last night."

Mr. McDaniels raised his eyebrows and glanced at Bob, who gave a sputtering sigh.

"What is that?" asked Mr. McDaniels. "Is that slang for getting high? Did you try a cigarette or get into the wine cellars, Max?"

Mr. McDaniels smiled uncertainly as Bob began to laugh, nearly subsonic chuckles that vibrated the glass panes of the dish cabinets.

"No, Dad," said Max. "Nothing like that. Ms. Richter had Cooper take David and me to an empty beach last night—a couple hours from Rowan."

"Yeah?" said Mr. McDaniels, the smile disappearing from his face as Max told him the story. He kept the tale brief, omitting the gruesome details of the husband's head in the basket. Max's father listened attentively, his expression alternating between anger and shivering curiosity.

"And what was the point of all this?" asked Mr. McDaniels when Max had concluded.

"Cooper said it's to get students used to being near the supernatural," explained Max. "David got sick because he's never been exposed. It didn't affect me as much, because of what I went through last spring."

Actually, Max thought his experience in Marley Augur's crypt was enough for a hundred Acclimations. The aura radiated by the undead blacksmith had been a far more malevolent force than the nausea-inducing presence of the woman's ghost.

"Bob, did you know about this?" asked Mr. McDaniels, turning to the craggy-faced ogre.

"No," said Bob. "I have never heard of one being Acclimated so young."

"Yeah," said Max hastily. "Most students do this when they're eighteen."

"Just before they're assigned," added Bob, frowning now as he diced another basket of tomatoes.

"Assigned to what?" asked Mr. McDaniels.

"Official duty," said Bob ominously, with an anxious glance at Max.

"Over my dead body," breathed Mr. McDaniels, removing his apron and heading for the door.

"Dad," cried Max. "Where are you going?"

"To find Ms. Richter," huffed his father, disappearing out the swinging doors.

Max groaned and buried his head, listening to the static that now hissed from the radio.

Despite his father's angry departure and an exhausting afternoon, Max found it impossible to resist the splendor of the Welcome Feast. The Manse was lit from within like a jewel as thousands of candles flickered from carven alcoves, casting a rich gleam on silver polished to spotless perfection. Students filed into the dining hall by class to take their seats, looking as scrubbed as the silverware in their formal uniforms. Max took a seat next to David, whose brow was furrowed in furious concentration as he wrestled with his crooked tie. David grunted hello as Max craned his neck at the tables where the Fourth Years were taking their places. Max scoured the faces until he found Julie Teller, a pretty girl from Melbourne with whom he had exchanged letters over the summer. His stomach clenched into a funny knot as Julie met his eyes for a moment before she quickly looked away and resumed a conversation with the girl next to her.

"Julie, Julie," muttered Connor, taking the seat next to Max. "What's going on with her?"

"I don't know," said Max. "I thought something—I mean, we wrote each other and stuff this summer—but she walked right past me in the foyer."

"Women," said Connor sympathetically. "I can't figure them out either, mate. Hey, Lucia?"

Lucia's dark eyes flashed at them from the far end of the table.

"Why won't you go out with me?" called Connor.

"You are a filthy pig-dog," said Lucia with cool disdain, eliciting peals of laughter and applause from a gaggle of nearby girls.

Connor shrugged and turned back to Max.

"See? By the way, Mr. Sikes took care of everything—those Sixth Years don't know squat about any witch. They probably don't even remember who Cooper is!" he added with a chuckle.

Before Max could reply, there was the clinking of spoons on crystal as Ms. Richter swept into the dining hall, followed by three adults Max had never seen before. They took their places among the faculty and staff, Ms. Richter's proud face looking happy but careworn in the candlelight.

"Please stand," she said in a clear, strong voice that filled the great hall.

Max stood, glancing at David, who had abandoned his tie and stuffed it in his pocket.

"This is a House of Learning," said Ms. Richter, "and today is the Day of Return, when teacher and pupil reforge their bonds and resume their progress on the path."

The faculty and students raised their glasses.

"This is a House of Learning," she continued, "and today is a Day of Remembrance, when we gather to honor our past, embracing both its joys and sorrows."

Again, the glasses were lifted in salute.

"This is a House of Learning and today is a Day of Renewal, when Rowan welcomes a new class bringing with them life and promise to grace these halls and grounds."

Max watched the First Years fidgeting nervously at the nearby tables. His voice joined those of the older students and faculty.

"We welcome them with open arms. We will help them on the way."

The assembly raised their glasses toward the First Years. Max, David, and Connor clinked glasses before draining the mouthfuls of wine and reclaiming their seats. Ms. Richter waited for the noise to die down before she continued.

"A new school year should be greeted with renewed energy, enthusiasm, and purpose, and I hope that each of you has returned to Rowan restored in body and mind to do your best. With the exception of our newest students, each of you has undoubtedly noticed that the campus has undergone significant changes over the summer. I wish to address the cause for such changes and quell the misinformation and rumors that I know are rampant."

Max felt a stir of whispers through the dining hall; the older students looked grim and attentive.

"As many of you know, a great evil has been unleashed through the long and secret efforts of the Enemy. That evil is Astaroth, the very same entity that drove us to these shores over three centuries ago. We have never faced a more formidable foe, and our field offices have already reported a dramatic rise in Enemy activity. Given these developments, things at Rowan will operate a bit differently this year, and I would like to introduce three special guests whom you will see about campus from time to time."

Ms. Richter gestured to the three strangers seated at the table behind her.

"Allow me to introduce Yuri Vilyak, Commander of the Red Branch."

A tall, formidable-looking man with silver hair and the flat black eyes of a doll stood and smiled at Ms. Richter before bowing to polite applause.

"What's the Red Branch?" whispered Max.

"I don't know what the Red Branch is," said David, "but I've seen Vilyak's name before. He was Director before Ms. Richter. I think he was voted out of office."

"Amulya Jain, Chair of the Prometheus Scholars," continued Ms. Richter.

Ms. Richter stood aside as an Indian woman in a brilliant scarlet sari and wire-rimmed spectacles stood and bowed before the students. David sat up and squinted at the beaming, willowy woman, who now took her seat once again.

"I've heard of her," he said, glancing at Max. "The Prometheus

Scholars are the very best Mystics in the world. She must be very good."

Max raised his eyebrows but had to swallow his question as Ms. Richter introduced the final guest, a lean middle-aged man in glasses and a black suit and tie.

"Our last guest is not a graduate of Rowan and is indeed outside our Order altogether. I have asked him here because he is an old friend and we will have need of old friends to face the challenges ahead. Please allow me to introduce Jesper Rasmussen, Chief Architect and Engineer of the Frankfurt Workshop."

The man listened with an amused expression, rubbing his hand distractedly over a completely hairless head throughout Ms. Richter's introduction.

"Clockwork marvels," murmured David. "That's how Miss Kraken described the Workshop. I don't think she likes what they do."

"Miss Kraken doesn't like *anything*," said Max, glimpsing the instructor, who watched Mr. Rasmussen with thin-lipped disapproval. Cynthia shushed him from several chairs over, and Max spent the rest of Ms. Richter's opening remarks studying the stained-glass windows and their many-colored panes while thinking of his Course training with the Agents earlier in the afternoon. They had been Junior Agents—just a few years out of Rowan—and although they had meant well, Max had found them to be patronizing before they started and painfully slow once the scenario had begun. More than once, Max had been forced to wait during his simulated mission for another member of his team to catch up as they navigated a labyrinth of tunnels and converged on the target—a hostage guarded by a band of tusked *oni*, fearsome and cunning Japanese demons. Once the team had eliminated the sentries and taken strategic positions, Max's instructions had been to wait for the team leader's signal. He had seen an opportunity, however, and chose instead to create a diversionary fire and leap into the chamber. As he had anticipated, the *oni* were too slow. Max had cut them down and freed the hostage in less than a minute, earning the team a much higher score than if he had acted on orders. Unfortunately, the team leader did not appreciate Max's initiative, and Max had been forced to endure a furious lecture about strategy, discipline, and unnecessary risks.

The lecture was forgotten, however, as food began to arrive, carried out on silver platters by a combination of Fifth Years and fauns in formal dress. As the fauns approached, Connor promptly flipped his napkin on the floor and dove down to get it. While he lingered beneath the table, Connor's charge, a Normandy faun named Kyra, marched past their table, her delicate features dripping with indignation.

"Why are you hiding from Kyra?" whispered David.

"Shhh!" hissed Connor, waving David away. "Don't draw her attention over here—she'll do something terrible to our food! She said she might!"

"Why?" asked Max, watching the faun soften her stride to deliver a platter to a table of delighted First Years.

"Thinks it's beneath her to be waiting on the likes of us," whispered Connor, peering over the table and slipping back into his seat. "Normandy fauns are right proud. I tried to explain it was just twice a year and how I wait on her all the other days, but she doesn't see it that way."

"How'd you get her to come at all?" asked David, watching as Kyra flicked a murderous glance at a First Year who had the nerve to point at her hooves.

"I bribed her," confessed Connor. "Said I'd get her a real tiara."

"And how exactly do you plan on doing that?" asked Max. The answer dawned on him almost immediately. "Mr. Sikes?"

Connor cackled mischievously and thumped the table with his fist. "Yes indeed, my friend! Should be getting it tonight—little fellow even promised to wrap it with a pink bow! Not even Kyra can stay mad after that!"

"You know, that imp will have to *steal* that tiara," said David, waving his fork at Connor. "An imp can't just make a tiara out of thin air—it's coming from someplace. This isn't good."

"Oh, give it a rest, Davie," pleaded Connor, reaching for a basket of warm focaccia. "Please? For me? Nobody who owns a bleedin' *tiara* is going to go hungry if it turns up missing."

Even David had to laugh. Without further ado, the three joined in the feast.

Lately, Max found that he was always craving food. It went beyond mere hunger and was, instead, an all-consuming need to feed a body whose demands for energy were becoming insatiable. David and Connor watched in silent awe as Max wolfed down plate after plate of tenderloin, chicken, string beans, and barley. When Max finally polished off a heaping mound of pasta shells swimming in Bellagrog's succulent red sauce, the ravenous hunger faded.

"Impressive," said Connor, wiping his mouth. "But you're wasting valuable time with this whole chewing thing. You should just learn to unhinge your jaw—you know, like a python. Maybe Sir Alistair can teach you. . . ."

Max made a face at the mention of Sir Alistair Wesley, Rowan's Etiquette instructor.

"No more Sir Alistair for me," replied Max. "I'm out of Etiquette and Diplomacy this year—they changed my schedule.

They've got me in Advanced Combat Training with the Sixth Years instead."

"Lucky you," said Connor, "but I wouldn't tell Sarah. She'll think they're sending you to the front lines."

Max nodded heartily in agreement while slipping a grilled chop onto his plate.

Dishes were now being cleared and a variety of desserts were set on the table, including Bellagrog's picture-perfect soufflés. David ordered coffee from a passing faun, ignoring the creature's disbelieving snort.

"Since when do you drink coffee?" laughed Connor.

"I'm tired and I need to stay up," replied David, stirring a cube of sugar into the porcelain cup. "I'm spending some time in the Archives tonight. Kraken got me access . . . er, *authorized* access," he added quickly, after Max raised an eyebrow. "I need to learn whatever I can about the Book of Thoth and Bram's Oath. The witches will be back in a few weeks, and I want to be ready."

"Yeah, but Richter and Kraken didn't know anything about Bram's Oath," said Max. "What makes you think there's anything on it in the Archives?"

"It's worth a look," said David. "The Archives aren't a little bookcase—they're huge, and there are lots of vaults. Nobody at Rowan has seen everything that's in there, much less understood or analyzed it all."

"But you're planning on it?" asked Connor.

"I've got my ways," said David lightly. "Ways that don't require Mr. Sikes . . ."

David pushed back from the table to wander about the dining hall. He stopped to examine a glistening portrait of a dour-faced burgher, swirling his cup of coffee like an old hand and ignoring the sniggers of several Third Years. Moments later, Max saw Amulya Jain, the visiting Scholar, approach David. The sniggers at the nearby table stopped immediately, with the students now curiously focused on their dessert. David and the Scholar were soon engrossed in conversation; Max could tell David was absorbed by the way he shifted his weight from foot to foot.

"C'mon," said Connor, tugging at Max's elbow. "Let's go say hello to the First Years. Gotta get them to sneak out tonight. It's tradition, you know," he said with a wink.

"Nothing to do with the *Kestrel*," insisted Max. The previous year they had been duped into sneaking out and spending the night aboard Rowan's ancient ship, the *Kestrel*, only to be thrown into the churning ocean when it was suddenly tossed about by something that screamed and wailed in the water. The experience had been terrifying and earned them an entire day of detention cleaning out the stables.

"Naw," said Connor dismissively. "Been done already. I've got something better in mind—something harmless."

When Max arrived at the rows of First Year tables, he immediately regretted his decision. There, sitting with the First Years, were Anna Lundgren and Sasha Ivanovich—two of three older students who had bullied Max the previous year. The third and worst of the bunch, Alex Muñoz, had been lost the previous spring—buried beneath a mound of stone and earth when Marley Augur's tomb had collapsed. Max knew Anna and Sasha blamed him for the loss of their friend.

"Here they are!" crowed Sasha as Max and Connor approached.

"These are the ones we were telling you about," said Anna, speaking to the huddling First Years in a conspiratorial tone. "Connor's the one on the right—he's just trash and not worth your worry. But Max? I'd stay clear of Max. Max is a murderer—killed our friend in cold blood."

Max felt his cheeks burn as the First Years looked at him, dumbfounded.

"You're kidding," laughed a heavyset boy with a mop of red hair.

"Wish I were," said Anna, her pretty blue eyes glittering with malice. "But ask anyone here and they'll tell you that Alex Muñoz is gone and Max McDaniels was the very last person to see him alive."

"What a load of bull!" snapped Connor, pinching his nose and waving his hand in the direction of Sasha. Several First Years grinned and giggled. "Don't listen to these two jokers—worst pair of prats in this whole place! Rowan heaped honors on Max when he got back! You'll see his name above Beowulf's Gauntlet—written in fiery script, clear as day."

"So it isn't true?" squeaked a small black boy with glasses.

"Well," said Connor, scratching his chestnut curls, "technically, that last bit *is* true, but they're leaving out lots of important stuff! Max ain't a murderer, for God's sake—that's crazy!"

"That's *just* the word I was looking for!" said Anna, her smile turning sickly sweet. "Crazy. I think that's how I heard a Sixth Year describe Max just this morning after breakfast. . . ."

Max bit off his reply and sighed, realizing that Anna was trying to bait him.

"Welcome to Rowan," he said quietly, walking away from the First Years and leaving Connor behind to argue with Anna and Sasha. The cavernous hall seemed stifling. He thought about tracking down Julie again but quickly put the idea out of his mind—that terrible force within him was stirring and now was not the time to ask why she seemed to be avoiding him. Instead Max stopped and leaned against a pillar whose gray stones had been worn smooth by the centuries. He considered the presence lurking within him. Ms. Richter called it Old

Magic; Miss Boon and the witch called it Cúchulain. Whatever its proper name, it was a force that had summoned terrible things to Max's doorstep, and he was determined to keep it under control.

"I'm my own person," he whispered, scratching the pillar with his thumbnail as Bob introduced Mum's sister, Bellagrog Shrope, to enthusiastic applause.

When the cheers subsided and the students began climbing up the curving steps, Max turned to see if he might catch Julie. Instead, he saw Commander Vilyak standing at his elbow. The man smiled, but his eyes remained dead as he took a long, hard look at Max.

"You're Max McDaniels," he said decisively. "I'm Commander Vilyak." As Max shook the proffered hand, he saw that the inside of Vilyak's wrist had some sort of tattoo. Vilyak caught Max staring at it and grinned, removing his cuff link and pulling back his sleeve so Max could get a better look. He saw an image of a red hand, raised in greeting, bound by a slender cord. "That's the mark of the Red Branch," Vilyak said proudly. "Ever seen it before?"

"No," said Max, strangely fascinated by the simple emblem.

"They're very rare," the man said fondly. "Only the top twelve Agents in the world get one of these. You know one of them, I think."

"Cooper?" asked Max.

"Yes," said Vilyak, smiling. "William Cooper is a member of the Red Branch. And he has told me a great deal about you, my young friend. Making your acquaintance is the only reason I'm here, what with things as busy as they are. Fortunately, everything Cooper reported has been confirmed."

"I don't understand, sir," said Max. "We've just met."

"I took the opportunity to review your scenario from this afternoon," said Vilyak, shifting to a more businesslike tone. "I watched it several times."

"Oh," said Max, reddening. "That. Well, I guess I should have followed orders. . . ."

Vilyak leaned forward and spoke, enunciating each word very carefully. "It was brilliant." The man clapped Max on the arm and gave him a parting wink. "Orders aren't for everyone, Max. Don't let them tame you too much—it's not your nature. I'll be in touch, eh?"

"Okay—er, thank you, sir!" said Max, flushing with an unexpected rush of pride. Vilyak joined a passing flock of senior faculty, and they departed in a slow procession of navy robes. Max craned his neck one more time, searching for Julie, before dashing up the stairs and out the Manse's door. Nick might have awoken by now, and Max felt like running far and wide in the warm summer night.

Nick was indeed waiting as Max emerged from the Sanctuary tunnel. The lymrill crouched in the tall grass, swishing his coppery tail and finishing the remains of a particularly large and juicy rat. Nick's eyes peered up as Max stepped into the clearing, two points of reflected moonlight shining bright among the deep greens of the darkening field. Giving the rat a final nudge, the lymrill licked its muzzle clean and stood to dig at the thick turf with its lethal, curling claws. With a sudden happy mewl, Nick bolted away, kicking up clumps of grass as he ran, and Max chased after.

By the time Max trudged back to the Manse, the campus was dark. A conspicuous exception, however, were the windows of Ms. Richter's office. Light streamed from a slim gap in the drawn curtains, spilling onto the flagged patio. Shapes moved across the opening—apparently there were several people in the Director's office. The drapes parted momentarily and Max saw Dr. Rasmussen standing at the window, surveying the orchard while speaking rapidly. With a scowl, the leader of the Frankfurt Workshop pulled the drapes shut once again. Max glanced at his watch; it was well past midnight. He wondered what would necessitate such a late meeting.

Max soon discovered the reason. In a wood-paneled room off the Manse's foyer, some two dozen pajama-clad students were gathered in stunned silence before a large television. Julie Teller was among the group, wedged into a leather couch and looking horror-stricken as she stared at the screen. A bleary-eyed anchorman was speaking, his tone eerily calm.

"Today's events are an unprecedented tragedy. For those viewers just joining us, five world leaders are dead and several others are missing under highly suspicious circumstances. While few details are available at this time, authorities believe the incidents to be linked and are acting accordingly. All domestic and international air travel has been temporarily suspended, as has trading across most global exchanges. The president has been moved to an undisclosed location and will address the American people later today. . . ."

Max stood speechless as the report went on to detail the ministers, presidents, and premiers who were dead or missing. There did not seem to be any pattern of wealth, politics, or popularity of the leaders. They were scattered across continents and regions, representing nations rich and poor. When the anchorman began to repeat his report, Max crossed quickly over to Julie and knelt next to the sofa.

"When did they start reporting this?" he asked her quietly.

She glanced at him as though gazing through a ghost. Her

face blanched, and she scooted off the couch to hurry from the room. Utterly perplexed, Max followed and called after her, but she ignored him, scampering quickly across the foyer and up the staircase toward the girls' dormitories. Max stood in the foyer, staring at the gleaming floor, while Julie's steps pattered away.

Other footsteps—quick and purposeful—sounded from the corridor that led to Ms. Richter's office. Cooper emerged into the foyer. Without so much as a glance at Max, the Agent strode out into the night.

~ 4 ~

THE RIDDLE AND THE RED BRANCH VAULT

Two weeks later, Bellagrog was holding court, as she was wont to do in the late afternoon. Max could hear her contagious laugh rumbling in the distance as he walked toward the Manse on a day when wood smoke was in the air and the leaves were tinged with orange and yellow. A splendid white goose waddled alongside him, pausing periodically to ensure that the dozen goslings behind them were keeping up and staying out of mischief.

"So, no words of wisdom?" asked Max. "I mean, we wrote each other all summer and now she won't even look at me. . . ."

"I won't pretend to understand teenage girls," sighed the goose. "I've seen over two hundred classes come through this school, and while times change, the teenage girl remains a fickle, mysterious beast. You should find yourself a nice selkie."

Max smiled as Hannah buffeted him playfully with her wing.

"You're too young to be heartbroken," she continued. "That job's been taken by this gorgeous goose who was left high and dry with twelve mouths to feed! Forget all about her, honey."

"I'll try," sighed Max as Hannah began veering off the path toward her nest on the edge of the orchard. He was reluctant to leave her company. "Do you want to sit on the patio?" he asked hopefully.

"Why?" asked Hannah, her voice becoming shrill. "To fawn over that revolting hag while she spins her lies and stories? Not on your life! That one's always nosing around the nest and cooing after the goslings. Like I don't know she'd toss 'em back like popcorn first chance she got!"

The goose waddled off, calling after her children, who came scurrying back to join their mother. Max strolled through the orchard, peering up at row upon row of apple trees, whose golden fruit signified graduates of Rowan who had passed away. More laughter sounded ahead as he emerged from the orchard to find Bellagrog sitting on one of the flagstone patio's benches, swirling a generous glass of brandy while she entertained some twenty students. Max's stomach made a funny flip as he spied Julie Teller sitting on a stone bench, flanked by a pair of girl-friends. The smile evaporated from her face the moment she saw Max, and she took a sudden interest in her sandals. Max's heart sank and he skirted the group, passing Mum, who was briskly sweeping fallen petals into little piles on the flagstones. The hag's face was curdled with indignation.

"Bel," she hissed, "I need you to hold the dustpan."

"Not now, Bea," rumbled Bellagrog, shooing away her sister. "You're interrupting me stories—"

Bellagrog cocked an eyebrow and caught Max reaching for the French doors.

"Max!" the hag sang. "Max, Max, handsome Max—pull up a seat or I'll crack yer back! Bwahahahaha! Was just breakin' out me stories before supper. Have a seat while Bea fetches her sis another splash of brandy."

"That's your fourth!" commented Mum acidly, propping up her broom and scurrying inside.

"When'd she get so clever with numbers?" laughed Bellagrog, gulping down the last amber drop. "Now, Max, plenty of room right next to yer ol' Auntie Mum."

Max did his best to smile as he squeezed onto the bench next to the swollen gray hag, who smelled like a nauseating mix of meat and mold. The other students giggled, but Julie looked mortified and merely stared at the ground. Bellagrog patted his knee and took a deep whiff of Max's upper arm, looking oddly distant as drool pooled behind her lower lip. A moment later, the hag blinked and fumbled for a pouch of tobacco, pinching off an enormous wad and stuffing it in her mouth just as Mum arrived with a crystal decanter.

"That's it, Bea," said Bellagrog, holding out her glass. "A little more . . . and a little more . . . and *that's* a proper glass!" The hag almost began to purr as she tipped back her drink. "As I was saying," she continued, "it wasn't no Sunday shower what made yer Auntie Mum pack her bags and hop the pond. Big things are afoot! Reminds me o' the summer of '40, when Nan sniffed trouble and moved us up to Shropshire before the bombs started fallin'. Mum was still in diapers yet!"

"Oh," cooed a Third Year girl, "I'll bet you were an adorable baby, Mum!"

Mum blushed and smiled appreciatively.

"Who said anything about a baby?" chortled Bellagrog. "She was a bloody teenager!"

Mum's lip trembled as the students burst into laughter.

"I never wore diapers in my teens!" she thundered.

"Have it your way, Bea," said Bellagrog with a wink. "Let's just call 'em 'training bloomers' if it'll make you happy. . . ."

More howls of laughter sent Mum gathering up her things with frantic gasps and mutters. Max felt a pang of sympathy for Mum as she gave her sister a murderous stare and stormed inside, slamming the French doors shut.

"Always had a thin skin, Bea did," said Bellagrog with an indulgent smile. "Anyway, it was right pretty country near Shropshire. Plenty to eat, too, with all the men off fighting the war and . . . er . . . leaving their families. . . ."

Bellagrog gave Max a sheepish shrug as her audience began whispering to one another and scooting away. She snapped her fingers to reclaim their attention, leaning forward to continue in a throaty whisper.

"Let's just say it was easy living for the Shropes, while those hags what stayed near London had an awful hard time of it. The moral of me little tale is that any blubbering fool will go a-runnin' once it rains, but it takes a smart old bird to find a cozy nook soon as the wind goes still and quiet. And it's quiet in the world, my lovelies—radio ain't singing me tunes, telephone's out half the time. Soon, dark nasties will be digging into cellars. . . ."

"Dark nasties . . . like *hags*?" quipped Connor, poking his head out from the French doors.

This brought a laugh from the group, but none laughed

louder than Bellagrog, whose whole body shook with mirth while she wiped a tear from her crocodile eye.

"Aye, nasties like hags," she allowed with a final, convulsive chuckle. "But other things, too—vyes and hobgoblins and older things much too terrible to mention."

Max knew the hag reveled in trying to frighten them, but he also saw that there was wisdom and hard experience in her words. Bellagrog was a survivor; it was evident in the way her small red eyes darted about, constantly filtering her environment into threats and opportunities.

"Sorry to interrupt," said Connor, "but Mr. McDaniels asked me to look for you—they need you in the kitchens."

"Well," said Bellagrog, swirling her brandy and downing it in one huge swallow, "it's nice to be needed, ain't it? And it's awful nice to be here snug and cozy with the likes of you while it's getting dark outside. Stay with me, my wee ones, and we'll wait it out right here—backs against the wall and brandies in hand!"

With a creak and a snort, the hag eased herself up, followed toward the French doors by the assembled students. Waiting for Julie, Max said her name and tapped her on the shoulder. Without so much as a sideways glance, she breezed past him.

"What is the *matter* with you?" shouted Max.

Several students turned and gaped at Max. But Julie wasn't one of them. She walked away, her shoulders as stiff and straight as a church pew. Red-faced, Max opened his mouth and shut it again, turning toward Connor. The Irish boy shrugged and stepped closer, sniffing at Max's armpit.

"Mystery solved," he declared.

"Shut up," said Max, sinking into an antique chair, utterly perplexed.

"You know," said Connor thoughtfully, "we could TP her room, leave a flaming bag on her doorstep—the possibilities are virtually endless. Of course, there are easier ways. . . . "

Max exhaled and glared at his friend, whose face was now alight with scheming.

"I've told you a dozen times," said Max, "I don't want to use Mr. Sikes."

"That's just 'cause Davie scared you off his services," said Connor. "He's really a help."

"When I need a lemonade, I'll let you know," said Max.

"No," said the Irish boy thoughtfully, "he's a lot more useful than that. He *listens* to me."

"If he's so great, why don't you have him make Lucia fall madly in love with you?" said Max, smiling. Connor blinked and shook his head.

"No, no—I mean, if I went whining to Mr. Sikes every time Lucia told me to bugger off, he'd stop answering my calls."

"He *has* to answer your calls," said Max pointedly. "He's a demon."

"Well, he can't make Julie fall in love with you," Connor said quickly, pausing between chimes as Old Tom sounded six o'clock. "I, er, already asked him about that sort of nonsense. I have something else in mind. A brilliant idea—and I *know* it will work."

Max looked at him impatiently.

"Forget all about her," said Connor.

"That's it?" asked Max, walking off toward the dining hall. "That's your brilliant idea? Hannah beat you to it."

"No," said Connor, tugging Max to a halt. "I mean *really* forget about her—wipe her clean from your memory."

"I don't want that imp in my head," said Max.

"Why?" asked Connor. "He only does what you want him to."

"I don't know," said Max.

"Just *talk* to him," pleaded Connor. "If you don't want to do anything, you don't have to."

"Okay," said Max. "Tonight, after dinner. But don't tell David."

"Don't you worry about that," said Connor happily. "I'm just glad you wised up and are willing to consider his invaluable services. I've aced every assignment this year!"

"You use him to *cheat*?" asked Max, raising his eyebrows.

"Naw," said Connor. "I wouldn't call it cheating—he just sort of looks over my shoulder and nudges me in the right direction now and then. I'm doing the work!" added Connor in response to Max's dubious expression.

The two dashed off to dinner, where David proved to be absent for a seventh consecutive night. Every night for the past week Max had heard his roommate tiptoe back into their room from the Archives in the early morning hours and collapse onto his bed for an hour or two of sleep.

While David was nowhere to be seen, Julie Teller had unfortunately chosen to sit at the next table. Glancing occasionally at her throughout the meal, Max mused sadly that soon she might be nothing but a random face in the hallways.

Max had just caught Connor watching him, the Irish boy chewing thoughtfully on a piece of asparagus, when he felt a tap on his shoulder. He turned to see Commander Vilyak standing over him.

"Hello there," said the Agent with a thin smile. "How are things?"

"Oh, hi," said Max, standing up to shake his hand. "I mean, fine, sir. Things are fine. Er, Commander Vilyak, this is my friend Connor Lynch."

Vilyak gave Connor an acknowledging nod as Connor stood and said hello. Max swelled with pride as Julie's table abruptly halted their conversation to take note of someone as senior as Vilyak stopping to speak with two Second Years.

"Are you from Ireland, Connor?" asked Vilyak.

"Yes, sir," said Connor. "Dublin."

"Well met, indeed," said Vilyak, bowing. "Max, you of all people should know that the Red Branch hails from Ireland— the country holds a special place in my heart."

"Why should I know that, sir?" asked Max.

"The Red Branch comprised the finest warriors of Ulster. Cúchulain himself was their greatest champion. Miss Boon might say you were born to our Order." Max frowned at the amused gleam in the man's flat black eyes. He did not like that his Mystics instructor was sharing her hypothesis that Max might be Cúchulain reborn. "In fact, I thought the young Hound of Rowan might like to see something of particular interest tonight. Something in the Archives."

"What's that, sir?" asked Max.

"Ooh!" interrupted Connor. "Are you going to take Max into the Archives?"

"If he has a mind to go," said Vilyak.

"Can I come, too?"

Vilyak laughed and patted Connor on the arm.

"I admire your enthusiasm, but I'm afraid I'm already bending the rules by taking Max," said the Agent with a sympathetic smile. "Sorry to disappoint you."

Connor looked crestfallen.

"What do you say, Max?" asked Vilyak. "Care to see some of Rowan's secrets?"

Connor practically writhed with jealousy as Max nodded eagerly.

"Connor, I'll talk to you later about that thing," said Max as he followed Vilyak out of the dining hall. Max paused to get a last glimpse of Julie and was surprised to see her watching him from her table. He looked away and hurried to keep pace with Vilyak's long, brisk strides.

Once outside the Manse, they walked along the garden paths toward Old Tom and Maggie, positioned like two great gray stones overlooking the sea.

"So," said Max, "I heard you used to be Director, before Ms. Richter."

"That's true," said Vilyak. "I was Director for six years, but I'm happy to have all of that behind me."

"Really?" asked Max. "Why is that?"

"A desk is no place for me," said the Agent, turning his doll's eyes on Max. "Out in the field is where I belong—hunting our enemies. As wonderful as Rowan is, it is just a little corner of what we do. Commanding the Red Branch is my true calling."

Vilyak led Max into Old Tom, climbing the stairwell to the third floor and down to a side passage that housed several seldom-used classrooms. Producing a large key from his pocket, Vilyak unlocked the door to Room 313. Max peered inside and saw nothing but a dusty room with some two dozen desks, several bookcases, and a smudged, swiveling blackboard on a wooden stand.

"After you," said Vilyak.

"But I thought we were going to the Archives," said Max.

"This is the way to the Archives," said Vilyak simply.

Max hesitated, then went inside. Vilyak stepped in after him and promptly locked the door. The man laughed when he saw the suspicious look on Max's face.

"Don't be nervous," laughed Vilyak. "The Archives won't open unless that door is locked."

Stepping over to the blackboard, Vilyak placed it flat on the floor and reached for a piece of chalk. Upon its dusty surface, the Agent wrote: *By right and necessity, Commander Vilyak requests access to the Archives.* Smiling at Max's curiosity, Vilyak lifted the blackboard away from the floor as though lifting a cellar door. Max leaned closer and saw a dimly lit staircase descending far out of sight.

"Whoa," said Max, reaching his hand into the space that had seemingly not existed a moment before.

"Follow me," said Vilyak, stepping down onto the first step. "Don't worry about the blackboard—the room will rearrange itself."

"Did *we* build the Archives?" asked Max, climbing down after Vilyak. Every student was aware of Rowan's curious origins and how it had been raised several centuries earlier by forces older and stronger than their own. Trails might change or disappear; peculiar will-o'-the-wisps might appear in the woods accompanied by faint and distant laughter. Students were often warned to avoid anything strange, any unexpected occurrence that might suggest a sudden pulse of the Old Magic that had laid the school's foundations. These events were unpredictable and potentially dangerous, and Max realized many of his classmates viewed him in much the same light.

"No, we did not build this," answered Vilyak, his voice echoing off gleaming marble walls as they continued steadily down the steps. "The scholars believe that the Archives are actually the oldest part of this school—the very heart of this whole campus. The most important books and relics that could be salvaged from Solas or collected since are stored here. Watch your step as we go—some of the stairs are quite worn."

Down and farther down went Max until he lost count of the steps. Old Tom could be heard ringing eight o'clock, but the chimes sounded as though they might be miles away. The air was warm with sudden drafts, and the walls were slick with moisture. Max imagined that they were descending into the bowels of a living thing, ancient and strange and riddled with magic. The powerful presence within him began to awaken and stir.

"Well, we're here at last," said Vilyak, coming to a halt after the last step, which emptied into a large room of rose-colored marble. Max gasped at the sight of two massive shedu flanking a tall door of shining brass that bore the Rowan seal. The shedu were enormous—fifteen feet tall, with the bodies of colossal bulls and human heads bearing tall crowns of bronze. They might have been statues until one suddenly swiveled its head to focus its blank, unblinking stare upon Max.

"Don't be afraid," said Vilyak, taking Max by the elbow and walking him forward. "Is this your first experience with shedu?"

"No, sir," breathed Max. "One of my classmates has a shedu charge, but he's a lot smaller than these."

"Shedu are ideal guardians," said Vilyak, reaching up to pat the chest of the stony creature that stood aside to let them pass. "They need little food or sleep and are highly resistant to trickery and Mystics. They'll let you pass since you're with me, but I'd advise you never to try to enter the Archives on your own. A shedu will not understand."

"Got it," said Max, inching past the imposing creatures.

Vilyak pulled the heavy brass door open and stood aside as Max poked his head within.

"Welcome to the Archives, Max. It is the heart of Rowan and the wealth of our people."

Max stood speechless in the doorway for several moments and gaped at the gargantuan space. Far larger than a cathedral, the Archives stretched out before him in a gleaming array of tables and cases and books—thousands and thousands of books arranged around sweeping balconies that rose up and up in a gentle spiral until Max's gaze fell upon a lighted fresco depicting the School of Athens hundreds of feet above them. Sturdy vaults with circular doors were set into recessed nooks around the oval room, the walls of which were hung with paintings and tapestries of every color and description. Slump-shouldered scholars sat alone or huddled at tables, poring over ancient-looking books and stacks of parchment as thin as tissue.

Max heard several coughs echo in the cavernous space and grinned to see David sitting small and hunched at a table next to a statue of Aristotle. A mound of books and papers lay next to a steaming coffee mug.

"That's my roommate," whispered Max to Vilyak.

"Ah, the famous Mr. Menlo," said Vilyak, peering with curiosity at David. "Yes, I've heard all about him. Go say hello if you like, but hurry back, please. I haven't much time."

Max strode into the room, ignoring the curious stares and whispers of the scholars who peered from behind dim lamps and thick spectacles. David's small, drawn face turned and blinked impatiently when Max tapped him on the shoulder. As he turned, David clumsily tried to palm a slim vial filled with a shimmering silver liquid.

"Max!" David exclaimed, rubbing his eyes. "How did you get down here?"

"Commander Vilyak brought me," said Max, gesturing at the Agent who stood near the doorway. Max glanced at the food wrappers, coffee mugs, and little pillow on the seat next to David's. "You moving down here?"

"I might as well," sighed David. "But it's been paying off. I've discovered something—something *very* important."

Max heard a noise behind him and turned to see Vilyak gesturing impatiently at his watch.

"David, I've got to run."

"Come back when you're finished," whispered David urgently.

"I'll try," said Max over his shoulder, ignoring David's imploring look while he hurried back to Vilyak.

"How is your friend?" asked Vilyak, guiding Max along the room's perimeter.

"Er, fine . . . tired, I guess," replied Max. "He's been spending a lot of time down here."

"Doing what, might I ask?" inquired Vilyak, raising an eyebrow.

"Research—Bram's promise to the witches. Have you heard about it?"

"I have, and rest assured, the two of you aren't going anywhere," said Vilyak with steely conviction. "You're far too important for us to hand you over like some sort of carnival prize. It's out of the question, and Richter knows it."

Vilyak patted Max on the shoulder and steered him toward a massive vault whose shining door of black granite was stamped with the same red hand and cord that was branded upon the Agent's wrist. Max's fingers twitched, and he gazed long and hard at the door.

Something inside was calling to him.

"What's in there?" asked Max quietly.

"The tools and treasure of the Red Branch," answered Vilyak. "All reserved for the exclusive use of our members." The Agent placed his palm against the great red seal. A moment later there was the muted rumble of stone sliding across stone and the massive door swung open to reveal a rich golden glow within. "Care to see?"

Max nodded and stepped past the Agent into a warm room of pale stone strewn with Persian carpets. The glow was coming from the reflection of several lamps on the scalloped curves, points, and edges of an armory the likes of which Max had never seen. Shirts of smoky nanomail were arranged next to medieval helmets that peered from behind a set of lacquered armor. Max stopped to gaze at a brilliant sword with a golden pommel that lay unsheathed on a red velvet cloth.

"That's Joyeuse," said Vilyak, smiling. "The sword of Charlemagne. Some would have you believe it was buried with him or resting in the Louvre, but we know better, eh?"

Max gazed at his reflection mirrored in the blade until something else caught his eye—the same gruesome-looking knife Max had seen only weeks before. It lay on a shirt of coarse woven cloth, its notched, wavy blade covered in what appeared to be dried blood.

"I've seen that before," whispered Max. "Cooper had it with him when David and I were brought to see Dame Mala."

"The Kris of Mpu Gandring," said Vilyak. "Indonesian—from the ancient Singhasari kingdom. It has an evil history. I won't touch it, but Cooper favors that one. It's failed him only once." Vilyak gestured to his face, alluding to the scars and burns that had transformed Cooper's pale features into a waxy mask.

"What happened to him?" asked Max suddenly. "I've never had the nerve to ask."

"I'm sure he'll tell you the full story someday," replied Vilyak. "I will say, however, that it's related to why I brought you here this evening. You see, Max, we have many things in the vault of the Red Branch, but our most precious relic is broken. Cooper tried to fix it, but he failed. I think you might someday succeed. Would you like to see it?"

Vilyak gestured toward a dark corner in the very farthest reaches of the vault. Max felt a tingling in his stomach. Whatever had been calling to him surely lay in that corner, amidst its chests and cases.

"What is it?" asked Max, his voice hoarse and dry.

"Have a look for yourself," said Vilyak. "You know it far better than I."

Max pressed forward. Gliding past an open chest of gold doubloons, he saw what Vilyak had intended him to find.

There, propped against a cracked wooden wheel, Max found a sharp spearhead attached to a thick length of gray, splintered bone. He knew in an instant that this barbed, murderous thing had been calling to him—beckoning him forward like a siren's song.

Vilyak came to stand behind him.

"That, Max, is what remains of Cúchulain's favorite weapon—his *gae bolga*. It is the greatest treasure that we of the Red Branch possess. As you can imagine, its pedigree and properties make it priceless."

Max remembered the tales he'd read of Cúchulain. The spear was made from the bones of a sea monster and given to Cúchulain by those who lived beyond this world. According to the stories, it was a devastating weapon; a wound from the *gae bolga* was always fatal.

"Do you think you could use something like this?" asked Vilyak, his tone slow and cautious.

Max paused and considered the question, which hung suspended in the vault's still air.

"I thought these things were reserved for the Red Branch," replied Max, finally glancing back at the weapon. "I'd have to be a member, and you said there can be only twelve."

"That's true," said Vilyak quietly, "but one among our ranks is retiring—too old now to be of creditable service. You are young, Max, but I have never seen one so gifted. You have already been blooded. Extraordinary times may necessitate exceptions, wouldn't you agree?"

Max reached for the broken spear. He wanted to test the weight of it in his hand.

"What on earth do you think you're doing?"

Ms. Richter's voice shattered the tranquility of the vault. Max jerked back his hand and turned to see the Director in the vault's doorway with arms folded and gray eyes ablaze, angrier than Max had ever seen her. Vilyak turned to face her.

"Explain yourself, Commander," seethed Ms. Richter.

"Good evening, Gabrielle," said Vilyak casually. "How nice to see you. I'd be happy to answer your question, but this vault is reserved for the Red Branch. If I were a stickler, I'd say you were trespassing. . . ."

Max's jaw fell open. The Director stood absolutely still, her attention fixed on Vilyak, who returned her stare with a patient smile, his black eyes fathomless and unblinking. Ms. Richter cleared her throat.

"Max, you will step out of this vault immediately. Commander Vilyak, you are to return overseas at once and rendezvous with your squad in Paris. Another politician is missing, and there are power outages all over Europe. The situation is rapidly getting out of hand. You will take command of local field offices as you see fit."

"Of course, Gabrielle," said Vilyak, standing at attention and leading Max out of the vault. Ms. Richter stepped aside as Vilyak closed the vault door, then patted Max on the shoulder.

"Thanks for visiting with me, Max. I'll see you later. Be good and study hard, eh?"

"Yes, sir," mumbled Max, shrinking under the laser-like focus of Ms. Richter's keen eyes. Vilyak smiled and spun on his heel, making for the door without a parting glance or word for Ms. Richter. The Director watched him go, then turned to Max with a sigh.

"I look before me and see a student," she said. "What does Commander Vilyak see?"

"I don't know," said Max, looking beyond her at the door's red seal.

"I think you do, Max."

"A recruit, I guess," Max replied, his cheeks burning hot. "I'm sorry."

Ms. Richter gave a gentle smile, her gray eyes shining silver as their crow's-feet crinkled to tight creases. It was such a hard face, but Max thought she must have been quite beautiful when she was younger.

"You're getting so big," she said. "You're almost as tall as I am now, and it's only a year ago that I had to stoop to look at you. We've been through a lot this past year, haven't we? I know I've been very busy, but it's time we had a talk."

"Yes, ma'am," said Max, exhaling now that he knew the Director was not angry with him. "But I should tell you that David's found something important—he's sitting right over there."

Ms. Richter raised her eyebrows and walked toward David's table with Max in tow. David was just pouring himself another cup of coffee while studying a golden talisman that he dangled from a finger.

"David," groaned Ms. Richter, "how many times do I have to ask you not to drink coffee, much less bring it into the Archives?"

"I'm careful," David said defensively, still examining the

talisman. "And besides, I can't stop—coffee is the greatest invention of all time!"

"Yes, well, as much as I'd love to debate the point, Max said you might have found something significant?"

"*Very* significant," said David with a sober nod, "but I think we should talk somewhere else."

Ms. Richter turned and narrowed her eyes at a nearby table of bearded scholars who were taking great pains to overhear their conversation.

"Very well," said Ms. Richter. "Let's move to one of the reading rooms."

With just the slightest uplift of her finger, Ms. Richter raised David's books and papers into the air. These followed behind the trio in a floating procession as the Director led Max and David into a snug little room off the second-floor balcony. The books and papers followed them inside, arranging themselves on a large table. Ms. Richter motioned for Max and David to sit in a pair of comfortable armchairs while she closed the door firmly behind them.

"Now," she said, "what's all this about? I didn't think I could fit any more excitement into one day!"

"The witches are telling the truth—Bram *did* promise three people to them," said David quietly. "But it gets worse."

"Go on," said Ms. Richter, her mouth a tight, straight line as she waited.

"The Book of Thoth exists, and he's looking for it *right now*," continued David, playing with the strange talisman that lay on his palm.

"*Who* exactly is looking for it?" asked Ms. Richter.

"Astaroth," whispered David. "But it gets even *worse*!"

"David, would you please tell me what *is* the worst of it?" snapped Ms. Richter.

"Bram hid the book away, but one other person knew how to find it. . . ."

David glanced at Max and an icy, sinking sensation began to pool in Max's belly.

"Let me guess," said Max. "Marley Augur."

"Marley Augur," confirmed David with an ironic smile. "Strange as it sounds, though, we actually have Augur to thank for tipping us off that the book's in danger. He made this for Bram before he turned traitor."

David held out the talisman, a golden disk on a slender chain engraved with an eight-pointed sun. Max squinted as David cupped it in his hands. The sun was giving off an unmistakable glow, as though a firefly were trapped inside it.

"The talisman indicates if the book is safe from Astaroth," said David. "According to Bram, it shines if the book's in danger—can you see it glowing?"

"Yes," said Ms. Richter, peering intently at it. "How have you come to know all this?"

"I found a letter from Bram," said David. "It was filed away with a bunch of other papers under 'Indecipherable.' "

"So how did you manage to decode it?" asked Ms. Richter.

"Thanks to Maya," replied David, referring to his charge, a gazelle-like creature called an ulu. Reaching into his sweater pocket, David produced the mysterious vial of silvery liquid and a slim paintbrush. "These are a few drops of Maya's blood," he explained. "An ulu's blood can be used to translate just about anything if it's brushed over the words and the proper spells are spoken. That's one of the reasons ulus are so rare—they were hunted down by Mystics and scholars, so now they're almost extinct. What those awful people learned the hard way, though, is that the ulu has to give its blood willingly. If you take it by force, its composition changes to a very strong acid—strong enough to burn through whatever precious text its captors wanted to translate."

"I see," said Ms. Richter, glancing at the vial.

David began digging impatiently through the pile of loose papers and maps until he procured a delicate, yellowed piece of parchment. He thrust it at Ms. Richter.

"Director," said David, "whatever happens with the witches, we have to get the book before Astaroth. Nothing else is more important!"

Ms. Richter took the parchment from David, holding it by the corners as she scanned it several times. With a brief nod, she handed the letter to Max. He blinked at the parchment's dense grid of black-inked symbols. It was utterly incomprehensible until slowly, gradually, silvery words bobbed to the surface and made the message clear.

> March 15, 1648
> It escapes me why heaven and earth should conspire to conceive such a perilous thing, but the Book of Thoth exists and must be forever hidden from those who would betray its secrets. For the present day, I have ensured the book's safety, though I buy it at an awful price. May God forgive me as I barter lives that are not my own!
> And yet, three lives—no matter how blessed—are but a pittance to preserve man's freedom. We have had a brush with apocalypse, for Astaroth had learned of the book's location and resolved to take possession through guile or murder or

war. The Demon is uncommon cunning and
long has he sought this book and studied
the arts that would deliver up its
secrets. Perish the thought of the book in
Astaroth's keeping, for with it he might
shape the world according to his will and
rule the fates of men. My own struggle
with the Demon is coming and it is
against his wickedness that Elias Bram
shall be tested.

I pray the book may lie veiled for
eternity, but time may bring strange tides
that lay bare a thing thought hidden.
Enclosed in this letter is a clever
talisman, crafted by Augur, who is my
confidant in these matters. Its face
shall shine in equal measure to the book's
peril from the Demon who covets it.

Should the Book of Thoth be at risk
once again, the solver of my riddle may
yet rescue it from harm. I dare not write
in plainer prose lest the Enemy come by
this letter and all is lost. If you should
succeed in finding the book, loath should
you be to use it! Follow the path of
wisdom and surrender it to safety where
it may lie quiet till the end of days....

Beneath where Teuton kings were
  crowned
There is a key with notches four
To steer my steed beyond the sun
And safely knock on heaven's door.

For there the book doth lie with those
Who sleep beneath both hill and tree.
But keep in mind, dear Sorcerer,
No spell will pry its secrets free.
        In haste,
        Elias Bram

Max handed the letter back to Ms. Richter, who slipped it carefully into an archival box. David reached out to hand her the talisman, but Ms. Richter shook her head.

"No, David, I'd like you to hold on to that just now. You've done some excellent work, and I can't think of anyone whom I'd rather have in possession of that talisman for the time being. Have you committed this letter to memory?"

"Yes, Director," said David.

"Good, because I need to take the original and share it with several colleagues immediately. I'd like you to begin working on Bram's Riddle and see if you can make sense of it. I'll be working on it, too. The witches arrive in two weeks' time. Given the circumstances, I am going to invite others to that meeting."

"Are we going off with the witches, Ms. Richter? Should we pack our things?" asked David with just a tiny hint of humor.

"Not just yet, David," said Ms. Richter with a weary smile. "I would ask that you have faith. And Max?" Ms. Richter looked at the dark-haired boy as she stopped at the door.

"Yes, Ms. Richter?"

"I would ask that you have patience," said the Director softly. "Your greatness shines for all to see, but the Red Branch is not for one so young. They are invaluable and we honor them, but theirs is grim and solitary work. I would spare you such a life until you're of an age to choose for yourself. Commander Vilyak is an excellent Agent, but he is ambitious and ambition can cloud even the finest judgment. No one else can wield the weapon of Cúchulain . . . it will be waiting for you when you're ready. Goodnight."

Max and David said goodnight as Ms. Richter closed the door behind her. David tapped the talisman with his finger, squinting at the sun on its face.

"What was that all about?" he asked.

"Nothing," said Max, digesting Ms. Richter's words. "Vilyak showed me a vault and some weapons, and Ms. Richter thinks he's trying to recruit me."

"Is he?" asked David, glancing up from the talisman.

"I guess he is," sighed Max.

"Beware the flatterers of the world," said David, wagging his finger, "for what is music to the ears may be poison to the soul."

"Who said that?" asked Max.

"I did," said David, his eyes twinkling as he reached for a book on German history.

Max shook his head and stood up from his chair.

"Are you going to be here all night working on the Riddle?"

"Yes indeed," said David, thumbing through the book. "I'll be here until the witches throw me in a sack and cart me away."

"Don't even joke," said Max, poking his head out of the reading room to glance at the door to the Archives. "Do you think those shedu will eat me if I leave here alone?"

"I don't think so," said David, stifling a yawn. "They're more concerned with who gets in than who gets out. Do you want me to walk you up?"

"No," said Max, gazing out the door and up at the frescoes high above. "I'll be fine. If you find anything out, tell me right away—even if I'm sleeping."

"Will do," said David, giving a little wave before burying his nose back in his book.

Max hurried out of the Archives, past the stony shedu, and up the many stairs to emerge once more in the gloom of Room 313. By the time he arrived back at his room, he noticed that the door was ajar by the tiniest of slivers. Walking cautiously inside, Max saw Connor lounging with his textbooks by the fireplace on the lower level. On the table stood Mr. Sikes, dressed impeccably as ever and clasping his hands expectantly.

~ 5 ~

DARKMATTERS

Max took comfort in the fact that he had walked this path many times before. Etched in his memory were the lane's muddy grooves, its gentle rise, and the slow curve that would bring the grand house into view. And there it was, a jagged silhouette on the hill whose narrow windows spilled warm light into the evening. As usual, the wolfhound was waiting for him. It padded slowly from the underbrush to block his path, a monstrous, tangled thing of gigantic proportions that stopped and appraised him in the twilight.

As the hound approached, something caught Max's attention. There, hidden behind the trunk of an alder tree, was the small, slim form of Mr. Sikes. Max scowled at the imp's luminous cat's eyes.

"Go away," Max murmured. "You're not supposed to be here."

"Just ignore me," purred Mr. Sikes, raising a tiny finger to his lips.

Max would have argued, but the hound was almost upon him, bigger than a horse and smelling of wet fur and earth. Its great, panting head loomed above Max. Holding his breath, Max braced himself for the question that he knew would come.

"What are you about? Answer quick or I'll gobble you up!"

Max hesitated.

True to its word, the hound's jaws yawned open and Max was swallowed up in one great gulp. He shut his eyes as the hound's teeth crunched closed behind him. For several dizzying moments his body seemed to slide, limp and languid, down the beast's gullet and into the soft, spongy bed of its belly.

When Max opened his eyes, he glimpsed that Mr. Sikes was still watching from the safety of the alder tree. A low growl sounded from Max's throat; he swung his heavy head full round to glower upon the little imp. Mr. Sikes retreated farther into the shadows.

Shifting his weight, Max dug a massive paw into the soft earth.

With a sudden pop Mr. Sikes transformed into a field mouse and fled up the path in a series of zigzagging hops. Max gave a roar and chased after, running with terrible speed on his four legs as the mouse made for the lights of the house.

The intrusive imp was not nearly quick enough.

Mr. Sikes had gained the front steps when Max overtook him, seizing the mouse in his jaws as his momentum brought them both crashing against the door. Scrambling to his feet,

Max growled and gave the mouse a sudden shake, tossing its body far out onto the wet grass.

The door opened behind him, and light streamed out onto the lawn, spotlighting the small, still form of the mouse.

"Max, what have you done?"

Max whirled at the sound of his mother's voice. She stood in the open doorway, hand in hand with his father. She was just as he remembered her. Max felt a sudden stab of longing to come inside the house and join them.

Something in his mother's features stopped him, however. Her dark eyes widened as she raised a trembling hand and pointed beyond him. Max turned to look again at the lifeless lump of Mr. Sikes, but the mouse was gone.

There, on the grass, lay the curled, broken body of Alex Muñoz.

Max screamed.

He awoke to see David standing by his bed, holding a lamp and looking frightened.

"You were dreaming," his roommate said. "You're okay, you know."

"Sure," croaked Max, blinking at the twinkling constellations and the lamp's reflection in the glass dome. He flung the sweat-soaked sheets away from him and propped himself against the headboard. The disturbing details of his dream, so vivid a moment earlier, began to fade. He was almost certain, however, that he had seen Mr. Sikes. Max had no idea why the imp would have been visiting his dreams, but he was strangely loath to share the incident with David.

"It's past four," whispered David. "The witches will be here soon. I'm going to watch for them if you want to come."

Max swung his legs over the bed with a nod and minutes later the two were creeping down the dormitory's hallway, wrapped in sweaters and blankets to guard against the morning chill. They found a suitable perch in a cozy nook on the third floor where lead-paned windows looked out onto the front lawn and drive. There was no hint of sun outside, just a dull wash of chalky gray that extended to the horizon. Max rested his forehead against the cool window.

"How's the Riddle coming?" asked Max, fogging the glass while David studied a small slip of paper.

David shrugged.

"Some of it is easy. 'Beneath where Teuton kings were crowned' is obviously a reference to Frankfurt, Germany. Frankfurt's where German rulers were elected and it's the headquarters for the Workshop. The other stuff is a little trickier."

"What does the Frankfurt Workshop have to do with it?" asked Max.

"They're not Rowan," said David, flicking the paper with his finger. "And I think that's *exactly* why Bram would have left a piece of the puzzle with them. He obviously thought the Book of Thoth is dangerous—he'd want to ensure that no one person or group could get it by themselves. By scattering the means of reaching it, he'd ensure it could be obtained only through cooperation, and that's likely only if the book's really in danger. It's pretty smart, actually—"

David cut his sentence short and stood up to gaze out the window as a dozen crows suddenly flew from the direction of the gate. The birds circled and wheeled before skimming over the grounds to perch on Maggie's roof. Several moments later a team of four black horses emerged from the dark wood, pulling an ornate red coach. The coach eased its way across the gray landscape until it came to a stop near the fountain below them. The horses tossed their heads, rolled their eyes, and breathed great clouds of steam, but the gleaming carriage remained closed and shuttered.

"It's like a jewelry box," whispered David, pressing his nose to the glass.

Max saw someone hurry down the Manse's front steps. It was Miss Boon, wrapped in a blue shawl and looking miserable. She stopped before the coach and gave a low, solemn bow. A red door promptly opened, and four hooded shapes slipped out to follow the young Mystics instructor inside. David turned from the window and stepped quickly down the hall.

"Now that they're here, we'll have to hurry," he said. "Come with me."

"Where?" asked Max.

"To the clock tower," David replied, scurrying away. "There's something I have to do, and I might not get the chance later."

"But they'll be coming to get us soon!" hissed Max.

"That's why we have to hurry!" whispered David, disappearing around the corner.

Minutes later, Max understood why Miss Boon had looked so glum. It was a raw, wet morning, and he shivered as he stamped the morning dew off his slippers and braced himself against the gusts that swirled about Old Tom. Max and David stood on a fenced balcony just outside the clock's face, obscuring its hands of weathered copper as they clutched the railing some 150 feet above the gray-green lawns below.

"What are we *doing* up here?" asked Max, his teeth chattering.

David ignored him and arched his back over the railing to squint up at the tower's sharp-pitched roof.

"Can you give me a boost up there?" he asked.

Max craned his neck at the steep angle of the roof and its

slick, wet shingles, then looked at his clumsy roommate. Even a mountain goat would have difficulty navigating that roof.

"Are you crazy?" he asked. "You'll slip right off!"

"You're probably right," mused David. "Higher is better, but I guess this will have to do."

"Do for what?" asked Max, pulling his blanket closer as a particularly furious gust came whipping in off the sea.

David did not answer him, but instead leaned far out over the balcony and raised a hand toward the ocean, whose gray waves crashed and sent high plumes of spray into the morning air. To Max's surprise, his roommate began to sing a soft, lilting song.

It was not like any song Max had heard before. The words were strange, as were the notes that periodically dipped unexpectedly or jumped to another key altogether. Max ignored the wind that howled and raged about him. He felt warm and content, losing himself in the hypnotic song that tempted him to sleep and drift along with the world's storms and currents until his body would unravel at last and become a bit of stone or sea.

A mist rose slowly from the ocean. Tatters of fog came sweeping over the cliffs to run like swift rivers along the walkways and gardens. Soon, a layer of mist, as soft and white as lamb's wool, blanketed the grounds and treetops. By the time David's voice trailed into silence, Max could hear that a crowd had awakened and gathered in front of Old Tom. As though shaken from a trance, David opened his eyes and suddenly raised his arms like a conductor. There was a low roar and the mist swirled clockwise, forming a great funnel at its center that expanded outward like the eye of a hurricane.

Max heard several startled shouts followed by the distant opening and closing of doors and windows. People had been gathering far below, but now they scattered as the mist was pushed out to the edges of the campus, rising higher and higher until it seemed Rowan had been uprooted and set within the clouds, hidden and secret from the world.

The sound of hard, hurried footsteps came from the tower's stairwell; a moment later Miss Boon's head burst into view. The young Mystics instructor was out of breath, her short brown hair clinging to her round face. She glanced at Max before narrowing her eyes at David.

"What have you done?" she asked sharply.

"I've hidden us," said David wearily. "The old spells were fading. No enemies will be able to find us now—by map, by road, or by sea. Rowan has disappeared."

Miss Boon stepped out onto the balcony and gazed out at the grounds and the towering dome of white mist that rose hundreds of feet into the air, filtering the rays of the morning sun that now peeped above the horizon like a sliver of gold.

"Go back down, David," she sighed, wiping condensation from her glasses. "We'll talk about this later. You too, Max. You're both to dress in your formal uniforms and wait in your room until Cooper comes for you. You are to do *nothing* else until that happens. Lord knows how the witches will seek to profit by this!"

Max and David slinked back inside and crept down the stairs, past the clock's gears and chimes, which smelled of oil and age. There was a large crowd gathered outside the steps.

"What did you do?" shouted one angry student.

"Make it go away!" called another.

"Make *them* go away!" screeched Anna Lundgren, stabbing a finger at Max.

"That's quite enough," commanded Miss Boon as she shepherded Max and David through the dense throng of bewildered students, scholars, and faculty. Max felt a tug on his sleeve and looked up to see a pretty girl with brown hair and freckles clutching a camera.

Max merely blinked at the unfamiliar girl before he was promptly swept along by Miss Boon and the curious crowd that closed in behind them. They were marched up the broad stairs and down the long hall to their room. Mr. McDaniels was waiting inside.

The knock came sooner than expected. Max answered the door, clean and scrubbed in his pressed Rowan uniform. David and Max's father came up the steps to find Cooper standing in the doorway.

"It's time," said the Agent softly. "The Director requests that you say nothing at all during the proceedings. It is important that you agree to this. Can the Director have your word?"

"Some kind of nerve," huffed Mr. McDaniels. "We're supposed to sit still like church mice while a bunch of strangers and witches decide our fate?"

"That's correct," said Cooper with a stoic nod. "If you don't like the terms, you can wait here and someone will inform you of the outcome."

"No," said David quickly. "We want to go—we can be quiet."

"No matter what?" Cooper asked.

"No matter what," replied Max.

Cooper led David and the McDanielses down many stairs, far below the Manse's dining hall and kitchens, until they reached a long hallway lined with polished suits of armor from various ages and civilizations. Max was surprised to see government security personnel in black suits standing outside the door along with a handful of Rowan Agents. They stood aside and opened a gleaming wooden door as Cooper approached.

"Remember your promise," Cooper warned as he ushered them inside.

Max felt his father's comforting hand on his shoulder as he stood on the threshold of a large room with a high chandeliered ceiling and an enormous circular table of malachite at its center. Some two dozen people sat around the table and many more were seated in chairs at the room's periphery. All were staring at Max and David. Cooper led them to three seats along the far wall, in between Miss Boon and Nigel Bristow, the man who had recruited Max to Rowan. Max tried to return Nigel's smile, but he felt numb inside as Ms. Richter stood to commence the proceedings. He soon learned that there were not only representatives of Rowan and the witches in attendance but also members of the Frankfurt Workshop and senior officials from a dozen governments.

"It has been nearly one thousand years since these three Orders have sat at table together," began Ms. Richter, "and I am grateful to all who have come. This meeting is born of grave necessity, and I hope that today we might transcend old feuds and grievances and unite in common purpose to face the peril before us. From beyond the grave Elias Bram has warned us of this danger, and it is his Riddle that troubles me today—*not* his Oath, which has brought our sisters on such a long journey."

An ancient witch in a black frock, her skin covered with those same strange symbols, rose to her feet. She was older than Dame Mala, with steel-gray hair and amethyst eyes that were now narrowed at Ms. Richter.

"What trickery is this?" demanded the witch in a hoarse voice, stabbing a ringed finger at the Director. "We are here for our rightful due and will not have our demands so lightly cast aside!"

"Very well, Dame Mako," said Ms. Richter. "In order to

move this council along to more pressing matters, I am prepared to state our position on the issue."

Scott McDaniels squeezed his son's forearm. Max held his breath and leaned forward to listen as the whole room grew still with a crackling air of expectation.

"Having consulted my advisors and having determined the legitimacy of Bram's Oath, I do hereby honor his pledge and surrender Max McDaniels and David Menlo to the Witches of the Eastern Range."

The room exploded in commotion.

"*What?*" Mr. McDaniels thundered, rocketing out of his chair. "Over my dead body!"

Mr. McDaniels was quickly intercepted by Mum, who abandoned her coffee cart to block his way with her short, squat body. She was joined by Nigel and Miss Boon, who managed to ease Max's father back into his seat. The real commotion, however, was taking place beside Ms. Richter. Commander Vilyak had stood and was leaning close to the Director. His face was crimson, and his massive hands were balled into tight fists. Max could not hear what he was saying, but the Director was unmoved.

"Agents Cooper and Yamato, please remove Commander Vilyak from these proceedings."

"You don't have the authority to remove me!" spat Vilyak, smacking the table hard with his hand. "This is an outrage and an utter abuse of your position!"

"Thank you, Commander," was Ms. Richter's calm reply. "That will be all."

Commander Vilyak glanced over his shoulder at Cooper and a female Agent who were standing behind him. Slowly, an icy calm came over him; his eyes became as flat and dead as a doll's once more. He glanced at Max before turning to face

Cooper, his comrade in the Red Branch. To Max, it seemed that a silent conversation was taking place between them. After several moments, Vilyak permitted himself to be led from the room. The door was closed, calm was restored, and for the first time the reality of Ms. Richter's words dawned upon Max.

They were leaving Rowan.

Max glanced at the cluster of shrouded crones at the table. They whispered to one another with obvious pleasure, beaming at Max and David with sharp-toothed grins and something resembling motherly affection. Max's father looked clammy and bloodless; even David looked shocked.

"I understand that this comes as a surprise to some," said Ms. Richter, failing even to glance in Max and David's direction. "And we are deeply grieved to say farewell to our students. While circumstance dictates that we sever their ties to this school, we hope and trust that Scott McDaniels will also be permitted to live among the witches with his son."

"Of course," said Dame Mako with an obliging nod toward Mr. McDaniels. "He will be received with honor."

"Then they will be free to leave with you as early as tomorrow morning," said Ms. Richter. "And now we must move on to more pressing business—the escalating evil that plagues the world now that Astaroth is free. . . ."

Max sat in stunned silence while ministers and senators shuffled papers and reported on troubles in their home countries. It was a grim recital of assassinations, plane crashes, train derailments, and crop failures. Angry mobs were gathering outside capital buildings; desperate refugees were stampeding toward the borders of the world's wealthier nations. Power stations had succumbed to mysterious fires, and it was becoming clear that the Enemy had long been infiltrating a number of governments. The numbers were staggering: a billion people without electricity, two billion without access to television or radio. A short black man in a gray suit reported that more than sixty governments were on the verge of collapse, their countries facing civil war. Miss Kraken spoke Max's mind when she interrupted an ample-bellied senator with a southern drawl.

"These reports can't be correct," she snapped. "As bad as things are, the newspapers haven't reported anything even approaching these proportions of catastrophe!"

The senator glanced at his watch and cleared his throat. "For the past six weeks, all relevant television programs, newspaper reports, and radio broadcasts have been subject to government approval."

"You're censoring the facts?" asked Miss Kraken incredulously.

"We are acting in the best interests of our citizens," replied the senator. "I'd remind you that the only reason we don't have blood in the streets in *this* country is because we are keeping potential misinformation from causing outright panic."

"We are doing the same," added an official from Moscow. "There are terrible reports from the countryside. Terrible! No one needs to hear, much less see, such stories and images. An entire village near Lensk was wiped out two days ago. Monstrous shapes have been sighted in the woods—rumors of ogres and werewolves are rampant. Despite our best efforts to calm the public, we have a crisis. Farms and villages are emptying. The people are fleeing to the cities—cities with little electricity or food. And winter is coming. Things have not been so bad for Mother Russia since the Great War."

Max squirmed in his seat as the tales of horror went on. His problems seemed tiny in light of all that was happening outside Rowan's gates. Perhaps Bellagrog had been right—now seemed a good time to find a snug, hidden corner and wait out the squalls and storms of the world.

It was Jesper Rasmussen, the bald, skeletal spokesperson for the Frankfurt Workshop, who stood next. His voice was dry and metallic; a nearly colorless tongue flicked out periodically to wet his thin lips.

"Forgive my ignorance," he said, "but it seems that we are attributing the present, ah, *misfortunes* to Astaroth. The Workshop still questions whether or not the Demon has returned, much less whether he is to blame for any of this. The current crises seem a bit sudden and dramatic for one known to spin his webs with slow patience."

"And so he did, Dr. Rasmussen," said Ms. Richter. "And so he was caught. Astaroth did indeed bide his time, but before his plans were complete, Elias Bram realized that a single mind and malice was orchestrating events to its satisfaction. Once Astaroth was revealed, we were able to frustrate some of his plots. Astaroth will have learned his lesson. He will move quickly if he is able."

Dr. Rasmussen shook his head as Ms. Richter spoke.

"*If* he is able. That is no small consideration. We have no proof that the Demon is even capable of assuming a physical form."

"Of that we *do* have proof," interrupted Dame Mako, rapping a sharp nail on the table and drawing Rasmussen's attention. "I have seen him."

Stunned silence filled the room. Max heard the crack of Dame Mako's fingers as she clasped her bony hands together in a supplicating gesture.

"He came to see us a fortnight ago," said the witch. "Perhaps we should have sent messages, but we thought it wiser to wait until Rowan proved true and honored Bram's Oath. The Demon came to us when we were gathered by the council fires."

"What did he want?" asked Ms. Richter softly. Her face was ashen and grave.

"He gave greetings," said Dame Mako. "He reminded us that he had once honored our ancestors and wished to rekindle the truce that had existed between us. His servants brought many gifts—jewels and hides and oil for the winter."

"I trust you did not accept them," said Ms. Richter.

"Ha! We are not so rich as you," laughed the witch. "Of course we took them! And we'll take more, too, as long as it's given freely and the Demon leaves us be!"

"He gives nothing freely," said Ms. Richter. "To visit the esteemed witches is a long journey. Astaroth did not seek you merely to lavish gifts and praise."

Dame Mako listened carefully to Ms. Richter's words and consulted briefly with the wizened crones who had accompanied her. Her wild eyes burned brightly as she gazed from face to face among the assembled politicians, Agents, and Mystics.

"The Demon covets the book he sought long ago," the witch rumbled. "The very book that Bram took from us and for which he delivered these Blessed Children to our keeping. He seeks the Book of Thoth."

"And why should the Demon seek this book?" asked Dr. Rasmussen.

Dame Mako glared at the Workshop representative. "All things have a truename," she rasped. "Every human, every bird and beast and flower, has such a name. This name is secret—it is what gives a thing shape and spirit and binds it to this world. According to legend, the Book of Thoth is a living record of all truenames since the world was birthed."

Jesper Rasmussen scoffed loudly and snapped at Mum for more coffee.

"So it is a phone book? A list of all the truenames of history? Of what possible value is that?"

Dame Mako scowled at the tall, gaunt man who smirked from behind his steel spectacles.

"It is priceless to the one who can decipher it," replied the witch calmly. "With the proper spells, the knowledge of an entity's truename conveys absolute mastery of that thing. A mountain, a person, even an *idea* can be reshaped, enslaved, or utterly stricken from this world as though it had never existed. Within the Book of Thoth lie the very blueprints to this world's past, present, and future."

"Ah, so it is DNA, is it?" asked Rasmussen, his eyes twinkling. "A bit of this, a bit of that, and we can rearrange the world how we choose? How delightful."

"Foolish man," snapped the witch. "With the Book, Astaroth would have us at his mercy."

"So it is a weapon," probed Rasmussen.

"It is whatever you wish it to be," replied Dame Mako quietly. "It holds the secrets to life and death and time, Dr. Rasmussen. Can you understand that?"

Max tried to imagine such a thing but found it hard. He looked at David, who seemed to be following the conversation very closely as he drained a second coffee. Dr. Rasmussen offered the witch a sour stare and seemed to mull several possible responses.

"Bah!" he said at length, removing his glasses to clean them with a cloth. "Who has seen or tested this book? No one can decipher it, and yet it holds the power to snuff our lives and shape our fates? What a convenient thing to possess—all one must do is brandish the book before one's enemies, and they will flock to your banner lest they be stricken from the record. No wonder Astaroth seeks its whereabouts! This book is a bogeyman capable of frightening even the high and mighty! Surely, Director Richter, you do not believe such an artifact exists."

Ms. Richter sat quietly while Mum refilled Rasmussen's coffee cup. When she spoke, her words were measured.

"I am confident that the book exists, that it is to be feared, and that it is in danger. For the first two, I rely upon history and the warnings of Elias Bram. For the third, I rely upon Dame Mako and the discoveries of our own David Menlo. Dr. Rasmussen, you have heard the tales of Prince Neferkeptah?"

"I can't say that I have," sighed Rasmussen, rubbing his temples.

"He was the last mortal to truly possess the book, and it destroyed him. Astaroth, however, is *not* mortal, and I am convinced that we must do everything possible to ensure that the book never falls into his hands."

"So where precisely is the god-awful thing?" asked a British minister.

"Just the question on my mind," echoed a senator.

"I don't know," said Ms. Richter simply.

"Then what is the point of wasting our time on this?" snapped the Russian official. "I have airplanes grounded with no fuel! Someone or something has ripped up a thousand miles of railroad track, and yet I'm supposed to focus my attention on a book? A book that we don't even know how to find?"

"I recognize that we all have pressing concerns," said Ms. Richter, "but if Astaroth gains possession of this book, our present worries will seem trivial indeed."

"Well," said Dr. Rasmussen, "it seems highly unlikely that Astaroth will find the book. After all, your people were the last to possess it, and even you do not know where it is."

Rasmussen looked pleased with himself until Ms. Richter beckoned for David to come forward. Hundreds of eyes followed Max's roommate as he walked, unhurried, to stand next to the Director.

"Ladies and gentlemen, allow me to introduce David Menlo. It is David whom we have to thank for finding and deciphering several of Bram's papers that concern this matter. When Bram hid the book, he confided the secret of its location to one other person. This person was Marley Augur, a member of the ruling council at our former school. It grieves me to say that Augur betrayed our Order and was instrumental in freeing Astaroth this past year. We must assume that Astaroth is privy to any secrets that Augur possessed. Within Bram's papers, David has discovered further proof that the book is in danger."

Ms. Richter motioned for an aide to dim the lights as David unbuttoned his collar and reached inside his shirt to retrieve the talisman that hung on a chain around his neck. In the darkened room, the talisman shone like a fiery coin, noticeably brighter than when Max had last seen it.

"Before he became a traitor, Marley Augur fashioned this talisman to warn Bram if the Book was in danger. Since we have discovered the talisman, it has burned brighter each day."

Max watched the talisman swinging gently back and forth on David's finger. The room was utterly quiet.

"We are in gravest peril," said Ms. Richter softly. "Not merely the organizations and countries represented here, but every man, woman, and child on this earth. We must marshal all our resources and we must do so immediately. I would now ask all who are not seated at this table to please withdraw so that the senior members of this council can decide upon an appropriate course of action."

Max felt very insignificant indeed as he was swept out of the room alongside his father and David amidst a crush of aides, Agents, scholars, and minor dignitaries. His senses swam with the smell of damp coats, the sober chatter of shocked officials, and the gleaming eyes of the witches who followed him out the door. Nigel was waiting for them when they emerged into the hallway. The Recruiter looked on the verge of tears.

"I don't know what to say," he said, flapping his arms helplessly. "I honestly never thought it would come to this. I am so terribly sorry, Scott."

Mr. McDaniels nodded and shook Nigel's hand. The frail blond man retrieved a silk handkerchief from his jacket and blew his nose. He gave a guilty laugh and dabbed at his eyes.

"Can I at least help you pack?" asked Nigel. "Share a laugh or two? I could send an Agent out for some Bedford Bros. thingies. . . ."

"That would be nice," said Max, smiling at the memory of that strange and wonderful night when Nigel's tests had confirmed the special spark within him. "My dad and I will meet you there. We're going to get Nick."

"Max, I don't think you'll be able to do that," said Miss Boon from behind them. "Nick and Maya are extremely rare—perhaps the last of their kind. We can't let them go."

Max whirled at the young instructor, who met his furious stare with calm reserve.

"I thought we were rare, too," he seethed.

Several nearby scholars and diplomats ceased their conversations at the commotion. Miss Boon gave a sad smile.

"Max, I am heartbroken at the Director's decision," she said soothingly, "but I also helped research the curse that would have befallen us. We have no choice but to honor Bram's Oath. I am sorry."

"That's fine," snapped Max, ignoring Nigel's gentle tug at his elbow. "But we're not leaving without Nick and Maya. We took an oath, too, you know."

"I'll speak to the Director," promised Miss Boon. "Meanwhile, I'll leave you to organize your things. Unfortunately, you are not to speak to any student about today's council—including your departure tomorrow morning."

"You mean we can't say good-bye to our friends?" asked David.

"I'm so sorry," replied Miss Boon, avoiding his gaze. "Given the situation's sensitivity, it's out of the question."

"Sensitivity?" scoffed Mr. McDaniels. "You've got some nerve using that word."

Miss Boon straightened and gave a curt nod to the group.

"Nigel, I trust you will escort Max and David to their room. Good-bye and good luck."

"Good-bye, Miss Boon," said Max quietly, dipping his head as his anger was replaced by a sudden pang of sorrow. The young Mystics instructor swept down the hallway, scattering scholars and bull-necked security personnel in her wake.

That evening, Max watched Nick rummage through a bag of Bedford Bros. Crispy Snacks while Nigel and Mr. McDaniels snapped shut the clasps of an overstuffed suitcase. David was still absent, having gone to the Archives to return several grimoires before saying good-bye to Maya in the Sanctuary. Despite Ms. Richter's permission for the boys to take their charges with them, David had decided that Maya should stay behind, having concluded that the ulu's frail constitution was poorly suited to life in the witches' mountain camps.

It was well past midnight when David returned, looking

drawn and sad. He ignored Nigel's efforts to cheer him up and instead went about folding his clothes and packing his medication into plastic bags.

An hour later, Max was sitting by the fire, listening to Mr. McDaniels explain each and every photo in the McDaniels family photo album to Nigel with painstaking detail. The Recruiter's eyelids were fluttering when Max thought he heard the sound of their door opening upstairs. Max glanced at David, but his roommate was now fretting over which remaining books to take, having already stuffed his enchanted pack with nearly all of his worldly possessions.

"Did you hear the door open?" asked Max quietly.

Nigel blinked and looked up gratefully from the photo album. "Come again?" he asked.

"I think someone's upstairs," Max whispered.

Nigel frowned and scooted off the couch, walking to the foot of the stairs.

"What on earth are you doing here?" asked the Recruiter, addressing someone on the landing above.

Max gaped as the tall, skeletal figure of Jesper Rasmussen descended the stairs.

"Answer my question, man," said Nigel sternly.

From his coat pocket, Dr. Rasmussen produced a slim gun and pointed it at Nigel. The gun hardly made a sound, but Max heard Nigel mutter a surprised "Oh!" before collapsing to the floor. With silent horror, the group watched a pinprick of blood expand into a small crimson stain above Nigel's heart.

Max leapt to his feet.

"Don't be foolish," warned Dr. Rasmussen in a quiet, calm voice. Max followed the man's gaze to where a small dot of red light now danced on Scott McDaniels's forehead. "As quick as you are, Max, I can shoot your father before you can lay a finger on me. If you and David fail to do exactly as I say, he will die. Do you understand?"

David nodded; his mouth was agape with shock. Max merely stared at Dr. Rasmussen, his anger bringing the man's features into sharp relief. Turning from Rasmussen's triumphant smirk, Max glanced again at Nigel's slumped form. His hands began to shake.

"Max," pleaded his father, "don't."

"Very wise of you, Mr. McDaniels," said Dr. Rasmussen. "For the moment, you have saved the life of your son. If you wish to continue living, however, you must come closer."

Max's father nodded and walked stiffly toward the heavy-lidded, skeletal man. His round face was shiny with sweat; he raised his hand in a steadying gesture.

"Just don't hurt anyone," pleaded Mr. McDaniels. "There's no need to hurt anyone."

"I will determine what is needed," replied Dr. Rasmussen coolly. "Ingest this, if you would."

From his breast pocket, Dr. Rasmussen produced a silver sphere the size of a pinball. He tossed it to Mr. McDaniels, who caught it with a puzzled expression.

"What is it?" said Mr. McDaniels suspiciously, inspecting the silver sphere.

"Your medicine," replied Dr. Rasmussen. "Take it like a good boy. You have three seconds."

"Dad, don't!" exclaimed Max. "It's poison!"

The red laser centered on Mr. McDaniels's forehead. Dr. Rasmussen began to count.

"Three . . . two . . ."

"Dad!"

Mr. McDaniels closed his eyes and swallowed the metallic ball. He grimaced as he strained to force it down. After several seconds, he gasped. "It's doing something to me!"

"Yes," said Dr. Rasmussen with a slow nod. "The discomfort will be over shortly. Listen very carefully to what I have to say. You have ingested an explosive, Mr. McDaniels. It is, as we speak, affixing itself to the lining of your stomach so that it cannot be removed or expelled without killing you in the process. It is programmed to detonate every two minutes unless it receives a coded transmission from the computer in my brain. If I am unable or unwilling to transmit this code, you will die. Fortunately for you, I am a reasonable man. I will continue to spare your life provided you, Max, and David follow my instructions to the letter. Do you understand?"

"Yes," said Mr. McDaniels. Sweat poured off his body, and he gave a sudden gag. "What about Nigel?" he asked, glancing at the Recruiter's crumpled form.

"He is already gone," muttered Dr. Rasmussen. "And we have little time. Max and David, you are to bring only as much as you can carry on your backs. Pack warm clothes and be quick. We are leaving in five minutes' time."

"What about my father?" Max growled. "He'll need things, too."

"We shall see," replied Dr. Rasmussen with a shrug. "The clock is ticking, my young friend."

Three minutes later, Max and David stood breathing heavily with hiking packs stuffed full of woolen sweaters and socks and flannel underwear. Rasmussen nodded toward Nick, who was crouched and bristling behind a potted palm.

"Most interesting," said Dr. Rasmussen, as though peering through a microscope. "Bring the lymrill, too," he added casually while reaching inside his jacket.

From his pocket, he produced a folded square of a strange, shimmering gauzy material. With a deft flick of his wrist, the cloth unfolded until it was the size of an enormous bedsheet. Almost instantly, the sheet disappeared as though it were completely transparent.

"This device bends the visible light spectrum," explained Dr. Rasmussen. "It will hide us as we exit the dormitories. Once we have descended to the foyer, I will make myself visible and depart as usual. When my driver opens the door to my car, you will hurry inside before me. The cloaking device is also sound-dampening, but please believe that I will know if you try to call out, signal, or deviate from my plan in any way. The consequences will be swift."

Minutes later, they were all moving quickly down the hallway, clinging to the opposite wall while a pair of Third Years chatted in a doorway. Nick's claws dug into Max's chest while the confused lymrill trembled and clung to his body. Max grimaced and held on fiercely to the base of Nick's tail as it strained to shake and rattle. The awkward procession continued in terrified, gasping steps until they reached the bottom of the stairs. Dr. Rasmussen held a warning finger to his lips as he slipped outside the cloth and strode forward into the foyer, where Mum was muttering to herself and dragging a mop unevenly across the tiles. She glanced up as Rasmussen crossed toward the door.

"Oh, hello, sir," she said, giving a brief curtsy.

Rasmussen glanced down at her as though she were something he might flick off his shoe.

"You're the serving hag, aren't you?" he asked dryly as he pushed open the double doors.

"Yes, sir. Me and my sister," said Mum, sniffing suddenly as though she had a cold. She paused a moment. "Is there anything I can do for you, sir?"

"Yes," said Rasmussen, pausing by the open door while Max, David, and his father scurried past him. "Learn to make proper coffee."

With that, Rasmussen closed the door behind him and moved quickly down the steps, passing Max and the others in the process. A sleek limousine was already waiting with a uniformed driver standing at attention by one of the doors. Max held his breath as a pair of Agents casually approached from behind the Manse.

"Leaving already, Dr. Rasmussen?" asked one.

"Can't be helped," replied Dr. Rasmussen, motioning for his driver to open the door.

"Would you like to see the Director?" asked the other. "I don't believe she was aware that you planned to depart this evening."

Dr. Rasmussen offered the pair an icy smile and paused before the open door. Max, David, and Mr. McDaniels scuttled inside the limousine, practically toppling onto one another as they collapsed onto its deep leather seats.

"Do not disturb the Director," said Dr. Rasmussen with a dismissive air of authority. "She is a busy lady, I am a busy man, and these are busy times. I will contact her tomorrow. Goodnight, gentlemen."

Dr. Rasmussen slipped inside, and the driver closed the door. Sitting up, Max caught a glimpse of Mum standing on the front steps, leaning against her mop with a puzzled expression as the limousine pulled away.

Mum knows we're here, Max realized. He thought of the hag's sudden sniff in the foyer; Mum's sense of smell was sharper than a bloodhound's. Max glanced at his father, who sat rigid against the backrest as the two Agents approached the hag. *Oh my God,* pleaded Max as his pulse began to pound. *Don't set off an alarm, Mum!* He squirmed for a better look, but the limousine eased around the fountain and he lost sight of the hag.

"Stay beneath the cloth until we are outside the gates," muttered Dr. Rasmussen, glancing at his watch with a satisfied smile. "We are precisely on time . . . good, good."

The car wound about the drive and out toward the ocean, where the mist David had conjured hung in the air like a spectral curtain. Max craned his neck around to see the yellow lights of the Manse, Old Tom, and Maggie twinkle out of sight as the limousine bent to the right, plunging into the wood and through the thick walls of stone to where the great gates opened to let them pass.

"Where are you taking us?" asked Max, glaring at Rasmussen.

"Be silent," muttered Rasmussen while he typed swift keystrokes into a handheld computer.

Several minutes later, the limousine came to a halt outside a white clapboard church on the outskirts of Rowan Township. Rasmussen motioned for them to get out; Max noticed that the driver had turned the lights off but kept the engine running.

"Hurry," said Dr. Rasmussen curtly. "There may be spies nearby."

The man led them around the church to a small cemetery in back. Reaching into his overcoat, he placed a small metal disk at the base of a weathered headstone.

"You will wait here," he ordered. "This device is a trigger whose global position has just been set to this precise location. If Mr. McDaniels strays more than ten meters, the explosive he has ingested will detonate. Do you understand?"

"Yes," said Max, stepping between Rasmussen and his father. "What are we supposed to do?"

"Wait here," replied the man, casting a long glance at Nick. "Someone will come for you. Now I must go. Give me the lymrill."

Max retreated a step as the man approached; Nick squirmed in Max's arms, and his quills stiffened.

"Don't touch him," warned Max.

"You're in no position to argue," muttered Rasmussen distractedly, extending a gloved hand.

Nick writhed; moonlight flashed on his claws, and Rasmussen cursed as blood spattered onto the grass. Rasmussen clutched an arm that had been slashed from wrist to elbow.

"Stupid animal!" hissed Rasmussen. He fumbled in his coat pocket for a slim device that hummed as he waved it over the wound. The flow of blood promptly stopped.

"It's not his fault," whispered Max. "Don't hurt him."

Dr. Rasmussen's features contorted briefly into a taut scowl. Slowly, he regained his composure while the wound on his forearm knitted itself whole like a closing zipper. He drew himself up and gave Nick a loathing glance.

"Don't wander off," he said icily, backing slowly out of the cemetery and slipping around the church. Max heard the car door close, followed by the low purr of its engine receding into the night. They were alone.

"Dad," said Max, turning at once. "Stand right next to that thing!"

Mr. McDaniels did as he was told, cradling a hand against his belly as he slumped against the gravestone. Max handed Nick to David and hurried over to his father.

"It's going to be okay," said Max soothingly, mopping away the beads of sweat that dotted his father's forehead. "We'll figure out how to get that thing out of you."

Mr. McDaniels groaned and squeezed Max's hand.

"Poor Nigel," muttered David, stroking Nick and setting him down onto the ground, where he curled into a ball and nibbled his tail.

Max tried to ignore David; it was all too overwhelming, and he could not focus on anything but the issue at hand. David sniffled and leaned close to inspect the slim, circular device resting on the gravestone.

"Don't touch it," hissed Max, shooing David away.

"I won't," said David. "But—"

A snapping twig cut David short.

Max whirled to stare at the stand of birch trees just beyond the cemetery's low fence. Something peeped from behind a tree and shuffled back deeper into the wood.

"David, stay with my dad," breathed Max, easing his father behind the shelter of the gravestone. He straightened and began walking slowly toward the trees.

"Who's there?" he called, scanning the trees for movement.

Nothing answered.

Max reached the fence and peered into the darkness; he locked onto a pair of startled blinking eyes. Quick as a flash, Max hopped the fence and darted into the forest to tackle the bulky figure, which shrieked and collapsed beneath him.

"Don't hurt me!" squealed a familiar voice.

Max rolled the figure over and squinted at the creature squirming helplessly beneath him.

It was Mum.

"What are you doing here?" breathed Max, helping the roly-poly hag to her feet. Mum brushed several leaves out of her hair and plucked a crushed wicker basket from the ground.

"I wanted to know what you were doing," she sniffed, flinging the ruined basket into a bush. "I smelled you, your yummy father, and that awful thing sneaking off with that mean man. Mum wanted to see what was so secret."

Max stooped to Mum's height.

"Does anyone else know that you're here?" he asked, taking hold of her shoulders.

"The gate guards," she muttered hesitantly, "but they think I'm out collecting mushrooms."

"Do you usually leave Rowan to collect mushrooms?" asked Max in a panic.

"Not just for mushrooms," she explained, examining her fingernails. "I also like to hide and sniff the tourists. Every year they're a little fatter, you know. . . ."

Max groaned and released her.

"Mum, go back home and keep this to yourself," he sighed, walking back toward the cemetery. "Promise me."

"I will not!" cried the hag, hurrying after. "I saw that you've got packs. You're going on a camping trip, and Mum's coming, too!"

Max ignored her, casually hopping the fence. Mum grunted and threw herself over, rolling like a barrel over the top and spilling with a crash into a clump of weeds.

"Who is that?" asked David, peering from around the gravestone.

"It's me, you hideous awful thing," hissed Mum, falling in step behind Max, who ignored her. "I need a vacation and I'm coming on your camping trip."

"We're not going on a camping trip," Max stated firmly.

"Oh no?" asked Mum, toeing David's pack with her blocky shoe. "Then what are you doing?"

"We don't know," replied Max angrily. "We're supposed to wait here and we can't leave or my dad will get hurt. And since when do you take vacations?"

Mum paused a moment. Her beady eyes began to fill with tears.

"I never needed a vacation," she said in a trembling voice, "but *she's* made a shambles of my life!"

Mum began to cry, great quivering sobs that soon escalated into outright bawling. She flung herself across Scott McDaniels's mountainous form, burying her wet snout in his chest.

"Who's made a shambles of your life?" croaked Mr. McDaniels, straining weakly to lift his head away from the greasy topknot that now tickled his nose.

"Bellagrog!" shrieked the hag, scratching at her tear-streaked cheeks. "She's ruined everything!" The hag sobbed again and practically tunneled into Mr. McDaniels, burying her face in his armpit.

"Have you tried to talk to her?" asked David.

"Talk?" asked Mum, lifting her head and swiveling her eye around to look at David. "You can't *talk* to Bellagrog—she don't listen. And you can't get rid of her, neither! Sniffs out all my little traps and poisons, she does!"

"Mum, you tried to poison your sister?" asked Max incredulously.

"They were very *humane* poisons," replied Mum with an indignant sniff. "With her out of the way, things could return to normal. Just Bob and me and your pa, happy as clams, and no more 'Let's make Bea a laughingstock'!"

Mum dissolved into more quivering sobs, punctuated by a sudden explosion of flatulence.

"Dear Lord," wheezed Mr. McDaniels, trying to loosen her grip upon him.

"Hmmm," said Mum, sniffing the air with interest. "I might need to duck in the woods for a bitsy."

"You do that," said Max, peeling the hag off his father,

careful not to upset the detonation device Dr. Rasmussen had left behind. Once Mum had waddled off out of earshot, Max leaned close to David and his father.

"We have to get rid of her," he whispered. "She could put you in danger, Dad."

Mr. McDaniels nodded.

"I feel bad for her," said David decisively.

"Get over it," said a man's voice.

Max whirled at the sound; Cooper was standing next to the church, dressed all in black with a heavy pack on his back. Next to him stood Miss Boon, wrapped in a dark shawl. The two approached cautiously, glancing periodically in the direction of the road.

"What are you doing here?" asked Max, flushing with a strange mix of shock and relief.

"Rescuing you," replied Miss Boon dryly. She knelt down to examine Rasmussen's device.

"Don't touch that," said Max. "It's—"

"I know what it is," said Miss Boon, "and your father will be just fine."

Before Max could say another word, Miss Boon depressed the device's glowing display, which then faded to black. Mr. McDaniels heaved a sigh of relief.

"Is it over?" he asked. "Or can this thing in me still go off?"

Cooper knelt over Mr. McDaniels.

"You only swallowed a casing," explained the Agent quietly. "Its core was hollow. It'll stay in you, but it's harmless."

"But what about Nigel?" asked Mr. McDaniels with visible relief on his face.

"Nigel's fine," replied Miss Boon with a small smile. "Unconscious and probably in for a headache, but nothing more."

"What was Rasmussen doing, then?" asked Max, hoisting Nick into his arms.

"Kidnapping you," replied Cooper.

"Ah," said David, rubbing his arms. "Brilliant."

"What's so brilliant?" croaked Mr. McDaniels.

"Rasmussen isn't associated with Rowan," said David, an admiring glint in his eye. "If he took us off Rowan's campus against our will, then Richter can't be held responsible for violating the terms of Bram's Oath. It's a clever way of avoiding the curse."

"So we hope," confirmed Miss Boon, crossing her fingers.

Just then, a hideous scream sounded in the distance, sending a primal chill down Max's spine. The cry trailed off into a note of despair. With a shriek, Mum came fleeing out of the woods, hoisting her bloomers up under her flowered dress.

"What's that terrible noise?" she cried, her eyes white and round with terror.

"The witches," replied Cooper quietly, tightening the straps of his pack. "They know Max and David are gone. Wait here till daylight, Mum. Then find your way back to campus."

"I'm not staying out here with witches about!" protested Mum. "I'm coming with you or I'll tell everyone what you've done!"

The hag crossed her meaty arms while Cooper paused to consider her.

"We don't have time for this," concluded the Agent in a flat voice. The shift in Cooper's tone alarmed Max. Clearly, the Agent had concluded that Mum was an obstacle to the success of his mission; obstacles were to be removed with brutal efficiency. The hag gave a stubborn snort, apparently oblivious to her danger.

"She's coming with us," said Max quickly, putting himself between Cooper and the hag.

"That's right," said Mum with a snort. "I'm camping, too!"

"This is no camping trip," spat Cooper, glancing at Max. "This is a DarkMatter operation."

"Ooh!" said Mum excitedly, clapping her hands. "Even better!"

Just then, a bird cawed loudly above them. Max's head swiveled up and he gasped.

Perched on the church's pitched roof were hundreds of black crows, crowded together in row upon row of glittering eyes and sharp, steely beaks. Their heads bobbed and their talons clacked as more birds arrived to join them.

"Max and David, get your packs," whispered Miss Boon. "Quickly now."

Max did as he was told, keeping his attention riveted on the birds while Cooper helped his father to his feet. One of the birds hopped to the edge of the roof and cocked its head inquisitively at them. Max winced as it began to caw. Moments later, others began to join in, by twos and threes, until their shrill voices split the night in a frantic chorus.

A cold wind bent the trees low. Max froze as another blood-curdling scream sounded from the direction of Rowan.

The witches were coming.

~ 6 ~

THE *ERASMUS*

"I *satu!*" hissed Cooper, and flames erupted from the church roof. The crows were swallowed up in shimmering waves of light and heat that rose high into the night. Several of the birds managed to escape, flapping frantically away while the others burned in a squawking pyre of crisped flesh and singed feathers. The roof groaned and sagged as embers shot high into the air like fireflies.

"Why did you do that?" gasped Mr. McDaniels. "That'll bring 'em straight here!"

"Those crows are familiars," muttered the Agent. "A witch

can see through its familiar's eyes, and we can't afford to be followed."

Just as Cooper finished speaking, horrible screams erupted through the night, bloodcurdling howls of rage and pain and despair. Mum clamped her hands over her ears and fell quaking to her knees. David looked terrified and tugged at Cooper's sleeve.

"Cooper, if each crow is a familiar, then there must be—"

"Hundreds of witches nearby," said the Agent with a grim nod. "We need to move. *Now*."

Max ran along with his father as the group dashed through the woods, following Cooper on a course that steered them toward the coast, but well away from Rowan. Nick bounded along with Cooper, stopping periodically to give a quizzical look at Max, who ran alongside his sputtering father. Miss Boon brought up the rear, hurrying David and Mum along as they wound a frantic path through the wood. Brittle branches scratched at their faces, leaves crunched underfoot, and the wind shook the treetops.

When they had run nearly a mile, Mr. McDaniels stopped and sagged against a peeling birch. More screams sounded throughout the woods behind them, and Max began to panic. He tugged at his father's hand.

"Dad," he pleaded, "c'mon."

"I can't," wheezed Mr. McDaniels, shutting his eyes in a fit of coughing. "I can't run another step. Keep going."

"No!" said Max, waving David and Mum along. Miss Boon stopped and knelt next to Mr. McDaniels.

"We can't stop here," she panted.

"I have to," protested Mr. McDaniels with a defeated shake of his head. He slowly opened his eyes, but he seemed to look through Miss Boon and gaze at the woods behind them.

His eyes abruptly widened: there was a witch some thirty feet away.

The witch stumbled blindly among the trees with her hands outstretched, swatting branches aside and searching the empty spaces before her while she muttered to herself. Her tattooed skin was deathly pale and her eyes were caked with dark blood.

"You're close," she moaned, veering toward them. Her hands snatched at the air as she shuffled toward them in several lunging steps. Max glanced at Miss Boon, but his Mystics instructor stood rigid. She merely gaped at the corpse-like figure, seemingly transfixed as the witch shuffled closer.

"You *are* close," croaked the witch, rubbing her blind eyes and giving a dull moan. "Stay where you are," she whispered, creeping closer as more screams sounded in the distance.

"Miss Boon," whispered Max.

Miss Boon gave no reply. Mr. McDaniels made a funny gurgle and squeezed Max's hand. The witch was now only two paces away, stretching out for them with a hideous, eager smile.

Suddenly, there was a dull thump.

A blank look of shock appeared on the witch's features. She stumbled once before crumpling to the ground, where she grasped mechanically at the cold soil. Max felt a pang of sympathy as the witch's motions subsided to little more than feeble twitches. With a sudden shudder, the witch rolled onto her side, her mouth swinging open like a loose hinge as Max spied the dull black handle of a knife protruding from her neck.

Cooper stole out from some nearby trees, crossing to them quickly and retrieving his weapon from the witch's body. He glanced at Miss Boon with unconcealed contempt before turning his attention to Mr. McDaniels.

"Can you run?" asked the Agent.

Max's father merely blinked stupidly, never taking his eyes

from the crumpled witch several feet away. Without a word, Cooper removed his pack and tossed it to Max. The tall, wiry Agent hoisted Mr. McDaniels to his feet, slinging the bigger man over his shoulder like a swollen sack of grain. Max hefted Cooper's pack and tugged at Miss Boon's hand. She mumbled something unintelligible before trotting alongside him. They hurried to keep up with the Agent, who ran steadily up ahead.

Within a quarter mile, they joined David, Mum, and Nick at a thicket where the wood dwindled to meet an open stretch of dunes and sparse grass. The ocean was close and Max could hear the low roar of the waves despite the periodic screams that sounded behind them. Cooper glanced up at the luminous clouds that raced across the black night. Max knew what Cooper was thinking: they would be exposed as they crossed the open field under the bright moon.

More screams filled the night. Cooper shook his head.

"We can't wait," he muttered, as though to himself. He turned to the group. "Everyone all right? You there, Mum—all right?"

Mum looked near tears but managed a nod.

"Good girl," said Cooper. "Follow me, then—quick as you can."

They dashed out into the open. Nick bounded alongside Max while the boy scanned the earth and sky behind them, expecting a host of black-robed witches to come hurtling after them. They clambered down a shallow bluff, arriving at a narrow beach where a rowboat rested on a small mound of sand and broken shells. Cooper set Max's father down and dragged the rowboat toward the black, briny chop. The Agent waded into the water and beckoned impatiently at them to get in.

The lymrill was first, bounding through the foam and

shallows to leap into the boat as if the whole experience were an exhilarating adventure. Max helped his father along while Miss Boon, regaining her composure, offered David a steadying hand as the small blond boy climbed aboard. Clambering in after his father, Max suddenly realized that Mum was still waiting on the beach.

"Mum," hissed Cooper. "Get in the boat!"

"I'm afraid of the water!" she shrieked, tearing at her hair and sinking to her knees.

"Have it your way," said Cooper, pushing the rowboat past a sandbar.

"I can levitate her," offered Miss Boon, swiveling in her seat.

"No," said the Agent quickly. "Mystics leave a trace. They'd know we came this way. She comes or goes on her own."

Mum watched them go, her swollen, puffy eyes blinking helplessly as Cooper guided the boat through a shallow wave. More screams sounded in the distance. Muttering obscenities, Mum clamped her hands over her eyes and plodded after them. The Agent swung her up and into the boat, where she promptly clung to Mr. McDaniels as if he were a great, woolly life preserver. When Cooper had pushed the boat past the shallow surf, the Agent hopped in and began rowing the little craft out to sea. The passengers shivered and huddled close to one another while the wind raged, the sea rolled, and spray crashed over the bow.

The cold slap of a wave woke Max from his slumber. He had sunk low amidst the wet baggage, hugging his sweater tight for warmth. Nick had been sleeping on him, but now the lymrill mewled in annoyance and shook the water from his quills. Max blinked and recovered his bearings. All trace of land had faded from view, and their little boat seemed all that remained in a vast, empty world of water. Even the crying of the gulls had faded until the only sounds came from Cooper dipping the oars in and out of swells that rolled on for as far as Max could see.

An hour later, Miss Boon sat up and hissed, disrupting the hypnotic squeak of the oarlocks. Cooper glanced over his shoulder at a ponderous black shape that now loomed ahead, gradually emerging from the fog. A sudden stab of white light cut through the gloom to fall directly upon them.

Miss Boon fidgeted, but Cooper rowed them steadily toward the dark shape and its bright, disembodied light. To Max, it looked as though some enormous sea creature had risen silently from the depths to assess a potential meal with a round and roving eye. As they approached, however, he saw that the mysterious shape was no monster, but merely a battered trawler. Faded white paint identified her as the *Erasmus*. A low greeting sounded from her deck as Cooper brought the rowboat alongside. A ladder was lowered and Cooper tossed the first of their packs up and over the rail.

Moments later, the group had clambered on deck, standing off to the side while Cooper spoke quietly to the captain, a stout, whiskered man in woollen cap and coat. Max held Nick and stood close to his father, looking out at the motley, inquisitive faces of the fishermen who eyed them curiously as they sipped from steel thermoses in the pre-dawn chill. Cooper pressed a slim packet into the captain's hand, and they were promptly motioned toward the captain's quarters.

Leading them down below, Cooper closed the hatch above them and rummaged through a sea chest to produce several woollen blankets. The cabin itself was snug and warm, with dark wood paneling, benches bolted to the floor, and a round table lit by an overhanging lamp. Mr. McDaniels and Mum collapsed heavily on a narrow bunk. David sniffled and distributed the blankets while Cooper set a kettle to boil on a small electric burner.

"What are we doing here?" asked David, sitting on a chest and shivering beneath his blanket.

"Hitching a ride," replied Cooper, squeezing his long legs beneath the table. "I've used this ship before. The captain is trustworthy."

"Cooper," said Miss Boon, sitting tall and clasping her hands, "I really do think we should contact the Director about this. . . ."

"We'll do no such thing," muttered the Agent, reaching for his pack. His scarred features resembled a mask of molten wax in the lamplight. Ignoring Miss Boon, he focused his hard blue eyes on Max. "Now that we're aboard, Max, I need to know something."

"What is it?" asked Max.

"Can I count on you?" asked Cooper simply.

"Of course you can," said Max, confused.

"You froze back there," said Cooper, frowning. "That can't happen again."

"I . . . er, I thought Miss Boon was going to—" Max began, feeling defensive.

"Miss Boon is a *teacher*," interrupted Cooper, speaking of the Mystics instructor as though she were back at Rowan arranging desks. "This is not a class. This is not the Course or an exercise. We are out in the open. You can never hesitate like that again when you're in danger. Do you understand?"

"I didn't even have a weapon," protested Max, feeling his cheeks grow hot.

"We can fix that," said Cooper, reaching for his pack. From

deep inside one of its pouches, he retrieved an item wrapped in soft black cloth. Max felt a queasy tingling in his stomach as Cooper pushed the bundle toward him. The cloth fell open, revealing a broken length of dull gray bone topped by a gleaming black blade.

"What is that?" asked David, stretching his neck like a turtle and squinting for a better look.

"It's the Spear of Cúchulain," said Max quietly, gazing at the broken relic.

The snapped shaft made it more of a long-handled dagger than a proper spear, but broken or not, its edge shone razor-sharp, and the barbs at its base looked murderous. It was a terrifying weapon; there could be no half measures with such a thing. It was made to take the life of one's enemies, not subdue them. Max resisted a powerful but unsettling urge to lift it from the table.

"I don't want my son having something like that," growled Mr. McDaniels, peering at it from where he sat on a narrow bunk. It was the first time he had spoken since his sighting of the witch. "You keep that yourself, Cooper."

"I'd like to," the Agent replied, "but I can't use it, mate. It won't even let me hold it."

With a grim smile Cooper reached out to lift the broken spear with his bare hand. The weapon immediately slid across the table as though repelled by a magnet. It tottered at the table's edge before slipping over the side. Instinctively, Max reached out to catch it.

It was a good deal heavier than he expected, possessing a weight that tended to gather behind the blade. As he held the weapon, Max felt it grow hot like a poker left to warm among the embers. The heat swam up his wrist to spread and blossom throughout him. Max shuddered. He had never felt quite this way before, not even when he had discovered the tapestry. He felt as wild and powerful as a storm. He felt invincible.

Miss Boon gasped and shot a glance at Cooper.

"Did you push it over the edge?" she asked with a shrill note.

"Max," said his father sternly, "put that thing back on the table."

Cooper ignored Miss Boon and fixed his pale eyes on Mr. McDaniels instead.

"Max is young, Mr. McDaniels, but we need him," said Cooper. "Rowan needs him. The Red Branch needs him. No more playtime. We need Max activated."

"*Activated?*" asked Mr. McDaniels incredulously. "He's a boy, not a robot."

"True," said Cooper, "Max is not a robot. But he might be the greatest hero of this age and our only chance at retrieving the Book of Thoth. Just as David might be our only chance at finding it."

"Nonsense," interjected Miss Boon sharply. "Max, put that thing down this instant."

Max met her gaze and shook his head.

"But it's mine," he replied evenly. "It is my right hand and the dread of my enemies. For I am the Hound of my people, and the day of my wrath is coming."

The blood drained from Miss Boon's face. Cooper nodded to himself. David merely watched Max with a sad, understanding smile. But it was Mr. McDaniels who broke the ensuing silence. His words were slow and hesitant.

"Son," he asked, "what did you just say?"

"What?" asked Max, swiveling in his seat.

"Max," said Miss Boon quietly, "you were speaking Old Irish just now. May I assume that you've never studied it?"

Max nodded. He had simply opened his mouth and the

words were there, as natural and necessary as breathing. He glanced warily at the black blade in his hand.

"We both heard him, Boon," murmured Cooper. "He's *meant* to have it."

The young teacher blinked; color returned to her face in a flash.

"The only thing that is 'meant,' Agent Cooper, is for us to keep Max and David from the witches," she snapped, employing the dry staccato she reserved for particularly dense students. "We will escort these three to the London field office and wait for further developments as planned."

"The plan's changed," said Cooper, striding back toward the hatch door and climbing up several steps. Max heard him bark an order in Dutch before he returned to the cabin, locking the hatch behind him. The deep rumbling of diesel engines shook the table as the boat groaned ahead through heavy seas. "You can skip off to London, but you'll need another ride," he said. "The Americans have grounded all flights, and this vessel's headed to Germany. We arrive at Hamburg in two weeks, so you might as well get comfortable."

"But if we swing by England, I could take you to visit Shrope Corner," said Mum, piping up cheerfully.

"Mum, *please* be quiet," said Miss Boon, rubbing her temples as she began pacing the cabin. Suddenly, she stopped and stabbed an accusatory finger at Cooper. "Did Vilyak put you up to this?"

The Agent gave her a dark look but said nothing.

"You answer me," demanded Miss Boon, enunciating each word with icy precision.

A numbing stillness permeated the cabin. The Agent watched the young teacher impassively for a stretch of silence that made Max squirm and Mum scoot back against the wall.

Nearly a minute passed before Cooper reached into his coat to produce a folded sheet of paper. He handed it to Miss Boon, who practically snatched it from his fingers. Her mismatched eyes—one brown, the other blue—devoured the document, scanning it several times from top to bottom. She blinked in quick succession.

"Would you like to authenticate it?" asked Cooper.

"No," she said quietly. "I can see it's authentic."

"What is it?" asked Mr. McDaniels, leaning forward to squint at the paper. "What's it say?"

Miss Boon frowned and cleared her throat. " 'I, Gabrielle Richter, authorize Agent William Cooper of the Red Branch to make any and all decisions regarding DarkMatter operations B011 and A002. Any resulting decisions are Agent Cooper's and his alone. Both the Director and Rowan's executive council disavow all knowledge of his plans or actions. All field offices and personnel are to provide any assistance that Agent Cooper may require. Violators will be subject to disciplinary action according to statute COC47.' "

"So he's in charge?" asked Mr. McDaniels.

"It would seem so," muttered Miss Boon, returning the edict to Cooper. "Although I can't imagine why the Director would do such a thing. . . ."

Max studied the weapon in his hand once more before placing it back on the black cloth. The warmth began to drain slowly, reluctantly, from his body.

"Why shouldn't Cooper be in charge?" he asked.

Miss Boon glanced at Cúchulain's spear. She made no attempt to mask the condescension in her voice.

"Because, Max, Agent Cooper is a professional killer who should not be making decisions about your well-being. He doesn't *care* about your well-being; it's not his nature. In fact, there are so many unacceptable aspects of this arrangement, I don't know where to begin."

Cooper merely folded the black cloth back over the *gae bolga*. He stowed the bundle back in his pack and pulled the drawstring tight.

"Just do your job, Miss Boon, and we'll all be fine."

"And what *is* my job?" replied the young woman with a prim, unblinking smile. "It seems I've been misinformed as to my purpose on this little expedition."

"It sure ain't to scrap with witches," growled Cooper. He stretched out on the floor, kicking off his boots. "You're here to give the boys a proper education."

Miss Boon snorted in disbelief.

"So the Director has me along to be their *tutor*?" she asked. "And how did I get to be so lucky?"

"Kraken's too old to make the trip," yawned the Agent, pulling his cap low and bringing their conversation to a close. His chest began to rise and fall with slow regularity.

Mum giggled from the corner, earning a furious glance from Miss Boon.

"Mum, I believe the water is boiling and there is some sort of vile flavored tea in that indecent mermaid canister. Kindly make tea for three. I expect you and Mr. McDaniels will want to get some sleep."

"I don't like tea," said David.

"You do today," snapped Miss Boon, sweeping a stack of charts off the table and tearing several blank pages out of her leather journal. With a tight mouth and brisk precision, she drew a perfect triangle that was soon filled with a maze of inter-secting lines. "Now, Max, why don't you come here and point out Euler's line. I'm sure David can provide us with its equation."

"Is that geometry?" croaked Mr. McDaniels.

"Yes it is, Mr. McDaniels," she replied. "Care to join us?"

Max's father promptly disappeared beneath his blanket.

For the next week, no one spoke of Cúchulain's spear or Max's strange outburst in Old Irish as the ship pressed on toward Germany. Cooper and Miss Boon managed to settle into a routine of chill formality while Max and David did their lessons or played cards with Mum and Mr. McDaniels. Although few of the sailors spoke English, many were good company and seemed accustomed to transporting unusual cargo. They laid bets on Mum or Nick for rat hunting (Mum always cheated; Nick always won) and broke out in cheerful song whenever the curtain of cold, gray clouds cracked a wink to permit a glimpse of sun. During these moments Max would lean far out over the rails to watch his shadow racing over the emerald sea before the sun disappeared and the waves darkened again to slate. It was after one of these interludes that Max spied David sitting alone, looking oddly shrunken in a borrowed sweater. He was perched on a mound of coiled ropes, hunched over a thick book bound in cracked red leather. Max wandered over, his mood lightened by the peep of sun.

"You look like you're going to hatch something," said Max, thumping the nest-like mound with a playful kick.

David smiled and tapped the book with his finger. "Actually, I *am* hatching something."

Max plopped next to David and tried to peer at the page, but David covered it as a pair of crew members strolled past, smoking cigarettes. David returned their wave but did not talk until they had passed out of earshot.

"That one speaks English, you know," he whispered, inclining his head at a lean, red-bearded man. "I don't know why he tries to hide it. I've caught him spying on us, and last night he slipped out during dinner to check the radio."

"But the radio's dead," said Max with a frown. "What would he be listening to?"

"I don't think he's using it to listen," said David with a side-ways glance. "I think he's trying to transmit—to send someone a message. . . ."

Max swiveled to look as the man leaned out over the rail. He regretted it immediately as a pair of small green eyes darted up to meet his own. The man abruptly flicked his cigarette over-board and strolled away toward the bow.

"Have you told Cooper?" asked Max.

"Not yet," said David. "I want to find out what he's doing and I don't want Cooper to make him suspicious. Anyway, we don't have to worry about him using the radio and tipping any-one off."

The blond boy smiled and produced a handful of red and yellow wires from his pocket. He lay them in a jumble on the nest of ropes, a satisfied expression on his face.

"That's great," said Max, "but what if *we* need to use the radio? It sounded like things are bad in Europe, and Cooper will want to get any information he can."

"I think we can get information another way," said David, again tapping the book.

Max braced himself as the ship rolled over a swell, glancing at the book's hand-lettered title of peeling gold leaf.

THE CONJURER'S CODEX OF SUMMONS
VOL. XI: THE SPIRITS PERILOUS
RECOMPILED AND TRANSLATED BY MAGDALENE KOLB, 1901.

"That book sounds dangerous," Max murmured warily.

"I've used dangerous books before," replied his roommate with a shrug. "Besides, this one's very valuable."

"What's in it?" asked Max, peering at the bizarre symbols and nightmarish images that flickered past as David riffled quickly through the cream-colored pages.

"Incantations," whispered David, glancing up and down the deck. "Powerful spells to call upon certain spirits."

"Imps and stuff?" asked Max, wrinkling his nose. "I thought you didn't like Mr. Sikes."

David shook his head impatiently and cast another glance toward the bow. "No, nothing like Mr. Sikes. Any Mystic can call on him if they have the right incantation. These spells are for different things. Ancient things. Things like—"

"*Astaroth?*" blurted out Max, louder than he'd intended.

David nodded and put a finger to his lips. He flipped the book to a page with an exquisite engraving whose central figure appeared to be a man with a handsome, sleepy face framed by dark, curling hair. The figure was sitting on a raised throne and seemed bemused as he listened to a long line of petitioners—crowned kings and bearded scholars lugging carts of astronomical equipment and alchemical contraptions. Astaroth's face looked considerably more youthful than the visage Max had seen appraising him from the Rembrandt painting. At a second glance, however, Max discerned that there was something eerily similar about the eyes. Max would never forget the fathomless black eyes that had blinked at him from inside their gilded frame: they had been ageless and numbingly non-human. Max tore his gaze away from the image to read the neat script on the facing page.

Of all the Spirits Perilous, Astaroth is most wise and cunning and veils his malice beneath a pretty cloak. Loath should thou be to summon him, unless thou be strong and know thy limits and wear a ring of silver true. For the Demon will seek to ensnare thee and keep thee past the witching hour when his strength doth wax with moon and tide and he may slip within thy circle. When he is called, beware his many shapes, for the Demon may be present and the unwary summoner knows it not! As a rooster he hath appeared, and as a wolf with baleful eyes, and as a viper black and coiled. The wise Sorcerer will call upon him and speak these words: "Noble Astaroth, pray favor thy petitioner with wisdom from under hill, beyond the stars, and beneath the deepest sea," for the Demon adores courtesy and is boastful of his knowledge of arts and letters and all manner of secrets. He will reveal himself and answer thy questions. But beware! Though Astaroth never lies, he will twist truth and will lead the unwary astray, so it is the Demon who is master. . . .

A shadow fell across the page. David snapped the book shut as the two whirled around to see the red-bearded sailor standing over them. A knowing smile spread across his hard face as he took a long draw off another cigarette.

"Tsk, tsk," said the sailor, grimacing to reveal a row of yellow teeth.

David cringed as the man stretched a gloved hand toward them.

Instead of snatching away the book, however, the sailor's fingers closed around the mess of wires that lay on the rope. He removed his gloves and began to untangle them.

"These belong to *Erasmus*," he said in a heavy accent. "Maybe bad boys don't know, but things are very bad in Europe, yes? Radio tells us where we can go. Understand? No more mischief—Karl is watching, eh?"

He wagged his finger at them and clomped on down the deck with a satisfied smirk.

"At least he didn't seem to know what the book is," said Max, exhaling a moment later. "And now we know he speaks English."

David nodded but said nothing. The corners of his mouth tightened as he fastened the book's clasp and slid it under his sweater.

"What are you going to do with that?" asked Max.

"Nothing yet," David said crossly. "It'll have to wait now that Karl's watching us. This isn't the place to do it, anyway."

"Do what?" asked Max, feeling a sudden tremor of cold race down his spine.

"Summon Astaroth, of course," replied David, bracing himself as the trawler's bow rose up the face of a gray-green swell.

Late that night, Max was smooshed against the wall of the control room while the crew of the *Erasmus* continued to pile inside. The captain bellowed for quiet while Karl fiddled with the radio, adjusting a knob with the tiniest of movements to scan through the shortwave frequencies. For several minutes only static crackled through the tinny speaker. Frowning, the men spooned at leftover bowls of a pungent fish soup thickened with flour.

Max heard Mum cry out suddenly. A crewman groaned as the hag elbowed him aside and tunneled to the front.

"Something's comin' through!" she shrieked. "Shut up, shut up!"

Max shut his eyes and strained to listen. There was indeed a voice crackling through the interference, as though calling to them from another world. It was a woman's voice, with an English accent, and it spoke in a calm and even tone. The static subsided and the voice could be heard.

". . . from emergency headquarters outside London. All citizens of the European Union are required to report to their nearest government office for registration, emergency supplies, and further instructions. Foreign travel is forbidden. Those who fail to register or attempt to leave any member country will be arrested. Any individual found to be harboring any unregistered persons is subject to arrest. Your cooperation during this difficult time is greatly appreciated. This is a message from the BBC, transmitted from emergency headquarters outside London."

A quiet patter of voices filled the cabin as the announcement was repeated. While those who spoke English translated for their shipmates, Max watched as Cooper slipped through the crowd for a quiet word with the captain. Karl continued fiddling with the radio, but Max saw him glance occasionally at Cooper and the captain, as though he were listening. Max hurried toward the door, where Miss Boon and Mr. McDaniels were standing.

"What's this mean, Dad?"

"I don't know," said his father, squeezing Max's shoulder. "It doesn't sound good."

Max turned quickly to Miss Boon.

"What's Cooper telling the captain?" he asked.

"I wish I knew," muttered his teacher. "I'm sure we'll find out soon. Meanwhile, it's late. David's already gone to bed and so should you."

"But there might be more news!" Max protested. He glanced again at Karl and lowered his voice to an urgent hiss. "And I don't trust that guy by the radio. David and I think he's spying on us."

Miss Boon stood on tiptoe and clucked her tongue.

"I'm on it," she muttered. "If there's any more news, I'll be sure to tell you. Now off to bed—or else we can get a head start on tomorrow's lessons."

Max began to speak, but Miss Boon flicked him a look that quashed all protest. His father yawned and slung an arm over Max's shoulder.

"I'm going to turn in, too," he said. "Claim the cot before Mum snares it!"

David was not asleep when the McDanielses climbed down into the cabin. He was standing shirtless before a small vanity mirror that was bolted to the wall. He held a lamp in his hand, creating a ghostly effect on his mirrored face. His reflection shifted its gaze to watch them descend.

"Whatcha doing, David?" asked Mr. McDaniels, glancing at David's messy pile of blankets in the corner. "Can't sleep?"

"No," said David, reaching for his shirt. His voice sounded oddly detached. "I had my last surgery three years ago today, you know."

"I didn't know you'd had surgery," said Mr. McDaniels, shooing Nick off the cot.

David smiled. "Heart surgery," he said, turning around to reveal a long pink scar down the center of his chest. "Actually, a heart *transplant*," he clarified. "Three years ago . . . it was my second one."

"I didn't know that," exclaimed Mr. McDaniels, leaning forward to peer at the scar while Max placed Nick inside a padded crate. Max had seen it before, but his roommate was always quick to hide it. Now David stood exposed, considering the pale line of tissue with a distant expression. He traced his finger along the scar.

"Two other people died so I could live," he murmured. "It makes me sad sometimes."

"No," rumbled Mr. McDaniels sympathetically. "That's not the way to look at it, son. Those poor souls' time had come. I think they'd be happy to know they gave you a chance to live. They get to live on through you! The way I see it, you've done each other a favor."

David smiled appreciatively and dimmed the lamp to the radiance of a nightlight before wriggling back beneath his blankets. Max said nothing, but slipped off his shoes and climbed into his own makeshift bed near the kitchenette.

"There's so much happening," David said, his voice sounding very small, even in the snug cabin. "There are times when I don't think I can stand it anymore. I know what you heard on the radio. They're starting to do the same things in America, too—it's all too terrible to even think about."

"How could you know all that if you've been down here?" asked Mr. McDaniels.

David didn't reply.

Max listened to the low whine of the ship's engines and wondered just whom his roommate had been speaking to. He scanned the cabin for the red book, but it was nowhere to be seen. Several moments passed before David spoke again.

"I try not to think of my mom, but I can't help it," he said, his voice as tense as stretched wire. "I want to know she's all right."

Max stopped looking for the red book and propped himself up on an elbow. This was the first time David had mentioned his mother since she had moved and left no forwarding address the previous year.

"She is, David," said Mr. McDaniels soothingly.

"Adults *always* want to say things are fine, even when they don't know," David sighed. "I'd rather *know* if something's bad than just believe that it's good."

Mr. McDaniels grunted. "That's interesting. I think you and Max are cut from the same cloth. Me? I'd rather believe the best. Maybe I'm a fool, but it keeps me afloat."

Max heard the jingle of keys and change as his father rummaged about for his wallet.

"Turn that lamp up a bit and come over here, David. You too, Max."

Max and David converged on Mr. McDaniels's cot and sat on its edge. In the soft yellow glow of the cabin, Mr. McDaniels looked like a sleepy bear, warm and content in his nightshirt of striped flannel. He held a small photograph gently at its corners.

"I want to show you my Bryn," he said softly.

"I've seen pictures of Mrs. McDaniels before," said David, hugging his knees. "Max has pictures of you all back at Rowan."

"No," said Mr. McDaniels, "those pictures are of *our* Bryn McDaniels—my wife and Max's mother. This is *my* Bryn."

He handed the faded picture to David, who scooted over to make room for Max. The photo was of Max's mother and he had never seen it before. She had been quite young when it was taken—younger even than Miss Boon. Dark eyes, brimming with laughter, flashed up from her newspaper as she lounged at an outdoor café. She had the same proud bearing as Max, the same sharp cheekbones and shining black hair.

"This is the woman I fell in love with," said Mr. McDaniels, "and the woman who loved me back even though she was way out of my league. Most beautiful creature I'd ever seen. And smart! I swear, David, the woman knew everything—she'd even give *you* a run for your money!"

The cot shook with Mr. McDaniels's chuckle. Max looked hard at his father, whose eyes were shining like those of a happy little boy. Scott McDaniels sighed and thumped David on the knee.

"I haven't seen my Bryn for a long time now. In my heart of hearts, though, I know I'll see her again. That gives me hope, and hope keeps me going."

"I don't know," said David slowly. "Hope seems like it could be a dangerous thing, Mr. McDaniels. I think it could drive me crazy or distract me from what I have to do."

Mr. McDaniels started to answer but stopped at the sound of footsteps coming down the hatch. Cooper stood on the bottom stair holding an armful of canned food.

"Pack up your things," he said quietly. "We're heading straight for the mainland. They're intercepting all boat traffic in the Channel. We'll have to make for Frankfurt by land."

"Where are they dropping us off?" asked Mr. McDaniels.

"Spain," muttered Cooper, letting the cans spill from his arms into an open pack.

"*Spain?*" groaned Mr. McDaniels. "But that's hundreds of miles away from Germany. Can't they drop us off any closer? It doesn't make any sense!"

Cooper stepped quickly over to their cot and slid the captain's locker out from beneath it.

"That's exactly why we're doing it," muttered the Agent, plucking a fancy-looking cheese and some smoked venison from the captain's private stores. The Agent stood and glanced impatiently at the three of them still sitting huddled on the bed. His eyes fell on the photograph cradled in David's palm. The Agent tilted his head for a better look.

"Ah!" said Mr. McDaniels, brightening once again. "Admiring my pretty lady, are you? That's my wife, Cooper. Max's mother."

Cooper blinked. His cold blue eyes flicked from the photograph to Max.

"A strong likeness," said the Agent with a curt nod.

Miss Boon and Mum came down a few minutes later, and the six of them set to gathering up their sweaters and books, cooking pans and food. While they packed, Max bit his tongue and tried to file away the questions that crowded his mind. More than once, he caught Cooper glancing at him, confirming what he already knew: this was not the first time Cooper had seen Bryn McDaniels.

~ 7 ~

THE SPANISH BOOKSELLER

It was nearly dawn when the captain knocked on the cabin door to tell them it was time to depart. Max yawned, scooped Nick into his arms, and followed Cooper up the steps. Most of the crew was crowded on deck, lining the starboard rail and staring out at the ocean. A strange light danced and flickered on their faces. Clutching Nick close, Max stepped between two of the sailors and gasped. The ocean was on fire.

A cargo ship was lolling on its side in the pale sea, spewing a bright torrent of flame and black smoke into the pale morning. It looked like the old whaling images Max had seen in books:

a harpooned giant that had rolled onto its side, expelling the essence of its life in one final gasp. Floating blobs of burning oil dotted the sea like lily pads, eerie and beautiful as they bobbed and flickered on the swells. Max searched for passengers or crew but saw no one.

Beyond the burning vessel was a dark, rocky shore that extended out to the north until it dwindled away in a light blue haze. In the far distance, another ship was burning. What must have been a monstrous inferno appeared as small and harmless as a guttering candle.

Cooper had some quiet words with the captain before addressing the group.

"This is where we get off," he said, shouldering his pack. "Captain's worried about mines, and I can't blame him. Make sure you— Mum, let him do his job!"

The hag scowled and released the arm of a crewman whom she'd come to fancy. Color returned to the young man's face. He nodded to Cooper appreciatively and joined his fellows in lowering a cumbersome lifeboat over the side. Max and the rest clambered down the rickety ladder and piled within it, steadying the small craft as it rolled on the gentle swells, bumping against the larger ship.

Max helped his father push their boat away from the *Erasmus*'s side. Once away, he settled into his seat only to hear someone call his name. He glanced up to see the red-bearded sailor leaning over the rail. A cold, knowing smile spread across the man's face as he lit a cigarette and bid them farewell. Max glared back while Cooper took the oars and began rowing them toward shore. They gave the burning ship a wide berth, and soon the *Erasmus* was lost behind the veil of oily smoke that swept across the sea.

"Cooper, that man with the red beard—"

"Is just now marking his chart so he can report to his superiors where we've landed," interjected the Agent. "Spies will be looking for us in Lisbon."

David swiveled in his seat.

"Why would he tell them we're in Portugal? Is he on our side?"

"Not at all," replied Cooper. "He's most certainly in the employ of the Enemy—or the witches. He'll tell them we're in Lisbon because Miss Boon implied that's where we are," replied Cooper. "I nearly believed it myself. Your teacher has a talent for suggestion."

"You bewitched him?" asked Mr. McDaniels.

"A crude expression," said Miss Boon, sitting noticeably taller among the baggage. "But yes, I had a few words with him after you'd gone to bed. A revolting man."

"Lisbon's not that far," said Mr. McDaniels. "Why not just tell him we were in Chile?"

"Plausibility is the key to effective suggestion, Mr. McDaniels," explained Miss Boon. "Did you hear that, boys?"

"Yes, Miss Boon," replied Max and David in chorus.

"Oh, forget your silly lessons," sniffed Mum, sinking lower in her wrap. "Blabbing away while I'm heartbroken. I'll *never* forget that sailor, mind you! He was such a wonderfully dumb and handsome thing. Practically *begged* to come with me . . ."

Cooper rowed steadily toward the empty shore.

"And what would you have served him with, Mum?" asked the Agent.

"Ooh! Let me think," cried the hag, sitting up straight and clapping excitedly. "He had a delightful aroma—like a great juicy pork chop! Sweet potatoes would garnish him proper, or a dollop of me old Nan's spinach—" The hag paused midclap. "Of course, Mum speaks theoretically. . . ."

Miss Boon raised an eyebrow.

"I hate to admit it, but Mum's making me hungry," piped up Mr. McDaniels. "What's the plan when we reach shore? Nice people on the *Erasmus,* but not much in the way of real grub."

"We've got canned food until we reach Salamanca," replied the Agent.

"And how far is that?" asked Mr. McDaniels.

"A hundred miles or so," replied the Agent, steering them around a bobbing trunk.

Mr. McDaniels groaned.

"We need to avoid any place that might require us to register," explained the Agent. "We're fugitives, Mr. McDaniels."

"But from *whom*? That's the question," murmured David.

Max turned to gaze at the quiet shoreline of dark rock and tide pools. Now that they were closer, Max could see small houses dotting the cliffs, squat little structures with unlit windows.

"Who would live here?" asked Max. "It seems so deserted."

"Fishermen," replied Cooper, squinting over his shoulder. "And there are even few of them in these parts. The nearest city is Santiago de Compostela."

Max clawed through his pack for the atlas Miss Boon had brought along. He searched the index for a map of Spain. In the northwest corner of Spain he spied Santiago de Compostela; Salamanca was to the southeast.

"Why are we going to Salamanca?" asked Max. "If we're headed to Germany, shouldn't we cut across the northern coast?"

"A fair question," said Miss Boon, leaning close to study the map herself.

"Two reasons," muttered Cooper. "We want to avoid coasts

and borders—that's where surveillance will be concentrated. Second, there's someone in Salamanca I need to see."

"And who might that be?" asked the young teacher.

"An old friend," replied the stoic Agent. "David, what's the status of your trinket there?"

David reached into his shirt and lifted out Bram's golden talisman. No matter how he turned it in his hand, in the early gloom it shone as bright as a sun-baked coin.

For several days, the six walked along a dusty road that bordered a field of languishing, half-harvested wheat. There was a medieval quality to the countryside—old trees and ruins and rough granite jutting up like teeth from the fading green hills. The land was beautiful but lonely. On the first day, they had seen a little girl and boy peeking out from a golden wood, but the pair had fled at the sight of them and they had seen no one since. The structures they glimpsed had been abandoned, from pillared granaries and old stone houses to red-tiled buildings that dotted the rolling landscape. A cold November wind blew through the swaying stalks, punctuated by David's singsong voice reciting the riddle.

> *Beneath where Teuton kings were crowned*
> *There is a key with notches four*
> *To steer my steed beyond the sun*
> *And safely knock on heaven's door.*

"Do you understand the Riddle?" asked Max to Miss Boon.

"I have hunches," replied the teacher, sipping from a canteen. "I agree with David that Bram probably entrusted this Key to the Workshop. Though actually German kings were only *chosen* in Frankfurt—they were crowned in Aachen."

"So why do we need the Workshop at all?" asked Max. "Why not go straight to Aachen?"

"And where should we look?" asked Miss Boon with a small smile.

Max pondered that for a moment. A key sounded like a small thing, and a small thing could be hidden nearly anyplace—inside a box or a book or a paving stone.

"I don't know," he admitted.

"That's why we need to start at the Workshop," said Miss Boon.

"But at the meeting, Rasmussen didn't even believe the Book of Thoth existed," said Max. "Why would he be so skeptical if his own Workshop holds the key to finding it?"

Miss Boon stopped to raise an eyebrow at him. The answer dawned on Max in a flash.

"He was lying!" Max exclaimed, remembering the dry, sardonic expression on the man's face. "He was only pretending not to know anything about it. They must want to find it themselves!"

"A distinct possibility," said Miss Boon. "This explains why we must be very careful when we arrive. Rasmussen helped us keep you from the witches only because it served his interests."

"Why would he care what happens to David and me?" asked Max, watching a large bird circling high above a distant farmhouse.

"He cares very much," replied Miss Boon. "The Workshop's relationship with Rowan is a fragile one, but there is peaceful and periodic cooperation. The witches, however, are another story. The witches are sworn enemies of the Workshop, Max. Rasmussen is well aware that you and David might become powerful adversaries should the witches obtain your services."

Max heard a groan behind him and turned to see his father

ease himself down onto a large rock. While Mum had complained often throughout their long days of walking, Mr. McDaniels had soldiered on with an air of quiet determination. Max admired his father's grit, but knew that the miles were taking a hard toll on his big body. He winced as his father peeled off his sock to reveal a doughy foot riddled with blisters. Cooper stopped up ahead and walked back toward them.

"I'm sorry," gasped a red-faced Mr. McDaniels as the Agent stooped down for a look. "I know we just stopped a few hours ago."

Cooper nodded and produced a little jar of light yellow ointment from his pack.

"Moomenhoven balm," he muttered. "It'll numb the pain and patch you up."

Cooper took a small dab from the jar and rubbed it into the foot, causing Mr. McDaniels to exhale with relief. He furrowed his brow and began wiggling his toes.

"This is good stuff!" he suddenly exclaimed, his cheeks flushing pink. "Those Moomenhovens could make a fortune if we brought this goop to market."

Mum promptly plopped next to Max's father.

"I want some, too," she declared, tugging off her thick-soled clog to reveal a gray-green foot with three sharp toes. David looked curiously at the misshapen wedge; Nick sniffed at it and mewled. Cooper shook his head and screwed the lid tight.

"Everyone's feet hurt, Mum," said the Agent. "Put your shoe back on. This balm's for emergencies."

Max tuned out Mum's bickering protest as something caught his attention. Up the road, a dull haze was rising into the air. Something was approaching.

"Cooper," said Max, a warning note in his voice.

The Agent's head whipped up and followed Max's pointing finger toward the cloud.

"Off the road," snapped the Agent, reaching for his pack. *"Quick, quick, quick!"*

They hurried off the road, running through the field of short-cropped wheat to a neighboring field where the grain had been left untouched. Breathing heavily, Max pressed himself flat to peer through gaps in the tall, graying stalks. He could hear the heavy, unmistakable rumbling of a diesel engine. Moments later, a large white truck eased into view, kicking up a fine cloud of dust in its wake. It slowed to a stop near a lone oak tree. Several men in work clothes climbed out of the back and trudged to the passenger side of the truck's cab. Each carried a rifle and wore a bright red armband about his upper arm. One of the men pointed at a small, dark object ahead. Nearby, Max heard Cooper curse.

There was Mum's blocky little shoe, lying by the roadside.

The shoe was retrieved and handed over to the person in the passenger seat.

The truck door promptly opened, and a tall man stepped out. Although he also had an armband, he was dressed more formally, wearing an olive-colored trench coat and black fedora. He strode quickly to where Mum's clog had been and stooped to examine the ground. The man in the fedora then stood to his full height and surveyed the fields where they lay hidden.

He called to one of the rifle-toting men, who hurried over. The two conversed while the cold wind rose and shook the surrounding wheat. Nearby, Nick's metallic quills began quivering. Max spied a rat wandering casually amidst the stalks.

"No," whispered Max, seizing the lymrill and hugging him close against his body. Nick gave an angry snort and struggled

for a moment, giving Max a painful nip in the process. Max gritted his teeth and stroked the coppery quills on Nick's belly until the rat wandered off and Nick finally went still. Max held his breath and peeped through the wheat.

The man in the fedora was scanning the surrounding countryside with binoculars. Long minutes passed before he slipped them back in his trench coat and turned on his heel, walking back toward the truck. Seconds later, the truck made a slow U-turn and sped back up the road.

"No one move," Cooper hissed. "Keep quiet till I'm back."

Cooper crawled away through the tall wheat while Max lay on the hard ground, breathing slowly and trying to ignore the dull throbbing in his hand where Nick had nipped him. Almost an hour passed before Cooper returned; not even Mum had dared break the silence in all that time.

"You can get up," he said quietly. "They stopped farther up the road, but they're gone now." The Agent hefted his pack and slung it back over his shoulders.

The rest clambered to their feet, shaking off the dust and bits of wheat. Mum looked abashed.

"I'm sorry about my shoe," she croaked. "Have I gotten us in trouble?"

"Remains to be seen," said Cooper. "They know *someone* was here, and that man in the hat clearly has some sort of authority."

"He was a vye, you know," said Mum.

"How do you know that?" asked David nervously.

Mum gave the air an audible sniff, flaring her large, wet nostrils.

"Were they all vyes?" asked Max.

"No, just the tall one," said Mum conclusively. "Couldn't you smell that the others were scared silly of him?"

Max shook his head.

"I don't even know why you've got those things," said Mum, giving Max's nose a contemptuous glance.

"If he's a vye, wouldn't he have smelled us, too?" asked Miss Boon.

"We were downwind, dear," explained Mum. "And his sniffer's no match for a hag's."

"Can someone please tell me what a vye is?" asked Mr. McDaniels, rubbing his arms and giving a nervous glance up the road.

"Shape-shifter," replied Cooper. "Highly intelligent. Looks something like a werewolf in its feral state."

"But vyes are bigger," added Max.

"And they've got awful, squinty eyes," volunteered David, making Max's father grimace.

"All true," said Cooper. "If that was a vye, then I've got little doubt they were looking for us, specifically. We must have been seen and reported."

"Those two children?" asked Miss Boon.

"Most likely," said Cooper, scanning the countryside that was quickly darkening to dusk. "I shouldn't have let them go."

"They were *children*, Cooper," said Miss Boon with a warning tone in her voice.

"No, Miss Boon," replied the Agent. "We just assumed they were."

The Agent gave Mum a thick sock to cover her bare foot and led them far from the road.

Five days later, Max stood on the banks of the river Tormes and contemplated Salamanca. The city was lit from within like a brilliant jewel: a conspicuous blaze of golden light after many miles of navigating the dark Spanish countryside.

The city was alive with not only light but music. The distant blare of trumpets and horns and drums carried across the chilly night.

Cooper had taken them on a detour around the city so that they might enter from an unexpected direction. It was clever, Max acknowledged, but now they were required to cross an ancient Roman bridge for entry, and a narrow way was easily guarded.

"Why do you think it's so light?" asked David. "It's like they're celebrating something."

"I don't know," said Cooper, setting down his pack and rifling through several pockets. He produced the black velvet bundle that held Cúchulain's spear.

"Can you slip this up your sleeve, Max?" he asked.

Max glanced at his travel-worn father. Mr. McDaniels looked gravely at the black shape but nodded his approval. Max reached inside the velvet wrap and removed the broken spear.

"Careful now," said Cooper. "It's still very sharp."

Max loosened his shirtsleeve and slipped the weapon inside, along the inside of his right arm. Even broken, it was a bit too long, extending several inches past his elbow, so he would be forced to keep the arm straight. The cold blade began to grow warm against his skin.

Cooper wrote an address down on a slip of paper and handed it to Miss Boon.

"We're going to use Mystics to disguise ourselves," he explained to them. "I'll enter first, ahead of you, in case they have means of detecting illusions. If anything should happen and we get separated, take them to this address. Will you do that, Miss Boon?"

"Of course," said the young Mystics instructor, swallowing hard and gazing across the river.

"Mr. McDaniels, you'll have to carry Nick."

Max's father groaned a moment later as he hoisted the improbably dense otter-sized lymrill into his arms. "He must be a hundred pounds!" he huffed before lapsing into awed silence. Cooper was murmuring words in a low strange language while river mist snaked up over the banks to envelop them. The golden lights of Salamanca were obscured for a moment until the mist washed over them and dissipated into the clear night sky.

"Say nothing unless absolutely necessary," said Cooper. "Follow me."

As they walked along the river's edge, Max felt utterly exposed. Cooper walked up ahead of them, tall and terrifying with his black knit cap over his white, scarred face. A pair of Spaniards wearing red armbands stood at the entryway to the bridge, passing a bottle between them. Cooper did not give their pistols a second glance and merely offered a pleasant wave as he strode past.

Miss Boon wiped pearly beads of perspiration from her forehead. "Just follow me," she whispered, and the group approached the bridge.

"*Buenas noches, abuelita,*" said one of the guards, nodding at Miss Boon. He was very young—no more than a year or two older than Max and David. He tipped his cap and waved them past the gates. As Max walked past, he glanced at the young man's armband and saw that it was not merely red but included a circular white design. Max had time to catch a star and several strange symbols that were reminiscent of an illustration he had seen in the *Conjuror's Codex,* but he dared not look closer. Up ahead, Cooper was already halfway across the bridge, a dark silhouette against a golden wall of light and music. When Max crossed over to the other side, it was like nothing he had ever seen.

The city was filled with people: young people, old people, all singing and dancing to a blaring cacophony of music played by musicians stationed at every corner. It was almost midnight, but young children ran giggling through the streets. Others were running, too. Max saw tall costumed figures whose faces were hidden behind masks painted in the likeness of grinning, mustachioed men with rosy red cheeks. Atop their heads, they wore tall, spade-shaped hats that rose and fell as the frightening figures ran like a phalanx through the crowds.

Max saw Cooper stop to cheer a masked passerby before striding ahead onto a wide street lined with buildings constructed of a sandy stone. Max made to follow him, but a trumpet blared nearby and he instinctively clapped his hands over his ears. Max saw immediately that his movement had caught the attention of a masked figure that had been running past. It stopped abruptly and swiveled its head to gaze at Max.

"Stay calm," said Miss Boon, squeezing Max's hand as the dead-eyed mask bobbed toward him.

Max's heart pounded in his chest. The hideous mask hovered just inches from his face.

"¿Es tu hora de acostarte, muchacha?" cackled the figure's high voice. Its gloved hand swung forward to tap him on the shoulder with a wooden baton. Just then, a gaggle of children ran screaming past Max, and the figure lumbered off after them. Max watched as they disappeared down a side street, and his eyes fell upon several men in trench coats and fedoras surveying the scene from beneath a café awning.

Miss Boon tugged at his sleeve, and Max followed her down the street where Cooper had disappeared, the group swimming against a tide of revelers.

THE SPANISH BOOKSELLER ~ 159

They followed Cooper at a cautious distance, passing by a great university. Its doors had been torn off their hinges and lay broken and splintered against its archways. As they walked, Max saw that many buildings had been destroyed, gutted and burned in a panorama of broken glass and charred stone. Other buildings were intact, and Max quickly noticed that these all displayed the same symbol as the red armbands. Some of the marks were painstakingly perfect in their symmetry; others were scrawled in haste upon thresholds or windows in a seeming mad dash for compliance.

They walked for several more blocks before Cooper finally stopped at a small bookstore built of the ubiquitous sandy stone. Its windows were dark, with Astaroth's sigil painted carefully upon the door.

Glancing up the street, Cooper gestured at them to come quickly. Max shivered and rubbed his arms while Cooper rang the bell. There was no answer. Cooper frowned and pressed the bell again. Another phalanx of masked men ran past them to the crashing accompaniment of a round, jolly man playing cymbals down at the corner. Cooper watched them go before pressing the bell again with rising urgency.

A light appeared at an upstairs window. Half a minute later, the door opened. A white-haired man with intelligent eyes and thick glasses stood in the doorway. His mouth sagged in irritation as he reached into his trouser pocket to flick a few coins onto the step. He gave them a stern, disapproving glance before turning away to close the door.

"We need shelter, Brother Lorca," said Cooper quickly.

The man's eyes widened as though he'd seen a ghost.

"Which of you is William?" asked the old man gruffly, blinking from face to face.

"I am," said Cooper, inclining his head.

"What's my one true love?" inquired the man, snapping his fingers impatiently.

"You have two," responded Cooper. "The wines of Rioja and the incomparable María."

The imperious scowl tightened to a twinkling smile; the door opened wide to admit them.

Max crowded into a small foyer while the white-haired man closed the heavy door and locked it. A woman's voice called from the top of an elegant staircase that rose and twisted out of sight.

"¿Quién está allí? ¡Envíelos lejos!"

"Tut, tut," scolded Señor Lorca, with a sharp laugh. "Come down, María. It is William and some friends, although he looks prettier than when I saw him last."

Cooper nodded, and turned the group's attention toward their reflection in a nearby baroque mirror. There they stood—two aging men, a plump nurse, an elderly woman wrapped in a brown shawl, and two girls no older than six. The plump nurse pointed.

"Is that *me*?" asked Mr. McDaniels.

"In the flesh," said Cooper.

Mr. McDaniels turned away from the mirror and looked himself up and down.

"But I look normal," he exclaimed, wiggling his fingers and examining his clothes.

"Mirrors reflect all illusions," said Cooper. "Very useful tidbit, that."

Max waved at himself in the mirror. A bundled, black-haired girl with round cheeks waved back. Everyone wore red armbands—even the children.

"Did anyone follow you?" asked Señor Lorca, bolting the door.

"No," said Cooper, stealing a peek out the bookshop's front window while drawing a pair of heavy crimson drapes. The Spaniard grunted his approval and herded the group through a large, two-story room of gleaming, glassed-in bookcases filled with old manuscripts, texts, and tablets. As they filed toward the rear, Max saw that the front of the building was dedicated to the bookstore but that the back rooms were private living quarters. They arrived at a large, comfortable kitchen with frescoed walls, cascading plants, and gleaming copper cookery.

"Ooh!" said Mr. McDaniels, eyeing a large cheese and a hanging ham.

Señor Lorca chuckled as he lit several candles and placed them on a sturdy table of sanded oak. Collapsing into a chair, the old man peered at the group standing assembled in the kitchen doorway.

"William, put your trickery aside so I may see you," he rumbled.

Cooper murmured several words. Max didn't feel anything different, but the old man sat straight up and gasped as his attention focused immediately upon Max and David.

"You've brought *them* here?" he asked. "This is a strange omen," he muttered, glancing at a worn wooden staircase.

"You know them?" asked Cooper quietly. "You know their faces?"

Señor Lorca nodded gravely, rising to his feet.

"I do. And I welcome you, David Menlo and Max McDaniels. I am honored."

Señor Lorca shuffled forward for introductions. There was a quiet dignity to the man, an elegant assuredness to his movements and a sharp, handsome profile unbowed by age. As they shook hands, Max saw a dozen faded scars on the man's papery skin. After pecking Mum on the cheek, Señor Lorca stooped and blinked at Nick, who sat on his back haunches sniffing the kitchen's delicious aromas.

"My heavens," he said. "Is that a lymrill?"

"Yes, sir," said Max.

"What a marvelous creature," said Señor Lorca, reaching out a hand to stroke Nick's quills. Nick's tail rattled, and he unfurled his lethal, curling claws to stretch luxuriantly, scoring the kitchen's worn red tiles in the process.

"Nick—no!" scolded Max just as an elderly woman arrived at the foot of the stairs, wrapped in a blue silk robe. She looked puzzled, alternating her gaze between Nick and the group.

"Bah!" the old man chuckled, waving off the damage. "Everyone should be so lucky as to have a lymrill in their kitchen. Please meet my María."

The woman smiled politely but hurried through the introductions until she reached Cooper.

"My William," she cooed, pulling off his black cap to hold his face in her hands. She gazed up at him, searching his face with tender affection, while Cooper's pale, scarred features writhed into something approximating a grin. The woman patted his face and prodded his belly. "Too thin," she said with a conclusive frown. "Someone is starving my boy."

"Shhh, María," said Cooper. "Mum's a cook."

Señora Lorca glanced over at Mum, whose scowling face would have curdled milk. The woman laughed and took Mum by the arm, leading the indignant hag into a side pantry. "You are a cook, eh? Then you can help me fatten him up!"

A half hour later, even Mr. McDaniels waved off a final pass at leftover fabada, a rich stew of pork and sausages and buttery beans in a savory broth. Señor Lorca watched with obvious pleasure on his creased face, refilling Mr. McDaniels's glass with a strong red wine.

"That is your first real supper in some time, eh?" asked the Spaniard.

"Delicious," rumbled Max's father, dabbing his mouth.

"Good," said Señor Lorca. "I like to watch you eat. Reminds me of when I was younger. Now, I just peck, peck, peck like a bird." The old man rolled his eyes and sighed. "Are you tired, my friend?"

Mr. McDaniels gave a groggy nod.

"I'm sleepy, too," croaked Mum, sitting on several cushions. "I miss my cupboard."

"We have many beds and several baths, but no guest cupboard," laughed María. "We do have a linen closet you might like. I will show you."

Mr. McDaniels and Mum shuffled off after Señora Lorca; her husband's shining eyes watched them go. The old man sighed and patted Cooper's arm.

"It is good to see you, William. Now, perhaps you will tell me why you bring these two to me."

"Cooper," interjected Miss Boon, "perhaps we should discuss what is suitable to share."

"It is all right, Miss Boon," said Cooper gently. "Antonio has saved my life many times over."

"Does he have security clearance?" asked Miss Boon, stirring a cup of black coffee.

Señor Lorca looked at Miss Boon with an amused expression. He pushed back from the table to pluck a framed photograph from an antique side table. He handed it to Miss Boon. The young Mystics instructor peered at the photo and shot a startled glance at Cooper, who looked uncomfortable.

"Yes," said Señor Lorca, "that is our William and myself, some years ago."

Max leaned close to Miss Boon for a glimpse. There was Señor Lorca, receiving a medal from Ms. Richter in what looked to be a great hall. In the photograph, Señor Lorca's hair was darker and the line of his jaw had a finer cut. But it was not the younger version of Antonio de Lorca that made Max stare; it was Cooper.

Max only knew the figure was Cooper from the Agent's distinctive stance—hands clasped patiently with his head tilted in thoughtful repose. Max blinked and looked again. In the photo, there were no scars, no patchwork of shiny skin and ruined features. The young man at Señor Lorca's side was strong-featured and roughly handsome, with a boxer's nose and brilliant blue eyes that gazed with pleasure upon Señor Lorca's medal.

"That is an old photo, Antonio," said Cooper, taking it gently from Miss Boon and placing it back on the side table. Señor Lorca grunted and rolled up his sleeve. Max leaned forward to peer at a red tattoo, dull and faded as a bruise upon his wrist; he had seen that mark before.

"Wonderful," sighed Miss Boon, resuming her air of tart skepticism. "*Another* member of the Red Branch. Should I take this as a confirmation that Commander Vilyak is dictating our mission?"

"I know nothing about your mission, Miss Boon," said Señor Lorca. "But you are not the first visitors I have had today."

"Who came to see you?" asked Cooper, sitting once again.

"The witches' representatives here in Spain," replied the old Agent, pouring himself a coffee. "This morning. I thought it was more of those crazed children and masked fools—*os peliqueiros*—knocking on my door, insisting we join the festival. Ever since the Demon visited the city, they have been wandering in from the countryside, acting as though every day is Carnival. Salamanca has gone mad."

"Astaroth has been here?" asked David, sitting up straight.

"Yes, my boy. Three weeks ago. He arrived and addressed the people in the Plaza Mayor. It is because he has chosen to 'bless' Salamanca that the city has electricity. There are to be a hundred days of festivals."

David made a curious face and excused himself from the table. He returned with the *Conjurer's Codex,* laying it out before the wizened Agent.

"Did he look like this?" asked David, pointing to the engraving.

"Yes," said Señor Lorca, wiping his glasses with a napkin. "Perhaps not so youthful, but this is a very good likeness. Where did you get this book?"

"The Archives," said David. "In the forbidden section."

"Clever boy," said Señor Lorca, peering again at the engraving.

Miss Boon snatched the red book up from under Señor Lorca's nose and scanned its cover. She closed her eyes and took a deep breath.

"David," she said. "Please tell me you haven't . . . *done* anything."

David remained silent; Max thought of the mysterious knowledge David seemed to have acquired their last night aboard the *Erasmus.*

"David Menlo," said Miss Boon. "Promise me this instant that you will not attempt any of the summoning spells in this book."

David said nothing; he merely folded his hands in his lap and stared at a yellow ribbon of wax that had dripped down a candle.

"Promise me, David," repeated their Mystics teacher, tapping a hard nail on the table.

"I can't do that, Miss Boon," said David meekly, avoiding her eyes. "It says that Astaroth is bound to tell the truth and—"

"Then I will keep it safe," interrupted Miss Boon, snapping it shut and placing it on her lap.

David's head whipped up. He opened his mouth as if to speak, but slowly closed it once again. Cooper leaned over to glance at the cover before flicking his eyes back at Señor Lorca.

"What did the witches want?" said the Agent, changing the subject.

"These two here," said Señor Lorca casually, waving his spoon at Max and David. "The witches suspect that Rowan has attempted a clever ruse and is using a disavowed Agent to take custody of these children. I knew nothing of it and said so. They seemed to think you had been in Portugal, but now believe you are in Spain. I've been promised the witches' eternal gratitude if I should keep a lookout for you." The old man shook his head and sipped his coffee.

Miss Boon shifted uncomfortably in her seat. Max glanced about the old house nervously.

"How do the witches know this address, Antonio?" asked Cooper quietly.

"We have helped each other in the past," replied Señor Lorca. "They have been useful to me in my old age."

"Did you let them into the house?" asked Cooper.

"I know what you are thinking, but rest assured there are no witch familiars here—no little spies hiding in the corners," said Señor Lorca. "I am old, but I am not blind to that silly trick, William."

Cooper nodded, but stood and paced the room.

"Coming here was a mistake," he said abruptly. "This house

will be watched. I'd hoped to rest here several days, but that is impossible."

Inwardly, Max sighed. He was tired of walking and sleeping in tents; a few days in a warm bed sounded very appealing, but he knew Cooper was right.

"And where will you go?" asked Señor Lorca.

"Germany," said Cooper.

"Ah," said Señor Lorca, tapping his fingers together. "Be careful, William. They're no better than the witches. But if you must be off, perhaps I can be of some use."

Cooper looked at his comrade with an expectant air.

"There are some trains running again," said Señor Lorca. "Government trains—top officials only. You could be in Germany in two days."

"Can you get us on one?" asked Cooper.

"My contacts are good. And with your talent for illusion . . . Yes, I think it's possible," concluded the old Agent. "Let me make inquiries first thing tomorrow morning. With some luck, you could be on the evening train to Paris, and from there on to Germany. Agreed?"

Cooper glanced at Miss Boon before giving a slow nod to Señor Lorca.

"We must know by noon," said Cooper. "We'll be gone otherwise."

"That gives me nine hours," said Agent Lorca. "Get some rest while you can, my friend."

Señor Lorca blew out the candles and led them up the back staircase to the second floor and a richly appointed hallway that gleamed with Spanish paintings. They passed one door and heard Mr. McDaniels's slow, rumbling snores. Mum's one shoe rested outside the dark wood of a hallway closet. Max and David were given a spacious room toward the front of the house with a private bath and two small beds stacked with white towels and blue pajamas. While David filled the bath, Max placed the Spear of Cúchulain on his pillow and wandered over to a pair of arched windows. Peeking through the drapes, Max watched masked figures steal down the cobbled lanes and alleys like grinning rats in a great maze of stone and light.

~ 8 ~

THE RED OATH

The next morning, Max wandered out of the kitchen, where Señora Lorca and his father were emptying the Lorcas' pantry of hams and cheeses and breads. These were deposited into David's battered but seemingly bottomless backpack, which had been magicked the previous year. While Mum wrapped sandwiches in waxed paper, Nick sprawled sphinx-like on the old red tiles and methodically devoured a set of old spoons. Max was restless. He trudged through the dining room, where David was arguing with Miss Boon. *The Conjurer's Codex of Summons* lay upon the table; Miss Boon's fingertips rested lightly on its crimson cover.

"Have you seen Cooper?" Max asked.

Miss Boon's bright, mismatched eyes flicked from David to him.

"Not since dawn," she said. "I'd imagine he's out scrounging for information. Speaking of which, I'd like to have a brief lesson once you've eaten."

"Where's Señor Lorca?" asked Max, ignoring the prospect of an impromptu class.

"Looking into rail passes," said Miss Boon. "We'll start the lesson in fifteen minutes."

"Hmmm," said Max, wandering out the door to a snug den paneled in dark wood and accented with yellow throws. He examined a little bronze statuette and several more photographs before slipping through the door that separated the private rooms from the bookshop.

The blare of horns and crash of cymbals continued to invade the house as they had throughout the night. The room was dark; only a thin slice of daylight slipped between the curtains' crimson folds. Max walked slowly around the perimeter, stopping at a tall bookcase whose contents were labeled by a brass plate: INDEX LIBRORUM PROHIBITORUM.

"Can you read Latin?" asked a voice behind him. Señor Lorca was standing at the far end of the room, removing a black overcoat. His white hair was swept back off his face, cheeks pink from the November chill.

"Yes, sir," said Max. "It says these books are forbidden."

"And so they were," said the old Agent, arriving next to Max and gazing through the glass case. "Centuries ago, the Church started making a list of books like these, their Index Librorum Prohibitorum. The stuff of heretics—blasphemous! To own one of these one risked much—imprisonment, excommunication . . . and worse. During the Inquisition, anything was possible."

"But I've heard of these writers," said Max, thrusting his hands deep in his pockets. "Kant, Voltaire, Locke . . . what's so dangerous about them?"

Señor Lorca chuckled; his eyes twinkled like dark coppers.

"Nothing is more dangerous than an idea. Ideas bring change and people fear change very much." He opened the glass case to retrieve a bound, delicate-looking manuscript entitled *De Revolutionibus Orbium Coelestium*. "Do you know what Goethe said about our friend Copernicus? The same Copernicus who concluded that our little earth was *not*—heaven forbid—the center of the solar system?"

"No," said Max.

"Mist and smoke," whispered Señor Lorca, conjuring a hovering orb of white vapor with a cardsharp's flick of the fingers. He blew into it, a gentle exhale that plucked at its edges until the ball dissipated to nothingness. " 'So many things vanished in mist and smoke! What became of our Eden, our world of innocence, piety, and poetry; the testimony of the senses; the conviction of a poetic-religious faith?' Do you understand what Goethe was saying?"

"I think so," said Max. "Copernicus challenged the way people viewed the world."

"And thus themselves," said Señor Lorca, tapping the manuscript before stowing it back behind the glass. "And that is very frightening, Max. Frightened people become capable of terrible things. Astaroth understands this very well. Ample evidence is in the streets."

Several knocks and laughter sounded at the front door.

"Ignore it," whispered Señor Lorca, raising a finger to his lips. "It is more of those idiot children summoning residents to festival. They will go away."

There were more knocks and a child's voice called out something in Spanish before Max heard the sound of running footsteps retreating over the din of distant music.

"Is it awful out there?" asked Max.

"It is," replied Señor Lorca with a grave nod. "My beautiful old university is destroyed—something unspeakable has taken up residence within it. The professors have been arrested. It is always so in such times, and I am old enough to remember others. Fortunately, my errand was worthwhile." The Agent sighed and produced a thick stack of stamped documents and papers.

"Will those get us to Germany?" asked Max.

"I hope so," said Señor Lorca. "I called in many favors. If they fail, William will look after you. He is most capable."

"It's so funny," said Max, thinking of Cooper. "I never think of him as having another name or . . ."

"Or another face?" asked Señor Lorca with an understanding smile.

Max nodded.

"I know," said the old man, sidestepping to another shelf to gaze upon the first editions arranged in neat rows. "It is hard for the young to believe that their elders were once foolish and beautiful, too." The old man bent down to smooth the fringe on an ornately woven rug. "Our William was the finest young Agent Rowan had seen for some time. He tells me that the Spear of Cúchulain has been entrusted to you."

"Yes," said Max. "It's upstairs."

"An ugly thing," said Señor Lorca, rising with a disapproving frown. "It made our William ugly."

"What does it have to do with Cooper?" asked Max, walking over.

The old Spaniard's eyes gazed at Max's reflection in the glass case.

"That weapon is broken," said Señor Lorca. "Fearsome, yes, but not at full potency. Cooper sought one who might mend it and make its magic whole."

"And who was that?" asked Max.

"The Fomorian," replied Señor Lorca, letting the syllables roll slowly off his tongue. "An ancient giant who hides still on the Isle of Man. It is the last. We hunted the others to extinction. The Fomorian is a great craftsman and of the Old Magic. He understands the secret makings of such a thing."

"And Cooper took the spear to him?" asked Max quietly.

"He did," sighed Señor Lorca. "And you have seen the result. It was I who found him—we did not think he would live." The old man shook his head at the memory.

"Fomorians must be awful," said Max.

"The most terrifying presence I have ever experienced," said Señor Lorca, closing his eyes. "I never saw the giant, but I *know* it saw me. A most peculiar feeling, Max—a sudden realization that Death was very near and my time on this earth had finished. I'll never know why it let us leave."

"Did you go back with more Agents?" asked Max.

"No. There are some things that should be left alone."

Señor Lorca opened his eyes and looked sharply at Max as if suddenly remembering that he was there.

"I want to give you something," he said abruptly.

The old man crossed the room to another bookcase, opening its glass door and removing an early edition of *Don Quixote*. He flipped the book open and let his fingers wander the page as though reading Braille. The bookcase slid back into the thick stone wall, revealing a small room behind it.

"What's in there?" asked Max, his interest piqued by glints of gold and the smell of age.

"Everything but my María," laughed the old Agent, slipping

inside. Max heard the clinking of metal and a sound as if the man was rummaging through boxes. Señor Lorca emerged a moment later holding a long-sleeved shirt of gunmetal gray. Its surface seemed to swallow up the daylight peeking in from the curtains. As Lorca spread it between his fingers, Max perceived slender white runes and symbols woven into the fabric like moonlit cobwebs.

"Is that nanomail?" asked Max, fascinated, as he ran his hand over a surface smoother than soap.

"A singular set," said Señor Lorca, holding it up against Max's frame. "It is my second skin and has a very special provenance. Damascus steel and spider's silk and many holy relics are bound within it. It will protect you, Max. Long ago I claimed it from the Red Branch vault, as was my right. Now I surrender it unto you, as a brother in arms."

"I'm not in the Red Branch," said Max.

"But you are meant to be," said Señor Lorca. "I am old and my service is finished. It was no accident that Cooper brought you to my doorstep, Max McDaniels. You are *meant* to take my place among the twelve. You were born in March, were you not?"

"How did you know that?" asked Max, narrowing his eyes.

"Because I was, too," said Señor Lorca. "The twelve members of the Red Branch are all born of different months and their powers wax and wane with the seasons. You are a child of March—the month of storms and war in the old calendars. Those gods will favor you as they did Cúchulain."

The old man stared down at Max like a cracked and weathered statue. Max felt another presence in the room. Cooper stood in the doorway.

"Should I do it?" asked Max.

Cooper said nothing; he merely stared at them, reading the scenario with a flat expression.

"Would I report to Vilyak?" asked Max.

"We all ultimately report to the Director," said Señor Lorca. "Our members are wanderers upon this earth—no field office, no true home save Rowan, and it may be long years before one glimpses the solace of its gates. Are you prepared to do your duty?"

Max's mouth was dry as dust. He nodded. Señor Lorca gripped Max's wrist with his long, steely fingers.

"In the name of St. Michael and Conchobar mac Nessa do I, Antonio de Lorca, declare Max McDaniels as my heir to the Red Branch and bestow upon him my title, lands, and duties. May he be a true and gracious champion—noble of bearing, fair in judgment, and terrible to the foes of Rowan. Does he accept this honor?"

Max paused. The sounds from the street faded to a hush. His attention zeroed in on the faint ticks of a nearby clock. His voice was strong and solemn.

"He does—he does accept this honor."

As soon as he finished speaking, Max felt a searing sensation in his right wrist, as though a hot brand had been pressed against it. Despite the pain, he made no sound for the long minute that followed. When Señor Lorca released him, Max saw his skin marked with the dull red symbol of the Red Branch—a red hand surrounded by a slender cord. Señor Lorca smiled at him and removed his glasses to wipe a tear from his eye.

"I have worn that mark so long, I feel almost naked without it," he said, lifting his sleeve to reveal a blank, bony wrist. "You have done me a great favor, Max. I am old and ready to meet my fate."

"I don't understand," said Max.

"Now that the mark has left him, Señor Lorca will pass on," said Cooper. "He is over two hundred years old. It is his time."

Max gaped at Señor Lorca, who merely smiled and nodded at him.

"I was born the very year Napoleon marched into my country—born into war and that is how I shall go. For over one hundred and sixty years I have been a member of the Red Branch. Those who bear that mark must make many sacrifices, Max, but it brings pleasure, too. Without that mark, I never would have met my María, no?"

Max thought of the plump, kindly woman making sandwiches in the kitchen. If what Señor Lorca was implying was true, she would soon be a widow. His stomach felt empty.

"I—I didn't know," he stammered, scratching at his wrist.

"No regrets, eh?" said Señor Lorca, handing Max the shirt of nanomail. "Put this on. You can wear your sweater over it."

Max did as he was told, pulling the long shirt of nanomail over his strong, wiry frame. It shrank and clung to him, as warm and taut as though he'd been encased in a living membrane. He twisted his torso, and the nanomail bent with him, smooth and supple. Moments later, Max pulled his black sweater over his head; only a thin sliver of gunmetal peeked out from beneath.

"You are now an Agent of Rowan and a member of the Red Branch," said Señor Lorca, looking Max up and down. "I embrace you as a brother."

The old man creaked down and hugged him, smoothing the black, curling hair away from Max's forehead the way his mother had when he was younger.

"Go retrieve your weapon, boy," said Señor Lorca, turning to close the door to his secret cache. "It has been waiting a long

time for its true keeper. Tell the others to wait in the cellar—
there is a secret passage there. Ask María to open it while I have
a word with William."

Max hurried back through the den and up the stairs to the
room where the spear was waiting. Arriving back in the kitchen,
he found Miss Boon looking snappish.

"I thought I said fifteen minutes," she said.

"Sorry," said Max. "Got caught up. Señor Lorca's back.
Cooper, too. We've got rail passes," he added, evading her stern
glance. "Señora Lorca?"

The elderly Spanish woman was bustling back and forth
from the kitchen to the pantry. She stopped abruptly, holding an
armful of bread.

"¿Sí?" she asked with an expectant smile.

"Señor Lorca asked for the cellar passage to be opened," said
Max. "We're to wait down there."

She blinked, but the smile remained frozen on her elegant
face.

"You are sure?" she asked slowly. "My Antonio told you
this?"

"Yes," said Max, puzzled at her reaction. A queasy feeling
rose in his stomach as he watched her smile grow taut. Señora
Lorca crossed herself before splashing cold water on her face.

"Come quickly," she murmured, taking a kerosene lantern
from the pantry.

"What's this all about?" whispered Miss Boon as Max helped
his father carry their bags down the dark cellar steps. David,
Mum, and Nick had already curved around a bend in the steps,
their footsteps sounding heavy and hollow on the old stone.

"I don't know," said Max. "There's some sort of secret—"
Boom!

The whole house shook and trembled. They froze like frightened mice on the stairs.

"What was that?" screeched Mum.

"Quick, quick!" cried Señora Lorca from far below. "Follow me!"

Max put his father's hand on Miss Boon's shoulder and squeezed past them.

"I'm going to see what's happening," he said.

"Max!" hissed his father. "Come back here!"

"I'll be back—keep going," replied Max, springing up the stairs.

He ran into Cooper in the hallway. The Agent's face was grim. The unmistakable sounds of a struggle could be heard from the front of the house.

"Turn around," commanded the Agent.

"Where's Señor Lorca?" asked Max breathlessly.

"Ensuring our escape," said Cooper, seizing Max's wrist and pulling him back toward the kitchen.

"No!" growled Max, twisting out of Cooper's grip and dashing toward the front of the house.

He was not prepared for what he saw.

Señor Lorca stood in the center of the bookstore, surrounded by laughing children who clung to his legs and arms while he fought off a mob of grinning peliqueiros, who swung their great, heavy batons in wild arcs. A dozen of the masked figures already lay sprawled on the floor, but more were flooding through the front door. Señor Lorca staggered as a baton crashed down on his head from behind. The old Agent roared and a brilliant blue incandescence writhed about him, sending the children scattering away. Blue and purple flames swept up to the ceiling; there was the sound of breaking glass, and several of the heavy bookcases came toppling down. Max saw a great wolf shape back into the foyer as Señor Lorca pressed the throng of *peliqueiros* back in a furious offensive.

An iron grip clamped on Max from behind.

"Obey orders!" seethed Cooper, wrenching Max backward with terrible strength and dragging him toward the kitchen. The smell of smoke permeated the air, and Max heard a chorus of shrieks near the front door. Once in the kitchen, Cooper barricaded the door with the heavy wooden table and a china cabinet in a jarring crash of broken plates and glass and pottery. Pushing Max through the cellar door, Cooper slammed it shut behind them. Whirling around, the Agent ran his hands along the door's edges, murmuring quietly. What spell Cooper had placed on the door, Max did not know, but its contours began to glow with deep-sea phosphorescence.

Down the steps they ran, to the cool, dry cellar stacked with rows of wine bottles and the accumulated clutter of many generations. Ahead was the dim light of Señora Lorca's lamp. She blinked past Max and Cooper, staring at the dark staircase from which they emerged. Cooper placed his hands gently on her shoulders.

"He is not coming, María—not this way. He will find you if he can."

Señora Lorca appeared dazed. A series of emotions flickered across her face while heavy footsteps thudded above them. The ceiling groaned under the weight of something enormous, whose bulk sent a slow, shivering tremor through the house.

"What is that?" asked Mr. McDaniels, clutching Max and David to him.

Cooper ignored him. "Please, María," the Agent said to the elderly Spanish woman. "Antonio would want you to go."

Blinking away tears, Señora Lorca nodded hastily and led them to one of the wine racks toward the rear of the cellar. She reached inside its cobwebbed depths. More footsteps and great shrieking yells sounded above them. Smoke began to seep down into the cellar.

"María, are you sure that's the right one?" asked Cooper, his voice eerily calm.

"I think so," she said, furrowing her brow. "Antonio made me remember it."

Mum began to sob. Miss Boon murmured to her quietly while Cooper ran back to peer up the stairs. Señora Lorca strained and thrust her arm deeper into the wine rack. There was a grating noise, and the wine rack slid several feet across the stone floor. An open space was revealed—short, steep steps that led down to a dim tunnel. Max gagged at the smell of sewage.

"You must hurry!" cried Señora Lorca. "It will close again in a minute."

Cooper ran back, and they squeezed down the narrow opening. Señora Lorca peered at them from above.

"María," hissed Cooper, beckoning. "Come down here!"

"I'm going to find Antonio," she said, turning away from them. The mechanical workings of the heavy rack began grinding shut again. Cooper's face darkened. In a blurry burst of speed, the Agent shot up the steps and enveloped the old woman like a trapdoor spider, dragging her down into the sewer. Señora Lorca gave a howl before subsiding to muffled, shaking sobs as the opening ground to a close.

For nearly an hour, they splashed and staggered along in a dark and nauseating reek. Miss Boon conjured a small orb of shimmering green and gold that floated ahead like a will-o'-the-wisp, revealing smaller tunnels that fed cold water into the main. At length, Cooper stopped at the base of a corroded iron ladder that rose fifteen feet to the street above. Mr. McDaniels retched quietly against the wall; even Nick snorted with disdain at a pair of sewer rats that scurried past. Cooper squinted at a map tucked among their papers and passes.

"This is it," he said conclusively, glancing at his watch. "The next train leaves for Bilbao in an hour. David, can all our things fit in your bag?"

David broke from a fit of wheezing coughs. "I think so," said Max's roommate, peering curiously into his battered backpack.

Cooper stuffed their packs into the backpack one by one, zipping it shut and slinging it over his shoulder. Climbing silently up the rusted ladder, he lifted its heavy covering and peered out. A flicker of annoyance crossed his features and he held up a finger for them to stay put. The Agent crawled out of the sewer on his belly until he had disappeared from view. Ten seconds later, his face appeared in the opening.

"You can come up."

They climbed the ladder, sputtering and gagging, into the bright afternoon. They were in an alleyway; two *peliqueiros* were sprawled in the street, unconscious. Cooper held one of their stout wooden batons under his arm. He pointed to a nearby spigot while he riffled through the bundle of documents.

"Wash off as best you can," he commanded, glancing down the alley.

Distant music floated in the air while they took turns at the spigot, splashing cold water over their shoes and pant legs until even Mum was satisfied that the odor had faded. Poor Nick huddled under the spigot, cold and miserable, while Max combed the water through his thick quills. He was careful to keep the red mark on his wrist concealed beneath his sleeve.

"These are your papers and passports," Cooper said. "Memorize your name and likeness. You are with the German ambassador. You are his aides and you are returning from a diplomatic conference. I will be the ambassador and speak for the group. Do you understand?"

They nodded as Cooper distributed the documents. He paused when he reached Señora Lorca. "We need to get you out of Salamanca, María."

"I will do no such thing," muttered Señora Lorca, squeezing the water from the hem of her skirt. "I am not leaving."

"Please, María," said Cooper.

The old woman shook her head defiantly.

"Where will you go?" asked Cooper quietly.

"My sister's."

Cooper glanced down at the motionless man lying at his boot. He said nothing for several moments. Señora Lorca gently took his hand.

"Go," she urged. "I do not blame you, William."

"I will try to come back and find you," said Cooper, kissing her on the forehead. Walking among them, Cooper spoke quickly in Latin, tapping each of them on the shoulder. The illusion complete, he shouldered David's bag and strode quickly down the alley.

"*Vaya con Dios,*" whispered Señora Lorca, waving farewell as they hurried away.

Twenty minutes later, Max sat in a luxurious compartment on a private train for public officials. He gaped out its clean glass window. Black-cowled witches wove through the crowds milling about the station. Workers in red armbands swarmed like ants over tall scaffolding that enclosed the beginnings of a towering statue. Thin-lipped officials surveyed the work, fedoras pulled low while they scribbled on their clipboards. Small blue-faced goblins with long beaks and red gums scurried past on urgent errands. Squat, swaddled hags examined the goods in a street vendor's cart. From the top floor of an apartment building, some-thing with white, larval eyes peered out from a broken window. Trumpets blared, voices sang, and drums boomed while they sat in silence.

"Are you all right, Cooper?" asked Miss Boon hesitantly as the train began to move.

The Agent sat across the compartment. His face was stone.

"The Book, Miss Boon," he said quietly. "All that matters is the Book."

The train picked up speed and glided like a silver snake into the east.

~ 9 ~

CLOCKWORK MARVELS

The train rolled on past abandoned farms and highways and swept up among the sloping shoulders of the Pyrenees. If Cooper slept, Max did not see it. The Agent sat upright, his eyes thin slivers of ice as he listened for the approach of conductors, police, or any of the other myriad officials. He managed to meet these individuals outside the door of their compartment, barking at them in a variety of languages with a stern, officious air. They crossed into France with a dull stamping of papers. A mob of dirt-smudged youths charged the train at Bordeaux, breaking several windows with chunks of hurled cement. The train stopped for some time in Paris, the city's center as brilliant as a fallen star amidst the blackened wreckage of its smoldering out-skirts. Many people boarded there; heavy boots sounded in the corridors. Gray and brown fedoras bobbed past the compart-ment window. The train went on.

"I don't understand," said Max, watching small flakes of snow melt on the window. "All those governments—the mili-tary, everything. It's like they never even fought back. I didn't know anything like this could happen."

"Militaries and governments are only as strong as the people who run them," said Miss Boon. "The Enemy has always infil-trated such organizations, but we severely underestimated the extent."

"Do you think they've infiltrated the Workshop?" asked Max.

"It's possible," said Miss Boon. "They infiltrated Rowan, after all, when they got to Mr. Morrow. I don't think much of Jesper Rasmussen, but I doubt he's working with the Enemy."

"Whatever happened with Rowan and the Workshop?" asked Max. "Didn't we used to be part of one Order?"

"Long ago, there was no Rowan, no Workshop or witch clans," explained Miss Boon. "Together, we numbered in the thousands—tens of thousands, according to the histories and YaYa's accounts. During the Middle Ages, bitter disputes arose over our direction. And the inventions kept coming—water mills, clocks, compasses, cannons. . . ."

Max nodded, noticing that the opportunity to teach seemed to relax Miss Boon. She sighed and plucked a stray hair from her sleeve before continuing.

"Some feared it was only a matter of time until science and technology eclipsed our arts and we risked enslavement to those who mastered them. We must embrace technology, they argued, devote ourselves to its study lest we fall into ruin. There were others who viewed such ideas as heresy, outraged over the notion that we might turn away from the Old Magic that distinguished us among humankind. Factions developed and bloody power struggles ensued. The extremists from both sides were driven off to pursue their passions in other corners of the world. The technologists built their Workshop, and the witches fled to the mountains. Neither has wholly forgiven us for choosing the middle road. They hate each other with a passion."

"Have you ever been to the Workshop?" asked Max.

"No, but I was offered an internship," answered Miss Boon. "They offer one periodically to Rowan's top student, but I declined. I don't mean to boast, but I *was* valedictorian that year. . . ."

"Have you ever been, Cooper?" asked Max.

The Agent nodded. Miss Boon's head swiveled.

"Dear God, please tell me you weren't a valedictorian, too."

"No, Miss Boon," said Cooper, scratching at a shiny patch of scalp. "Far from it, I'm afraid. You're the only valedictorian here."

"Thank the Lord!" said Miss Boon, folding her arms and settling back contentedly.

Max heard a thin wheeze followed by another. Cooper was laughing. His shoulders shook. Miss Boon turned red but managed to look mildly amused. Mr. McDaniels started chuckling, too. A moment later, the four of them were laughing together. Mum cracked her crocodile eye and glared at them, but David went right on sleeping.

"What's so funny?" demanded Mum, scrambling to her feet. "Are you laughing at me?"

"No, Mum," said Miss Boon. "We're laughing at *me*."

"And I was having a nice dream, too," said Mum crossly. "Bellagrog and I were making a big vat of our holiday eggnog. Three parts bourbon to one part nog, just the way she likes it. . . ."

"Sounds like you miss her, Mum," teased Max, poking the hag playfully in the ribs.

"She's a beast!" protested Mum, swatting weakly at Max's hand. "But I do miss my cupboard and my cooking and the oven that works just so."

"And Bob?" chided Max.

"Yes, yes, and Bob too . . . the stupid clumsy oaf," grumbled the hag. "Half the school's probably starved to death! He can't do anything without me, you know."

"We know," they said in unison.

Cooper fished through David's pack and produced a large bar of chocolate that he'd taken from the *Erasmus*.

"I thought those were all gone!" said Mr. McDaniels, now very much awake.

"Had to hide one from you," replied Cooper. "For emergencies."

The Agent broke the bar into pieces and doled them out— even Nick received a small wedge, which he sniffed gingerly before swallowing.

"What about you, Miss Boon?" asked Cooper, chewing his chocolate thoughtfully. "What do you miss?"

"What *don't* I miss?" said the Mystics instructor with a sigh. "I miss teaching. Fires in the great hall. Reading on Maggie's steps. And, dear Lord, a regular bath!"

"I miss my friends," said Max. "And Hannah and the goslings. Geez, I wouldn't even mind seeing Renard!"

"*Monsieur* Renard," corrected Miss Boon.

"I miss Maya and the Archives," David said, peeping from beneath the arm flung over his face.

"What about you, Dad?" asked Max.

Mr. McDaniels flushed. He drummed his fingers on his barrel chest.

"The Beefmeister 2000."

Max and David howled with laughter.

"I wonder if I'm still receiving monthly shipments of meat," said Max.

"Well, you *should* be," huffed Scott McDaniels indignantly. "I paid for them in advance."

"Sorry, Mr. McDaniels," giggled David. "I don't think the deliverymen can find Rowan anymore."

Max envisioned the great veil of mist David had conjured from the sea. He tried to imagine what was happening at Rowan Academy, whether classes were continuing and the students were safe. He wondered how his own country was coping with the sudden changes in the world. Real news was so hard to come by—he did not even know if a president occupied the White House.

A knock sounded at the door; a dark shape filled its small window.

A vye was peering into the compartment. Yellow, feral eyes wandered from face to face.

"Dear God!" gasped Mr. McDaniels, gripping his seat.

"It doesn't see you, Scott," said Cooper evenly. "It sees six German diplomats. Just be still."

Cooper strode to the door and opened it.

"*Gute Nacht*," said Cooper, staring up at the vye.

"*Gute Nacht*," replied the blue-black vye. It ducked under the doorway, clutching a clipboard against its trench coat. Its matted fur was damp; one clawed hand was bandaged and bloodied. Max held his breath. He felt utterly exposed, as though he were hiding in plain sight. It seemed impossible that the vye would not see him for what he was—a thirteen-year-old boy clutching a lymrill that had instinctively balled into a defensive mass of bristling quills.

Max felt for the spearhead that he now kept in his sleeve. It was warm to the touch and hummed ever so slightly. The vye glanced at him; Max fidgeted and coughed. Snapping his fingers under the vye's nose, Cooper reclaimed its attention with an authoritative stream of rapid-fire words. The vye bared black-gummed fangs and glared at the Agent for several long seconds. Affecting boredom, Cooper crossed his arms and tapped his shoe impatiently. A nearly subsonic growl rumbled in the vye's throat as it fumbled for something in its coat. Their documents were stamped and returned to them. The vye muttered something to Cooper before stalking out of the compartment, shutting the door firmly behind it.

"Is it really gone?" asked Mr. McDaniels.

"It is," said Cooper, slipping the documents back into his coat.

"That's the most god-awful thing I've ever seen," sputtered Mr. McDaniels.

"Why wasn't it disguised?" asked Max.

"Because they're getting cocky," said Cooper. "Vyes don't like human form—makes their eyes itch. I told him we didn't appreciate the sudden scare and that I'd speak to his superiors."

"You're kidding," said Mr. McDaniels.

"No," said Cooper, peering outside the window. "That was a good reminder to be on our toes. We've just passed Strasbourg and are crossing into Germany. We'll be in Frankfurt by dawn."

The Agent spied the empty chocolate wrapper on the floor and stooped to snatch it up, thrusting it deep within his pocket before taking the seat nearest the door.

Dawn arrived with a steel-gray sky and a sporadic drizzling of sleet that rattled on the roof. From a distance, Frankfurt seemed undamaged—no trails of black smoke rose into the air, as at

Bilbao and Tours. The train pulled into a station of metal and glass with a great domed roof. Nick mewled unhappily as Max stowed him in David's backpack. Cooper stood by the door and looked them over.

"Stay close behind me as a group. Don't speak to anyone. A receiving outpost of the Workshop isn't far—we must hurry without drawing attention to ourselves."

They filed out after Cooper, squeezing through the narrow corridor past bleary-eyed officials. The station was nearly empty; just a few coffee-sipping men and women loitered near another track under the bored gaze of a slouching policeman.

Cooper strode purposefully for the exit while they trailed behind him like dutiful aides. As they neared one of the exits, a middle-aged woman ran up to Cooper.

"*Oskar!*" she said, embracing him. "*Wie geht es Ihnen?*"

"*Danke, gut,*" replied Cooper stiffly, removing her hands. "*Es tut mir leid, aber wir sind spät.*"

The woman's smile faded. She turned and watched them go with a puzzled expression. In his peripheral vision, Max saw the policeman straighten and stare at them.

"Cooper," he hissed.

"Keep walking; stay calm," said the Agent without breaking stride.

They stepped out the main exit into the cold gray morning. Hurrying past several commuters, Cooper led them to a street crossing, where they were forced to wait at a traffic light. An undisguised vye stood waiting across the street, looking utterly out of place amidst the automobiles and buildings.

A car honked to their left. Max turned to see a sleek silver limousine idling at the curb. The driver stepped out and addressed them.

"*Guten Tag, Herren,*" said the driver, holding open the door.

Cooper stared at him. The light changed, and the vye began padding across the street.

"*Doktor Rasmussen sendet Grüße,*" said the driver, glancing nervously at the approaching vye. He beckoned at the open door. Offering a curt nod, Cooper led them quickly to the car, where Max piled in after his father. The door was locked and they pulled away from the curb. The vye peered at the license plate but continued on toward the station.

"Welcome to Frankfurt," said the driver, accelerating past several cars with diplomatic plates. "I speak English and I can assure you that your disguises are no longer necessary."

"How do you know who we are?" asked Cooper quietly.

"I don't," replied the driver. "I can only definitively say that Scott McDaniels is in this car. I assume the rest of you come from Rowan as well."

"The pill," muttered David, nudging Mr. McDaniels. "That pill Rasmussen made you swallow . . . it must have been a—"

"Homing device," replied the driver with a satisfied smile. "Yes, we've been following your progress for quite some time."

In a blur, Cooper leaned forward and pressed his knife against the driver's throat.

"Have you been sharing that information?" the Agent whispered.

"I'm quite sure I don't know what you're talking about," the driver replied in a steady voice. "We have already aided you twice now. Dr. Rasmussen is eagerly awaiting your safe arrival."

Cooper said nothing and kept the knife still. The driver did his best to appear calm, but Max saw tiny beads of sweat forming on his forehead. Cooper muttered several words; Max felt a slight tingling as the illusion drained away. Sitting up in the backseat, Max saw his own face reflected in the rearview mirror.

"Look at me," said Cooper.

The driver glanced at the Agent. His eyes widened in shock at the waxy, scarecrow face hovering inches from his own. Cooper's voice was deadly calm; his Cockney accent thickened.

"If I find that the Workshop is responsible for the death of Antonio de Lorca, I'm going to hold you personally responsible, mate. Do you understand me?"

The driver swallowed hard and nodded. Miss Boon put a hand on Cooper's arm and gently guided the knife away.

"You said Dr. Rasmussen is awaiting us?" she asked.

"Yes, madam," said the driver, looking back at her gratefully. "You are to be his honored guests."

Mum made a disbelieving face, but Miss Boon shushed her. Max opened David's pack; Nick practically leapt into his face. The lymrill nipped Max hard on the finger and circled into a peevish ball.

"Is that the lymrill?" asked the driver, trying to glimpse Nick in the rearview mirror.

"How do you know Nick's a lymrill?" asked Max.

"Dr. Rasmussen described him," said the driver. "A most interesting creature."

The driver drove them past a government building and on a circuitous route through the city. They ended up, however, at a parking garage only a few blocks from the train station. The driver waved at the attendant, who promptly lifted the gate. The car plunged into the dimly lit structure and proceeded to wind its way down. When it reached the lowest level, the driver accelerated smoothly toward a dead end of gray concrete. The speed pushed Max back against his seat, but the car made no sound.

Cooper fidgeted and gripped the backrest.

"What are you doing?" he growled, leaning forward once again.

"Please remain calm," replied the driver. "The increased speed is necessary."

They raced past thick pylons and stalls filled with expensive automobiles. The speedometer crept past 120 kilometers per hour. Their acceleration was so smooth it seemed they were stationary and the wall was racing toward them. Mum shrieked and covered her eyes. Mr. McDaniels hugged Max and David to him.

They sped right through the barrier.

For a brief moment, the car went dark. When he could see again, Max whirled around in his seat and watched the wall rapidly receding in their wake.

"So it was an illusion, then," said Cooper, finally easing back in his seat.

"Not at all, sir," said the driver. "That wall's solid enough to stop a tank."

"I don't follow," said Miss Boon, prying Mum off her.

"Nanotechnology," replied the driver. "We've adjusted its properties to admit objects traveling at the appropriate speed. A smidgeon slower and . . . splat!"

"Cool!" said David, joining Max at the back window. The automobile was descending at a steep grade on what appeared to be a four-lane highway tunneled deep into the earth. Slim blue lights lined the rock walls at regular intervals.

"You boys will like the Workshop," said the driver, smiling. "There is lots to see, and Jason Barrett is anxious to get reacquainted."

"How is Jason?" asked Max, excited to see his friend, a recent graduate of Rowan.

"Very well," said the driver. "A most promising young

man—working with our engineers in Applications. Altogether very thorough with his research."

"You're doing *research*?" asked Miss Boon incredulously. "Now? Haven't you been affected by all that's happening?"

"Self-sufficiency is our driving creed," replied the driver. "We don't need your food or power plants or communications networks. We've already solved those problems."

"I wonder why Dr. Rasmussen should eagerly await our arrival," said Miss Boon with a prim smile. "It seems the Workshop has everything it needs."

"We are self-sufficient but not discourteous," said the driver, expertly guiding them down a slow, spiraling descent. The car leveled out and he accelerated at a rate Max had never experienced before. They rocketed through the tunnel in a blur of polished rock and streaming lights. The speedometer read 350 kilometers per hour as they whirred through another wall, this one made of gleaming black metal. Then the car slowed to a purr, and the driver wheeled it toward a massive pyramid of smooth, sheer rock that was set at the center of an enormous cavern.

Max gazed in mute astonishment at the scale of the space and everything within it. The pyramid must have been a mile wide, with a pair of monstrous silver doors set into its face. A dozen other tunnels emptied into the cavern, feeding toward the great pyramid; some were hundreds of feet in diameter. The driver eased the car to a stop among a host of identical vehicles parked near the towering entrance.

"How far down are we?" croaked Mr. McDaniels, following Max out the door and rocking back on his heels to survey the space.

"Approximately seven kilometers below sea level," responded the driver. "Nearly twice as deep as a diamond mine. But we have spaces deeper still."

Miss Boon waved her hand through the air and rubbed her fingers together.

"But it's cool here," she said. "It should be hot—*intolerably* hot this far down."

"We learned long ago to harness the heat and pressures at such a depth," chuckled the driver, leading them toward the towering silver doors. "Where you perceive a threat, we recognize an opportunity. The geothermal heat we capture and convert from this site alone could power a major city."

"I'll bet Vincenti would love to see this place," whispered Max to David, referring to Rowan's technology specialist.

"Your Joseph Vincenti would have little interest in what we do here," echoed a voice ahead of them.

Jesper Rasmussen stood at the threshold of an inconspicuous opening next to the gargantuan doors. A smile creased his skeletal, hairless features. "You see, your Joseph Vincenti makes Devices. We make machines. I think you can tell the difference." He laughed and walked forward to greet them. "I'm sorry we cannot open them for you," he said, waving at the colossal doors behind him. "It's quite a sight, but I could hardly justify the energy expenditure. My colleagues would think I'm getting vain." He stopped and gave a short bow to David and the McDanielses. "It is nice to see you under less dire circumstances. Welcome to the Frankfurt Workshop."

"Hmph," said Mr. McDaniels, shaking the proffered hand.

"What do you think of our little home?" asked Rasmussen, gesturing at the looming monolithic structure. "What you see is ten times greater than the pyramid at Giza and you're only glimpsing half."

Max imagined the gargantuan structure extending far below the smooth rock flooring at his feet. He felt infinitesimal.

"Let's get you settled, then," said Rasmussen, dismissing the driver and steering David forward. Mum reached out and clutched Max's hand as they followed Rasmussen through the small side door that might have been an entrance for insects.

They were led into a dim white room with a steel door at the opposite end.

"This will take but a moment," said Rasmussen, closing the door to the outside. "A sterilization procedure. We've become very cautious about contamination from microorganisms. You won't feel a thing."

As he locked the door, the room was illuminated with rapid pulses of light like thousands of camera flashes firing one after the other. Shapes swam before Max's eyes; Nick howled and raced around the room's perimeter. The flashes abruptly stopped, and a green light appeared on the steel door's handle.

"Your eyes will recover momentarily," said Rasmussen. "My apologies for the duration, but we've never had to sterilize one of her kind before. I'm sure the hag understands."

"Oh, indeed I do, sir!" said Mum, clasping her hands and offering a low curtsy. "We hags are indeed a filthy lot! I'm much obliged to you for zapping me crawlies!"

"Not at all," said Rasmussen, strolling forward to have his iris scanned.

As they filed out of the room, Max caught Mum scrabbling furiously at her nose. She dragged her finger along the wall, leaving a shiny trail. She shrugged at Max and waddled after the group, humming with satisfaction.

"We'll first get you settled," said Rasmussen, leading them down a short corridor that opened into an enormous atrium. Max blinked and exchanged glances with his father; he could have sworn they were outside. Live redwood trees and sequoias rose hundreds of feet in the air, creating halos of shade from warm sunlight that filtered through glass panes far above.

Dozens of people were sitting at circular tables, chatting over tea or huddled in quiet conversation around schematic drawings. Woven baskets of fresh fruit were arranged in neat rows beneath the open window of a cozy café built of rose-colored stone. Max breathed in deeply and felt the oxygen-rich air sharpen his senses.

"Are those trees real?" asked Mr. McDaniels.

"Of course they're real," replied Rasmussen proudly. "Only the sunlight is simulated."

"Do they sell coffee there?" asked David, meandering toward the café.

"Any coffee you might care to try," said Rasmussen. "But it's not for sale. Nothing at the Workshop is for sale. Just tell Natalia what you would like."

"So I suppose those great big apples are just there for the taking?" asked Mum.

"Of course."

"And those croissants there? I guess I could just stuff my mouth full of 'em?"

"If that's what you wish."

The hag's small red eyes darted greedily around the atrium.

"And that handsome bloke sitting by the rosebush? I suppose I could simply—"

"Mum!" hissed Miss Boon. "Behave yourself."

Dr. Rasmussen laughed.

"I know you have had a long journey. I'll be sure to have some refreshments sent to your rooms."

"*Room,*" said Cooper. "One room will suffice."

"Cooper," whined Max and David together.

"We've been stuck together an awful lot," said Mr. McDaniels, craning his neck about. "Maybe a little space to spread out wouldn't be such a bad thing."

"One room," repeated Cooper, ignoring them. "And we'd be obliged for a bit of rest. As you said, we've had a long journey."

"As you wish," said Rasmussen, offering a curious smile. He beckoned to a tall woman wearing a trim gray outfit. "Can you please take our guests to a suite in the VIP quarters?"

"Of course," said the young woman. "Please follow me."

They were taken to an elevator bank that was unlike any Max had ever seen; the elevator was a sort of smooth oval pod that was propelled along without any appreciable sense of friction. They traveled at a steep trajectory before suddenly leveling off to skim smoothly along a white plastic tube lined with rows of shiny silver disks like the suckers on a tentacle. A violin concerto played from a hidden speaker.

"Er, are you Mr. Rasmussen's secretary?" asked Mr. McDaniels.

"I'm a physicist," replied the woman coolly.

Mr. McDaniels blushed and coughed into his fist.

"Have you seen what's happening aboveground?" asked Miss Boon.

"Not personally," replied the woman. "I've never been aboveground."

Max's jaw dropped. Even Cooper glanced up in interest.

"You mean you've *never* left the Workshop?" asked Miss Boon.

"I understand that must sound odd," said the woman, "but there's never been a reason to leave."

"So you've never seen a hag before?" asked Mum, giving a regal turn to present her bulbous profile.

"Of course I have," said the woman, glancing at her watch. "There's a stuffed specimen in our Biology Museum, and we have a dozen genetic samples on record."

Mum's eyes widened in shock; her lower lip began to quiver. "You've got a hag *stuffed* in some dusty museum?"

"The museum is perfectly clean."

"You scrawny little—"

Miss Boon clamped her hand over Mum's mouth while the gray hag flushed green. Max was impressed that Miss Boon could keep a hold on Mum, who was notoriously strong for her size. After several furious seconds Mum stopped struggling.

"Are you going to be polite?" asked Miss Boon firmly.

Mum glared at the teacher but nodded. The hand was removed and the hag leapt to her feet.

"It's my cousin Gertrude!" Mum bawled. "Gertie went on holiday twenty years ago and—"

Miss Boon sighed and snapped her fingers before Mum's spitting, hissing mouth. The shrieks and accusations ceased as though Mum had been unplugged.

"Thank you," said the woman as the pod came to a gentle stop. "I'll take you to your room."

For all of the Workshop's emphasis on machines, Max found their room surprisingly organic. Its palette was light, its textures were natural, and the internal geometry converged to pleasing curves. It had two large bedrooms and baths and a common room complete with burning fireplace. The woman touched a screen that was set into a wall of burled hardwood.

"Just address the monitor if you have any requests," she said. "I have to be returning to work."

Cooper nodded and shut the door behind her.

"Assume everything we do and say will be seen and heard," he muttered, opening David's bag and unpacking their things. Hoisting his own pack, Cooper disappeared into one of the bathrooms to shower. Max and David followed Mr. McDaniels into one of the bedrooms, where they collapsed onto a huge soothing green comforter. Nick leapt up on the bed to nestle between the McDanielses. Scratching the lymrill's silky ears, Max closed his eyes and drifted to his first satisfactory sleep in a month.

He awoke to the sound of Mum's voice speaking shrilly from the common room. Max glanced at his watch—he'd been asleep for five hours.

Padding into the next room, Max saw Mum standing before the computer screen, near a serving cart mounded with picked bones and discarded gristle. The hag had evidently just bathed; her wet hair was pulled into a topknot, and an enormous white bathrobe trailed behind her as she paced back and forth.

"That's right," she confirmed. "And six more hams on the bone. Honey-glazed."

"Will that be all, madam?" asked the beleaguered-looking woman on the screen.

"And perfume," Mum thundered, shooting a finger toward the ceiling. "Something expens—"

Cooper strode to the computer screen and banged it off.

"I wasn't finished!" hissed Mum.

"Get dressed," said Cooper. "We're not on vacation."

The Agent ignored Mum's departing curses and threats as he pulled on his shirt of nanomail. He looked tired; there was a purplish tinge to the skin beneath his undamaged eye.

"Are you all right, Cooper?" asked Max.

Cooper nodded and reached for the wavy-bladed kris. He oiled its blade with a black cloth before strapping the scabbard to the small of his back. He reached for his black sweater and sniffed it.

"They have plenty of clean clothes in the closets," offered Max.

"Threaded with audiowire and filament cameras, no doubt," replied Cooper. "Stick with what we brought, eh? Whether it needs a wash or not."

Cooper glanced at the door to the room where David and Mr. McDaniels were sleeping. He crossed over and shut it before taking a seat at a small dining table near the fire. He beckoned for Max to sit.

"How do you feel?" asked Cooper.

"Fine," said Max. "Hungry, but fine."

"We haven't had much time for training," muttered the Agent. "Do you feel sharp? Capable, I mean."

"I do," said Max, puzzling at the man's earnest tone.

"That's good," said the Agent, rubbing his hands together. "That's very good."

"Cooper, what's wrong?"

The pale blue eyes darted away from Max to stare at the fire. The Agent seemed to choose his words carefully.

"We all have a purpose," said Cooper. "I used to think mine was to be alone—to hunt Rowan's enemies and keep dark things where they belonged. I was wrong. My true purpose has been to keep you safe—you and David, your father and Miss Boon. Even Mum."

Max began to speak, but Cooper held up a finger to silence him.

"A time may come when I cannot keep you all safe. You are inexperienced, but you are a member of the Red Branch and you have been blooded. As of this moment, I am assigning you a most important objective."

The Agent pushed a thin slip of paper toward Max. There were only three words, but they sent a chill down Max's spine.

PROTECT DAVID MENLO

"Throw it in the fire," muttered Cooper.

They watched the paper blacken and curl and dissolve to ash.

"Well, at least it's straightforward," said Max, trying to lighten the mood.

"Straightforward, yes," said Cooper. "But not simple. It must be your reason for being. Nothing can come between you and this objective."

Cooper inclined his head toward one of the bathrooms, where Mr. McDaniels's booming baritone could be heard from the shower. Max pondered several scenarios.

"You mean if I had to choose—"

"There is no choosing," said the Agent, shaking his head. "There can be no hesitation. Your objective is clear."

Max glowered at Cooper.

"I will look after him, Max," offered the Agent. "You know that."

Max nodded, looking hard at Cooper. "I do. But there's one more thing I want to know."

"And what's that?"

"Did you know my mother?" asked Max simply.

Cooper blinked but sat perfectly still. They stared at each other for several seconds.

"Why would you ask me that?" asked the Agent slowly, rising to retrieve a bottle of water from a slim silver refrigerator.

"I saw your face when my dad showed you the photograph," said Max. "You've seen her before, haven't you?"

A vein throbbed in Cooper's forehead. He sipped slowly from the bottle.

"Yes," he said quietly. "I have seen your mother before."

"Where?" demanded Max.

"I can't answer that."

"Where is she now?" demanded Max.

"I can't say," said Cooper evenly.

"You don't know or you can't say?" said Max, his face growing hot. He jabbed a finger at the Agent. "She's dead, isn't she?"

"I don't believe so," replied Cooper.

"What's that supposed to mean?" hissed Max.

There was a sharp knock at the door. Cooper strode over to answer it but Max seized his arm.

"Answer me!"

Cooper's face darkened and he straightened to his full height. Turning, he gripped Max hard by the shoulders.

"I think she's alive because her apple hasn't turned to gold. And that's all you'll get from me, do you hear?"

The words struck Max like a physical blow. Cooper released him and went toward the door. Max's hands began to shake. A tremendous, terrifying surge of energy snapped through his body like a whip.

Breathing deeply, Max shut his eyes for a moment and sought to calm himself.

His mother was alive. His mother had attended Rowan.

Max's mind flashed back to his memories. He had never seen his mother do anything unusual—nothing to suggest she had any capabilities in Mystics. She had certainly never mentioned Rowan. So many questions. He opened his eyes and saw Dr. Rasmussen standing in the doorway, looking at him curiously.

"Are you ill, boy?" asked the man. "You don't look well."

"I'm fine," croaked Max.

"I trust you're comfortable here," said Dr. Rasmussen, glancing at Cooper's stained clothing with mild amusement. "And I see you've already managed a bite," he added, glimpsing the culinary carnage.

"No," sighed Cooper. "Just Mum."

"Ah, the hag," said Dr. Rasmussen, frowning. "Curious travel companion. If you're ready, I'll give you a brief tour of the Workshop. Then we request your company at dinner."

Minutes later, they had piled into another one of the floating pods and were whisked off on brisk rounds of subterranean wheat fields and orchards and greenhouses, all illuminated by artificial sunlight and manned by robotic, spidery farmhands or actual humans who enjoyed the activity. They glided through monstrous foundries, past coiled energy converters, and beneath shuttered research labs that protruded like rock ledges in the hollowed enormity of an old salt mine. Surfaces were clean, people moved with unhurried efficiency, and everywhere was the low drone of white noise.

"How many people live in the Workshop?" asked Cooper as the pod slowed to permit a team of scientists to cross the way.

"That's classified, as I'm sure you understand," replied Dr. Rasmussen.

The pod rose several levels and accelerated forward into a well-lit hall the size of an aircraft hangar. Max fidgeted and glanced at Mum as they passed biological exhibits. Gargantuan skeletons of whales and dinosaurs were suspended in glass cases, their mouths yawning wide to reveal fine-combed baleen or six-inch teeth. While they hovered past tree sloths and octopi and marmosets and water buffalo, Mum's face was pressed against the pod's window.

Dr. Rasmussen continued his dry commentary. ". . . of course, many are now extinct, but we have preserved all available genetic material in cryogenic bins located beneath each exhibit.

With this we are able to incubate and resuscitate any species whose reappearance is considered desirable. For example—"

"Where's the hag?" blurted out Mum.

"I beg your pardon?"

"The hag, the hag!" shrieked Mum. "I want to see her."

"Very well," said Rasmussen. The pod hummed along toward a vast wing labeled EXOTICS.

This gallery was dim, brightened primarily by the exhibits themselves, whose glass cases were illuminated from within.

"Now this is interesting," said David, sitting up.

Max gaped at a russet-plumed cockatrice whose petrifying eyes had been removed. A mottled Okinawan hobgoblin glared straight ahead, its sharp-toothed mouth frozen in a mischievous leer. They passed a Baltic ogre and a serpentine naga. David and Max craned their necks to glimpse the shadowed face of an enormous giant clad in heavy skins. It must have been thirty feet tall, with braided black hair, and several eyes sparkled from beneath its craggy brow like semiprecious stones. The giant's head and limbs were massive and rough-hewn, as though it had crawled out of some bubbling vat of primal clay and cooled before it could be properly shaped. It was the most hideous thing Max had ever seen.

"What is that?" asked David, scuttling to the rear of the pod to get a second glance at its label.

"A Fomorian giant," replied a disinterested Dr. Rasmussen. "Thoroughly brutish and mercifully extinct. We purchased that specimen from Solas in the sixteenth century."

Max glanced at Cooper, but the Agent merely stared straight ahead. They had passed several more cases of various giants and ogres and trolls when Miss Boon suddenly exclaimed, "Excuse me, but did that lamia just blink?"

"Ah, Lilith is a great favorite among the schoolchildren,"

chuckled Dr. Rasmussen, bringing the pod to a halt. The pod door slid open, and he stood aside to let them out. They stopped at a respectful distance from the ten-foot cube. The lamia's hooded eyes surveyed them with disdain. It had the porcelain face and torso of a beautiful woman but the lower body of a green-skinned constrictor that moved ever so slowly in a thick series of coils.

"You keep *live* specimens here?" asked Cooper.

"Certain creatures, yes," said Dr. Rasmussen defensively. "They're critical to our research. Without that research, you'd have no Course, my friend."

"You built the Course?" asked Max.

"Of course we did," said Dr. Rasmussen proudly. "Not quite cutting-edge anymore, but I daresay it still meets your needs—even those of your top Agents."

Cooper nodded and stepped closer to the glass. The lamia's snake trunk now wrapped sinuously around its body. Blood-red lips smiled and parted to reveal triangular white teeth.

"Ever have one escape?" asked Cooper.

Dr. Rasmussen scoffed.

"Never. Our containment chambers are impenetrable. A lamia is a minor consideration. After all, we have afrits and marids and all sorts of *diaboli minora* similarly imprisoned."

"You're joking," said Miss Boon, looking ashen-faced.

"Not at all," said Dr. Rasmussen, gesturing toward distant rows of bronze-tinted cases. "Your own Scholars inscribed the original pentacles in the mid-nineteenth century, I believe."

"Bother all that!" shrieked Mum, flapping her hands impatiently. *"Where's the hag?"*

"Two aisles over, three cases down," muttered Dr. Rasmussen.

Mum galloped away, skidding around a gleaming exhibit of a half-grown chimera.

Moments later, a bloodcurdling wail, like a broken siren, rose to a frenzied pitch before subsiding into pitiful sobs. The group hurried over to find Mum curled into a weeping ball at the base of a brightly lit exhibit. Within the case was a particularly pasty, gap-toothed hag in a floral sundress, toting a large woven handbag. Her features were frozen into an expression of revolted shock and horror. Max glanced at the nameplate: PEDIVORE TERRIBILIS.

"Murderers!" howled Mum. "Oh, my poor Gertie. Cut down in the prime of life."

"My condolences," sniffed Dr. Rasmussen.

Mum scrambled to her feet and launched herself at Dr. Rasmussen. Mr. McDaniels intercepted the sputtering, cursing hag.

"We'd better take Mum back to our room," said Miss Boon quietly.

"Another transport is on its way," said Dr. Rasmussen, tapping a translucent screen on his watch. He flicked an irritated glance at Mum, who now clung to Max's father like an inconsolable koala. They stood in awkward silence for the next minute until a sleek pod hovered before them.

"I'll take her," said Mr. McDaniels, lumbering toward the open door with his sobbing burden.

Mum's face whipped up from Scott McDaniels's shoulder. Her face contorted in fury.

"I'm going to get you, Rasmussen," she hissed, taking a long sniff. "Hags *never* forget!"

The door slid shut, and the pod reversed smoothly out of the gallery.

"Charming creature," remarked Dr. Rasmussen, turning on his heel. "Shall we?"

"I hope we don't see a stuffed lymrill," whispered Max to David. "Nick would go berserk."

PEDIVORE
TERRIBILIS

"You won't see one because we don't have one," called Dr. Rasmussen from up ahead. "Your Nick is the only specimen I've ever actually seen. He's priceless, really."

Max frowned and ran to retrieve Nick from where the lymrill was standing on his hind legs to examine a plump were-rat specimen. Seconds later, their pod had reversed out of the gallery and rejoined one of the disk-lined tubes.

They glided along for several minutes until the pod eased to a stop and they stepped out into a clearing where a Grecian temple opened onto a small sunken amphitheater ringed by olive trees. Several dozen young children sat on the steps, listening to an elderly woman who was demonstrating an antique-looking device that resembled a sort of vise. The woman pulled the handle, which turned a large screw that, in turn, lowered a metal-faced woodblock, pressing it tight against a sheet of parchment. The children clapped as the woman removed the parchment and displayed an inked broadsheet.

Max stared at the children. They looked almost identical; dark olive skin, bright blue eyes, and close-cropped black hair.

"Our youngest students, learning the basics," said Rasmussen, stepping out.

"Are they clones?" asked Miss Boon, squinting at them.

"Of course not," said Dr. Rasmussen. "We do practice some eugenics, of course, but we have a healthy respect for nature as well. Some genetic traits are controlled; others are left to chance. We find it maximizes advantageous characteristics while still allowing for evolutionary outliers."

The man smiled and inclined his head deferentially toward Max and David.

"But you wear glasses," said Miss Boon. "And you're—"

"Bald." Dr. Rasmussen smiled. "Totally hairless, actually—*alopecia universalis*. All evolutionary disadvantages, I know, but it's a law at the Workshop that only nonengineered humans can attain certain levels of seniority. It's an important safeguard against the temptations of total optimization. That could lead to dangerous levels of genetic convergence, an evolutionary no-no."

He led them around the rim of the amphitheater, strolling toward the columned temple.

"Hello, Dr. Rasmussen," chimed the children.

"Hello, children," he said, waving amicably. "What have you got there?"

"Gutenberg's press," said a proud-faced girl, holding up a sheet of freshly inked type.

"And what's so special about it?" asked Dr. Rasmussen.

"It used movable, durable type to create a mechanical printing process," answered the girl.

"So what?" asked Dr. Rasmussen with an irreverent shrug. "Why should we care?"

The girl blushed and sat down. Her immediate neighbor stood and continued.

"A mechanical printing process was much more efficient than handwritten manuscripts. Information and ideas could be disseminated more easily, democratizing knowledge and creating a primitive network effect."

"Excellent," Dr. Rasmussen said, clapping. "And what permitted this transformation?"

"A machine," crowed the children.

"And what *is* a machine?" asked Dr. Rasmussen, feigning ignorance.

"A machine is any device that transmits or modifies energy to perform useful work," chimed the children.

"Carry on, then," said Dr. Rasmussen, waving good-bye and strolling casually toward the temple. Max and David followed behind, glancing back at the children, who had clambered up to the top steps to watch them with open, curious faces.

"Dr. Rasmussen," called Miss Boon. "Please stop for a moment."

"What is it, Miss Boon?"

"This tour's very enlightening, but I'm curious that you've never once asked the purpose of our visit."

"But I know the purpose of your visit, Miss Boon. You seek something secreted here by Elias Bram—something to do with the Book of Thoth."

"Well, yes," said the teacher, blinking rapidly. "I happen to think it's in Aachen. You see, Charlemagne's tomb is located there, and it might—"

"It is not in Aachen," said Dr. Rasmussen with a dismissive wave of his hand. "It is here. We have found a chamber constructed by Bram."

"Have you got it, then?" asked Cooper quietly.

"No," said Dr. Rasmussen. "Try as we might, we haven't been able to open the chamber."

"How's that?" asked Miss Boon. "It seems you have a machine for everything."

Dr. Rasmussen smiled coldly. His small, reptilian eyes shifted from her to David.

"We don't need a machine, Miss Boon," he said. "We need a Sorcerer."

~ 10 ~

BRAM'S KEY

They followed Dr. Rasmussen to the temple, passing through a six-columned peristyle and into the clean marble structure. A richly laid table was set at the center, around which were seated a dozen Workshop officials. One young face was conspicuous among them, and Max found himself waving back to Jason Barrett, who had risen with the others as they arrived. Jason looked much older than the last time Max had seen him—like a full-grown man. He strode forward to greet them.

"Max, Miss Boon, it's great to see you!" he said in his southern drawl, tousling Max's hair and shaking Miss Boon's hand politely. "Man, you're getting big," he said, giving Max a jab on the shoulder, glancing curiously at the nanomail peeking from his sweater. Introductions were made. From people's titles, it seemed the Workshop was organized into three main divisions: Energy, Matter, and Applications. The Rowan visitors shook hands with the heads of each and their direct reports before the group was seated. As the meal was served, Max was delighted to see that even Nick had been provided for—a deep tureen of slim metal ingots kept the lymrill noisily occupied. Max poked dubiously at a tofu dish masquerading as meat while Rasmussen initiated conversation.

"We are most indebted to Rowan for paying us such a timely visit," said Dr. Rasmussen, raising a glass of cabernet. "Indeed, I must admit we have become a bit exasperated by the problem."

"And what exactly is the problem?" asked Miss Boon.

"Bram's Chamber," replied the head of Energy. "Its door has proven inexplicably difficult."

"I can't make heads or tails of it," said Jason Barrett, passing a curry dish to Max. "And it's ruined a lot of equipment. It's wound with magic, but whatever binding spell's on it is way out of my league. I think it'd give even ol' Kraken fits."

"*Miss* Kraken," said Miss Boon icily, eliciting a hasty apology. She turned her attention to Dr. Rasmussen. "I'm curious that you simply happened upon this chamber, Doctor. If I recall you seemed to doubt that the Book of Thoth even existed."

Dr. Rasmussen held up his hands in a guilty, supplicating gesture.

"What else could I do, Miss Boon? I was skeptical, yes, but in which direction should I err? If the Book does not exist, we have indulged a wild-goose chase. If it does and we permit Astaroth to pursue it at his pleasure, then we have let laziness endanger us. As a leader, I cannot permit the latter. Following our council at Rowan, I consulted my advisors. We discovered that Elias Bram did indeed spend considerable time here in 1646. Old schematics revealed that he had assisted us in hollowing out some of the lower levels, including some shafts that were later discontinued and sealed off long ago. We opened them and found something most unusual."

"Bram's Chamber," said Miss Boon.

"Indeed."

"We should like to have a look at it," said Miss Boon.

"After supper, we should very much like you to," said Rasmussen, opening another bottle of wine. He shifted the conversation to other topics, predominately the status of major cities and population migrations across the continent. Max ate quietly, trying to keep up with the engineers' various reports while Jason bombarded him with questions about the witches and Rowan. Jason's questions were pleasant but puzzling—he seemed oddly detached from the situation aboveground.

"Jason, is your family okay?" asked Max, abandoning the tofu brick in its sauce.

"Actually, they're here," he replied, attacking a bowl of greens. "Everyone—aunts and uncles, too. Soon as things started going bad, the Workshop brought them in."

"Wow," said Max. "I guess that's a good thing."

"They've adjusted to this place easier than to what was happening outside," said Jason with a sober nod. "Apparently things were getting mighty strange at home. My uncle had a farm— swears something was calling to him from his well."

Max grimaced at the thought. The field offices must have been working nonstop—if they were even still investigating such minor curiosities. Max was anxious to see Bram's Chamber and heaved a private sigh of relief when dessert was served.

Once David had finished a jaw-dropping fifth cup of coffee, the meal was brought to a conclusion. In the commotion of the group rising from their seats, Jason casually leaned close to Max.

"Keep a close eye on Nick," he whispered.

"What?" asked Max, but Jason merely began speaking to a Senior Matter Specialist about some recent conductivity tests. Max looked anxiously for Nick, who was now dozing in the tureen with a belly as round and taut as a pumpkin.

"Do you know how he does it?" asked a willowy woman to Max's right.

"Excuse me?"

"The lymrill," she said, pointing at Nick. "How his body metabolizes food and metal alike."

"I have no idea," said Max.

"Fascinating," said the woman, "to think that it possesses some process or enzyme that can convert common metals into something extraordinary. Have you ever plucked one of his quills?"

"No," said Max, appalled. "I don't think he'd like that."

"Hmmm," said the woman, eyeing Nick thoughtfully.

"And I'd hate to see what would happen if someone tried," added Max pointedly. "Nick's a tank."

The woman smiled and drifted away to where Dr. Rasmussen was gathering them at another pod bank at the rear of the temple. A transport glided forward from a queue of several. Artificial sunlight reflected on a shallow fountain, sending shimmering bands of gold dancing on the pod's silver surface. Max gazed up at the Grecian masks and statues that adorned the temple space. It was all too surreal. He scooped Nick up from his slumber and slung the heavy body across his shoulders like a recent kill, much to the amusement of Dr. Rasmussen.

The pods glided one after another, banking out of the temple and down a long tube that seemed to run along the pyramid's periphery. Veering gently to the right, they suddenly plunged down a raw, wide mineshaft of dark rock and winking crystals. Max felt his stomach gurgle; David had closed his eyes and was humming quietly to himself.

At last the pods began to decelerate, arriving at a hollowed chamber half the size of a gymnasium. Fluorescent lights were scattered about an intricate latticework of temporary supports and braces. Formidable earthmoving machines and drills lay off to the side; Max noticed the massive bits had been worn down like spent erasers. Two dozen engineers were already there, scouring blueprints and diagrams from a mobile workstation of computer screens and some sort of hologram projector. They appeared exhausted, turning to stare at the new arrivals with blank expressions. Max looked past them to where a round stone door was set into the rock face.

"Any new developments?" asked Rasmussen cheerfully.

"No, sir," said a cadaverous-looking woman with close-cropped white hair.

"Well. I've brought you some new tools," said Rasmussen. "Perhaps you'll give our guests a summary of what we've learned to date."

The woman folded her arms.

"Well," she said lightly, "what we have here is a door. A door with no handles or visible hinges. A door that our sensors say is made of mere granite, and yet it causes our hardest drills to crumble like cheese—when we can even position them close enough to touch it."

"Why is it difficult to get a drill close?" asked Cooper.

"I was hoping you could tell me," she snapped. Removing a

metal stylus from her front pocket, she lobbed it toward the door. It stopped in midflight and dropped to the floor as though it had struck an invisible wall.

"What about a laser?" asked Miss Boon.

The woman glared at the Mystics instructor.

"Yes, we'd managed to think of that, too," she answered, following a pregnant pause. "The resulting explosion killed three engineers and nearly collapsed the tunnel. Perhaps the young lady brought a can opener?"

Miss Boon sighed and turned to Dr. Rasmussen.

"May we have a look?"

"By all means," he replied. "Please forgive Dr. Braden—she's not accustomed to obstacles more immovable than herself."

The woman nodded with stiff formality as Miss Boon swept past with David in tow. Max felt a flash of admiration for the young instructor, who seemed utterly uncowed by the formidable engineer. He and Cooper were following behind when David suddenly stopped. He removed Bram's talisman and passed it back to Max.

"It's tugging at my neck," he explained. "If you're wearing metal, you should stay right here."

Max and Cooper looked at each other; both were wearing nanomail, and Cooper always carried several weapons. The area ahead was suddenly illuminated by a pair of spectral white orbs conjured by Miss Boon. She and David stood before the circular door, which was some ten feet in diameter and carved of a grayish green stone flecked with bits of black. In the center of the door was the profile of an ibis-headed figure that Max knew to be the Egyptian god Thoth. The door's outer edge was carved with a dozen cat-sized ants in a frozen march around the perimeter. Between the ants and the image of Thoth were thousands of hieroglyphs that had been inscribed with surgical precision.

David and Miss Boon conversed quietly while Dr. Rasmussen and the other senior officials came to congregate behind Max and Cooper, just beyond the reach of the force emanating from the door. Miss Boon levitated several feet off the ground to peer at some inscriptions near the top; David backed away to survey the whole. As their examination lapsed into mysterious silence, Dr. Braden began to grumble. For several minutes, David did not move, standing quietly with his hands clasped behind him as though admiring a work of art. Suddenly, David clapped his hands. His young voice rang off the walls.

"Little myrmex, little myrmex, awake! The Sorcerer has come and recalls you to life."

Nothing happened.

" 'Sorcerer' indeed," sneered Dr. Braden. "Now, perhaps we can get back to—"

"Shhh," muttered Rasmussen, holding up a finger. "Something's happening."

Indeed, something was happening. A fine powder began running down the door in rivulets. Max squinted and watched the stone surrounding the carven ants dissolve to reveal a dozen shiny black bodies underneath. The enormous ants shook off the remaining bits of masonry. Elbowed antennae trembled, mandibles clicked, and they began marching along the edge in an orderly clockwise procession. Dr. Rasmussen clucked his tongue and turned to Dr. Braden with a victorious smirk.

"See? I told you the little one was held in high esteem. Miss Boon, is the door opening?"

Miss Boon walked over, leaving David to resume his studious pose before the door.

"No, Dr. Rasmussen," she replied. "There are many spells on this door—David's only let it know that someone wishes to enter. It is still locked."

Dr. Braden glared at Jason Barrett.

"Why couldn't you do that?" she demanded.

"It's not Jason's fault," interjected Miss Boon. "The incantation may be as simple as a nursery rhyme, but it depends on who's speaking. That door would not listen to me. I don't think it would listen to anyone but David."

"But he's a child," scoffed Dr. Braden.

"Dr. Braden," said Miss Boon, "surely someone as educated as yourself doesn't need me to explain that small things can possess tremendous energy."

"Of course not," said the engineer.

"Well, you're looking at the most powerful Mystic the world has seen in nearly four hundred years. Since Elias Bram, as a matter of fact. In my opinion, David's not even really a Mystic—he's a true Sorcerer."

"What is the difference?" asked Dr. Braden, plucking at her chin.

"Mystics can cast spells," said Miss Boon simply. "Sorcerers often won't bother with such rote necessities—their energies and instincts are so great that they can simply improvise what they need. They are exceedingly rare."

Dr. Braden opened her mouth and then clamped it shut.

"Is *he* the reason that Rowan has disappeared?" asked Dr. Rasmussen.

"He is," said Miss Boon.

"I see," said Dr. Rasmussen admiringly.

David turned on his heel and walked over to them with his hands thrust deeply in his pockets. His young features were quiet and composed. Behind him, the ants continued in their tireless march.

"I'll need some quiet, so it would be best if you all left now," he said, his eyes staring at the floor.

Dr. Rasmussen chuckled.

"We quite understand—we're being too noisy. You'll have absolute silence, young man."

David shook his head.

"I'll need privacy and a book. I think Miss Boon knows which one."

Miss Boon locked eyes with David.

"Are you quite certain about that?" she asked cautiously.

"Quite."

"David, I don't want you down here alone," said Cooper quietly.

"Max can stay," said David, wandering back toward the door. "Oh, and I'll want coffee—lots of it, please. Plenty of sugar and cream."

Dr. Braden started to object, but Rasmussen silenced her with a furious glance.

"If I've learned to respect anything, it's the demands of genius," he said. "Of course David can have whatever he desires. We will give him his privacy." The man reached into his pocket and handed a slim communications device to Max. "Press this if you need anything. I expect that you'll notify us immediately if the door is opened?"

Max glanced at Cooper, who nodded his acquiescence.

"Everyone out," said Dr. Rasmussen, ushering the engineers back toward the transport pods.

"Tell my dad not to worry," said Max, handing Nick and the talisman to Cooper.

Miss Boon gripped Max's arm tightly and leaned close.

"Max, I don't know what David's planning to do, but that book is *exceedingly* dangerous. . . ."

Cooper placed his hand over the teacher's hand and gently removed it from Max's arm.

"We need to trust David, Miss Boon," he said quietly. "Let's get him what he needs."

Chewing a nail, Miss Boon gave David a decidedly maternal glance before turning to follow Cooper.

The pods departed and Max slumped to the floor, resting his back against a hulking drill while David stood bathed in the ghostly white glow of the orbs. The small blond Sorcerer did not move until the *Codex* and coffee arrived, and even then he seemed utterly oblivious to the presence of anyone else. He stirred the cream and sugar into the thermal carafe and paced back and forth, muttering soundless words and flipping through the red book with the casual air of a bookstore browser. Max yawned and eyed the rows of heated coffee cylinders. The *click-click-click* of the marching ants filled his ears. He turned from David to scan the dark cavern, lit here and there by soft halos of fluorescent lights. By the time David began to chant, Max was already drifting to sleep.

He awoke to a much brighter chamber. David stood within a protective circle that burned as blue as an arc welder's flame; he leaned close to examine the door, clutching the open book to his chest. He was flanked by two other circles—pentacles that burned like red phosphorous. The ants were marching faster now. Max stood to his feet.

"Don't come any closer," ordered David, without turning. "Stay behind the line."

Max glanced down and saw a faint, shimmering line in the floor, just beyond Dr. Braden's stylus.

"How is it coming?" hissed Max.

"It's coming," David replied wearily. "The overall solution isn't that complex, but it's tedious, and the spells multiply if you're not clever enough to—"

David broke off abruptly, speaking a sudden flurry of words in Egyptian.

"Sorry," he muttered before continuing. "You have to speak the proper words of command at precisely the right time, like aligning the tumblers of a lock. Otherwise the requirements multiply."

"What's with the circles?"

"There are two very powerful demons in this room. The pentacles are to confine them, naturally. The circle's to protect me. That line is to protect you."

David held up a finger as he bobbed his head in some silent count before speaking a command in Greek.

"I don't see any demons," Max said, rubbing his arms as chills cascaded down his spine.

"Maybe not," said David. "But they see you. Stay where you are."

"What're they for?" asked Max.

"Doing the grunt work," replied David. "They're solving the trickier binding spells and parsing out the final commands so I can speak them at the proper time. Very helpful, actually."

Max lapsed into silence as David continued, periodically raising his small fist and uttering words that sounded nigh unintelligible. As Max watched, he began to discern subtle disturbances above the two pentacles. The air above them seemed to shimmer and distort periodically, like waves of summer heat rising off a highway. From far off, Max thought he could hear indecipherable whispers and mutterings—eerie, gibbering voices that played tricks on his ears. The march of the ants achieved a frantic cadence.

"Come here," said David with an air of calm command. "I need your help now."

Max crept forward but stopped at the faint line drawn into the floor.

"But I thought—"

"Stay where you are!" shrieked David, his body jerking suddenly up and off the floor as though he were a marionette. His feet landed dangerously close to the edge of the protective circle, and his body swayed about to face Max with milk-white eyes. Max stood utterly still. David's eyes clamped shut, and he bent over, straightening slowly as though gathering his energies. He lifted his chin with an imperious air and seemed to gaze coldly upon something within one of the pentacles. Glancing at the *Codex,* he read from it in a strong voice.

"Thy service complete, I consign thee to the places beyond this earth from which thee may not stir without proper summons. Disobey and you shall be cast into Oblivion."

Max exhaled as the pentacles began to dim; faint whispers faded to silence until all evidence of the menacing visitors had gone. David stood breathing heavily, his face shiny with sweat. Turning back to face the door, he seemed to follow the path of one particular ant as it marched. When it reached the top of the door, David whispered one final word of command. The ants promptly leapt off the door to land in a chittering, churning jumble at David's feet.

The great stone door shuddered.

"David, get away from it!" yelled Max.

David looked back at him, tottering wearily like a punch-drunk fighter.

Hundreds of tons of stone toppled forward in a slow, murderous arc toward David's defenseless head.

Max leapt.

With a deafening boom, the door crashed into the rock floor, sending up stinging chips of granite and effectively disintegrating the mindless, clicking ants. Max and David lay sprawled to the side, coughing in the choking plumes of dust that rose like a mushroom cloud. When the ringing in his ears subsided, Max pulled David to his feet, brushing bits of rubble and debris from the dazed boy's face.

"Don't tell Miss Boon what happened," David whispered before his legs buckled beneath him. Max felt about David's cold, rubbery wrist for a pulse. He laid David on the floor, balling his own sweater beneath his roommate's head. Fumbling for the device Rasmussen had given him, Max pressed it frantically.

"Why, hello," purred Rasmussen's voice.

"We need a doctor," panted Max.

"Is the door open?" asked Dr. Rasmussen.

"Yes! *But we need a doctor now!*" Max screamed.

"Of course," came the calm reply.

Max threw the device against the wall and began pacing the room, feeling utterly helpless as he watched David's chest rise in slow, ponderous breaths. It seemed an eternity before the first pod arrived with a host of eager-looking engineers, including Dr. Braden. A physician and several attendants arrived in a second pod moments later.

The physician was a kind-faced woman with jet-black hair. She hovered over David, examining his vital signs by hand while her attendants placed sensor pads on David's wrists, chest, and temples.

"Where's Cooper and Miss Boon?" asked Max when Rasmussen arrived.

"In your room asleep, I'd imagine," he replied casually. "It's four in the morning. What seems to be amiss, Patricia?"

The physician at David's side frowned and examined a small computer screen.

"He has an erratic heartbeat—very weak."

"He had a transplant," volunteered Max. "Two, actually."

"Hmmm," said the physician, exchanging a grim glance with her colleagues.

"Do something!" yelled Max.

"For God's sake, control yourself, boy," muttered Rasmussen impatiently. He stepped past them to stand on the toppled stone slab. The repelling force seemed to have dissipated when David broke the spell; engineers were hurriedly rolling machines and monitors toward the dark tomb-like opening. Meanwhile, the physician quietly relayed instructions to an assistant, who selected from among a dozen long syringes filled with an ashy-looking substance. At the physician's nod, the assistant suddenly plunged one of the long needles straight into David's chest.

"What is that?" cried Max, hovering over them. David's leg kicked suddenly and thumped on the rock floor.

"Medicine," one of the assistants assured him. "Microscopic robots to structurally patch and strengthen his heart."

"Is it *hurting* him?" asked Max urgently.

"If he were awake, he'd be in quite a bit of pain," explained the physician patiently, "but fortunately he's unconscious. Normally, we'd administer anesthesia, but not under these circumstances. You did the right thing to call for us."

Max heard Rasmussen's voice sound behind him.

"If the boy is bothering you, Patricia, we can have him removed."

The physician never had a chance to answer. Rage consumed Max; he whirled on Rasmussen. A moment later, the skeletal man had sunk to his knees, gazing up in sputtering terror as Max held him by the throat.

"H-help!" croaked Rasmussen, his face turning blue.

"This 'boy' just might snap your neck," Max hissed. The power that surged through him was both terrifying and exhilarating. He was vaguely aware of figures moving in the background and his peripheral vision. They seemed no more significant than the ants crushed beneath the door. Faint pinging noises could be heard as projectiles bounced harmlessly off his nanomail. Then a dull pain spread throughout his legs. Glancing down, he saw several small darts embedded in his thigh. Another hit. Then another.

Turning, Max spied a white-faced engineer pointing a device at him and fingering its trigger. But before the man could compress it, Max had released Rasmussen and closed the distance in two blurred steps. Wrenching the device away, Max crumpled its casing like aluminum. Its owner promptly fainted.

Another version of Max appeared in the room, triggering frantic shouts and waves of darts that ricocheted off the walls. A second phantasm appeared, then a third. While his doubles played havoc with the terrified engineers, Max slipped silently behind a machine from which he might ambush the largest group. Before he could, however, one voice rose above the others.

"Stop! *Please* stop!"

It was the physician. She was addressing one of the flawless illusions, which circled her and David. The phantasms stopped and studied her. Suddenly, they dissipated in a curl of black smoke.

"Everyone put away your weapons," commanded the physician, hurrying over to Dr. Rasmussen, who lay sprawled and coughing. "Where are you?" she called.

"I'm right here," said Max, stepping out from his hiding place.

The nearby engineers practically jumped out of their suits. They turned and backed away to the other side of the chamber.

The physician gazed at Max's legs in horror before barking

technical orders at her assistants, who had taken refuge behind a drill.

"What's the matter?" asked Max.

"We—we've got to get you to the hospital ward immediately," stammered the physician. "That's a fatal dose of tranquilizers. I don't understand how you're even on two feet."

"I'm fine," said Max, plucking one out of his thigh. "Just look after David."

Rasmussen sat up, massaging his neck. Much to Max's surprise, he was laughing.

"Lesson learned," he wheezed, clearing his throat in a series of rasping coughs. "I had no idea you—well, needless to say, I quite understand the witches' interest in you. My sincere apologies if I caused offense. Delicacy is a personal shortcoming."

"Dr. Rasmussen," pleaded the physician, "we must get him to the hospital."

"Does he look *ill* to you, Patricia?" snapped Rasmussen, brushing debris from his pants. He shuffled toward the crumpled curiosity that had been a functioning weapon only moments earlier. Picking it up between two fingers, Rasmussen peered at it intently.

"May I at least take *this* patient to the hospital?" asked the exasperated physician.

"Of course," said Rasmussen distractedly. "Thank you, Patricia."

"I'm going with David," said Max, remembering Cooper's command. Just the previous day, Cooper had entrusted Max with David's care, and already it seemed he was failing in his charge. He eyed the yawning chasm of Bram's Chamber, reluctant to abandon it to the engineers, who had already resumed wheeling equipment toward the door. But Max snatched up the *Codex* and followed David's gurney aboard the medical pod.

* * *

Several hours later, Miss Boon was furious. Max sat red-faced with knitted fingers while his Mystics instructor berated him for losing his temper. She paced back and forth, ramrod straight, uttering words such as *reckless* and *juvenile* and *imbecilic* with numbing regularity. Draped over the back of a nearby loveseat was Mum, who practically writhed with delight as Max was forced to recount the violent episode.

"What did his face look like when you was squeezin'?" asked the hag, interrupting Miss Boon.

"Not now," muttered Max.

"You should have given him a head-butt," said Mum authoritatively, offering a ferocious demonstration. "Knocks 'em straight out!"

"That's quite enough, Mum," snapped Miss Boon, spinning to address the hag, who fled cackling toward a bedroom.

Before Miss Boon could continue her tirade, the door to their suite opened. Cooper and Mr. McDaniels walked in, clutching a wobbly David between them.

"And that's another thing," said Miss Boon. "I want to know exactly what David did that has left him in this condition."

"I don't know *exactly* what he did," snapped Max. "I fell asleep."

"Ha!" snorted Miss Boon, digging in her heels.

"The good news is that David should be all right," interjected Scott McDaniels. "The doctor said he'd undergone a terrible strain and that it wasn't good for his heart. But some pills, some shots, some rest, and our boy should be good as new."

David smiled weakly.

"That's the only good news we have," said Cooper, replacing the talisman around David's neck and tucking it in the boy's sweater. "The Workshop recovered whatever was in that

chamber. There was a golem inside, but they managed to immo-
bilize and destroy it. Rasmussen wants a meeting to discuss the
situation."

"What's to discuss?" said Miss Boon, blinking rapidly. "It's
perfectly obvious that the Key is our property. Without David,
they'd still be staring at a stone door, for heaven's sake!"

"Bring your attorney, then," replied Cooper, shaking his
head. "Everyone else, pack your things and stow them in David's
bag. We might need to leave in a hurry."

"But—" began the young teacher.

"That's a direct order, Miss Boon," said the Agent stolidly.
"Max, get your weapon. You're to have it on you at all times."

"Yes, sir," replied Max, trotting back to the bedroom. He
tied the spearhead to his back, as he'd seen Cooper do, before
cramming the rest of their things into David's battered pack.
Nearby, Nick mewled and shredded a pillow before thrashing it
in his teeth like a terrier.

"Not a peep," muttered Max. "We'll have to feed you later."

The lymrill yawned and stretched his claws dramatically,
giving Max an acid stare before waddling out to the living room.
Several minutes later, an attendant knocked on their door, and
they glided away in one of the high-speed transport tubes.

They were escorted into a much more officious-looking
room. No charming fountains or columns or students here,
observed Max. Senior Workshop officials sat around a long
table of polished redwood. Armored soldiers stood at attention
along the dark-paneled walls. In the middle of the table,
propped up like a grisly centerpiece, was the severed head of
the chamber's guardian—an unseeing lump of cracked stone
whose rough, simple features might have been sculpted by a
child. Dr. Rasmussen sat at the head of the table, grinning from
behind his polished spectacles.

"Welcome, my friends," said Dr. Rasmussen, gesturing at the empty chairs. Max sat next to his father, cradling Nick in his lap. Jason Barrett sat across the way looking profoundly uncomfortable. "How do you like our new sculpture?" Dr. Rasmussen inquired, gesturing at the golem's head. "Dr. Braden's already taken the body to the museum. Quite the mindless, plodding creature, isn't it? We were a bit disappointed to find something so crude."

Cooper nodded.

"I understand you have something of interest?" asked the Agent.

"Indeed we do," said Dr. Rasmussen. "A most curious object."

Rasmussen lifted something heavy from the floor and placed it on the table before him.

Bram's Riddle had mentioned a key with four notches, but this object did not resemble any such thing. It looked more like a globe of silver rings supported on a short stand of smooth wood. Dr. Rasmussen gave one of the rings a playful spin.

"Do you know what this is?" he asked.

"That's an armillary sphere," said Miss Boon. "Invented by Eratosthenes in the third century B.C. An astronomical teaching tool."

"Indeed," said Dr. Rasmussen. "And what is it for, I wonder?"

Silence ensued. Max glanced at Cooper and counted the soldiers along the wall, as he had been taught. Rasmussen tapped a long, slender finger against the tabletop.

"I see," he said, frowning. "I find it curious that Rowan expects the Workshop's cooperation on matters great and small, but when we make a simple request for information you are as silent as the grave."

Cooper removed his cap, revealing the scarred, close-cropped skull beneath it. He examined the hat, plucking a bit of white thread from the black wool. Max felt Nick tremble. When the Agent spoke, his voice was calm and flat and terrifying.

"That object belongs to Rowan. Its purpose is classified. We're not leaving without it."

The tension around the table was palpable. Dr. Rasmussen looked genuinely perplexed. He blinked and ran his hand across his smooth, hairless cheek.

"Surely you meant that as a request and not some sort of primitive threat, Agent Cooper. I can't imagine that Rowan would arrive on our doorstep making such demands given all the Workshop has done for them. Such a threat would be ironic indeed, as we are in the company of two young gentlemen who, without our assistance, would now be eking out a miserable life with the witches."

"It belongs to Rowan," repeated Cooper.

"If it belongs to Rowan, why would Bram entrust its care to the Workshop?" asked Dr. Rasmussen. "Perhaps if we know what it's for, we can better gauge what to do."

"It's a key," said David, his small voice ringing like a clear note. He looked utterly drained. "That much we know from the riddle Bram left behind. And Bram stashed it here for a very good reason: to keep it safe and to ensure cooperation among the branches of the old Order. That's why you couldn't reach it without me. We have to cooperate or no one will get the Book but Astaroth."

Miss Boon nodded; Rasmussen appeared to listen carefully to David's words.

"If I recall correctly, Mr. Menlo, I believe you bear a trinket that monitors the Book's danger?"

David nodded.

"And what does the marvelous little trinket say?" asked Rasmussen.

David reached inside his sweater and brought out the talisman, laying it on the table. It was as dark and cold as lead.

"Perhaps we should just keep this Key here," said Rasmussen, shrugging. "It would seem the Demon is no closer to getting the Book than we are."

"We can't count on that," said Miss Boon quickly. "For all we know, there may be other ways to find the Book of Thoth. The Demon has Marley Augur in his service—Augur knew everything that Bram had done with it."

"And this Augur," said Dr. Rasmussen, touching his fingertips together. "He was one of *yours*, if I recall correctly? A member of some standing, I believe?"

"Yes," said Miss Boon, clasping her hands patiently.

"Hmmm," said Rasmussen. "That is troubling. Given the likelihood of disloyalty among your ranks, I can hardly conclude that this sphere or the Book would be safe with Rowan."

"That's absurd," said Miss Boon, leaning forward.

"Is it?" asked Dr. Rasmussen. "If my information is accurate, didn't Rowan have a traitor in their midst only last year? A Byron Morrow?"

Miss Boon glanced at Jason Barrett, who blushed and looked away.

"And wasn't this Mr. Morrow a teacher?" continued Dr. Rasmussen with an innocent smile.

"What's your point?" asked Cooper.

"Isn't Miss Boon a teacher as well?"

"Don't insult her," warned Cooper, his eyes as cold as a shark's.

"I wouldn't dream of insulting her," said Dr. Rasmussen. "I'm sure Rowan's teachers are the most talented, ethical individuals your organization has to offer. That's precisely my point, Agent Cooper—if even an exalted teacher can be corrupted, what can be said for the rest of your Order? Most unsafe guardians of such an artifact, I'm afraid."

Max glowered at Dr. Rasmussen. He imagined that no matter what words or argument one chose, the smiling Rasmussen would twist and shape them to his purpose. Miss Boon took a deep breath and rested her palms on the table.

"What would you propose?" she asked wearily.

Dr. Rasmussen leaned forward.

"We have discussed the issue and are prepared to let you have this contraption or Key or whatever it is in exchange for the lymrill."

"*What?*" exclaimed Max, clutching Nick to him.

Jason Barrett cleared his throat and spoke up. "Dr. Rasmussen, you have to understand that Nick isn't just Max's pet— there's a very special bond between them. Max took an oath—"

"Mr. Barrett, do not interrupt unless you wish your entire family returned to the surface."

Jason's face darkened; he shut his mouth and stared at the tabletop.

"In addition," continued Dr. Rasmussen, "we require blood and tissue samples from young Max McDaniels. When these have been obtained, this object will be surrendered to you. Given Rowan's professed need for its acquisition, I think our price is very reasonable."

"It's not just Rowan's need," interjected Miss Boon, motioning for Max to be still. "It's *humankind's* need, Dr. Rasmussen."

"So you say," said Dr. Rasmussen with a dismissive wave. "But we are quite comfortable where we are. Should the Enemy conquer every single continent, it will affect us not."

"You mean that you're not even going to fight?" asked Miss Boon incredulously.

"We've amassed a great deal of data and analyzed many scenarios, Miss Boon," replied Dr. Rasmussen with a shrug. "You have already lost, I'm afraid. Over seventy percent of the world's population is transitioning to rule under puppet regimes; the rest will soon follow. Government ranks are riddled with the Enemy's servants. Even those officials not part of the original conspiracy are quickly swearing allegiance. As far as the common people are concerned, they're too worried about starvation, civil war, and things scratching at their windows to muster a credible resistance. Through your arts, Rowan may manage to hide for a bit, but you too will fall. Our most generous estimates give you a year."

"But don't you see?" pleaded Miss Boon. "That's exactly why you should be helping us! If everything you're saying is true, the Book might be our only hope to destroy Astaroth!"

"Why do you assume it's in our best interest to destroy the Demon?" asked Rasmussen, spinning the sphere's rings once again.

Miss Boon simply stared at him.

"Because Astaroth is a terrible evil."

"Says who?" asked Rasmussen, visibly enjoying the exchange. "Theologians? Priests? Your Promethean Scholars? Ha! I can argue that mankind is a far worse calamity. Look at the evidence—an accelerating rate of species extinction, an appalling waste of precious resources, catastrophic impact on the atmosphere and climate. . . . These are all the result of humans arriving on the planetary scene just a heartbeat ago. We're worse than locusts, Miss Boon. A culling of man's population and planetary influence might be the very thing we need at this juncture."

Silence. Miss Boon pursed her lips; when she finally spoke, her voice trembled with anger.

"Dr. Rasmussen, do you *want* Astaroth to win?"

"The Workshop is neutral in the affair," he replied decisively. "We wish Rowan the best in its struggle and would appreciate a prompt reply regarding the matter at hand."

Max looked down at Nick, whose otter-like face was uncharacteristically serene and thoughtful. Max knew that the lymrill understood some basic essence of the conversation. Sharp claws curled and hooked into Max's sweater as the creature stood on its hind legs, balancing its forepaws against Max's chest like a baby. It craned its neck to peer down the table at Rasmussen.

"I can't," blurted out Max, with a pleading look at Miss Boon and Cooper. "I can't give Nick up to these people. They'll put him under a microscope or on a dissecting tray. I'd rather die."

"And I don't want you people having tissue samples of my son," said Mr. McDaniels, crossing his arms. "Creepiest damn thing I ever heard of in my life! What're you going to do? Clone him like a sheep?"

"*Take me!*" shrieked Mum, bolting suddenly out of her chair and running toward the head of the table. She was quickly intercepted by a soldier, who held the struggling hag firmly by the shoulders. "Take *me* instead!" bawled Mum. "Leave the boy and that poor stupid creature alone!"

Laughter erupted around the table. Dr. Rasmussen smiled and shared a twinkling, conspiratorial wink with his neighbors.

"Thank you for the generous counteroffer, but we must decline. We already have one hag, and that is quite enough."

"But I'm unique!" insisted Mum. "And I can cook!"

"Congratulations," sighed Dr. Rasmussen, motioning for

the soldier to escort Mum back to her seat. Throughout the episode, Max noticed that David had not moved, but was staring at the talisman on the table.

The chuckles subsided, and Rasmussen stood to rest his palms on the table.

"Come, my friends," he said. "We are all busy people. Do we have an agreement or not?"

None of the Rowan representatives answered. With the exception of a teary, indignant Mum, they were now all staring at Bram's talisman.

It was glowing.

Glowing was too strong a word. The miniature light was as weak and shaky as a dying bulb. But it was getting stronger.

"What sort of cheap conjurer's trick is this?" asked Rasmussen, bemused.

"I'm not doing anything to it," said David, peering closely at the talisman, which now shone with the luminescence of a full moon. Several engineers stood for a better view; Rasmussen made a curt gesture, and they promptly returned to their seats.

Three loud beeps suddenly sounded in the room. Glaring at David, Dr. Rasmussen reached into his pocket and removed a slim phone. As he pressed it to his ear, his face twisted into an irritated scowl. Motioning impatiently for the guard captain, Dr. Rasmussen issued soft-spoken orders while the engineers looked on in silence. The guard captain hurried out of the room, followed by a score of soldiers. Dr. Rasmussen removed his spectacles and massaged his eyes.

"My apologies," he said. "We've had a minor power outage in the northwest sector."

"Do you always send soldiers to fix a power outage?" asked Cooper.

"Not normally, Agent Cooper, but the northwest sector is a

particularly troublesome location for such a thing to occur. The museums are located there, you see. . . . Apparently several live exhibits have escaped," muttered Dr. Rasmussen. "Dr. Friedman?"

The thin woman Max had spoken to at dinner snapped to attention.

"Yes, Dr. Rasmussen?"

"Please take your team and locate Dr. Braden. Immediately. It seems the good doctor's homing beacon has become disabled and we cannot find her. Please ensure she is safe and accounted for."

"Of course," replied the woman, making a stiff exit. Max scanned the faces of the other engineers. They all looked frightened.

The room's lights suddenly flickered and went out. Emergency lights kicked on, giving the room a dim orange hue. Dr. Rasmussen issued another command, but no one moved. All eyes were fixed on the talisman, which burned hot and bright as a blacksmith's fire.

~ 11 ~

A MAN AT THE DOOR

They heard the first scream five minutes later. It was faint but unmistakable as it seeped through the paneled walls, a note of surprise that escalated a moment later to pitched hysteria before going silent. The doors were locked. Armored soldiers placed listening devices against the wall, which were attended to with unblinking concentration. Dr. Rasmussen spoke quietly into his phone while the burning light of the talisman reflected in the smooth ovals of his glasses. The man's mouth twitched and he placed the phone on the table.

"For the time being, we will remain here," he said. "It seems there are some safety concerns we must address before we can access the main command center."

"Do you need help?" asked Cooper.

"Very thoughtful of you, Agent Cooper, but we can manage," he replied. He pressed another button beneath the table, and the wall panels slid back to reveal an enormous screen depicting a score of separate images from around the Workshop. Max glimpsed the deserted café and redwoods; empty corridors; an abandoned lab where white-hot metals bubbled in dark crucibles. Rasmussen leaned back and spoke to the screen, issuing clipped commands that shifted some scenes and zoomed in on others until the whole was a disorienting matrix of motion.

"Victor," muttered Rasmussen, eliciting a prompt response from a doughy, bearded man seated at the table, "I'd like you to transmit Emergency Code Six to our residents via their implant chips. Authorization code is currently 49653C8625. Understood?"

"Yes, sir," said the man, typing rapidly into a computer.

Then something strange appeared on one of the screens.

Rasmussen uttered a command, and the image expanded to half the available screen. A figure was visible walking across a marble floor. It had the approximate shape of a human but was wrought entirely of flame. Billows of white smoke rose in waves from its shoulders; a trail of burning footprints smoldered in its wake.

"An afrit," said Cooper grimly.

"Is that bad?" whispered Mr. McDaniels.

Cooper, David, and Miss Boon nodded.

"A spirit of fire," explained Cooper. "Very tough. I'll bet our friends here bought him from the witches. Through an intermediary, I'd guess. Iran. Maybe Saudi Arabia."

Dr. Rasmussen gave Cooper an irritated frown before speaking softly into his phone. Placing it back on the table, he tapped his finger while the camera adjusted to follow the afrit, which paused at an exhibit of a narwhal. A dozen pods appeared at the bottom edge of the screen; black-armored soldiers swarmed out like hornets. The afrit ignored them, turning to inspect a nearby polar bear. Amidst a flurry of nervous shouts and commands the soldiers hurried into formation. They pointed an array of fearsome-looking guns at the preoccupied spirit, whose flames audibly hissed and popped in the background.

The soldiers fired.

Bolts of energy forked from the guns and converged at the afrit, slamming into its back. The fiery being lurched forward from the impact, melting the polar bear's glass case as if it were beeswax. Dr. Rasmussen smiled as the soldiers marched forward, firing another volley of bolts at the huddled afrit.

"Otherworldly or not, it appears to feel pain," he chuckled.

"Cover your ears," muttered Cooper, pulling his cap low and promptly following his own advice.

Max and the others did likewise.

The afrit stood and turned to face its attackers.

It screamed.

Even muffled, Max found the sound almost deafening—a high-pitched, inhuman cry of petrifying rage. Glass cases shattered into a million sparkling pieces; marble tiles popped from their settings as an apparent shockwave of sound and heat rushed over them. The soldiers collapsed and covered their ears; bolts of energy arced wildly as the afrit advanced. When the first soldier erupted in flames, Rasmussen hurriedly switched to another camera. Flecks of spittle flew as he hissed into his phone.

"All troops from north sector are to proceed immediately to the Biology Museum."

"You're sending them to their deaths," said Cooper. "There's nothing they can do."

"Thank you for your opinion, Agent Cooper."

"I'm going to find my family," said Jason suddenly, pushing back from the table.

"You will stay where you are, as required by Emergency Code Six," said Dr. Rasmussen.

Jason ignored Dr. Rasmussen, walking quickly to the doors.

"Restrain him," ordered Dr. Rasmussen, continuing to watch the screen.

Max looked on as the soldier barring Jason's way was knocked unconscious by the strong blond boy, who then wrenched the doors open and disappeared down the corridor. Several soldiers started to pursue, but Rasmussen screamed at them to remain where they were and secure the doors.

"It's no matter," he muttered, composing himself. "Let him go. We cannot be responsible for him if he endangers himself through his own stupidity." Rasmussen gazed sidelong at the fallen soldier with disgust. "I'm afraid our troops aren't quite up to Rowan's standards. We have emphasized other things here. I can assure you it will be remedied," he added, with an appraising glance at Max.

A flash of fire raced across one camera. Something brown and mottled lumbered by another.

"I'm not sure you're going to get that chance," said Miss Boon.

Dr. Rasmussen maximized the image from another camera, which was following something as it slithered slowly up a broad staircase. It was the lamia, Lilith. Her serpentine trunk rippled smoothly as she peered through an open archway. Seconds later, she disappeared inside.

"Th-those are the children's dormitories!" stammered a woman.

"I can see that, Dr. Bhargava!"

Dr. Rasmussen switched to another camera inside the

archway. Max jumped at the sight of the heavy-lidded, beautiful face filling the screen and peering at them. A forked tongue flicked between sharp teeth. Red lips parted in a slow, knowing smile. The image was suddenly lost in a blip of static before it went black altogether.

Dr. Rasmussen made frantic calls redirecting the north sector troops. No one answered.

"Where are those dormitories?" asked Cooper, unsheathing the wavy-bladed kris.

"Northwest sector, twenty floors up," mumbled Dr. Bhargava. "But the tubes are shut down. You'd have to go on foot."

"Hurry up and give me a map."

The trembling engineer tapped several keys and offered up a palm-sized computer to the Agent, who snatched it from her hands. "Stay here," he commanded before slipping out the door. Max heard rapid footsteps fading down the hallway before the doors were shut and bolted.

"How far is it?" asked Miss Boon.

"At least two kilometers," replied the woman, taking a deep, shuddering breath.

"Oh dear," said Miss Boon quietly, watching the images anxiously as Rasmussen scrolled through them. The screen was checkered with black rectangles as surveillance cameras flickered and failed.

A shiny bead of sweat rolled like a ball bearing down Rasmussen's smooth head to land on the collar of his shirt. He snatched up his phone.

"Dr. Friedman, *where* is Dr. Braden?"

The answer apparently displeased him; the device was slammed against the gleaming redwood. Bram's talisman sparked. Dr. Rasmussen stabbed an accusatory finger at the talisman and then at David.

"You're causing that, aren't you? *You're causing all of this!*"

David flinched at the accusation.

"Of course I'm not," he said quietly.

"Ha!" scoffed Dr. Rasmussen, smacking the table. "Afrits and demons and sorcerers—you're all the same. You should all be exterminated."

"Shhh!" hissed Dr. Bhargava as something dark went hurtling up the dormitory steps and disappeared inside. It was Cooper.

Max found the ensuing wait unbearable. He paced up and down along the table, watching the screen while his pulse fluttered like a rabbit's. Outside the door, he could hear the many footsteps of frantic engineers seeking shelter. Dr. Rasmussen ignored them, focusing instead on the camera stationed outside the children's dormitory.

In the shadow beneath the archway, something moved.

The thick coil of a snake bulged out into the hallway. Cooper emerged a moment later, dragging the bloated body of the lamia down the steps, where it lay in a limp mound of flesh, hair, and scales. Turning, the Agent stepped back to the doorway, which he sealed with a swirling nebula of energy that stretched across the opening like a thin film of oily water. He paused briefly to study the computer before he was gone, dashing down the steps and out of sight.

"Thank God," muttered Dr. Rasmussen, reaching for a bottle of water.

"Where is he going now?" Dr. Bhargava asked, searching the screens.

"To find that afrit, I think," whispered Miss Boon, sitting very straight and staring at the golem's primitive features.

"Well, he's certainly a brave man," remarked Dr. Rasmussen. "I'll grant him that. Although I don't see what good that knife will do him against that afrit. I've never quite understood why you people favor them so."

"That's easy," Max replied, glaring at the man. "Anyone can shoot a gun or push a button, Dr. Rasmussen. But a knife? You've got to get close to use a knife. It takes real skill and courage. You wouldn't know anything about it."

"Don't lecture me, boy."

"Cooper was right," snapped Max, surveying the assembled engineers and soldiers. "Bram's Key belongs to us, and we're *not* leaving without it. He's risking his life to clean up your mess while you sit here. I don't even know why we're bargaining with you. I could take it right now."

Twenty guns were leveled at Max.

"You tell them to point those somewhere else," said Max quietly.

"Max!" exclaimed Mr. McDaniels, lurching to his feet.

"Stay right there, Dad," said Max evenly. Slowly, he reached back for the *gae bolga* and drew it from beneath his sweater. It was warm at his touch and hummed like a tuning fork. "The brave doctor's going to tell them to lower their guns. Otherwise, there's going to be serious trouble."

Dr. Rasmussen looked at Max with very real fear stamped on his taut features. He glanced at his colleagues and cleared his throat.

"Put them away," he croaked to his guards.

The guns were lowered.

"We have a deal then," said Max, walking toward Dr. Rasmussen. The Workshop leader winced and several of the guards shifted uneasily as Max raised the *gae bolga* level with his chest. Drawing the razor-sharp blade across his forearm, Max let three drops of blood patter onto the table. Rasmussen watched them spread for a moment, before snarling to his neighbor.

"Don't just sit there! Get it in a container!"

Max lifted Bram's Key and stalked back to his end of the table, setting it before Miss Boon like a trophy. Taking his seat, he scooped Nick back into his lap and sucked at the cut on his forearm.

"What about the lymrill?" asked the other engineer, stoppering a small vial containing the blood.

Max glared at the man before returning his attention to the monitors. There was no sign of Cooper. Suddenly, the main lights turned back on; the pervasive hum of white noise returned. Three beeps sounded on Rasmussen's phone.

"Yes?" he responded. "Good, good. We'll have to look for her later—something probably happened at the museum. Double-check the golem exhibit. Things are looking up, however."

He placed the phone back on the table and took a deep gulp of water.

"Power's been restored," he said with a contented sigh. "Several escaped specimens have been destroyed, and the situation is coming under control. I believe it's now safe to proceed to Central Command."

"What about Agent Cooper?" asked Miss Boon softly. "Did they say anything about him?"

Dr. Rasmussen opened his mouth and clamped it shut again.

"I, eh, didn't think to ask," he said with a sheepish glance at Miss Boon.

"Just extraordinary," snapped Miss Boon, standing up abruptly. She slid the sphere back down the table toward Max. "I'm going to look for William," she said. "If I'm not back within the hour, the rest of you are to leave this hellhole immediately and proceed to the Berlin field office. If that *reptile* hinders you in any way, Max, you do whatever is necessary to get your father, David, and Mum out. Understood?"

"Yes, Miss Boon," said Max.

"Hazel, be careful, love," pleaded Mum, clutching Miss Boon's arm.

"I'll be fine, Mum," said Miss Boon, kissing the hag's topknot. With a farewell smile to David and the McDanielses, Miss Boon strode to the door. Flinging it open, she stopped dead in her tracks. Cooper stood on the threshold, frozen in the act of knocking. Smoke rose in lazy curls from his singed boots; dried blood streaked his chin. He blinked at Miss Boon.

"I—I was coming to find you," she stammered.

"Mission accomplished."

Cooper staggered as Miss Boon embraced him. For a moment, the Agent looked utterly bewildered; his scarred cheeks flushed pink. His gloved hand patted Miss Boon's back hesitantly while the teacher's shoulders shook with muffled sobs. A second later, Mum nearly tackled the pair.

"Did you manage to contain that thing? That afrit?" asked Dr. Rasmussen.

"I did," said Cooper, stepping inside amidst Mum's cries and triumphant whoops.

"Well, we're very grateful, of course," muttered Dr. Rasmussen.

Cooper nodded, while a number of the engineers hurried around the table to shake his hand and thank him for protecting their children. The attention seemed to make the Agent profoundly uncomfortable.

"We can leave now," said Miss Boon, straightening and wiping her face with a handkerchief. "We have the Key. We'll fill you in later."

Cooper's eyes flicked to the sphere and then to the burning talisman.

"Good," he said, crossing over to stow the sphere in David's pack. "I'm assuming we can hitch a ride out of here?"

"Yes, yes, of course," Dr. Rasmussen said, glancing once more at Bram's Key before the flap was closed and buckled. "It's the least we can do. Where would you like to go? We have a variety of options via tunnel."

"What are they?" asked Cooper, wiping the dried blood from his chin.

Dr. Rasmussen ticked them off on his fingers.

"Immediate options are Prague, Venice, Budapest, Amsterdam, Brussels, London, and Berlin."

"Which are still resisting?"

"Most are conquered; Brussels and Prague are still being difficult."

"Amsterdam, then," said Cooper, swinging David's pack over his shoulder. "The Enemy attention will be stronger where there's active resistance."

The Agent turned and jabbed a finger at Dr. Rasmussen.

"And I want that homing contraption out of Mr. McDaniels," added the Agent. "Right now."

Max glanced at his father as Dr. Rasmussen frowned.

"Oh, very well," he said, punching several more buttons on the keypad of his computer.

Mr. McDaniels burped, a prolonged, rumbling expulsion that apparently took him by surprise.

"Excuse me," he muttered, massaging his belly. He blinked several times and suddenly retched, clutching the edge of the table.

"Dad!" said Max, running to his father's side.

"He'll be fine," said Dr. Rasmussen. "Extrication is a bit unpleasant but harmless."

Mr. McDaniels grimaced like a toddler sipping cough syrup.

"It's crawling," he gasped. "It's crawling up my stomach!"

A formidable *bloop-bloop-bloop* sounded within his belly. David inched away. Mr. McDaniels gave a monstrous belch and promptly launched a silver ball on an impressive trajectory until it plunked unceremoniously on the golem's head. Tiny hooks retracted back into the device and its small green light slowly extinguished.

"Whew!" said Mr. McDaniels, loosening his belt. "I could use a beer."

"If you weren't in such a hurry, we'd accommodate you," said Dr. Rasmussen, swiveling to face the monitors. He eliminated the multiple views so that one image dominated the screen—that of a middle-aged man sitting in an enormous room filled with computers. Many engineers were busily occupied in the background.

"Hello, Sunil," said Dr. Rasmussen. "Thank you for taking post in my absence. I'd like to know casualty numbers if we have them."

The man nodded, his face grave.

"Ninety-seven dead, fifty-two injured, and one missing."

"Dr. Braden, I presume?"

"Yes, sir. May I ask why you've elected to open the main gates, sir?"

The thin smile on Dr. Rasmussen's face evaporated.

"What are you talking about?"

"The main gates, sir. They're opening as we speak."

Well, close them! commanded Rasmussen.

"Sir, you know as well as I do that they must open fully before they can be closed again."

Rasmussen swore and split the screen to include another view. From a camera in the main entry hall, Max watched the pyramid's great gates swinging outward. Each of the interlocking doors was over a hundred feet tall, sliding open on tracks that glistened with gears and machine oil. Max marveled at how smoothly they operated—each door must have weighed a million pounds, and yet they were opening without a sound.

"What are those?" asked Dr. Rasmussen, squinting at a bobbing field of lights beyond the gates.

Max drew a sharp intake of breath.

"Torches," said Cooper. "Thousands of them."

"Oh my God," muttered Rasmussen. "Sunil, broadcast Emergency Code Ten. Workshop is to be put on total lockdown—all residents are to proceed to nearest seismic shelters without delay."

The man nodded, and his image disappeared from the screen.

"Our defensive cordons have been disabled," Rasmussen whispered. "We're wide open."

Max gaped at the churning sea of torches that extended beyond sight. Horns blared and drums thundered as countless needle-fanged imps and winged homunculi and long-armed goblins chattered and shrieked in a semicircle outside the yawning gates. Behind them were thousands of vyes, some in trench coats, some in soldier's fatigues, all terrifying silhouettes of wolfish, matted fur. Beyond the vyes, huge shapes moved in the dim reaches outside the range of spotlights that now swept frantically across the jeering throng.

When the gates ground to a halt, two dozen gray-bellied ogres in horned helmets lumbered past the smaller creatures, lugging steel spikes larger than a man. Great mauls rose and fell in a jolting symphony of sparks. Moments later, the gates were wedged open with dozens of thick spikes pinning the doors back like crude metal stitches. The din from the monstrous rabble grew so great, the cameras shook.

Dr. Rasmussen had slunk so far down in his chair as to be nearly invisible.

"Why aren't they rushing in?" he gibbered. "What are they waiting for?"

The screams and roars and drums reached a fevered pitch. Torches began to part as the motley assemblage formed a corridor in their center. Something made its way slowly toward the gate. Max ran up to the screen as the lead figure came into view.

It was Marley Augur.

The traitorous blacksmith rode forward astride an enormous horse that had been barded for war. Swinging casually from a strap at his saddle was the same black hammer that had crippled Peter Varga and nearly killed Max. A cruel-looking crown of iron had been fitted to his skull; a fine mesh of black mail was draped over long, gaunt limbs whose flesh had eroded over the centuries. The revenant's head was held high, thin braids of white hair hanging at his temples. Hollow eyes danced with the flicker of corpse candles.

He surveyed the towering entryway, stopping his horse before the threshold. The image steadied as the din died away. A familiar voice, deep and terrible, called out.

"Come forth and pay tribute!"

All eyes in the room turned toward Dr. Rasmussen. He looked wildly from face to face.

"You can't possibly think I'm going down there!"

"Someone is," said Max, spying a lone shadow lengthening toward the open gates.

Dr. Braden emerged into view, appearing no bigger than a child as she stepped gingerly past the hunched, helmeted ogres leaning on their mauls. Augur watched her come, sitting patiently astride his restless horse. He acknowledged her with a solemn bow and let her pass. She disappeared into the silent horde, which closed around her as though she had been swallowed. Augur's voice rang out again.

"In the name of Astaroth the Wise, I do hereby demand Jesper Rasmussen to come forth and to bring with him Rowan's sons and daughters."

Dr. Rasmussen moaned and hid his face as Augur continued.

"If you arrive quickly, my lord shall be merciful—not one among us shall cross this threshold and we will leave you be. If you delay, we shall claim each firstborn among you. Cower and we will grind every last soul and stone to dust."

The effect was nearly instantaneous. Rasmussen was jerked to his feet by the engineers and soldiers, whom terror had transformed into a roiling, hysterical mob that kicked and beat him toward the door. Cooper swam through the mob and pulled Rasmussen away, shielding the man.

"*Get out!*" shrieked one of the wild-eyed engineers. "*Get out before they kill us all!*"

Max shooed Nick toward the door, ducking a hurled computer in the process. It shattered above his head. His father shielded David and Miss Boon as they stumbled out. Max yanked Mum along as the hag screamed obscenities and strained to throttle Dr. Bhargava, who had struck her with a briefcase. They spilled out into the hallway. The man Sunil, to whom Rasmussen had spoken, whirred around the corner in one of the gleaming pods.

"Take this and leave," he said, jumping out.

"Sunil, help me," pleaded Rasmussen, clutching his colleague. The man's expression remained strong and fixed as he stepped past Dr. Rasmussen into the control room, shutting the door quietly behind him. Rasmussen merely blinked in shock until Cooper pushed him into the transport. Max tugged his father's elbow as they all piled in behind.

"Dad, maybe you don't have to go," whispered Max, squeezing his father's arm.

Mr. McDaniels turned to his son and smiled with eyes as bright as sapphires.

"Of course I do."

"Main gate," muttered Cooper, tapping a white touch screen. His command made no difference. Someone else was steering. The pod careened down the passageway, merging abruptly onto a main tube that sped them toward the gate.

A funereal silence filled the transport pod. Cooper seemed preternaturally calm as he placed the kris across his lap and methodically double-checked his bootlaces and the fastenings on David's backpack. Cinching the straps a bit tighter, he handed the bag to Max.

"Keep this with you," he said quietly. "Don't give it up."

"What are you planning to do?" asked Mr. McDaniels hoarsely.

"I don't know," replied the Agent, looking out the window and breathing deeply.

The pod glided down the tube's moderate decline before banking smoothly around a turn that deposited them into the enormous entry hall. Redwoods stretched toward shafts of artificial sunlight as the pod skimmed past abandoned tables and chairs and the café, whose espresso machine sputtered plumes of steam. Far ahead were the gates—a tall rectangle of swimming torchlight where distant ogres seemed no more than matchsticks propped against the great silver doors.

The ogres appeared considerably larger as the pod approached. The monsters loomed twelve feet tall, with gnarled limbs, swollen bellies, and wet eyes that leered with piggish cunning from under gladiatorial helmets. Two dozen of them stood lining the open doors, careful not to extend even a toe over the gate's threshold. Beyond them, Augur waited astride a horse that Max now saw was no living thing at all but an undead construct of pale bone and sinew beneath its ornate plating.

The skeletal horse's teeth champed and ground together; bone slid smoothly over bone while the horse pranced restlessly from side to side in a jingle of plates and straps and stirrups. Nick took one look at the hollow eyes and made an agitated hissing noise Max had never heard before. Grizzly-like claws extended from between the lymrill's toes, and he scratched frantically against the windows.

"Don't look at them," said Max, squeezing his father's hand as the pod slowed to a halt.

Mr. McDaniels made a sound in his throat but did not respond.

Max began to sense the same terrible coldness he'd experienced in Marley Augur's crypt the previous year. It was an unnatural feeling, a cadaverous chill of icy bogs and frostbitten graves that crept up the fingernails and slid under the skin to tunnel deep within the marrow.

"I can't breathe," his father croaked.

Max was confident his father would persevere; he was more worried about David. His roommate looked like a small lump of uncooked dough that had been wedged into a corner of the pod. For all of David's uncanny knowledge and power, Max knew he had never experienced anything like this before. Marley Augur was a far cry from the lonely spirit they'd encountered during their Acclimation.

Cooper exited the pod, keeping his wary eyes on the ogres as the rest clambered out. The blacksmith was a terrible figure indeed as he looked down upon them, proud and grim as an ancient king. Beyond the horseman was a sea of sputtering torches and glinting teeth that waited in breathless silence.

"We've done as you've asked," Cooper said. "Remove those barricades so they can close the gates."

"You do not command here," said Marley Augur in a voice deep and cold. "These are the terms. You will lay down your arms and surrender the Key of Elias Bram, which we know you keep. The two sons of the Sidh shall depart with the witches, as was promised. The rest shall leave here and return to Rowan in order to arrange for its peaceful submission."

Mr. McDaniels looked past Augur at the assembled horde. "The witches don't sound half bad," he whispered, glancing at Max and David.

David coughed and shook his head. "We'll only consider the terms from Astaroth himself," said the small boy.

Max heard the ogres shuffle behind him, rumbling with laughter at David's demand.

The witch-fires in Augur's eyes flared with anger. "I speak for his lordship, you miserable whelp."

"You're a traitor to your people," said David, stepping forward to stand just before the monstrous charger. "You are beyond redemption and beneath contempt."

The ogres ceased their laughter. Mr. McDaniels crossed himself and shut his eyes; even Cooper gaped at David, who stood gazing solemnly at the revenant.

A green mist gathered slowly about Augur; Max knew it did not bode well. He hurried to David's side just as Augur hefted the murderous black hammer.

"Stop."

The command rang from far back in the cavern, issued in a musical tenor that rose from the throng of hideous vyes and hook-nosed imps. Augur froze and looked back as a small procession came up the aisle in a merry jingling of bells. A horn blared, followed by another and another until the cavern rang with their call. The armies began to cheer and stamp and resume their guzzling of plundered wine as the procession came into view.

Max saw that it was a delicate golden carriage, pulled by two black wolves the size of plow horses. The gilded coach rolled along, flanked by four deathly knights that looked to have been raised from some long slumber to serve whatever lurked behind the closed red drapes. Marley Augur scowled and wheeled his horse away from David as the tattered flags of conquered countries were raised on waving pikes. A great cry rose up among the assembled horde.

The sound was deafening, drowning out the jingling bells and Mum's muttered oaths and obscenities. The panting wolves brought the carriage to a stop, positioning the curtained window so that it faced them broadside. Max retched as a miasma radiated from the golden carriage, a nauseating smell of death and disease and brimstone. Several more trumpets sounded, and torches were raised in manic tribute before all subsided to silence once again.

Laughter sounded within the carriage. A soft tenor spoke.

"Do forgive the noise," it said. "They but halloo their names to the reverberate hills."

"What?" asked Mum, nibbling at her lower lip.

"It's Shakespeare," said Miss Boon quietly.

"Indeed it is, Hazel Benson Boon," said the amused voice. "I'd wager you're familiar with all his works. I wish you could have been with me to enjoy them at the old Globe. I was moved to participate in a performance or two, but I fear the bard disapproved of my Iago—felt I'd misinterpreted the character. I'm sure he knew best, of course. . . . And how are *you*, Max McDaniels?"

Max froze at hearing his name spoken by the presence within the carriage.

"I'm very pleased to make your acquaintance and to thank you personally for rescuing me," said the voice.

"I didn't rescue you," whispered Max.

"But you did," the voice insisted. "Without *you*, I'd still be confined within that depressing Rembrandt. So dark, so dreary. As a reward, you shall have the honor of accompanying me as an aide-de-camp before fulfilling your obligation to the witches. You have no objections, I trust, Dame Mako?"

Max heard the witch's voice inside the carriage. The old woman sounded terrified.

"Of course not, my lord," she said.

"I'm most grateful," said the voice. "And Max, is this the one who claims to be your father? Step forward, good sir, so I can have a look at you."

Sweat ran in little rivers down Scott McDaniels's face. He took two halting steps toward the golden carriage. The gauzy red drape was pulled back to reveal a pale white face inside.

For the second time in his life, Max looked upon Astaroth. The Demon was as pale as an apparition and radiated a faint luminescence within the carriage's dark interior. Black hair fell like two bolts of silk past his shoulders and onto white robes. The face was beautiful but shone as cold and dead as a mask. Black eyes crinkled into sickle moons of merriment as Astaroth tapped a serpentine rod against the carriage's door.

"Closer," the Demon whispered, beckoning with a playful smile.

With another shuffling step, Scott McDaniels stood a mere six feet from the open window.

"Hmmm," Astaroth mused, gazing up and down at Mr. McDaniels. "Max must be his mother's son—they always are," he added with a knowing smile. "And is the other one David Menlo?"

"He is, my lord," said Dame Mako, huddled beneath her robes on the opposite seat.

Astaroth slid closer to the carriage window and looked David up and down.

"You fancy yourself quite a summoner, don't you, David?" chided the Demon. "That's a dangerous business, my young friend. Do you see Dame Mako here?"

David nodded, his hands bunched into shaking fists.

"She's not terribly comfortable, as you can see. Dame Mako would far prefer to see me confined within a pentacle, but unlike you, she's wise enough to know it can't be done," said Astaroth, wagging a long-nailed finger. "For shame. Did you really think you could compel *me* to come running? That hasn't been managed for quite some time, my friend. Do you think you should be punished for your arrogance?"

"No," whispered David.

"Speak up, child."

"No," repeated David, furiously wiping away tears on his sleeve.

"Shhh," said Astaroth. "There's no need for that. Come closer."

David stood rooted to the spot.

"I had thought you might see the error of your ways, but here you remain stubborn and willful. Must your friends suffer for your arrogance?" inquired the Demon.

David shook his head violently, inching forward with muffled sobs. Shaking with rage, Max gripped the spearhead, but restrained himself at Cooper's glaring insistence. Mr. McDaniels came to Max's side and held his son close.

David's meager form approached the dark window with the white smiling face. The great black wolves turned their wet muzzles; the vyes leaned close with expectant grins. The Demon extended two white hands out the window as if to grant a blessing. Trembling uncontrollably, David placed his hand between them.

The two conversed quietly for a moment while the Demon squeezed and patted David's hand. Max strained to hear what was said, but could not. Suddenly, Astaroth laughed.

"Of course I shall grant your request, young David!" exclaimed the Demon. "You're just as tender and sweet as the first spring lamb! Augur, have the stakes removed and permit the quaking craftsmen to shut their doors."

At Augur's command, the ogres grunted and strained, using the handles of their mauls to pry at the barricades until they could be wrenched from the rock. Swinging the spikes onto their shoulders, the ogres lumbered forward, giving the harnessed wolves a wide berth as they assembled amongst the chattering imps and vyes. Almost instantly, the gargantuan silver doors began to close in a silent display of seamless machinery. David and Astaroth conversed privately throughout, to the Demon's apparent pleasure.

"Oh, but naturally we'll leave them be!" cried the Demon suddenly. "We might have kept the doors open, for all you need worry. I *always* tell the truth, as you well know from that unfortunate book. Aren't you a precious thing for inquiring?"

David nodded and took a long, shuddering breath.

"Are you going to hurt me?" he asked with a sudden, convulsive sob.

"Of course I am," said Astaroth, walking his fingers across David's palm. "You've been a naughty, prideful boy, and I'd be doing you a disservice to let such a thing pass. Now answer me a question. . . . Is this the *hand* that turned those awful pages?"

David nodded.

"And are these the *eyes* that read those terrible letters?" continued the Demon.

"Yes," squeaked the small boy.

"And I suppose this is the very *tongue* that formed those unfortunate words?"

David's shoulders shook fiercely as he mumbled something incoherent.

"The hand it is," concluded the Demon, lifting it for inspection. "Witness! I shall consume your sins, leaving you with eyes to see the good I do and a tongue to spread word of my mercy."

The Demon's mouth yawned impossibly wide, like a great serpent unhinging its jaws. David turned away.

The jaws snapped shut with horrific force. Max screamed; David crumpled as if he'd been shot. Tearing out of his father's grasp, Max ran forward to crouch by his roommate, whose hand had been severed at the wrist.

Astaroth looked down at David's unconscious face with thoughtful consideration.

"The deed is done, the wound is clean, and he is wiser for my gift," commented the Demon. "His sins are now forgiven."

Astaroth chuckled, while Max frantically examined David's injury. Where David's hand had been, there was no bloody wound, but merely a stump of pale, puckered skin. Not a droplet of blood could be seen.

"Don't be angry, Max," said the Demon in a soothing voice. "Help your friend inside the carriage and bring that most curious Key. With the exception of Dr. Rasmussen, the others may go and pave the way of peace with Rowan."

"But why do I have to stay?" shrieked Dr. Rasmussen.

"It's Dr. Braden's request," explained Astaroth with a sly grin. "I'd overrule her, but I'd say she's earned a bit of discretion, wouldn't you?"

Max felt a squeeze on his hand; David's eyes were small slits of pain. His whisper was frantic.

"Pull me away from him."

Max did as he was told, dragging his roommate away from the carriage. Gasping with effort, David drew himself up. Astaroth watched them from the window; his smile slowly disappeared.

"Stop this foolishness and get inside."

David glared at the Demon, leaning against Max with his injured arm bent against his side.

"*Solas!*"

His words were barely audible, but the effect was instantaneous. The cavern was suddenly illuminated with the light of a million flashbulbs—a blinding burst of light that made the vyes howl and the ogres roar with fury. Augur's horse reared, almost toppling the revenant, while the monstrous wolves snarled and tugged at the golden carriage. Spots swam before Max's eyes; he blinked rapidly to glimpse thousands of howling vyes blindly clawing at one another.

"Seize them," said Astaroth, humor giving way to cool reserve.

Before the nearest ogre could stumble forward, David thrust a finger toward the scowling Demon in the window and gasped a sequence of strange, terrible words.

"Ea bethu gaea volk qabar!"

Max lost his footing as the ground gave a sudden jolt beneath him. The cavern floor split open into a great fissure separating them from the Enemy. Several ogres toppled, bellowing, into the crack that yawned wider as the earth shook.

David screamed and great gouts of green-gold fire and molten rock roared up from the fissure, pluming higher and higher until they came crashing down like a wave upon the carriage and nearby horde. Screams and roars filled the air as flesh split and crackled. Max and the others were flung back by the rushing backlash of superheated air that singed their eyes and set their clothes to smoking.

Cooper wasted no time.

"On your feet!" he yelled, wrenching Mr. McDaniels and Miss Boon off the ground. Miss Boon retrieved Mum from where the hag had fallen into a quivering bundle. Max called out to Nick, who ran alongside as he carried David toward the rows of silver sedans parked to the side of the gates.

"What have you done?" shrieked Dr. Rasmussen. "He'll kill us all!"

Cooper ran back and seized the bewildered man, dragging him toward the silver car and launching him into the backseat, where he sprawled across the others. The Agent slammed the door shut and examined the ignition.

"Where's the key?" he muttered.

"You have to enter a code," sputtered Rasmussen.

"Tell me the code!" bellowed Cooper, punching the dash.

Max peered out the rear window. The wall of fire had subsided until only a few tongues of flame licked occasionally from the fissure. Beyond the fissure was a howling, writing mess of bodies, but the carriage seemed unharmed. Marley Augur and the deathly horsemen had pulled back some distance from the chasm and now galloped toward its edge.

"Cooper—" said Max.

Cooper's head whirled around; his eyes widened as the horsemen leapt the chasm in an arc of burning manes and smoking armor. The Agent cuffed Dr. Rasmussen.

"What's the damn code?" he shouted.

"Zero zero six five nine," blurted out the hysterical man.

Cooper punched the numbers quickly into a dashboard screen and the engine roared to life.

Max pushed David and his father down in the seat as the horsemen approached. Marley Augur lifted his hammer and leaned from the side of his saddle.

"Hurry!" Max yelled.

The sedan peeled forward just as Augur's hammer descended, crushing the trunk and sending the occupants crashing into one another as the back axle groaned. Cooper swore and swung the wheel around, accelerating rapidly around a column of other vehicles while the horsemen galloped just behind them. Mum screamed as a mailed fist slammed against her window, cracking it into a jigsaw puzzle of fragments. Pulling the wheel hard to his right, Cooper knocked one of the riders from his horse before yanking the wheel back to the left and hugging the pyramid's perimeter. Max watched the speedometer climb clockwise, pushing him back against the cool leather seat. The horsemen faded into the rearview mirror as they arrived at the side of the pyramid opposite the gates. None of Astaroth's forces had been stationed here. Three enormous tunnels yawned before them.

"Which do I take?" asked Cooper, downshifting.

Dr. Rasmussen's red-rimmed eyes blinked at their options as

he strained to peer through his broken glasses. "The left one goes to Amsterdam," he muttered. "The right to Berlin."

"What about the center?" asked the Agent.

"The Black Forest," said Rasmussen. "We have an emergency depot there."

"Behind us!" yelled Mr. McDaniels, staring white-faced out the rear window.

Racing up behind them were the horsemen and Astaroth's carriage, pulled by the rabidly snapping wolves.

Cooper shifted and stepped on the accelerator, speeding toward the center tunnel.

Max saw the Demon's white face appear out the carriage window; Astaroth extended a grasping hand toward them. Suddenly, the entire car bucked and lifted off the ground as though batted by an invisible hand, sending them spinning about like a top. They slammed back down in a grinding squeal of rubber and gears, the car careening wildly from side to side, while Cooper fought the wheel. The Agent barely managed to guide the car into the tunnel, shaving its right side against the entrance in a screaming shower of white sparks.

Miss Boon shook Dr. Rasmussen. "What's the exit velocity?" she asked.

"What?" said Dr. Rasmussen from where he hugged the floorboards.

"The exit velocity!" snapped Cooper. "To get through the barrier."

"Three hundred kilometers per hour," croaked Dr. Rasmussen. "You must be very precise!"

Max watched an imposing black wall grow larger as Cooper shifted and accelerated. Behind them, the horsemen and carriage had entered the tunnel in a distant flicker of burning manes and glinting gold. The car's engine whirred louder. Max saw the needle wobble toward the necessary number. Sparks and smoke billowed from the damaged rear. The car rattled and shook.

"Brace yourselves," muttered Cooper, struggling to keep the damaged vehicle straight as they hurtled toward the black wall. The engine began to whine; the needle seemed to hover and stick at 280 kilometers per hour. Cooper scowled and slammed his foot on the accelerator as the cabin was suddenly illuminated from behind. Max swiveled about to see the tunnel behind them engorged with fire. Flames leapt and raced along the tunnel walls, threatening to engulf the car as it strained to speed ahead.

The black wall filled the windshield. Max screamed and shut his eyes.

Nothing happened.

The car gave only a gentle shudder, going dark momentarily until they passed through the barrier. A dull roar, like distant surf, filled the cabin, but no flames managed to permeate the solid wall behind them. Rocketing ahead, the sedan fishtailed around a banking turn and climbed up the long, gentle incline that would bring them into daylight.

~ 12 ~

A Flying Fortress

The car managed to carry on for twenty miles before its engine whined and it began to meander drunkenly. They had seen no traffic, not even a glimpse of a pedestrian or villager, as they sped out of Frankfurt past homes and shops that offered no hint of light or chimney smoke in the cold, gray afternoon. Cooper wrenched the vehicle back into the proper lane, glancing warily at the rearview mirror.

"Is there anyone back there?" croaked Mr. McDaniels.

"No," said the Agent. "I doubt anyone will be coming."

"But Dr. Braden will know where we've gone," muttered Rasmussen darkly.

"I doubt she survived all that," said Cooper, shaking his head. "And with her gone, the Workshop is safe for now—they can't enter after Astaroth promised not to."

"Bah!" scoffed Dr. Rasmussen, settling into a quiet simmer.

The car labored across the countryside toward the Black Forest. As they sputtered along, Max glanced anxiously at his roommate. David was curled like a cat across Miss Boon's lap with his injured arm bent up and under his chin. His eyelids were closed tight, fluttering with fever, while Mum peered intently at his puckered stump, now smeared thick with Moomenhoven balm.

"Is he sick?" asked the hag, sniffing at David.

"I don't know, Mum," said Miss Boon, stroking David's blond head. "He's suffered major trauma and expended a tremendous amount of energy. He needs to go home."

"Is that where we're going, then?" Max asked hoarsely. "Back to Rowan?"

"I think so," said Miss Boon. "We need to get David to the healers and we don't know yet what to do with Bram's Key. Don't you agree, Cooper?"

The Agent nodded.

"But if we go back to Rowan, won't that trigger the witches' curse?" asked Max.

"I don't know," sighed Miss Boon, shooing Mum's flaring snout away from David.

Two miles later, the Workshop's car began belching smoke—guttering puffs of white vapor that streamed and fluttered into the dark woods. A grinding of metal on metal vibrated the floor beneath Max's feet. Rasmussen moaned and rocked the seat in front of him, coaxing the car forward in vain. Fifty feet later they had stopped; the vehicle gave a convulsive shudder, releasing a great plume of silvery water vapor.

"How far is that depot?" asked Cooper.

Rasmussen peered out at a street sign.

"Twenty kilometers at least," he said.

Cooper glanced at the dashboard's blinking lights and rubbed wearily at his eyes.

"We'll have to walk," he said, shutting down the engine.

"Can't you people conjure something?" snapped Rasmussen in irritation.

"I don't know what's around here or if we're being followed," said Cooper. "A witch or something else might follow any trail that Mystics leave behind. We walk."

Minutes later, Max waited by the roadside as Mr. McDaniels and Cooper returned from pushing the car off the road. The car had stopped smoking and now lay beneath a pile of branches and shrubs at the bottom of a shallow ravine. Cooper took David from Mum and Miss Boon, slinging the small boy over his shoulder, where he lay limp and still. Wet snow fell lazily from the sky as they trudged toward a rising wall of dark fir trees.

Max walked quietly, simmering in his thoughts, as the group hugged the winding road and the wind blew needles from the trees. Nick waddled alongside, straying off periodically only to reappear up ahead, peering expectantly at them as the afternoon gave way to dusk and then to a thin sliver of moon. The forest about them was utterly still; no birds called, no animals rustled amidst the branches or among the underbrush. When they passed a lone cottage with a broken door, Cooper peered inside.

"There's nothing you want to see in there," he said quickly before coughing conclusively into his sleeve.

A few stars were twinkling, scattered and faint overhead, when Rasmussen finally broke the monotonous scrape and shuffle of their feet.

"We're nearly there," he rasped, stomping his feet for warmth as he pointed to a fenced service road that sloped away into the trees on their right. As they approached in the dark, Max spied snow-spattered signs that warned trespassers to keep away. Rasmussen reached out to the door, which swung forward on its hinge. He kicked something in the snow and bent down to retrieve the remnants of a chain. It had been cut in two.

"Someone has already been here," he muttered, squinting ahead into the dark and thumbing the severed metal. They stood before the open gate for several seconds, amidst the rich smell of pine and the soft crunch of frost. Max looked closely at David, from whom heat radiated like a warming brick. Mum suddenly hobbled back onto the road and peered back the way they'd come.

"Trucks comin'!" she whispered. "Big ones!"

"Inside the gate," ordered Cooper, handing David to Mr. McDaniels and ushering them off the road and into the inky shadows beneath the trees. Max heard the low rumble of diesel engines; snowflakes drifted like luminescent plankton across the white shine of headlights.

"They're vyes," hissed Mum, sniffing the cold air.

"Dr. Rasmussen, lead them on," said Cooper. "I'll catch up."

They scampered quickly after Rasmussen, who seemed to swim through the dark with tentative swipes of his raw white hands. Mr. McDaniels huffed and sputtered under the burden of David as they trotted along. The forest closed behind them. No headlights could be seen; they heard no sounds from the road.

A half mile later, the path opened into a large clearing that Max felt before he saw; the black canopy gave way to the dim shades of night and muted stars. An airplane hangar, a long dark structure of domed steel and glass, sat in the midst of the clearing. Workmen's sheds dotted the landscape, and among these several bonfires burned, surrounded by many crouching figures who chattered and brayed in strange voices.

"Things must be very bad if the goblins are venturing out alone," whispered Miss Boon.

"Bleedin' cowards," agreed Mum, "unless they've got numbers."

Max peered out at a squat, sway-backed goblin with a curling nose and the twitching ears of a goat. It tottered away from the nearest fire to relieve itself behind a shed. Above the fire was the skinned and spitted body of a sickly-looking horse, rotating slowly while the assembled goblins sang and drank and cast strange shadows on the snow.

"Are they Astaroth's servants?" whispered Max, tugging at Miss Boon's sleeve.

"I doubt it," said the teacher, frowning. "I think they've just wandered down from the mountains or out from beneath some hill."

"What are they singing?" asked Max, trying to decipher the bits of words from the goblins' chorus.

"They're singing of trickery and deceits, dark gods and vengeance," said Miss Boon, frowning as a pipe began to play. Several of the goblins cavorted about the fire in a jerky, leaping dance while they tilted their small, horned heads to shriek at the sickle moon. Whether they called out in worship or fear or delight was lost upon Max as they circled about their spitted dinner and their chorus filled the clearing. Max gazed back into the woods, but there was no sign of Cooper.

"What's in that building?" whispered Miss Boon to Rasmussen.

"Transports," he replied. "Planes of all sorts."

"Can they get us to America?" asked Miss Boon.

"Yes, yes, of course," muttered Rasmussen. "Assuming they haven't been damaged."

"We'll just have to sneak by them the best we can," said Miss Boon.

"Oh dear," said Mum, squeezing Miss Boon's arm. "Wind's changing, and goblin sniffers would give me own a run!"

True to Mum's word, Max felt a cool breeze on his neck. It carried their scent out into the clearing as thick and rich as spilled soup.

The singing stopped.

The goblins turned from the fires to gaze at them, like curious hyenas inspecting a potential kill.

"So much for stealth," muttered Miss Boon. *"Run!"*

Max clutched the *gae bolga* as they dashed across the clearing. The goblins merely watched them for a moment, their small luminescent eyes blinking in surprise. Max saw one of the larger ones lope forward to rest its weight on its hands like a potbellied baboon. It scratched at a curling leather cap on its head and scowled at them with a mouth full of chipped teeth. With a guttural shriek, it suddenly bolted after them. Dozens of goblins followed suit, converging on the group as they fled toward the hangar.

The goblins surrounded them just as they gained the door. Rasmussen frantically punched numbers into a keypad while the others huddled around with their backs against the wall. Miss Boon muttered a spell, but a thrown rock sent her ducking low with a shriek, disrupting the incantation. The goblins leered close, gibbering and gnashing their teeth; bony hands swiped at the humans with increasing boldness.

The pointed, swollen face of the goblin leader emerged as he pushed through their ranks. Taking his place before the huddled group, the long-armed goblin spoke to Mum in a sly, rasping language. After several barking snippets, the goblin wagged a clawed finger at Mum and spoke in halting English.

"Three for you and three for the pot. Fair is fair, foul hag."

"What does that mean?" said Mr. McDaniels, kicking his foot out at a particularly brazen young goblin. Nick hissed and bristled at the creature, which retreated back into the throng.

"Goblins and hags work together sometimes," panted Mum, eyeing the lead goblin warily. "An old truce. He's striking a bargain, you see. Naturally assumes me to be the leader. If three of us are given up, then the rest can go. His name is Bnuublik and he's from Feldberg."

"*I don't care where he's from!*" bellowed Mr. McDaniels.

"What do they want with the three who are given up?" asked Max cautiously.

"Astaroth's armies have gobbled up everything for miles," explained the hag with a sympathetic shrug.

"Tell them to forget it," said Max, swinging up the sharp spearhead.

The goblin leader glanced at Max and raised his hand, speaking quickly to Mum.

"Wait!" cried Mum. "He's prepared to make another offer to the fierce one with the evil knife! Bnuublik says that they will let us go if we surrender He-Who-Looks-Like-a-Mound-of-Cheese and if I agree to . . . No," said Mum, frowning. "No, that can't be right."

The goblin calmly repeated himself.

Mum's face darkened.

"I'm *not* that kind of girl!" roared the hag, walloping the goblin, who somersaulted backward to the immense delight of his comrades. He scowled and rocked back onto his haunches, rubbing his mottled cheek.

Suddenly, a car horn blared in the distance, long and continuous as though stuck. Shouts sounded from far away; lights bobbed and flashed in the woods. Seconds later, Cooper hurtled into the clearing, dodging to the side just as a truck screamed past him, almost rolling over as it skidded to a stop in the snow. More trucks lumbered into the clearing; vyes in trench coats and red armbands spilled out the back. Scrambling to his feet, the Agent sprinted toward the hangar.

The goblins shrieked and scattered away, fleeing like frightened gibbons into the safety of the trees. Rasmussen resumed his frantic pecking at the keypad until the door swung inward to reveal a dark, cavernous space within.

"Inside!" shrieked Rasmussen, tugging at Mr. McDaniels's arm and waving at the others to follow. Cooper closed the distance between them while the vyes dropped down to all fours, black and gray blurs against the moonlit snow. Dashing inside to join them, the Agent slammed the door shut and pressed his weight against it. A tremendous impact jarred the door as the first vye slammed against it; metal hinges groaned, and the door frame gave a brittle shiver. Rasmussen and Mr. McDaniels flanked Cooper and the three threw their shoulders against the door as it dented inward under the weight of the vyes that snapped and cursed and raged against it.

"Hazel, bind this door!" grunted Cooper, wrenching back a hairy arm that thrust itself through the opening. There was a hideous crack and a bloodcurdling howl erupted from the other side of the door. Snatching back its injured arm, the vye let the door slam shut once again.

Max watched dark shapes dart past windows; a wolf silhouette pressed against the frosted panes, scratching at the reinforced glass. He turned to help Mum pull David away from the door, where Miss Boon was hastily scrawling invisible symbols in the air. The men staggered back as something large and heavy—an improvised ram of some sort—crashed into it from outside. Cooper hurled himself once again at the door, which was beginning to warp and buckle from the strain.

"There!" cried Miss Boon as the entry began to hum and glow with a soft iridescence.

"Are there any other doors?" asked Cooper of Rasmussen.

"One on the other side," gasped the man. "And the hangar entrance, of course."

At this, Max turned and gazed at the looming shapes behind them. Rasmussen hastily flipped on the lights, transforming the black, mysterious forms into a fleet of aircraft that appeared to be salvaged from earlier eras to comprise a sort of aviation museum. Max spied round-bellied bombers and delicate biplanes, broad-nosed cargo craft and troop carriers neatly arrayed in rows of matte green and gleaming silver. Behind him, the pounding came to a sudden halt. Cooper glanced warily at the door.

"I'm going to secure the other door. Rasmussen, get everyone aboard whatever we're taking. *Quick now!*"

The Agent dashed across the hangar, ducking under the wing of a World War II fighter. While his footsteps clattered away, Rasmussen trotted down a line of aircraft. He stopped at a broad-winged bomber that had an unobstructed path to the hangar doors. The engineer muttered to himself and counted their numbers on his fingers.

"This is it," decided Dr. Rasmussen.

"How many does this seat?" asked Miss Boon.

"Nine or ten," replied the man, eyeing Mr. McDaniels.

"Plenty of room," said Miss Boon. "We'll wait for Cooper."

Breaking glass showered onto the floor.

"There's no time!" Rasmussen cried, climbing aboard as three vyes squeezed through a second-story window across the hangar. The vyes leapt from the jagged sill down to the floor, scrambling to their feet in a sliding screech of claws to close the distance. Several more pushed their way, snapping and slavering, through the window.

A rumbling noise filled the hangar, a ponderous drumming of metal and wheels. At the far end of the building, Max saw the hangar doors sliding open. A gust of cold night air swept toward them with Cooper in its wake, yelling at them to board.

The bomber's hatch clattered open; Rasmussen had already disappeared inside. Mum shrieked and climbed on all fours up into the plane's belly. Nick leapt in after, retreating quickly into the gunner's seat, a small glass hemisphere attached to the underbelly of the plane. Mr. McDaniels and Miss Boon managed to carry David inside.

Propellers whirred to life and the plane strained against wooden blocks wedged beneath its wheels. Skidding to a stop, Cooper ducked beneath the bomber and wrenched the blocks away.

Several vyes had now reached the plane, which shuddered and rolled slowly forward. Cooper's wavy-bladed knife flashed; a vye howled and fell to the ground, snapping wildly at a wound in its belly. Max went to help Cooper, but the Agent waved him away with a furious command.

"Get David out of here!"

The Agent was now moving with blurred precision; three more vyes fell as Cooper placed himself between the open hatch and the approaching creatures. Rasmussen yelled from the cockpit.

"They've blocked our exit!"

Max ducked beneath the slow-rolling bomber and saw that the vyes had positioned two trucks as a barricade before the open doors. Flames leapt outside in the dark, sending white smoke up in sputtering waves. Max heard Cooper grunt as a vye closed its teeth on his leg; the kris whistled in a lethal arc. Disentangling himself from the heavy mound at his feet, the Agent whirled to glimpse the barricade at the hangar's exit before hurrying over to them.

"What should we do?" asked Max breathlessly.

"What I told you," huffed the Agent, seizing Max in a painful grip and practically hurling him through the bomber's hatch. Miss Boon met him at the doorway.

"Hurry and get inside, William," she pleaded.

Cooper paused long enough for a smile to flit across his ruined features.

"Got things to do, Hazel. Be well."

The Agent slammed the door shut and pounded twice on the plane's side. Max squirmed around his father and squeezed into the cockpit next to Rasmussen, who was guiding the plane slowly past several fighters. The trucks loomed ahead, blocking their way as more vyes streamed into the hangar. Max blinked as a brilliant flash momentarily blinded him.

"What was that?" asked Rasmussen, pawing at his eyes.

"Cooper," said Max, letting his eyes readjust. He blinked again and saw that the Agent had run up ahead of them and was weaving his way past blinded vyes to close on the rear truck blocking their path. The Agent swung himself up into the truck and disappeared inside. A vye was promptly thrown through the windshield, skidding across the hood before it lay still. There was a hideous squeal of metal on metal as Cooper rammed the other truck from behind, inching it forward.

"What's happening?" asked Miss Boon urgently from behind them.

"He's clearing the way," muttered Max, his spirits falling as more vyes converged on Cooper's truck, clinging to the bed and scrabbling for a hold on the doors and windows, apparently suicidal in their determination to reach the Agent.

Despite the onslaught, Cooper forced the other truck steadily forward in a shower of sparks. Smoke from outside now billowed into the hangar, filling the air with a filmy haze. Easing the throttle back, Rasmussen guided the bomber smoothly forward.

"Can we make it?" called Mr. McDaniels.

"I can hardly see," muttered Rasmussen, squinting through his broken spectacles.

A dark shape suddenly obscured their view; an enormous vye had climbed up onto the windshield and clung like a barnacle to the plane. Its muzzle contorted in a smile; a heavy palm smacked against the glass, creating a spiderweb of thin cracks. Rasmussen shrieked and braced himself as the vye reared back for the shattering blow.

It never came.

The vye was yanked unceremoniously from the windshield by an invisible force that left the creature momentarily suspended in midair, flailing like an overturned turtle, before it was suddenly flung away to thud against a neighboring plane. Max turned and saw Miss Boon behind him, her features furrowed with concentration.

"Did *you* do that?" asked Max, but his Mystics instructor merely squeezed past him. Hurrying into the cockpit, she placed her palm against the cracked windshield as Rasmussen pulled back on the throttle. While the plane eased forward, the spiderweb of cracks seemed to thin and diminish until the glass was whole again.

"Everyone strap in!" yelled Rasmussen, sending Max scurrying down to the ball turret, where Nick was stowed.

Sliding in next to the lymrill, Max saw the dark shapes of

vyes swarming all about them. Beyond the vyes, Max could see that Cooper's truck had now nearly rammed the other truck out of their way. A few more seconds and . . .

"Go!" shrieked Max, banging the hatch above him. "Go, go, go!"

The plane groaned forward; fighters and cargo planes rolled past. Vyes scattered as the plane picked up speed, hurtling out the doors and through trails of burning oil and smoke.

Seconds later, air rushed beneath the bomber's wings. The heavy craft bucked slightly and then leveled off, rising steadily above the dark clearing and its strange constellations of camp-fires. Looking below, Max saw Cooper's truck in flames, careen-ing wildly toward the woods while dozens of vyes galloped behind on the white snow. The plane lifted and banked to the right; the Black Forest fell away beneath tattered layers of clouds that hid the world beneath a veil of pale gossamer. Cooper dis-appeared from view.

Max sat perfectly still in the gunner's turret, clutching Nick and watching the wisps of cloud go racing by. Rummaging through David's pack, Max felt for the cool metal rings of the armillary sphere. Pulling it out, he placed it on his knee. The lymrill sniffed at it tentatively.

"Do you see this?" he asked quietly. "We came all this way for a bit of metal and wood. A key, says Bram. Not like any key I've ever seen. And it's cost an awful lot, hasn't it, Nick? Señor Lorca . . . David . . . and now maybe Cooper."

Nick mewled and nipped his finger.

"We'll be home soon," Max whispered, scratching the cop-pery quills and listening to the hum of the engines. Beneath his feet, the turret's windows began to mist with cold. His father handed down a blanket, which Max accepted gratefully. Wrapping himself and Nick in the deep green folds, Max lost himself in the drone of the bomber's engines. The night was black and the stars were bright as they flew west above a sea of clouds.

He awoke to hear Miss Boon puzzling over maps and arguing with Dr. Rasmussen. Bright blue sky and tufts of cloud raced below along with occasional peeks of ocean. Yawning, he clutched the blanket around him and wriggled like an inchworm out of the ball turret and toward the cockpit. Max glanced at his watch and had an alarming thought.

"Don't we need to refuel?" he called urgently.

"That's what I thought," said his father, rinsing his mouth clean into a metal cup. "The good doctor says they've modified the engines on all these planes—we could fly to America and back. Not that I want to."

"How far away are we?" asked Max.

"Close, apparently," said Mr. McDaniels. "That is, if we can find it. David might have done his work too well."

Max glanced at his roommate, who was sleeping beneath a mound of blankets and emitting a wheezy whistle as he breathed. Nearby, Mum grumbled and pulled her blanket tight around her ears. Climbing forward, Max stuck his head into the cockpit.

"I'm telling you that we're too far north," growled Rasmussen, purple-faced as he waved a map at Miss Boon. The two bickered back and forth over when they'd last glimpsed Cape Cod.

"But it's right on the ocean," said Max, reaching for the map. "Can't we just fly along the coast until we see it?"

"We've done that," snapped Rasmussen. "We managed a lovely glimpse of Kennebunkport, but no Rowan. It's as though it doesn't exist! Vanished!"

Max opened his mouth and closed it once again, choosing instead to look out the window where tatters of cloud and mist revealed a jagged coastline below. Max blinked. Rowan was right ahead of them; the copper weathervane on Old Tom was winking in the sunlight.

"But there it is!" blurted Max, stabbing a finger at the cockpit window.

Miss Boon and Dr. Rasmussen ceased arguing for just a moment to gape at the gleaming spire and snow-sprinkled lawns ahead. The black silhouette of the *Kestrel* looked like a toy anchored to a blue-gray sea. The two adults pressed against the window, speechless for several moments.

"That's impossible," breathed Rasmussen, tapping the compass. "We're at least a hundred miles north of Rowan."

"Fifty miles south," muttered Miss Boon, glancing at the map.

Rasmussen grunted and dipped the nose of the bomber toward the ocean, taking a long banking turn that brought them low over the waves and skimming straight toward the sheer cliffs.

"I don't suppose you have a runway handy?" asked Rasmussen.

Max envisioned the grounds' manicured lawns, English gardens, and well-tended hedges.

"Dear Lord," groaned Miss Boon. "Nolan's going to kill us!"

"Get back and buckle in," ordered Rasmussen sharply. "This is going to be bumpy."

Max hurried back into the fuselage and relayed the orders to his father and Mum. Sliding back into the turret, he buckled himself in just as the landing gear began to lower. Up ahead, the Manse tilted wildly as Rasmussen strained to steady the plane.

Max held his breath as the nose cleared the cliffs and splashed down onto wet snow.

Immediately, the bomber groaned and began lurching sideways, throwing up a spray of snow and dirt and grass as it screamed across the lawns. People scattered, rushing for the safety of the gray stone buildings. Brakes squealed and muddy snow spattered the turret's window as the Manse loomed ever closer.

"We're going to hit it!" yelled Max as the plane wobbled and skidded forward. The marble fountain was a mere fifty yards away. Max shut his eyes and covered his head.

Suddenly, their progress slowed—smoothly, wondrously, as though the intervening air were congealing into gelatin. Forces rippled through the plane, magic so strong that the hair on Max's neck stood on end. He opened his eyes a peek and saw that they had slowed to a crawl. The fountain's marble horses fixed him with a blank stare, shooting streams of water that shimmered and billowed in the cool air as the plane ground to a reluctant halt. Ms. Richter stood on the Manse's steps, eyeing them with quiet curiosity.

~ 13 ~

WHISPERS AT THE
WITCHING HOUR

The next morning, a Moomenhoven hurried past Max with a swish of her cow tail and a shy smile. David's arm had been dressed again in a wrap the color of sea foam. He lay nestled beneath a hand-stitched quilt and square patterns of morning light that peeped through frosted windowpanes. A cozy fire burned in a hearth of polished river stones by which a trio of Moomenhovens sat, plump in white aprons with dishtowels spread across their laps while they mixed ingredients for salves and ointments that were carefully smoothed into jars. Max enjoyed watching them. While the Moomenhovens were mute and seemingly identical, subtle shifts in their features hinted at individual personalities brimming with care, concern, and humor.

Max's eyes followed the cream-colored walls to gaze at the anonymous lumps farther down the ward. Ms. Richter had said most were relatives of Rowan students; they were just a tiny fraction of the refugees who had arrived at the campus. They had been shepherded to Rowan by overworked Agents and now crammed into every spare room that the Manse, Old Tom, and Maggie had to offer. Rowan had become a beehive of activity.

The ward was quiet, however. The only sounds were the occasional crackle in the hearth and the soft *tap-tap-tap* as herbs and roots and berries were patiently measured and mortared by the Moomenhovens. A loud, warbling snore joined in. Max reached across David's feet to nudge his father, who lay sprawled across a chair of worn brown leather. With a rumble, Mr. McDaniels flicked a crumb from his chin and continued to snore in a majestic baritone. Max quietly packed up the checkers board and retrieved a nibbled sandwich that had fallen from his father's hand to lodge against the armrest. The soft tapping ceased. The Moomenhovens put down their things and swiveled their heads toward the door. A loud, authoritative voice was coming down the hallway.

Bellagrog burst through the double doors followed by Connor, Sarah, and an anxious-looking Mum. In the weeks since Max had last seen her, Bellagrog had ballooned to enormous proportions. The hag swaggered into the room behind a belly that protruded far beyond the jut of her chin. Beetle-bright eyes took in the room at a glance; gray cheeks flushed pink with pleasure as she spied the McDanielses.

"There they are!" she bellowed with a whoop and a wave. Mr. McDaniels awoke with a snort and blinked at the hag, who now advanced upon them with tottering glee. "You don't call, you don't write, but ya can't hide from yer Auntie Mum!" crowed Bellagrog, wrenching Max out of his chair to crush him against her padded hip. "There's some what said you were goners, but I told 'em all to shut their yappers—my boys would be coming home right soon, and with buried treasure to boot! Bwahahahaha!"

A Moomenhoven planted herself before Bellagrog and put a finger to her lips. The hag scowled.

"What? Making too much noise, am I? Well, pardon a girl for being happy to see the McDaniels boys and little Davie here." Rolling her eyes, Bellagrog stabbed a finger at a trembling patient who peered out at the commotion from beneath a tented sheet. "Oi! You there! Am I botherin' ya? Am I interferin' with yer *healin*'? Bwahahahaha!"

The patient shook her head vigorously and disappeared beneath her blanket. With a throaty chuckle, the hag rounded on the Moomenhoven and swung a meaty arm about her shoulders. "See? Take a load off, girlie—I got everything under control. You just clippety-clop right back to yer nice cozy chair and let me see my boys." Her crocodile eye narrowed as she massaged the Moomenhoven's neck with fat, bandaged fingers. "You lot live on the fourth floor, don'tcha? Past the painting of the skinny milkmaids and the door with the rickety lock what needs fixin'?"

"Bel," Mum pleaded.

The Moomenhoven glanced at the others and swallowed.

"Thought so," said Bellagrog, scratching casually at her belly. "You Moomies sure are deep sleepers. . . ."

Horrified, the Moomenhoven hurried away to the protective embrace of her sisters. With a satisfied snort, Bellagrog plopped onto the foot of David's bed, giving the sleeping boy a passing sniff as she reached out to lovingly squeeze Mr. McDaniels's foot.

"I tried to stop her," explained Mum sheepishly.

"Heard you found Cousin Gertrude," interrupted Bellagrog, abandoning Mr. McDaniels's foot to peer intently at David's wrap. "Can't say I didn't see it comin' for ol' Gertie—didn't know her noggin from her caboose, that one! Bwahahahaha!"

"We're . . . eh . . . very sorry about your cousin," offered Mr. McDaniels.

"Don't be, love," said Bellagrog with a dismissive wave. "You ain't got anything to be sorry about. It's Bea here who ought to be ashamed. To think, a Shrope within' spittin' distance of the man who done it, and she don't even lift a finger!"

"I tried," snapped Mum. "There was lots happening—the timing wasn't right!"

"Well, it's out of your hands now, ain't it?" replied Bellagrog coolly.

"You know, we never would have made it without Mum," volunteered Max.

"That's true," said Mr. McDaniels, sitting up. "She sniffed out a vye in Spain."

"And heard the trucks coming in the Black Forest," added Max.

"And did some pretty fast talking with the goblins," said Scott McDaniels.

"Did she now?" asked Bellagrog, eyeing her sister.

"I did!" exclaimed Mum, nodding enthusiastically. She paced excitedly, twiddling her fingers. "You should have *seen* me, Bel! We were surrounded by 'em—vyes everywhere! Goblins, too! And handsome sailors! And what did I do when they started yammering? Well, I started a-head-buttin' and lettin' 'em all know that ol' Bea meant business!"

While Mum leapt to and fro, pantomiming fictitious exploits, Sarah and Connor pulled up chairs. Connor clapped Max on the back and began peppering the McDanielses with questions.

"Is David going to be okay?"

"Where did you get that plane?"

"What's happening outside?"

"Is it true you saw Astaroth?"

Max and his father tried their best to answer. Sarah listened eagerly, elbows propped on her knees, but Connor was impatient. The Irish boy was so eager for information that he interrupted them several times in his hurry to clarify points or ask follow-up questions. Sarah flicked him in the ribs.

"Give them a minute to catch their breaths," she said, giving Max an apologetic shrug. "He's been like this ever since we got our first-quarter grades," she explained. "Seems to think he's the only one capable of solving a problem. Mind your own business, Connor."

"Well, it's everyone's business, isn't it?" replied Connor indignantly. "For example, I heard you went off looking for something of Elias Bram's. Is that true?"

"Well, yeah," said Max, "but at first it was to get away from the witches. I guess there's a lot you don't know."

"*See?*" said Connor, glaring at Sarah. "Did you get whatever you were looking for?"

"Yeah," said Max, "I think so."

"Where is it?" asked Connor.

"We gave it to Ms. Richter—I think the scholars are studying it in the Archives," said Max.

"Wherever *they* happen to be," Connor added with a sour huff and a glare at Max. Connor had been peevish when Max had shared few details of his previous visit with Commander Vilyak.

Bellagrog pricked up an ear and turned from Mum's caperings. "The secret place with lots of books and blokes with beards?" she asked.

Connor whirled about.

"You've been there?" he asked. "You know where it is?"

"Course I do," replied the hag, picking at her bandaged fingers. "Followed a teacher down, didn't I? Coulda conked him on the crown and had him in a pot for all he knew! Bwahahahaha! Couldn't get in proper, but I got a peek all right."

"Why couldn't you get in?" asked Connor earnestly.

"Some big ol' boys stepped right in front o' me when I tried to slip past," she said. "Thought they was statues. Scared the daylights out of me—nearly filled up me bloomers!"

"Bel," hissed Mum, "you shouldn't be snooping around the campus—the Archives are off-limits."

"Well, ain't you a sweet, obedient thing," teased Bellagrog. "Bea Shrope confined to her cupboard! Don't go sniffing outside your cupboard, Bea! Dearie me, you might get a *scoldin'*! Sheesh—I'm surprised you ain't bottled up like Gertie!"

"Bellagrog, what did you do to your hand?" asked Max, changing the subject.

The hag scowled and thrust forth her bandaged fingers for all to see. "That bloody goose pecked me, she did! Here I am trying to make sure her wee ones don't go wanderin' off into the woods and she comes flying in outta nowhere, all feathers and beak. Crazy stinkin' bird."

"Ah," said Max, privately congratulating Hannah.

"Anyway," said Sarah, "we came up here to see you all and to see if Max wants to go to classes with us."

"That's nice of you," said Mr. McDaniels. "And I think it's a good idea. Go on, Max—I can stay here with David."

"Actually, love," said Bellagrog, cocking an eye at Max's father, "we need *you* in the kitchens. Lots of new mouths to feed, you know. Refugees and stragglers showin' up by the score every hour. Bob sent me to see if you could lend a hand—breakfasts, lunches, and don't forget the Yuletide feast's a-coming!"

"Oh," said Mr. McDaniels. "Well, I don't know . . ."

"Little Davie ain't going nowhere," said Bellagrog, shambling over to hover above David's peaceful face. Fat fingers pried David's eyelids open; the hag peered intently at his bright blue irises. "You going anywhere, love? No? Okay, then, be a good boy and stay right here. Bwahahahaha!"

The hag smoothed David's hair and sniffed him several times, squeezing his cheek with slack-jawed distraction, before suddenly striding off toward the door with the brisk air of a busy foreman.

"See you down in the kitchens, love," Bellagrog called over her shoulder. "Muffins and marmalade if you're quick; cinders sweepin' if ya dawdle!" With an apologetic curtsy to the huddled Moomenhovens, Mum scurried out after her sister.

Max bowed his head beneath a heavy jet of hot water in the third-floor bathroom. Over the sound of the water, he heard Jimmy's merry singing as the odd little bathroom attendant straightened up and restocked the shelves with toiletries.

Glancing down, Max saw the mark of the Red Branch burned into his wrist like a badge of blood. He dreaded the day he could no longer hide it from his father—or Sarah, for that matter. Ms. Richter had so far said nothing, only regarded him with a look of somber understanding. Images of Señor Lorca and Cooper ran through his mind. Cupping hot water and soap, he scrubbed at his wrist. Faster and faster he scrabbled and scratched and plucked at the mark until his skin was pink and raw. But the mark remained.

Connor was waiting in the hallway when he emerged from his room. Max zipped his coat and shook water out of his black tangles. The nanomail shirt and Cúchulain's spear were stowed beneath his bed; his hand now cradled a text on Mystics.

"Ready?" asked Connor. "We'll breeze in a few minutes late—sneak in the back so everyone can't bug you right away. Cynthia and Lucia have already told everyone to leave you alone."

"Sounds good."

"Everything okay? You seem . . . quiet, eh?"

"I'm fine," said Max, thinking of his mother and the witches' curse and Bram's Key. "A lot's been happening, and I have lots of questions."

Connor's face became uncharacteristically thoughtful.

"I heard people asking about Cooper—heard he didn't come back. Scared me silly, but I was always glad he was on our side, you know?"

Max said nothing and followed Connor down the hallway.

Outside, the morning was bright but muted behind David's great curtain of mist that rose shimmering above the sea like an earthbound aurora. A sprinkling of snow was on the ground; paths shone black and slick with the marks of many footprints. The plane had been removed, and the piled-up turf had been smoothed down once again. A few tardy students dashed past them, rounding the Manse and making their way through the orchard for the Smithy. Small snowflakes melted on his cheeks while Max paused to watch a group of unfamiliar adults and children stringing holly along the snowbound hedges. A little Chinese girl flapped a red mitten at him as Old Tom chimed nine o'clock. Max smiled and trotted off after Connor, who was hurrying along toward Maggie, tall and gray as she sputtered wisps of chimney smoke.

The Second Year Mystics instructor was Mr. Tavares, a short man with a gray-streaked beard and thick, square glasses. He stood before some thirty students, who were clustered along the lecture hall's bottom rows studiously copying a diagram on a dusty blackboard. The room smelled heavily of incense and wet boots; its walls were etched with strange symbols that thrummed and simmered with quiet energy. Max saw a hand wave from the back row; Cynthia, Lucia, and Sarah beckoned them over.

Mr. Tavares glanced up at Max, causing the other students to crane their necks and stare at him. Clearing his throat, the man hastily resumed.

"Now that you've copied Solomon's Circle, can anyone tell me what it's for?"

Rolf Luger shot his hand in the air.

"Protection against elemental spirits, greater imps, and minor demons. Duration is short—only one hour—but the summoner is not required to maintain eye contact with the summoned being."

"Very good, Mr. Luger," said the teacher curtly. "And why might one wish to summon one of the aforementioned spirits?"

"Any number of reasons," said a girl with black braids. "To send messages, acquire information, or bind it within an item to enhance its properties."

"Sounds lovely," said the instructor. "What's the downside?"

Connor raised his hand.

"A spirit can sometimes possess the one who summoned it. Using a summoned spirit for evil purposes increases the likelihood of such an outcome. Sloppy inscriptions and hasty contracts can also result in bad, bad things. Famous examples of misguided summonings include Dr. Faustus, Madam Lurie, and the Mad Dey of Oran."

Max frowned and thought of David in the healing ward. He wondered why David had failed to summon Astaroth and consequently been punished; it had seemed there was nothing beyond David's reach. He raised his hand; the teacher looked at him in surprise.

"Yes, Mr. McDaniels?"

"What does it take to summon a major spirit?" he asked. "A Spirit Perilous?"

"Hmmm," replied the teacher, tugging thoughtfully at his beard. "Where did you hear that old term? I don't think anyone's tried for some time. They were called Spirits Perilous for good reason, however. The last person I can think of to do something like that would have been Elias Bram, and then only those at the weaker end of the spectrum."

"But why?" asked Max, ignoring the many eyes upon him. "I mean, if the incantations and instructions are there, why wouldn't someone be able to do it?"

"Ah," said Mr. Tavares, "you've missed quite a bit this term, McDaniels. Perhaps one of your classmates can answer your question."

"The incantation only *contacts* the spirit," explained Cynthia patiently. "It's the power of the summoner that ultimately compels the spirit to come. If it's not compelled—"

Connor jumped in, interrupting Cynthia.

"If it ain't compelled, the spirit might show and clip the sorry blaggard or just let the poor chancer be. Most spirits won't bother with a thick summons since they're blow-ins to these parts and makin' a show can tie their knickers in a bunch."

Giggles ensued; Mr. Tavares sighed and tapped his foot while a grin spread across Connor's mischievous features.

"In English, please, Mr. Lynch."

"Of course," said Connor, sitting up and clearing his throat. "Most spirits are not native to this world, sir, and thus won't bother punishing an ill-advised summons, as the required manifestation might cause considerable pain and distress."

More giggles.

"Thank you, Mr. Lynch," replied the apparently unflappable

Mr. Tavares, who moved on to efficient dismissals of properly summoned spirits.

Max had many more questions but kept them bottled up while he borrowed paper and a pen from Cynthia. With careful strokes, he copied the diagram on the board.

By the end of the afternoon, Max had borrowed a great deal of paper. Second Year classes were significantly more challenging than those of the previous year. In a matter of weeks, it seemed Max had fallen far, far behind his peers on everything ranging from geometry and chemistry to ancient civilizations and poetry. Throughout the afternoon, he tried to pay attention, but he often found his gaze drifting to the floorboards where, deep below, Bram's mysterious Key was stowed, subject no doubt to the unblinking scrutiny of hunched, whispering scholars. He pictured its silver curves and intricate system of smooth-swinging rings, a masterly bit of craftsmanship. Puzzling over the sort of lock it might fit, Max played Bram's Riddle over and over in his mind.

Connor walked alongside him, whistling softly as they meandered past gas lamps that began to glow in the deepening dusk to light the icy walkways. Snow drifted down, slow and steady, like tiny stars falling from the firmament.

"Christmas is coming," said Connor suddenly.

"Hmmm?" said Max, startled from his thoughts.

"Christmas," repeated Connor, kicking snow from the base of a lamppost. "It makes me glad, is all—eggnog and songs and twinkling lights. Stupid, I know, but it's true."

"No," said Max slowly, "it's not stupid at all. What do you want for Christmas?"

"A kiss from Lucia," said Connor, laughing. "Without the help of her stupid frog!"

Max laughed, and it suddenly seemed as though all the

hopelessness and despair and sorrow were lifted from his heart. He breathed deep, letting the cold air tingle his nose. Tilting back his head, he gazed up at the evening sky and its faint stars. He felt a sudden urge to rise high, high among them.

"And what do you want, Max? What can jolly old Saint Nick bring you?"

Max thought of his mother and Cooper and Astaroth's white face and its malevolent smile. He thought of the silver sphere in the Archives and the hidden Book of Thoth.

"Answers," said Max.

"You know I can help you with that," said Connor, lowering his voice as they passed several teachers on the Manse's front steps. The great doors, resplendent with their deep carvings, were now hung with silver bells that jingled as Max pulled them open. The two boys ducked into the warm foyer, where there was light and noise and the promise of dinner.

Later that evening, while Max flipped through his notes on summoning, he registered a peculiar pause in the ticking of David's clock, as though the silent interval between ticks had been stretched a fraction longer. He glanced up at his roommate's dresser, its drawers still half-open from the night they had been forced to leave at gunpoint. It was a sharp reminder of David's absence, and Max stood to close them, one by one, sweeping the surface free of dust. Turning back to the table, he found himself staring into the pale yellow eyes of Mr. Sikes.

"Good evening, Master McDaniels," purred the imp, bowing low.

"How did you get in here?" asked Max, narrowing his eyes.

"You called me," said the imp simply, polishing its small gold pocket watch.

"No, I didn't," said Max.

"With apologies, I must beg to differ," replied the imp. "You were thinking of poor Master Menlo and your adventures in the Workshop and whether Agent Cooper knows the fate of your mother. Those are many burdens for one so young. It's only natural that you would wish for a companion who might listen to your troubles, and thus . . . here I am."

"I've got lots of people to talk to," snapped Max defensively.

"I'm relieved to hear it," said the imp. "But surely you don't mean your poor father. I can't imagine you would wish to inform him that Agent Cooper—a man he has trusted with his life—might be concealing information about his long-lost love."

"No," said Max, frowning. "I would never—"

"And surely not my own esteemed Master Lynch," interrupted the imp, guessing Max's next choice. "The master has many fine qualities, but I think we'd agree that discretion is—how shall we put it?—a 'development opportunity'?"

Max sighed and nodded in agreement. Mr. Sikes paced about the tabletop, tapping his chin as he considered other possibilities that were quickly discarded.

"Ms. Richter!" exclaimed Max, a note of triumph in his voice.

The imp nodded politely, but Max could sense its disappointment. He reddened.

"An excellent thought," intoned Mr. Sikes unconvincingly, "but I might have a number of reservations, not the least of which is that the Director has a full plate herself and might find her patience sorely tested if asked to put the world's concerns aside for the wants of a thirteen-year-old boy. And we must face the unpleasant truth, Max, that she has never really confided in you. . . ."

"Yes, she has," said Max defensively. "Last year—she showed me top secret maps and everything."

"She showed *you*?" asked Mr. Sikes slowly. "Or she showed David Menlo?"

Max fell silent and considered the imp's words. It was true that Ms. Richter often solicited David's opinion while Max was relegated to the role of silent spectator. His frustration must have registered with Mr. Sikes, for the imp quickly moved on.

"It's no matter," he said. "Besides, if we are agreed that Agent Cooper is concealing information about your mother, it only follows that the Director would be part of the cover-up." Mr. Sikes's voice became soft with sympathy as he studied the pain evident on Max's face. "Don't put all your faith in adults, Max—no adult ever *really* listens to a child. It's not their nature."

Max sat at the table and drummed his fingers.

"If no one ever listens to a child, why should *you* listen to me?" he suddenly snapped.

"Ah," said Mr. Sikes, "I said that no adult—no *human* adult—ever really listens to a child. But I am an imp. It is my nature to listen, young Max. It is what I do—I listen and serve."

"You can't do anything for me," muttered Max.

"Really?" asked Mr. Sikes, his eyes burning bright at the challenge. "What if I told you that I could save your life this very evening?"

"You think I'm going to die tonight?" asked Max, straightening.

"I'm quite sure of it," replied Mr. Sikes with a solemn nod. "Unless you listen to me . . ."

"Go on," said Max, unnerved by the calm assuredness in the little creature.

"You plan to try where David failed and summon Astaroth,"

continued the imp. "The summoning will be imperfect, but the demon will come of his own free will. And when he does, he will kill you, Max McDaniels. He will slay you where you stand and run wild through this school. Do you not think he is hoping for this very opportunity?"

"But how do you know this?" asked Max quietly.

"Max," sighed the imp. "The evidence is before me: a young man with difficult questions, hasty notes on summoning, and the seductive promise of a Spirit Perilous who knows many secrets and is bound to speak the truth. Do my instincts fail me?"

"No," said Max heavily, glancing at his scribbled notes with shame.

"Put embarrassment aside," said Mr. Sikes with an understanding smile. "It was a noble impulse, if dangerous. If I may, let me steer you from such a course and put our immediate energies into Mr. Menlo's recovery."

Mr. Sikes procured a cup of cocoa, and Max sipped it quietly while the imp drew close and spoke of moons and runes and mandrake.

For several weeks, Max sat at David's side and administered the slow healing spell he had crafted with Mr. Sikes. He kept to himself for much of that time, attending classes sporadically and focusing almost all of his attention on the slim ribbon of silk on which he inked one rune after another while standing under the moonlight atop Old Tom. The ink was a noxious blend of foul ingredients that Max prepared by hand under the watchful tutelage of Mr. Sikes. Each morning Max tied the ribbon about David's injured arm, and each evening he removed it once again and added to its potency high above the campus. The Moomenhovens paid little attention to Max on his visits, concerned as they were with David's condition, which had not improved despite their very best efforts.

One evening, when Max went to remove the ribbon following the Yuletide feast, he found Bob seated at David's bedside. The reformed Russian ogre had made it a habit to visit the comatose boy and read to him, his basso voice rolling slowly through the ward like the comforting call of a distant foghorn. Max did not want to interrupt and took a seat in a worn chair while the lanky ogre peered through his monocle in the amber lamplight. Bob tried sounding out a difficult word, a growl of annoyance vibrating deep in his throat.

"What does this say?" he finally asked Max, frowning and flipping the book around.

"Wenceslas," yawned Max, glancing at the old book of carols.

"Oh," said Bob, studiously finding his place once again on the page.

There was a soft rustle of sheets and David sat up, blinking curiously at the feeding tube inserted in his arm and the ribbon tied about the protective wrap.

"Cinnamon toast," he blurted. "Do you think I could have some?"

"David," said Max, sitting straight up in his chair.

Bob dropped the book; the ogre's toothless mouth fell open. He leaned close to David and patted the smiling boy's cheek with his tough, leathery hand.

"Toast? Bob will make all the cinnamon toast you can eat!"

With a clap, Bob lurched to his feet and strode over to a Moomenhoven, who was dozing beneath a woolly throw and a plate of goodies squirreled from the feast. The plump creature opened an eye and followed Bob's long, pointing finger toward

David, who was now wriggling his legs and examining his hospital pajamas. Springing up from the chair, the Moomenhoven fumbled for a thermometer and hurried over.

"I'm pretty sure that's the wrong kind," said David gently, pointing at the silvery probe.

The Moomenhoven blushed furiously and scurried off to find another.

"How do you feel?" asked Max.

David glanced at the space where his right hand used to be.

"I'm okay," he said after a moment. "I needed some time to recover. That spell almost finished me, you know." David smiled and began fiddling with the wrap on his hand. Round and round he spun his finger clockwise until the material and Max's ribbon both fell away, revealing a smooth, shiny stump.

"Not much to look at," he murmured, taking the proper thermometer from the hovering, apologetic Moomenhoven. He thanked her and promised to take his temperature momentarily.

"Does it hurt?" asked Max.

"No," said David. "But my body still thinks it's there . . . I can feel my fingers itching." He sighed and cupped the puckered skin with his remaining hand. "What's been happening here?"

"A lot," said Max. "Cooper's gone; he stayed behind to clear the way for us. I don't know what happened to him, but it didn't look good. I tried to find his apple in the orchard, but it isn't there. A Sixth Year told me once you're assigned to DarkMatter operations, they remove your apple—so no one else knows whether you're dead or alive." Max frowned and wondered which of the many orchard apples belonged to his mother.

"Rasmussen's here," Max went on. "He's taken up a room in the south wing near my dad's. You can see him sometimes sulking in his window or hear him yelling for his meals. I wish Cooper were here to shut him up—"

David hugged his knees and cut him off.

"Bram's Key—the Book of Origins. That's all that matters."

Max glowered at David.

"Cooper—"

"Did what he was trained to do," interrupted David. "No one was more focused on our objective than Cooper, Max. He would want us to finish the job. Where's the Key now?"

"In the Archives," replied Max heavily. "I talked to Miss Boon last night—they still don't know what it's for."

David nodded. "Any sign of the witches?"

"No. No one shows up here but refugees and whatever Agents have escaped from the field offices," said Max darkly. "Richter's spent most of our resources bringing people here. Vilyak's furious—says she's responsible for the fall of half our field offices. He's called for a vote of no confidence. Vilyak wants to be Director."

"Not while Bob is here," growled the ogre, towering over them. He bore a silver tray piled high with warm, buttery cinnamon toast. This he set on David's lap before easing himself into a seat. David began devouring the toast, speaking with a full mouth.

"Did you tell anyone—"

"Not yet," said Bob with a wink. "Little one needs rest, not visitors."

"Bob, please don't tell anyone I've woken up until tomorrow," David pleaded.

The ogre frowned.

"Is it mischief that you make?" he asked cautiously.

"No," said David. "I just need a bit of time without everyone pestering me. The first thing they'll do is stick me down with the scholars studying that sphere."

"But I thought you said that's all that matters," said Max.

"It is," said David, glancing sharply at him. "But the answers we need aren't in the Archives. . . ."

The ogre shook his head and pushed up from his seat.

"The less Bob knows, the better. I tell the Director at break-fast tomorrow."

David thanked Bob and watched the ogre lumber out, duck-ing beneath the archway and letting the doors swing shut be-hind him. Then his eyes returned to Max; his whispered words were urgent.

"Do you have my pack?" he asked.

"Yeah," said Max cautiously. "It's in our room."

"Good," said David. "Fill it with enough clothes for both of us—enough for a long time. Bring your spear and the shirt Señor Lorca gave you and meet me on the main path between the orchard and the Smithy. Will you do it?"

"Of course," said Max, his weariness evaporating. He felt a sudden urgency to consult with Mr. Sikes. "Where are we going?" he asked.

"I don't know yet," said David. "But I'll know soon enough. Just meet me on the path!"

David dutifully slipped the thermometer beneath his tongue as Max hurried from the room.

It was nearly eleven o'clock when Max stole from the Manse and crept down the salted steps, sticking to the shadows as he clutched David's enchanted pack. The campus was awash in moonlight, bands of bright snow and ice fringed by dark and fragrant pine. Far off Max heard the faint, cheery notes of Nolan's fiddle. Creeping off the path, Max stole for the cover of the orchard, weaving his way silently among the class trees until he had disappeared beneath the frail, sighing canopy that marked the border of the orchard and the wooded paths beyond. Max saw a white puff of breath billow out from behind a tree. David was waiting.

Max's roommate, still in his pajamas with the quilt draped over his shoulders, gave a start when Max slipped round the tree to tap him on the shoulder. The small boy grinned and asked Max if he'd brought everything they'd need.

"I think so," whispered Max, patting the bag. "I threw almost everything you own in here."

"Good," said David, peering up the path. "Now help me look for something—I'm sure it's right around here."

"What are we looking for?" asked Max.

"A coin," replied David. "I buried it around here last year."

"I remember," said Max, thinking back to his first day at Rowan, when he'd spied his strange new roommate inexplicably burying a coin where a small side path diverged into the wood. He scanned the ground where David was poking about the snow and hard, cold soil. "Didn't you bury it by a side path?" Max asked, seeing an overgrown path some twenty feet ahead.

"I did," said David. "But the paths move. That's why I buried the coin. There's Old Magic in these woods, Max—can't you feel it?"

Max shook his head and ran his fingers along an ancient beech. He felt nothing, but he knew there was something peculiar in these woods—he himself had once encountered strange lights and faint laughter. Ever since that incident, he'd been content to keep his feet firmly planted on well-trodden ways.

"Help me look," huffed David. "I know it's close."

Max crouched low near his roommate and plunged his hands into the cold snow, digging through frost and leaves and dirt in a wide sweep. For ten minutes they crouched in the cold, while their fingers scrabbled numbly at the hard ground.

"Can't you do a spell or something?" muttered Max in frustration.

"Not yet," coughed David. "I need to save everything I can."

"For what?" asked Max. "You haven't even told me what we're doing."

"I know," said David, grinning. "If I had, you might not have come. . . . Aha! Here it is!"

David produced a gritty coin in his remaining palm. He rubbed it clean of dirt between his thumb and forefinger, holding it up to the moonlight and peering closely at its date. Satisfied, he pulled the quilt closer about him and plunged into the woods at the exact spot where the coin had been unearthed. Max hurried after.

The woods closed behind them and the air grew colder. David said nothing, walking resolutely forward while Max crunched behind, pushing tree branches aside until it seemed they must have traveled quite far indeed. Max had no idea how far these woods extended. He imagined they should have reached the main road to town by now, but spaces at Rowan could be deceiving.

As they walked on, Max sensed a change in the woods. The air was getting warmer. The trees seemed framed in moonlight despite the dark, interlacing roof of dense branches above them. The unexpected fragrance of rose petals filled the air. Max stopped and gazed upon a broad clearing ringed by summer flowers. He kicked snow from his boots, gaping at thick green grass and fireflies that hovered lazily in the moonlight. Ancient-looking stones, cracked and weathered, were arranged in a circle. They towered above David, who walked gingerly among them with his quilt trailing like a king's robe in the grass.

"What is this place?" breathed Max, stepping out into the clearing.

"What time is it?" asked David, ignoring Max's question as he counted his paces across the circle of stones. Max glanced at his watch.

"Almost midnight," he said.

"We have to hurry," said David, letting the quilt slip from his shoulders. Max now saw that David was walking upon a smooth stone circle. It was some ten feet across, centered among the standing stones and fringed with toadstools and moss. David swept away bits of grass and dirt until the surface was clean, then stepped off the circle and pointed his small index finger at its perimeter.

A green flame, thin as a laser, burst through the stone and traced a slow, precise circle that glowed along the stone's perimeter. This done, several additional green flames seeped through the stone in a slow dance, carving powerful runes of warding. Max watched the summoner's circle form, slow and beautiful, as green and gold tracery flickered on the dark surface. This was no Solomon's Circle, Max could see readily enough; this circle was for other things.

"Step inside," said David, beckoning Max over. The two stepped over the circle's glowing threshold. The night was terribly still; even the trees seemed to be listening in breathless silence. A gleam caught Max's eye; he now saw a silver ring on David's finger.

"David," said Max, realizing his roommate's intent. "It's too soon. He'll hurt you again."

"Not here," whispered David, seizing Max's wrist in a sudden, fierce grip. "He'll have to come this time." Clearing his throat and shutting his eyes, David called out into the dark. "Noble Astaroth, pray favor your petitioner with wisdom from under hill, beyond the stars, and beneath the deepest sea."

From far, far away Max heard Old Tom's chimes strike

midnight. A warm breeze rose up in the clearing; branches shook in fits as the wind rose to a moan. Max swallowed hard as David's fingers dug deeper into his wrist. He felt horribly exposed. His heartbeat began to patter. As he swiveled his head about in a panic, a swaying branch suddenly caught his eye.

"Connor?" Max croaked, seeing his friend's astonished face peering at them from behind a tree.

"What are you doing?" asked Connor, his features alight with wonder. There was more movement and Max saw Cynthia, Sarah, and Lucia peek out from behind Connor.

"What are *you* doing?" Max hissed.

"We followed you," said Connor proudly. "I knew you were up to something—digging around your room like a badger and all."

"Get out of here—all of you!" pleaded Max, glancing at David's trancelike expression. "Something terrible is coming!"

Max whirled about to scan the woods as Old Tom struck the last chime and faded to silence. The air became deathly still once again and a noxious smell seeped into the clearing. The odor was sickly sweet—a smell of corpses and brimstone and syrupy perfume. Terrified, Max shook David. His roommate's eyes shot open. He blinked at Max, distracted, until he suddenly caught sight of their friends.

"Get in the circle," David said softly.

From the nearby woods, a branch snapped. Max saw a faint, shimmering light bob toward them from among the trees.

"Get in the circle!" David screamed.

Sarah bolted past Connor toward the safety of the magic circle. Her decisiveness seemed to drive the others into action. They burst from the woods, running in wide-eyed terror toward the protective ring.

Something else leapt into the clearing from the other end. Max's heart froze as he saw a grinning, masked *peliqueiro,* such as he had seen in Salamanca. It was dressed in scarlet, its dead eyes carved in crescent moons of merriment as it crossed the clearing quickly in pursuit.

Sarah leapt over the circle's flickering threshold, almost crashing into Max and David. Connor came next, followed by Lucia. Cynthia lagged behind as the masked figure hurtled across the clearing, inhumanly swift. She shrieked and leapt. A gloved hand snatched at her hair, tearing out several long red strands, but she landed with a thud at Max and David's feet. The summoner's circle burst into bright flame, illuminating the clearing in a sudden blaze of golden light. Trembling, the six children clustered together and turned to face Astaroth.

The Demon said nothing for some time as he stood just beyond the circle's perimeter. The mask's black eyes looked coldly upon them; he twined Cynthia's hairs about a finger. Pacing slowly about the circle, Astaroth patiently examined its every detail. Runes and symbols flared and hissed at his approach.

"Bene," said the Demon with an acknowledging nod. He pivoted on his heel to survey the tall stones. "A bit of a cheat, really, but I suppose it worked. Here I am. Do you know where these stones come from, David?"

"No," said David quietly.

"Orkney," said Astaroth, shimmering faintly in the moonlight. He thumped his fist affectionately against the megalith. "Old stones. They have old voices. But it was the very young voice that caught my attention. . . ." Removing the *peliqueiro* mask, Astaroth turned to gaze at them with his malevolent white face. He glanced at David's arm. "What does the young one require of me?" he asked sweetly. "I'll confess I'm a bit surprised,

David. After our last conversation, I didn't think I'd hear from you again. Have you called to make amends for the murder of my servants?"

"No," said David, trembling next to Max.

"Pity," said the Demon, pacing slowly about the perimeter again. The reek of Astaroth's presence was overpowering. Lucia gagged into her sleeve. Astaroth smiled. "You're a poor host, David. You should have brought silver rings for all. Max can bear it, I think, but the others are not made of such stern stuff."

"They're not supposed to be here," said David, glancing worriedly at his friends.

"But here they are," said Astaroth. "And now I have seen them. I know their faces. I know their names. And I even have a token of the young lady, have I not? Mischief can be mine, you know."

Cynthia gasped suddenly as the Demon unwound one of her hairs to stretch it taut between his delicate fingers. Crumpling to the ground, Cynthia writhed in a spasm of pain.

"Stop it," said David, seething.

"She must ask me," insisted the Demon, stretching the hair tighter.

"Please stop," gasped Cynthia, fighting off tears.

"Of course," said Astaroth, letting the hairs fall from his grasp. "Oh, don't be angry with me," said the Demon as Cynthia struggled to her feet. "It's your friend here who should bear the brunt of your wrath. He has endangered you, Cynthia. It's lucky for you that mere curiosity overwhelms me. . . ."

"Promise that you'll never hurt her again," commanded David, thrusting a finger at the smiling face. "Promise or I'll hurt you."

"My, my," said the Demon, with a cold glitter in his dark eyes. "My lesson has turned you cruel indeed. I had hoped that little incident at the Workshop might have sated your bloodlust, but apparently I was mistaken. A cruel, conniving thing you are, David Menlo! Very well . . . your summons compels three reasonable services from me. Shall a promise to Miss Gilley be one of them?"

David hesitated. Long seconds passed while Astaroth strolled about the perimeter, looking bored. The flames about the circle began to sputter and pulse. Max looked at it doubtfully.

"How long will the circle last?" whispered Max.

"One hour," replied his roommate.

"Don't forget what the *Codex* said," hissed Max. "Astaroth will try to stall—to distract us. He's already doing it, David!"

David blinked and glanced at Max. Astaroth was smiling patiently, holding a delicate black scepter fashioned in the form of a viper.

"Come, David," he chided. "You know how busy I am. This very country is poised to hoist my flag, and I'd hate to miss the ceremony. Shall Miss Gilley be spared my attentions?"

"Yes," blurted David. "Promise never to hurt Cynthia or permit her to be hurt by any power under your control. Agreed?"

"Agreed," said Astaroth, yawning.

"How do we use Bram's Key to reach the Book of Origins?" asked David.

"Ah," said Astaroth, pacing once again. "Now we come to it, do we not?"

The Demon chanted Bram's Riddle in a lilting, amused voice. "Not much of a poet, the esteemed Elias Bram, but it seems his purpose was served. Do you know what the notches are, David?"

"Yes," said David. "I think so."

"And?" said the Demon, beckoning playfully.

"Coordinates," David answered. "Coordinates for space and time."

"Bravo," said Astaroth with an acknowledging bow. "Three notches for place, one for time, and there the Book shall be! Do you even know what it is you're searching for?"

"Stop stalling," said David. "The question was how to use the Key."

"Simple," the Demon said. "The Key steers Bram's steed, silly boy."

"But YaYa's too old," said Max aloud, puzzling over how the sphere would fit on Rowan's Matriarch.

"*Not* the ki-rin," said Astaroth wearily. "Max, be a good boy and be quiet. You know what they say: better to keep your mouth shut and have others think you a fool than to open your mouth and prove it, no?"

Max's cheeks grew hot. For a moment, he forgot his fear and glowered at the demon.

"Save your anger," said Astaroth with a dismissive wave. "No broken blade will harm me, not even one wielded by you."

"The ship!" said David suddenly. "The *Kestrel*! Bram built it, didn't he? That's the steed from the Riddle."

Astaroth clapped, cold and hollow, while the firelight danced upon his smooth features.

"Upon its accursed figurehead you shall place the Key, David Menlo. A beacon it shall be to guide you on your way. But be warned, young Sorcerer—such a place as it leads to is not for little boys. You might find my company preferable."

"Be silent," commanded David.

"Is that your third request?" teased Astaroth, counting upon his fingers.

Max panicked. He could not let such a chance pass; his question rang out in the night.

"What happened to my mother?"

David whirled to look at Max. For a moment, the small boy's face contorted in anger.

Astaroth laughed.

"Aren't we constant as the northern star?" hissed Astaroth. "I'm almost moved. A boy who pines for his mother, for she did leave him, did she not? And where is she, I wonder? Ensnared by a prophet, I fear. And to think it was the same man who led the witches to you. Peter Varga is his name, although I imagine you'll assign him others less pleasant."

"What does Peter have to do with anything?" demanded Max. "Where is she?"

"She is far," said the Demon, his voice fading to a silken whisper as he leaned close to the circle's perimeter. "Far away, Max McDaniels. You must find the Book of Thoth before ever you find her. And as for Peter, well, he has only one eye on the future, does he not? A poor man's prophet, I fear. Cassandra would be shamed. Max, your mother sought the Sidh on a fool's errand for which she has almost paid in full."

"What does that mean?" asked Max, frantic. "How can I find her?"

"You shall not see your mother till you delve within Brugh na Boinne," replied Astaroth, his black eyes crinkling. "I daresay it should be home sweet home to you, young Hound, but you cannot simply knock at the appointed hour. You must take the other way. Best hurry or she will be lost, entombed within the Sidh. Time has strange tides and it would not do to linger. . . ."

"How do we get the Book once we've arrived wherever it is we're going?" interrupted David.

"Now, now," said Astaroth, wagging a finger. "I've fulfilled my part of the bargain. The ancient rules have been obeyed, and I take my leave. I have errands of my own, you see, and cannot stay for pleasantries. Goodnight, children. We will surely meet again."

Placing the mask on his head once more, the Demon walked slowly beyond the firelight of the circle, disappearing behind one of the stones and into the forest beyond.

"We have to hurry," panted Max, taking a step toward the forest.

David's hand caught him by the sleeve.

"Don't!" he hissed. "No one leaves this circle until Old Tom chimes one o'clock. The chime will dismiss Astaroth. Until it does, we can't be certain he's gone. He might be out there waiting for us."

Max froze and stared out at the dark trees. A sickly sensation hovered in his stomach. Was the Demon still lurking out there beyond the firelight? They waited in cowed silence. Sarah, Lucia, and Cynthia huddled together within the circle, not daring to move a finger toward its protective edge. Amidst quiet prayers, Connor crossed himself and shut his eyes tight.

When the chime sounded, distant and hollow, the circle's flames began to flicker and diminish. A sudden, furious gale swept through the trees, causing them to huddle together like rabbits on a stormy plain. The wind screamed across the clearing in a rush of torn flowers and bits of tree bark. Max felt Sarah's forehead press against his. Her hands shook uncontrollably, and Max squeezed them gently.

"He's gone, Sarah," said Max, mustering a smile.

"I'm sorry," she said. "We shouldn't have come. . . . We knew you were up to something and we didn't want to lose you again."

She burst into tears.

"He was whispering to me," she bawled. "The entire time he was speaking to you I could hear his voice whispering in my ear. He was telling me to push you out of the circle—push you out while your backs were turned. He promised so many things. And I *listened*! I'm so ashamed."

Sarah sobbed uncontrollably.

"Did he speak to the rest of you?" asked Max.

Lucia and Cynthia nodded. Connor said nothing but rocked back and forth, hugging his knees.

"Connor?" asked Max.

"I'm sorry we came," whispered the Irish boy, his voice hoarse. "It's all my fault you had to waste a question on us."

"You can make it up to us," said David, taking the pack from Max's hand and slinging it over his shoulder. "Tonight."

"How?" asked Connor, avoiding David's stern gaze and staring at the cold stone circle.

"You always wanted to see the Archives," said David softly. "Well, this is your big chance. We're going to swipe Bram's Key from under the scholars' noses."

Connor blinked and watched David stalk off toward the woods. "I've been a bad influence on that one," he concluded, rubbing his arms and hurrying after David.

Max helped Sarah off the stone and the four followed David and Connor. They paused only for a parting glance at the grim stones that jutted like broken teeth beneath the light of the pale gibbous moon.

~ 14 ~

BEYOND HEAVEN'S VEIL

Dr. Rasmussen's sharp, predatory face glared down at them from the light of his open doorway. Despite the late hour, the exiled Workshop leader was still dressed in rumpled work clothes, thumbing the handle of a pipe.

His attention locked on David.

"Up again, are you?" he asked, masking any surprise with cool reserve. He nodded at Max and didn't bother to acknowledge the others, who peered curiously at him from the shallow flight of stairs that concluded at his room. "Shouldn't you be sleeping?" he asked with a thin, mirthless smile. "It's Christmas Eve, after all."

"We need your help," said David.

"Of course you do," sighed Rasmussen with a frown. "That's what I get for assuming you were the serving hag."

"Her name's Mum, in case you've forgotten," said Max, glaring at the haughty man.

"Not her," sniffed Rasmussen. "The other one. Even more revolting, if that's conceivable, but she makes a passable cider. She's coming any minute, so you'd best run along before she spots you out of bed. I have work to do."

The man moved to shut his door, but Max wedged it open with his foot.

"It'll just take a minute," Max insisted, forcing the door open and walking inside. The others followed behind, mumbling hellos to the stunned and scowling engineer.

"Abominable child," muttered Rasmussen, closing the door with a snick. He marched past them and swept up a pile of papers and drawings that were stacked on a writing desk near the windows. Max was surprised to see the beautiful suite was a mess. Crusted plates and stained coffee cups were piled into corners, clothes were strewn about, and the air smelled faintly sour.

"Whew," said Connor, poking at a black dress sock hanging limply off a chair.

"I wasn't expecting company," said Rasmussen defensively, snatching the sock and tossing it toward a mound of dirty laundry. He folded his arms and glared at them. "What do you want?"

"Your displacement thingy," said Max. "The one that bends light waves."

Rasmussen twitched his nose as though it itched.

"And what would we be doing with it?" he asked.

"That's none of your business," said David. "We're asking you for a favor and I think you owe us one."

"Ha!" snorted Rasmussen. "Oh, the arrogance! I owe you? Because of *you*, I'm surrounded by bumbling idiots and malodorous hags! Because of *you*, my life's work has been ruined! I owe you nothing."

There was a sharp knock at the door. Rasmussen scowled.

"Of course she'd come now," he said in a simmering tone as he strode over to an antique chest buried beneath a mound of used towels. Reaching inside, Rasmussen retrieved the wondrous fabric and hurled it at Max, who snatched it out of the air and draped it over the others before slipping underneath. With a menacing stare, Rasmussen raised a finger to his lips and strode over to the door. Bellagrog stood outside with a serving cart.

"Evening, sir," she said amiably, pushing the cart inside. "Hot cider and toast, just like you requested. Put an extra drop of the good stuff in it, since it's Christmas and all."

Rasmussen stiffened and glanced at the children.

"Er, yes. Thank you, serving hag. That will be all."

Bellagrog ignored him, setting a silver tray on the writing desk and buttering his toast with brisk, efficient movements.

"I can do that myself!" said Rasmussen, red-faced, wrestling the knife from the potbellied hag.

"Awright, awright," said Bellagrog, holding her hands up. "I thought you liked me to do it, that's all. Never bothered ya before, did it?"

"Yes, well, things have changed," said Rasmussen, squinting as he set to buttering a piece of toast with inexpert stabbing motions. Bits of bread were flung into the air as the toast was chiseled into a pockmarked wreck.

Bellagrog merely watched him with a bemused expression. Her crocodile eye wandered up and down Rasmussen's spare frame. Her gaze became distant. When she spoke, her voice was hoarse.

"Ya got any family, Doc?"

"No," muttered Rasmussen, abandoning one shredded catastrophe and moving on to another.

"Well, I do," drawled the hag thoughtfully. "Sure, I got me wee sis right here with me, but Yuletide gets me thinkin' 'bout the others, too. They can drive ya batty, family can, but blood's blood."

"Very moving," said Rasmussen, oblivious to Bellagrog's cautious movements.

Max gasped as the hag suddenly slipped a massive cleaver out of her apron. Without a moment's hesitation, she lifted the heavy blade above her head and—

The cleaver froze, poised like a guillotine, above the unsuspecting man.

Bellagrog sniffed the air, nostrils puckering like a pig's. Her eyes widening with surprise, the hag gaped in the direction of Max and the others. Abruptly lowering the blade, she scowled and hid the cleaver in her apron's pouch.

"There!" said Rasmussen in triumph, holding up a reasonably whole piece of buttered toast.

"Bravo, Doctor! Well done, indeed!" crowed Bellagrog, applauding Rasmussen, who poured himself a mug of pungent cider.

"Yes, well, the others were clearly defective," said Rasmussen, glancing at the small mound of toast scraps. "You'll have to make more."

"In a jiffy," said Bellagrog with a low curtsy. "I believe that piece was toasted a bit more than the others, sir. I'll be sure the others follow suit."

"See to it," said Rasmussen, dismissing her with a wave.

"Shall we do your laundry tomorrow, sir?" asked the hag, pushing the cart toward the door.

"Yes," said Rasmussen, gazing imperiously about the room. "Yes, I believe so."

"Of course, sir. Trust your Bel to take care of everything. Merry Christmas, sir."

"Yes, yes. Merry Christmas," Rasmussen murmured, downing his cup in one smooth swallow.

With a parting glare in the direction of the children, the hag shambled out, pushing the cart before her. Rasmussen closed the door and spun on his heel.

"Well, you've got what you've come for, haven't you?" he said, fumbling through his pockets for a match. He lit his pipe, puffing at them with the impatient air of a peevish lord. "I'll expect it folded and placed at my door when you're finished. And don't think you don't owe me something in return."

"Sure thing," said Max, slipping out from beneath the cloth. "I'll even give you a tip for free."

"What's that?" growled Rasmussen, standing aside as the others filed past into the hallway.

"*Never* let Bellagrog in here again," Max warned. "Never be alone with her. Have someone else prepare your meals. That hag's crafty as they come and she wants your head on a platter. Literally."

Rasmussen snorted with laughter and blew sweet-smelling tobacco in Max's face.

"My, my, are you trying to *frighten* me?" he scoffed. "It's Christmas, not Halloween, miserable boy. Happy slinking about or whatever it is you Rowan students do at two in the morning. Off with you."

* * *

Max imagined they must resemble an awkward insect, twelve
legs moving out of sync as they bumped and jostled one another
beneath the displacement fabric. While the campus was quiet,
their precautions were warranted; they had to wait several times
for Agents or sleepless parents to pass on nighttime strolls.
Hurrying up the stairs of Old Tom, they wound their way along
the stairwells and down the halls until they reached Room 313.
David glanced down the hallway before placing his palm on the
door.

"Wait," hissed Lucia. "Why can't we just ask for Bram's Key
or whatever it is? After all, you two had it to begin with!"

"Don't chicken out now, Lucia," moaned Connor.

"Shhh," said Sarah. Footsteps sounded in the hall above
them.

"There will be too many questions, and there's no guarantee
they'll give it to us," said Max. "You heard what Astaroth said—
my mother doesn't have much time! We can't wait."

"But—" protested Lucia.

"What are you worried about?" whispered Connor incredulously. "Getting *detention*? Lucia, the whole world's going dark.
Or haven't you noticed? I don't think anyone's gonna lose sleep
over your permanent record!"

Footsteps sounded in the stairwell; someone was approaching.

"*Vola, vola!*" hissed Lucia, scowling and pinching Connor.

David muttered a word and tapped the doorknob three
times. It swung open on well-oiled hinges and David stepped
inside, hurrying over to the blackboard. He scratched at the
board awkwardly with his left hand before abandoning the
effort. Another command and the chalk bobbed into the air,
writing the necessary words in a bold hand: *By right and necessity, David Menlo requests access to the Archives.*

Max swiveled the board down and raised it once again to reveal the dark staircase below. In a quiet, even voice David gave the group brief instructions. Connor wrinkled his nose at the plan and shook his head.

"But we'll get caught for sure!" he said.

"That's precisely the point," muttered David.

"But I want to come with you," protested Connor.

"Me too," said Sarah. "You can't do all this alone."

David said nothing for some time. When he spoke, his eyes glittered with tears.

"We're not doing this alone," he said. "You're helping us right now. But you can't come with us—none of you can. There's no guarantee we're coming back."

Max said nothing as Sarah's eyes locked onto his own. He had already suspected the terrible truth that David voiced aloud. He squeezed Sarah's hand and kissed it as Cynthia removed her pearl necklace and enveloped David in a fierce hug.

"What's this?" he asked as she pressed the necklace into his hand.

"This was my grandmama's," said Cynthia. "You bring it back or I'll kill you!"

The six children laughed and hugged one another close again. Cynthia blew a long, lingering honk into her sleeve.

"We'll make you proud," she said, blinking away tears.

Max tightened David's pack on his shoulders as the group stole down the warm, wet stairs and into the living heart of Rowan.

At the bottom of the stairs, the shedu stood flanking the door, as massive and imposing as Max remembered. The guardians stared straight ahead while David slipped from beneath the sheet to approach them. Speaking softly, David bowed low and made a supplicating gesture. There was a low rumble as the creatures lowered themselves to the ground, still towering over David. Max held his breath; they could have crushed the small boy at any moment. Gradually, the shedu closed their eyes and rested their heads on the clean stone floor.

"What did you do?" asked Max, leading the others forward.

"I suggested they have a nap," said David simply. "They're under a powerful spell, you know, to keep them alert. Poor things haven't slept in centuries."

Max peered through the double doors to the Archives. There in the center of the main reading room was Bram's Key. Its silver was polished to a fine gleam; all about it were scholars huddled at surrounding tables strewn with charts and papers and parchments galore. Max squinted and saw Vilyak sipping coffee while he chatted quietly with nine men and women in dark nanomail.

"The Red Branch," Max whispered. "They're the best Agents in the world."

Connor gave a low whistle.

"This changes everything," whispered Cynthia. "Those are anything but scholars. How on earth are we supposed to fool them?"

"You don't need to fool them forever," said David. "You just need to be a distraction, nothing more. Who's going to be the lucky one to get things moving?"

"I'll do it," said Sarah.

"Maybe I should," said Connor.

"Please," said Sarah. "I'm way faster than you—you'll be nabbed in a heartbeat."

"Once you're caught, don't resist," Max said, peering out at the Red Branch. "Don't even joke around, Connor—I *mean* it. Surrender right away and demand to speak to Ms. Richter.

Those Agents are deadly serious. Don't give them any excuse to hurt you."

Lucia made a funny whimper; Connor swallowed hard.

Reaching into his pack, David removed a rolled-up pair of socks and squeezed it within his fist. The pair of socks suddenly grew and assumed a metallic luster. Seconds later, David held a perfect replica of the silver armillary sphere.

Sarah slipped under the blanket with Max and David while the others remained behind. Slowly, the hidden trio made their way into the Archives, creeping along the floor until they were crouched a mere foot from the table where Bram's Key was perched. Across the way, Vilyak continued his conversation with the Red Branch.

David handed Max the replica sphere. Both glanced at Sarah. The beautiful Nigerian girl nodded and set her jaw.

In one fluid movement, Sarah dashed out from beneath the blanket and snatched Bram's Key from its pedestal. There was a commotion as scholars sat up suddenly at their tables. Vilyak's black doll's eyes flicked onto Sarah. Before anyone could move, David flexed his fingers and Sarah shut her eyes.

"*Solas!*"

The room exploded in light. Scholars shouted and fell back from their tables; Vilyak and the Red Branch cursed, stumbling forward as the flash of light momentarily blinded them. Sarah dashed past Max, smoothly exchanging the real Key for the replica. Huddling close to a bookcase, Max and David waited for the scholars and Agents to stampede past them as Sarah bolted toward the entrance and the stairs.

Once they had a clear path, Max and David hurried for the opposite end of the cavernous room, walking quickly in lockstep beneath the displacement blanket. Behind them, Max heard shouts as Connor, Lucia, and Cynthia ran into the room. Sarah's voice rose above the din, yelling, "Catch!" There was a triumphant whoop from Connor, followed by more shouts and the crash of toppling furniture.

Once they reached the great spiral staircases that led up to the stacks, Max and David turned to see their friends pinned on the floor, each in the arms of two members of the Red Branch. Vilyak stood above them, red-faced and barking questions that echoed in the room's vast acoustics. Shaken scholars righted tables and lamps, stepping around broken chairs and a shattered vase.

David tugged at Max's arm and the two hurried up the steps, winding up and around the Archives' perimeter until they stopped, breathless, at a remote stack of dusty tomes and ribbon-bound papers.

"This is it," David wheezed, stowing the sphere in the pack on Max's back. "This is the secret way I used last year."

"I thought you said I couldn't follow you this way," said Max.

"We need to try," said David, catching his breath. Below them, Vilyak's anger echoed off the walls and filled the great space. "I'll go first to open the passage. Instead of going straight through, I'll try to stay inside to keep it open. Hurry after me."

Max nodded. Slipping out from beneath the blanket, David strode toward a stack of books on Divination. The books parted and let him pass with nary a ripple. Holding his breath, Max followed after.

He gasped as he felt his body suddenly squeezed under immense pressure. A faint clicking sounded in his jaw; there was a horrendous pull on his body as though a great and greedy giant were slurping him through a straw. The pressure in his head began to build. Strange lights swam before his eyes, and he feared his jaw would snap.

Suddenly, like a popping balloon, the pain was gone.

Opening his eyes, Max saw that he and David were standing on the path between the Manse and Old Tom. David's teeth chattered. It was still dark, but it was Christmas morning and the campus looked serene as snow fell, clean and cold. David and Max trotted off across the lawns, past twinkling lights and holly boughs, as they made their way toward the slippery steps that would lead them down to the sea.

The *Kestrel* loomed black and huge against the graying dawn. Her stout planks creaked as she rocked back and forth, restless in the choppy water that splashed and steamed against her sides. The two boys hurried along the packed sand, up the steps, and down the dock like a pair of fugitives. In one spring, Max cleared the distance between the dock and the ship. He swung the gangplank over the side, pushing it toward David, who waited patiently on the dock, still in his pajamas. A moment later, David scampered up the platform and onto the ship, his cheeks pink with excitement.

"We'll have to hurry," he said, taking Bram's Key from Max. *Boom!*

The *Kestrel* groaned as some force took hold of it. The prow rose high in the air like a bucking horse and crashed down again, knocking the two boys off their feet and jarring the sphere from David's grasp. Scrambling on all fours, Max dove for the sphere, which rolled and skittered toward starboard as the ship rocked nearly onto its side. He caught the Key by its stand, slamming painfully into the ship's guardrails.

A familiar wailing rose up from the black ocean depths. The ship began to shake and pitch violently. As they and their classmates had discovered the previous year, the *Kestrel* had an unseen and most disturbing guardian. A horrific, weeping wail rose to shake their eardrums and rattle their senses.

The boys clung precariously to the ship as it bucked and rocked. Freezing water crashed over the side to drench the two as Max crawled toward the ship's figurehead, squinting as snow and bits of ice whipped against his face in a sudden tempest. The wailing became an earsplitting scream.

"Hold on!" he yelled over the wailing and the crash of the waves. David had wrapped a bit of rope around his wrist and was slung about the deck. Max leapt over a barrel that had broken free from its fastenings and climbed the deck that rose again before him. Wind screamed through the sails and rigging as Max clambered forward. As the ship tapered toward the prow, he was able to seize the railing and pull himself up.

The figurehead, a stern-looking hawk carved of dark wood, bobbed just beyond reach. Max leapt and grabbed hold of it as the ship crashed against the sea again, nearly flinging him over the prow. A metal ring on the figurehead's arched back grazed Max's hand. His fingers felt the perimeter of a circle, carved like the lid of a jack-o'-lantern into the back of the figure. He tugged at the metal ring, but the lid remained fast—glued shut with grime and salt that had accumulated over the years. Max gritted his teeth and gave a tremendous pull, wrenching the lid open but throwing himself backward in the process.

He crashed onto the deck and braced himself to be flung overboard. Nothing happened, however. The terrible wailing subsided to a sigh, and the *Kestrel* settled back into its berth like a hen returning to its nest. A few residual waves slapped the ship's side, and then the ocean was calm. Max scrambled quickly to his feet, clutching Bram's Key. He turned to see David tangled hopelessly in netting like a towheaded fish.

"What made it stop?" Max asked as snow fell peacefully once again upon his shoulders.

"I don't know," panted David, untangling himself.

Suddenly, the ship was bathed in light as though a hundred spotlights had been turned upon it. Max shielded his eyes, stumbling toward the rail to see what was happening.

Standing on the beach, beneath floating orbs of light, was Ms. Richter, flanked by Commander Vilyak and other members of the Red Branch. Curious spectators were streaming down the stone steps, wrapped in robes and blankets to assemble on the beach. Max saw his father among them, hurrying down the steps with Bob, who clutched a lantern.

"Max!" his father called. "What are you doing? Is that *David*?"

"Hi, Mr. McDaniels," said David, waving weakly.

"David Menlo, explain yourself," said Ms. Richter, looking tired and grim.

"I'm sorry for all the trouble," said David. "But Max and I have to leave now. Don't be too hard on Connor and the others. They only meant to help."

"McDaniels!" shouted Vilyak. "Disembark from that ship immediately! That's a direct order!"

"Max," called his father, looking horror-stricken. "Please come down here."

"I'm sorry, Dad," said Max, ignoring Vilyak while he handed Bram's Key to David. "I'm off to find Mom."

"Then let me come with you!" cried Mr. McDaniels hoarsely, hurrying through the crowd and sputtering clouds of frosty air.

"You can't," said Max, shaking his head. "You can't come with me this time, but I'll find her. I promise! Look after Nick!"

Mr. McDaniels stopped, his mouth agape as he stared up at his son.

Vilyak barked an order to his Agents, who began striding purposefully up the dock's steps.

"*Stop!*" said Ms. Richter. The Agents halted at her command, alternating their gaze between the Director and Commander Vilyak. Ms. Richter turned from them and gazed back at Max. The Director gave a sad but understanding smile. Her voice carried, clear and strong, in the wintry air. "You carry our fortunes with you. Go with our blessings and look after David. You must be his keeper."

Max nodded and waved good-bye. Behind him, David lowered Bram's Key into the figurehead's opening. As soon as he did so, there was a single beautiful note, pure as a struck bell. It seemed to hover, taut and trembling, in the sudden stillness.

Max hurried over to stand by David. The two watched as the rings began to spin, each silvery orbit accelerating until the sphere became a single blur of silver. A shiver ran through the ship. Icicles from the masts and rigging rained upon the deck and shattered as the *Kestrel*'s great sails unfurled of their own accord. Lines snaked about, heaved to by brisk and invisible hands. As the topgallants were lowered, the mooring ropes snapped.

From the beach there was a collective gasp as the *Kestrel* lifted from the sea to hover in the air. David's face was aglow with excitement. Snowflakes clinging to his lashes, he gazed up at the sails as they rippled and stretched taut in the breeze.

Max glimpsed something fluttering near his ear. He turned and saw a gypsy moth with a singed wing spiral precariously onto his shoulder.

"You'll need me!" squeaked the moth, its feelers twitching in the cold.

With a quick glance at David, who remained transfixed by the *Kestrel*, Max plucked Mr. Sikes from his shoulder and stowed the imp in his coat's warm woollen pocket. The moth peered at him from deep inside, snug in its new burrow.

Banking slightly, the ship began to pivot and swing its prow slowly toward the open sea. Max ran back to the stern and looked out upon the assembled crowd. He spotted his father once again and waved, smiling through his tears, as the ship pushed off, sailing out over the dark ocean on a gentle rise to meet the sky.

~ 15 ~

AMONG THE SIDH

The two boys stood at the prow. While David rummaged through his pack for warmer clothes, Max stared out over the glittering ocean, speechless, while the ship sailed up toward winking stars and a moon that shone bright as a pearl. David poked his head through a fisherman's sweater and pulled on a navy woollen coat, slowly fastening the toggles with his left hand.

"Where are we going, David?" asked Max.

"I don't know," replied David sleepily, breathing deep and gazing up at the tall mast and its white, smooth sails.

Max yawned and marked the constellations in the sky as the ship rose higher. He peeked inside his pocket and saw Mr. Sikes, now in the form of a field mouse, curled up in a snug little ball. Max imagined he was curled up, too, warm in his sleigh bed, watching the stars through the glassy dome of his room back at Rowan. They sailed on, and the earth appeared no more than a miniature. Peering over the side, Max saw cities arranged like so many toys sprinkled over continents where moonlit clouds drifted like migratory herds. The air was cold and the stars impossibly bright as the *Kestrel* sailed on toward Orion.

"There's Betelgeuse," murmured David, pointing at a large reddish star. "And Rigel and Bellatrix. Some call Orion's belt the 'Three Magi,' you know. . . ."

Max nodded dreamily and hugged his coat closer about him.

The stars grew to the size of pumpkins and the moon seemed beyond all reckoning as it bathed the sails and deck in a milky radiance. Gazing over the side again, Max saw nothing below them: no clouds, no land, and no dark swirls of ocean. Then he became afraid, thinking that they might sail on forever, severing all ties to their world as they drifted into the ether.

Whether they had sailed for hours or days or a lifetime, Max could not tell. He was conscious only of the sky becoming thin, its matter stretched beyond capacity, until Max swore he could see tiny gaps in its delicate black weave. He laughed and clutched the rail, leaning forward as the slivers of color became bigger, revealing a hazy wash of blue and green.

Night gave way to day, and now the *Kestrel* seemed to glide upon currents of air and wisps of cloud that raced along the prow, like porpoises. A landscape came into view—emerald hills, tilled fields, and rivers that coursed and snaked through resplendent country. Small towns clustered about tall, slim castles unlike any Max had ever seen. The wind picked up, and the *Kestrel* began to buck and wobble.

They clung to the railings as the *Kestrel* shook and groaned, her timbers threatening to snap like matchsticks. Blobs of deep green became forests, forests became trees, and then the very treetops scratched at the *Kestrel*'s keel as she skimmed above them. There was a tearing sound, and Max saw the topgallants ripped from the mast, floating in their wake like sheets blown free of a clothesline. David yelled something, but Max could not hear him above the whipping wind and the furious rippling of the mainsail. The ship rolled slightly as it cleared the forest, dipping down toward the fields of a farm. Max threw David beneath him and covered their heads.

There was a sudden jolt, followed by another and another as the *Kestrel* bounced across the field like a skipping stone. With a terrible crack, Max felt the mainsail settle over them like a tented sheet as the ship slid across the field in a spray of cabbages and damp black soil. Groaning, the *Kestrel* came to a sudden halt, rolling onto its side and spilling the two boys onto the ground.

They lay there for several moments, breathing hard and regaining their senses. Max struggled to his feet and backed away from the ship to assess the damage. Snapped wood, frayed rope, and tattered sails had been left in their wake, a trail of nautical carnage. He peeked into his pocket to see Mr. Sikes trembling with fright but apparently unharmed and clinging on inside. Limping around the ship, Max saw that the *Kestrel*'s hull had been shorn away, leaving only a skeleton of her upper decks and what remained of her snapped and broken masts. David hobbled around to join him, scratching at an impressive lump on his forehead.

"Guess we'll have to find another way home," he said.

Max nodded, running his hand along a jagged hole of splintered wood.

"I wonder whose fields these are," Max said, glancing around. There was no person or building to be seen. "Probably best not to find out," he added, wondering how they could possibly explain a shipwreck amidst a stranger's cabbages.

"Where should we go?" asked David.

Max glanced up at the morning sun, rising in the pale sky. He removed his coat and stuffed it in David's pack, carefully stowing Mr. Sikes in his pocket while David surveyed the landscape. Straightening, Max followed David's gaze to a distant hill that rose high above its neighbors.

"Let's climb up there," Max suggested. "At least we can have a look around."

Shouldering their pack, Max led the way. The two hurried off the cabbage field, mindful not to cause any more damage, and walked instead along a packed dirt road that wound like a ribbon among low hills thick with wildflowers. At a small creek, they crossed a narrow footbridge, and then began to climb steeper hills while the sun rose behind them. Max's stomach growled and he came to a sobering realization.

"I forgot to pack food!"

"Oh," said David, nursing his bump and looking thoughtful.

"I'm an idiot," moaned Max, kicking at a stone.

David said nothing and continued walking. Max poked at his stomach and willed it into submission.

As it turned out, their destination was farther than it had initially appeared. Hours of brisk walking passed before they finally saw the hill looming before them. It seemed to be a landmark of sorts; other roads converged upon the hill, and Max spied something rocking in the wind at its crest. David had to pause to catch his breath several times as the pair climbed many switchbacks on their trek to its summit.

Once on top, Max saw that his choice had been a good one.

The rocking object he had seen was, in fact, a signpost, and the hill a sort of crossroads. From this height, Max could look upon rolling greenery and white-fenced fields that stretched to the horizon. For several moments, Max and David stood in silence, reading the strange names painted on weathered wood signs that pointed in eight directions:

SIDH FIONNACHAIDH
SIDH BODB
SIDH BRI LEITH
SIDH AIRCELTRAI
SIDH RODRUBÂN
SIDH EAS AEDHA RUAIDH
SIDH MEADHA
SIDH BRUGH NA BOINNE

"Which do we choose?" asked David.

"I don't know," said Max, stepping over to inspect them more closely. His eyes locked on the sign pointing to Brugh na Boinne—Astaroth had said he would find his mother there. Max was just about to speak up when he felt something scurry up his arm. Mr. Sikes whispered urgently, his whiskers tickling Max's ear.

"Danger approaches, Master McDaniels!" piped the imp.

Max turned to look back in the direction from which they'd come. There was someone in the distance, walking along the same road they had taken. Something about the far-off figure filled Max with loathing. Tapping David, he pointed at their apparent pursuer, who was now nearing the footbridge they had crossed only an hour earlier.

"We need to get moving," said Max.

"I agree," said David, shivering in the wind. "Which way?"

Max was about to speak again when the imp's urgent whispers made him pause.

"Not Brugh na Boinne!" pleaded the imp. "Not yet! It is to Rodrubân you must go!"

Max ran his hand along the sign pointing to Brugh na Boinne. He felt the mouse's tiny claws prick at his neck in protest.

"I vote for Sidh Rodrubân," said Max at length, succumbing to Mr. Sikes's urgent counsel.

"Why?" asked David.

"For one thing," replied Max, "it leads directly away from whomever that is. And it'll be hard to see us from up here." David looked out at the wooded paths beneath them, sloping away into the trees. He glanced back at the mysterious figure, which had now crossed the bridge and seemed to be gaining steadily.

David nodded and clucked his tongue in agreement. The two boys scurried down the slope, following the path as it plunged into a wood of tall beech and twisty oak.

Summer showers pattered softly on the leaves while Max and David stole along the forest floor. They had been walking for what seemed to be hours, trying to make good time, but pausing occasionally to marvel at the landscape around them. The air was clean and fragrant, the colors more vibrant than Max had ever seen. He felt as though he were experiencing trees and grass and flowers and clouds for the first time, marvelous shapes and hues that brimmed with life and vitality. Packed dirt gave way to clean cobblestones as the forest opened onto rolling hills where flocks of white sheep grazed on close-cropped pastures.

The sun hovered directly overhead when the two reached the crest of a hill crowned with cherry blossoms. A rabbit observed them on its hind legs, twitching its whiskers. Max eyed it hungrily, and it promptly dove into its burrow.

"How far do you think Sidh Rodrubân might be?" asked Max, thinking of dinner.

"No idea," said David. "Have you noticed how deceptive the distances are? Or maybe it's time that's deceptive. I don't know."

Max glanced at his watch, whose readings advanced and retreated seemingly at random. He turned to gauge the distance they'd already traveled, his eyes wandering west, where a silvery mist was settling in the hollows of the hills.

There he saw a chilling sight: the same dark figure, standing on a hilltop.

Max abruptly pushed David to the ground and flattened himself against the grass off the path.

"What—" sputtered David, flicking a cherry blossom from his nose.

"Over there," whispered Max. "On that hill. Do you think he's seen us?"

David gazed out at the figure that leaned on a tall walking stick. The two boys heard faint laughter carry toward them on the breeze. The silhouette acknowledged them with a wave and began a brisk descent down the hill. The blood drained from David's face.

"I know who that is," whispered David.

"Who?" asked Max.

"Astaroth," croaked David, pushing up from the ground.

"How could he get here?" asked Max.

David's reply was to run as fast as his short legs could carry him. Max followed his roommate, who gasped and sputtered with terror as they fled up the road until they had run what seemed to be several miles. David collapsed in a heap, wracked by a violent fit of coughing.

"I can't run anymore," he wheezed. "I have to rest."

Max nodded but looked warily behind them. He could feel terror rising—cresting—in a slow, sickly wave within him. He glanced at the crown of the last hill. The Demon had not yet come, but Max was suddenly aware that no birds called above and the docile flocks of sheep had retreated until they appeared as tiny dabs of ivory scattered at the horizon.

"Let's at least get off the road," said Max quickly, helping David to the far side of a great willow tree, whose branches over-hung a small green pond. David leaned his back against the trunk and took a slow, deep breath.

"This reminds me of the Sanctuary lagoon," he said with a weary smile.

Max reached into their pack for a towel. Dipping it into the cool water, he wrung it out and placed it on his friend's forehead the way his father did whenever he was sick.

"Five minutes," said Max, watching the hill. "Then we get moving again."

David shook his head.

"Running won't matter," whispered David, closing his eyes. "We might as well stay here."

Max did not like that idea. He peered around the broad willow and gazed back at the road. While David rested, Max waited, listening to the drone of crickets and the chirruping call of pond frogs. Fear continued to well up within him, as if a dropper of poison were filling up his mind. He had a sudden urge to hide, to dig down deep into the earth and wait until the pursuing evil passed them by. He glanced at David slipping into sleep, felt a frantic scurrying up his arm. Mr. Sikes's whiskers twitched with panic.

"We must keep going," hissed the imp. "This is a perilous place to rest!"

"Why?" asked Max, rubbing his eyes.

"He is coming!" squeaked the mouse. "It is the Demon that follows you!"

Max shook his head.

"David needs to rest," he murmured. "And I'm watching."

Closing his fingers about the *gae bolga,* Max leaned heavily against the tree and watched the lonely road. Mr. Sikes lingered a moment on his shoulder and then scurried back to Max's pocket with a squeak of reprimand. A breeze gently shook the willow branches. There was a soft splash in the pond and Max imagined that he was a frog, safe beneath the water and kicking about the reeds.

When Max awoke, a harvest moon hovered above and even the crickets seemed to be fast asleep. Glancing down, Max saw David sleeping peacefully at the base of the tree, lying on his side amidst the tall grass and mossy roots. Something bright caught Max's attention; reflections of firelight were dancing on the still pond. In a sudden panic, Max remembered their danger. He stepped away from the willow and peered out to survey the road.

There was Astaroth, sitting cross-legged on the cobblestones. Two rabbits had been skinned and spitted above a small, bright fire. The Demon's white face turned to look at Max, his black eyes glittering with amusement. Max felt Mr. Sikes trembling in his pocket.

"Well met, little Hound. I'd come to you, but I cannot leave the road."

"And why is that?" asked Max, gripping Cúchulain's spear tightly in his hand.

"A condition of my passage," replied Astaroth smoothly.

"Come and eat, why don't you? I have two fat rabbits to share, and you do look ever so hungry."

David had awoken and crept forward to stand by Max. Astaroth's eyes crinkled to slits; his aquiline features sharpened to a malevolent smile. He tapped his scepter on his knee, his voice soft and sibilant.

> *On the idle hill of summer,*
> *Sleepy with the flow of streams,*
> *Far I hear the steady drummer*
> *Drumming like a noise in dreams.*

"Awake again, young David? Good, good. I was just inviting Max to table."

David said nothing but looked upon the grinning Demon with mute terror. As if sensing his thoughts, Astaroth clapped his hands and laughed.

"Yes, yes, I know. No summoning circle to keep me at bay, is there? I suppose I could have *you* spitted on this fire if I wished." Astaroth's eyes crinkled. "But I did not interrupt my plans and risk a journey to the Sidh to punish two wayward boys."

"Then why are you here?" asked David.

"The Book is here," replied Astaroth simply, tending to the rabbits. "Instead of plying me with questions, you should thank me, David Menlo. You might have slept forever had I not called you back. As I warned at your summons, David, this is a perilous place for one such as you. The Sidh has many voices, and it is your nature to listen."

Astaroth laughed soundlessly while the rabbits sizzled above the flames.

"Come and eat," he said. "Though we seek the same prize,

upon this road you are safe from me. You have my word. I savor an honest competition."

David walked slowly toward the Demon and sat opposite him. For several moments, the two stared at each other while the fire crackled between them. Astaroth smiled and reached into the flames to slide the rabbits off the spit.

"Roast rabbit 'neath starry skies of the Sidh," he chuckled. "The romantic in me almost writhes with pleasure." He tossed the rabbits to Max, who took a wary seat by David. The rabbits smelled delicious, and the two boys tore into them with their fingers. Astaroth merely watched them, his face as still and smooth as porcelain. There the three sat, in silence, while the landscape darkened about them and the wind sighed through the grass. At length, Astaroth spoke.

"Of all your choices, this road was wisest, David," said Astaroth.

"I didn't choose it," said David. "Max did."

"Did he indeed?" exclaimed the Demon. "Perhaps I should have guessed your feet would lead you hither, Max McDaniels. Do you know who is Master at Rodrubân?"

Max shook his head.

"Ah, a bittersweet meeting it shall be," said Astaroth with a knowing smile. "Leave David to his quest and come away with me so I might spare you such heartache. A great captain you shall be—chief among my host when you are strong enough."

Now it was Max's turn to laugh.

"I'd rather die."

"There are far worse things than death," said the Demon, stoking the fire. "Perhaps someday you will reconsider."

Max said nothing.

"Look at yourself," said Astaroth, smiling. "So angry and spiteful. Old Magic brimming within you—a noble prince!—

and yet you do not know the slightest thing about yourself. Who *are* you?"

Max glowered momentarily at the Demon before gazing into the fire. Astaroth's words reminded him of the wolfhound that haunted his dreams: *What are you about? Answer quick, or I'll gobble you up!*

"I'm Max McDaniels," he said quietly.

"Bah!" the Demon cackled, his voice echoing in the blackness. "What is that but a name? A false name from a false father! You are no more Max McDaniels than I am. Max McDaniels does not exist! Max McDaniels has *never* existed!"

Max's hands began to shake.

"Be quiet," he whispered, seething. "You're a liar."

"No," purred the Demon. "I am not. I do not bait you, Max, but offer my sympathies. How many sorry souls have faded from the earth without ever truly knowing *who* they were and *why* they were here? It's not fair—none of it is! Rowan is mistaken to think I seek the Book of Thoth for my own benefit. I seek it for yours! Who but I can use the Book and share the secrets that should belong to all mankind? It is a cruel fate that your kind should be blessed with consciousness yet denied true understanding. Who *are* you, Max? Until you know your truename, you shall never know peace. Your existence will be but a false, aimless thing until you fade along with all the others before you."

The fire sputtered, sending a plume of bright sparks into the night.

"But why the destruction?" asked David softly. "Why are vyes and goblins and other dark things running wild? Why must every country bow and scrape?"

"Grim necessities," Astaroth said with a shrug. "I doubt not that there are many sad tales and that many curse my name, but

the greater good must be served. Mankind is within a genera-
tion, perhaps two, of self-extermination. What it needs is one
strong voice—a ruler blessed with knowledge and wisdom to set
things aright before it is too late. It is not conquest I seek but
pacification. I fully concede, however, that the Book is a more
elegant solution. By hindering me, David Menlo, you merely
prolong mankind's suffering. It need not be this way."

David shook his head and smiled at the Demon.

"Flectere si nequeo superos, Achaeronta movebo."

Astaroth's smile faded to a thin line.

"Post tenebras lux," he whispered in reply. "You know nothing
of hell, David Menlo, yet you may before the end. For the time
being, however, I fancy a bit of sport and would not have you lost
to the perils of the Sidh. Heed this before I go: Many forks lie
between you and Rodrubân. Always choose the right-hand road
or you will be lost. And though you thirst, drink from no stream
until you come to Rodrubân and win entry to its halls."

The fire suddenly leapt high, obscuring the Demon. Max
blinked and looked upon a great black wolf with pale yellow eyes
and a red, lolling tongue. In one leap, the wolf cleared the fire,
scattering Max and David as it landed between them to race
down the dark road. The boys huddled close to the fire, neither
speaking as they gazed upon the bright moon and a quiet landscape of hill and shadow.

The sun rose and set three times while Max and David walked,
subsisting on blackberries that grew wild on the hills. Heeding
Astaroth's warning, they resisted the temptation to drink from
clear streams whose babbling was a siren's song to their dry and
swollen throats. At every fork, they kept to the right, making
camp at night amidst the hollows of hoary trees, whose great
roots provided shelter from the wind. There had been no further

sign of Astaroth, and Mr. Sikes seemed content to slumber within Max's pocket. On the fourth day, the boys heard the blare of a distant horn. Forgetting hunger and thirst, they hurried up the sloping hill as fast as their tired legs could carry them.

As they neared the summit, something bounded over the hill and hurried past them. It was a hart with a rough red coat and eyes rimmed white with terror. Another deer bounded over the crest, followed by another and another. They landed lightly on their hooves, scampering past Max and David to flee for the safety of a wooded thicket.

Another horn sounded. Creeping to the hill's summit, the boys looked out upon a baffling spectacle.

Below them, two armies faced each other on a broad plain where the road forked yet again. Red and green banners fluttered, helmets gleamed, and tall spears glittered in the morning sun. Upon the third blast of the horn, a fierce battle was joined. For what seemed an hour, Max watched, speechless and horrified, as footmen were trampled, horses speared, and knights beheaded. Shouts and cries sounded from the field, whose verdant grass was churned into crimson mud.

Finally, from amidst the battle, a horn sounded once again. Those still standing and wearing green raised their weapons in victory, while those in red bowed their heads in defeat. Forming ranks once again, the survivors of each army marched to opposite ends of the field. David hissed and pointed toward the carnage in the center.

"Look! Look what's happening!"

The battlefield began to wriggle as though a sea of maggots were roiling beneath the noonday sun. Slain knights and footmen rose slowly to their feet, fetching lost weapons, limbs, and heads as they rejoined their fellows. Once the field was clear and the ranks restored, the horn sounded for the fifth and final time.

The red army made an orderly withdrawal down the left-hand road. The green army cheered as they left, clashing swords and spears against their great shields. Victorious, the green army marched from the battlefield, following the road that curved to the right and disappeared between two hills. Max and David followed them at a distance, climbing heights and scurrying down through tree-fringed valleys until they gazed upon the wondrous sight of Rodrubân.

Built of white stone on a broad green hill, the castle stretched tall and straight toward the sky, its seven spires flashing silver. Hanging from the walls were the same green banners the army carried: a white sun stitched onto a field of jade. Grazing herds of cattle and sheep dotted white-fenced pastures. Lush fields of wheat and apple orchards checkered the surrounding valley, irrigated by three meandering streams that funneled down from distant hills. The returning army marched down the cobbled road, passing neat rows of straw-thatched cottages until they came to a long suspension bridge that spanned a chasm before the castle gate. A horn sounded, the drawbridge was lowered, and the army marched across the bridge to disappear inside.

Max and David hurried down into the valley, sticking to the road and giving the long-horned bulls a wide berth as they chewed their cud. When they reached the first of many houses, they saw their first inhabitant of the Sidh. It was a woman, visible through her open doorway. She was sitting at a loom, weaving cream-colored cloth with fast, nimble movements. The woman stopped weaving and met their gaze. Easing up from her stool, she came to stand in the doorway and stare at them with eyes of brilliant green. Other faces began to appear in windows and doorways, some beautiful, some plain, all quiet and ageless.

The hard ringing from a smithy ceased; more doors were flung open and the street was soon lined with curious faces.

"Excuse me," said David, pausing to address a potbellied man wearing a cobbler's apron. "Who lives in that castle?"

No answer was given; the man simply stared.

"Does anyone know Bryn McDaniels?" called Max, looking from face to face in vain.

"Let's go," whispered David, tugging at Max's sleeve. The two hurried through the town, trailed by townsfolk who followed in a strange, silent procession.

When they arrived at the bridge, Max and David gazed up at the white walls looming over them. Far above, ravens circled the silver-tipped spires, dipping now and again to give a hoarse call. The townsfolk assembled in a wide semicircle, standing in the shade of apple trees whose boughs were heavy with fruit.

"Come on," said Max, stepping out onto the wooden bridge.

The bridge promptly bucked and flailed as if it were alive. From the far end, a great wave raced down its length to snap Max high into the air. For a moment, Max felt as though he was floating. Then he began to plummet, gazing in horror at the seemingly bottomless chasm beneath him. With a desperate grab, he seized the bridge's handrail and caught himself, dangling by his fingertips. Another shiver in the bridge spit him back onto the hard ground at David's feet.

"Are you okay?" asked David.

Max nodded, glaring at the silent, stoic townsfolk.

Laughter rang out from the castle, feminine and mocking. Max saw a figure standing on a crenellated battlement above the drawbridge. It was a young woman with wild black hair that whipped in the wind.

"Only heroes may cross," she laughed. "Not beardless boys who had best run home before they're missed and scolded."

Max reddened and climbed quickly to his feet. He stared out at the bridge, one hundred feet of heavy wooden planks swaying lightly in the breeze. Setting his jaw, Max stepped out onto the first plank, clutching the handrails tightly. He had almost made it halfway across when the bridge bucked once again, swinging him to and fro like a clinging insect. There was another decisive snap and Max lost his grip on the handrails, landing on his back with a painful thud. The bridge became still and Max withdrew in a frantic crab walk until he was back where he had started. Peals of laughter sounded from the walls.

"What is this creature that advances on two legs but retreats on four?" mocked the raven-haired maiden. "We shall have to add you to the lists!"

"Leave it be, boy," said a voice from behind Max. He whipped his head around to see the bearded cobbler step forward from the ranks of townsfolk. "That bridge has claimed many lives. You are brave to try, but try no more."

"Have you tried?" panted Max.

"We all have," replied the man. "Many seek the wisdom of the High King, but few pass beyond those gates. Thus we wait here, on the doorstep, until the day he sees fit to hear our petitions. You will be welcome among us. There is a home and work for you here."

"I can't wait," said Max, his anger rising as he spied the mocking figure on the wall. "I *will* cross that bridge," he seethed, rounding on the swaying span.

"Only weaklings trade in idle boasts," called the maiden. "Silence served you better."

David said something, but Max could not hear him. Blood drummed in his temples, and he began to tremble. Terrible, frightening energies consumed him. With two steps, Max leapt high into the air. The bridge rose to meet him, sinuous as a serpent. Landing far out upon the span, Max touched only for a moment before springing again. He arced beyond the bridge's perilous reach to land safely on the other side

"Open the gate!" he roared, raining three thunderous blows on the heavy timbers. Seconds later, there was the slow measure of clanking iron. He stood aside as the drawbridge was lowered, turning to address David, who watched in silence from across the way.

"Cross over," called Max to his friend.

David shook his head. "I can't."

Somehow, Max knew it to be true. David could not enter this place. He felt at his pocket, but Mr. Sikes was not there. Max glanced back for the furtive movements of a mouse or the faint flutter of a moth but saw nothing. Mr. Sikes had gone. With a farewell wave to David, Max turned and passed within the white stone arch of Rodrubân, withdrawing the spear that he had concealed beneath his sweater.

Once inside, he looked upon a broad courtyard where a single ancient oak was planted. Ringing the base of the tree was a fountain of clear water. The raven-haired woman stood before the fountain, tall and proud. Walking forward, she stopped before him and glanced at the *gae bolga* in his hand.

"Where did you get this?" asked the woman, staring at the broken weapon.

"It was given to me," replied Max coldly. "I am meant to have it."

"I am Scathach," said the woman, taking Max lightly by the arm and leading him past the oak and fountain until they had climbed many steps and crossed many halls. There was no sign of the army that had entered. A profound silence filled the castle. At last, they reached a long flight of marble steps that concluded at a pair of golden doors. Pulling them open, Scathach ushered Max inside a great hall hung with many tapestries. At the far end was a throne, and upon that throne was a figure bathed in radiance so blinding that Max immediately gasped and fell to one knee, shielding his eyes.

For long moments, no word was spoken while Max bowed low and listened to the pounding in his chest. Suddenly, a clear voice filled the hall.

"Scathach, what is this you bring?"

"I know not, my lord," she answered.

"Look at me, boy," commanded the voice.

Max forced his head up, gazing across the hall at the speaker. His eyes burned and ached, but he could not look away. Upon the throne, he saw a man with a handsome, youthful face. In his hand was a heavy spear; at his feet lay a great gray wolfhound. The monstrous hound was looking at Max. As it rose from the floor and padded toward him, Max nearly fainted. It was the very same creature from his dreams.

The hound came to a halt mere inches from Max's face. A low growl sounded from deep within its throat. Summoning all his courage, Max rose to his full height and stared back at the hound. The two stood for long moments appraising each other.

"Surely this is my kin," said the man at last, his voice calm and quiet.

"He carries this, my lord," said Scathach, lifting Max's hand to display the broken spear.

"Bring it to me," commanded the radiant figure.

At Scathach's bidding, Max walked forward, resisting the desire to turn away from the searing radiance. The hound walked beside him. Once he stood at the foot of the throne, the man extended his hand to receive the weapon.

"Strong and fair was he who bore this long ago," said the man, examining the blade. "Are you worthy of it?"

"I am," said Max, meeting the man's impassive gaze.

"How are you named?" asked the man.

Max paused a moment, glancing at the hound, before responding.

"I'm Max McDaniels."

The man bowed his head in greeting.

"You stand before Lugh the Long-Handed, High King of Rodrubân. You come seeking that which was entrusted to me. You are my son."

The man's words echoed in Max's ears. A flood of emotions welled up within him. Gazing upon the shining figure, Max knew he spoke the truth. Scott McDaniels was not his father; Max's entire life and identity had been a lie. Lugh rose from his throne to tower over Max, who stood only to his chest. There was no love or warmth in the High King's expression, merely a distant curiosity. Placing the broken spear on Max's palm, Lugh closed his fingers about the splintered haft.

"Scathach shall judge if you are worthy," he said.

"But I have no time for tests," protested Max, fighting tears. "There's so much I have to do!"

"You are not yet ready," said Lugh. He motioned for Scathach to lead Max from the hall; the audience was finished. Before departing, Max looked back to see the great hound settling once again at Lugh's feet. As Scathach closed the door, the High King issued one last command.

"Break him."

The moon waxed and waned and seasons changed while Max trained and suffered under Scathach, forbidden to leave Rodrubân. Under her tutelage, Max mastered many feats, but at a terrible price. In his room now, atop the highest tower, he gazed down at the town below, a twinkling of lights among the sable fields. Somewhere out there was David. For a moment, Max could not picture his friend's face, and it shamed him.

He walked away from the window and stared at his reflection in a mirror of polished silver. It was a handsome youth who stared back, but the eyes had grown hard. With a callused finger, Max traced a thin white scar that sliced from cheekbone to chin—one of many such souvenirs that now marked him.

There was a soft knock on the door.

Max turned as Scathach entered. She wore an embroidered robe of white linen and carried a green bundle of silk. This she lay upon the bed.

"Tomorrow, you shall depart Rodrubân," she said, avoiding his gaze.

"And where will I go?" asked Max.

"The others know," she said. "They will be waiting at the bridge at first light."

Max nodded and stepped over to inspect the bundle. Unfolding it, he saw the broken spear and Señor Lorca's shirt of nanomail. On top of the nanomail, however, was something else: a brooch of silver and ivory fashioned in the shape of a sun. Max examined it under the candlelight.

"What is this?" he asked.

"Something to remember us by," she said softly, kissing him once on the cheek. She turned and walked swiftly from the room, pausing for a moment on the threshold. "Never forget that you are the son of a king."

"Will I see him again?" asked Max.

"No," replied Scathach, shutting the door behind her.

* * *

In the morning, Max waited within the courtyard while the drawbridge was lowered. He stepped over the threshold and onto a fringe of wet grass. Waiting across the bridge was David, leaning against a farmer's cart pulled by a weathered mare, white in the muzzle. A bent, cloaked driver held the reins. In the distance, Max heard the ring of the blacksmith's hammer. He walked across the docile bridge to meet his grinning roommate once again.

"You're taller," said David, shielding his eyes from the sun.

"You look exactly the same," said Max, clapping David on the shoulder.

The driver rapped a stick impatiently against the cart.

"We must be going," croaked an ancient voice. Max turned to see a gray-haired woman, her face seamed and shriveled, peering at him from beneath a brown hood.

"And who are you?" asked Max.

"Caillech," muttered the woman, scowling and turning away to face the road before them.

David shrugged at the woman's rudeness and climbed into the cart, whose floor was strewn with hay. Max looked one more time upon Rodrubân. He hoped to glimpse a slender, black-haired figure standing at a window, but saw only ravens riding on the wind.

~ 16 ~

DRIFT AND MASTERY

The cart rattled along the worn cobblestones, pulled by the plodding mare. As the morning mists subsided and the sun rose high, they clopped past orchards, cottages, and a tall white tower that had come to ruin. Caillech was silent, merely clucking her tongue whenever the horse slowed to nose at a flower or nibble at the roadside grass. David had many questions, however, and listened with great interest as Max told him of his training and trials at Rodrubân. Max shared many things, but he said very little of Lugh and nothing of the paternal claim that troubled him.

"What about you?" asked Max. "What did you do all this time?"

"Chores and trades," said David, smiling. "I can fetch water, clean stables, feed animals, dye wool, and make a painful pair of shoes."

"Sounds awful," said Max.

"It's the happiest I've ever been," said David, uncovering a basket to offer Max an apple. "And I don't think it's boasting to say I'm the best one-handed cobbler in all the Sidh!"

Max smiled.

"What of Astaroth?" he asked, the Demon seeming a distant memory under the warm sun.

"Only rumors." David shrugged. "Occasionally, a traveler will arrive with tales of a strange being waiting at crossroads, jesting with passersby. Wherever Astaroth is from, it isn't from here. Even in the Sidh, I think they're afraid of him."

"And how did you . . . ?" whispered Max, inclining his head at Caillech's bent form, clutching the reins.

"Meet our friendly driver?" said David, smiling. "Last night I was cleaning the cobbler's shop when she knocked. Not so much as a hello. Just a 'On the morn, we fetch your prize,' and she pushed past me to sleep in *my* bed! Weird, I know, but weirdness is the way here—everyone coming and going on strange, secret errands."

"And where is she taking us?" asked Max.

"Brugh na Boinne," rasped Caillech, shooing away a horsefly.

Max sat up straight and turned toward their driver. Since his decision at the crossroads, that name had haunted Max's dreams: Astaroth had said his mother would be there.

"How far is it?" asked Max urgently.

"Far," replied the crone.

"Can't we go any faster?" asked Max, watching the nag's head bob in time with its plodding pace.

Caillech laughed—a low, mirthless croaking.

"There was once a man who saw Death staring at him in the marketplace," she muttered. "Afraid, the man stole a horse and rode as fast as he could to the next town. Once there, he took a room at an inn and locked himself inside. But there was Death, already waiting by the fire. 'How?' cried the man. 'How can you be here?' Death smiled and stood. 'I asked myself the same when I saw you at the marketplace, for it is here that I was to meet you.'"

Caillech laughed again and shook her head. Max said nothing, but glanced instead at David. His roommate seemed lost in thought, however, gazing quietly at the mossy remains of a wall built long ago.

For a stretch of days, they rattled along through sun and showers and wind as they followed the white road, winding through the green countryside. At times, they saw armies flying different colors, marching like glittering ants in the distance. When pressed for details, Caillech merely shrugged and said that the kingdoms of the Sidh often fought with one another. Max found the pace maddening; Caillech slept like the dead and on some days she couldn't be roused before noon. When awake, she was miserable company—chewing her lip in silence or muttering hoarse, cryptic replies to Max's many questions.

Early one afternoon, Max was jostled from his daydreams as the cart came to a halt. Caillech scratched her head and swiveled to gaze at the road behind them. She scowled and spat into the road.

"What is it, Caillech?" asked David cautiously.

"This is not the road to Brugh na Boinne," she said at length, looking past them.

Max exploded.

"What do you mean?" he cried, smacking the side of the cart. He stood and looked behind them. Theirs was the only road in sight.

"This is not the road to Brugh na Boinne," repeated Caillech.

"And it took you this long to realize it?" asked Max, incredulous. He buried his head in his hands. "Do you have *any* idea where you're going?"

Caillech stared at Max. Her dark eyes narrowed to angry creases.

"Do *you*?" she asked.

Max swallowed his reply; it took all his effort to smother his temper.

"Take the reins yourself or be still, you impudent child!" hissed the crone.

Max remained standing, staring at Caillech with rising anger. After a moment, David spoke.

"She didn't mean to take the wrong way," he said gently. "Sit back down, Max."

Max nodded but kept his eyes on their driver, who returned his glare with a defiant scowl. Sinking back into the cart, Max knitted his fingers behind his head and stared up at the sky. The mare snorted and they began the slow, laborious process of turning the cart around.

The miles passed and it was nearing twilight, but they had yet to see a crossroads. Even David's cheerful whistling grated on Max's nerves. Rolling onto his side, Max flicked his finger against the cart's rough planks and tried to smother his irritation. He sighed as the horse gave a tired whinny and the cart slowed to a snail's pace. Glancing up at the sky, Max saw they still had a smidgeon of sun remaining.

"We're not stopping yet," he snapped, shutting his eyes and rubbing at his temples.

"We are here," croaked the old woman as the cart rolled to a stop.

"And where is here?" snapped Max.

"Brugh na Boinne," replied Caillech.

Max cracked an eye open. David was standing up in the cart, gazing at something ahead of them. Sitting up, Max turned and blinked. The road had come to an abrupt end, tunneling into the side of a great hill studded with rocks and roots. Max climbed from the cart and stared.

"But we didn't come this way before," he said, glancing sharply at David. "And haven't we been on the same road this whole time?"

David nodded and shivered, rubbing his arms as the sun's last rays began to fade at the horizon. While the landscape darkened about them, a pale light glimmered from the hill's dark opening. Faint and veiled it began, but as the light grew stronger, its flickering luminescence spilled out from the hill like a welcoming light. A fire was burning inside.

A tingling arose in Max's neck and fingers, the same sensation he'd experienced when he discovered the tapestry.

Caillech stepped down from her seat and hobbled toward the cave's opening.

"What are you fools waiting for?" she hissed. Bent nearly to the ground, the old woman shuffled inside. Max took David's pack from the smaller boy and closed his fingers around Cúchulain's spear. Side by side, the two boys walked into the earth.

The road did not end at the hill but continued within it. Max and David's footsteps echoed off the cobblestones as they descended slowly, following a long, slow curve. Yellow firelight flickered on the walls, broken by Caillech's shadow, which looked misshapen and monstrous as she muttered and shuffled ahead of them.

At last, the road ended, terminating at a large cave deep within the hill. Many tapestries hung along the walls, illuminated by a massive brazier that burned at the cavern's center. Against the far wall was an alabaster dais and upon its smooth white surface were several objects.

"Behold!" croaked Caillech. "The Four Treasures of the Tuatha dé Danann and that which you seek!"

Following Caillech around the burning brazier, Max and David approached the dais. The crone pointed a bony finger at an enormous cauldron of etched bronze from which protruded a heavy shaft of wood.

"The Dagda's Cauldron," she muttered. "They say it can feed an army and raise the dead. And within it, the Spear of Lugh—deadly to all save his kin and so terrible, it must sleep beneath water laced with poppies. And there is the Sword of Nuada, Claíomh Solais," she gasped, pointing at a gleaming sword of silver. "And next to it, Lia Fáil—the stone that was kingmaker until Cúchulain himself split it in two!"

Max walked over to the stone, running his hand over its rough surface to the smooth, sharp plane where it had been halved. He glanced at the weapon he carried and wondered if it had done the deed long ago. David passed behind him, arriving at the last object on the dais.

There, suspended within a case of blown glass, was the Book of Thoth. David and Max peered closely at it. The glass distorted its appearance, but some details could be seen. It had a cover of tarnished gold, etched with hieroglyphs and the profile of an ibis-headed man—the Egyptian god himself. With a sharp intake of breath, David tried to lift the case. It did not move.

"Let me help," said Max, taking hold of the glass and giving a heave.

The case remained fast and the two boys were left staring at the Book as though it were a pastry beneath a domed cake plate. David gasped suddenly and fished frantically inside his shirt. He brought out Bram's talisman, holding it gingerly by its slender chain.

It was glowing a dull red, the heat within it intensifying even as they watched.

"We have to hurry," muttered David, wrenching the chain off his neck and tossing the hot medallion aside. "The Book's in danger."

Max stepped back as David began to chant. Strange words rang through the cavern, powerful spells that seemed to make the very earth hush and listen. Nothing happened, however, and Max saw that David was frustrated. His words became songs, lilting chants and melodies that saturated the air until it hummed with magic. Still the glass remained. The songs became whispers—slow, terrible words that echoed off the walls and whispered back, distant and mocking. David bowed his head and the echoes subsided to silence. He raised his eyebrows and glanced wearily at Max.

"I'm so sorry," he sighed. "I must have lost my touch."

Max had a sudden flash of memory.

"You haven't lost anything," Max cried, shaking his friend in his excitement. "Remember Bram's Riddle?" Max almost hyperventilated as he recited the poem's second verse.

> For there the book doth lie with those
> Who sleep beneath both hill and tree.
> But keep in mind, dear Sorcerer,
> No spell will pry its secrets free.

"You're right," said David, blinking slowly. "Magic won't open it at all."

"Whatever you mean to do, you must decide soon," muttered Caillech. "The door above is still open!"

The woman's words smacked of menace. Max turned and stared at the medallion.

It was smoldering now, issuing steady waves of heat.

Max felt a sudden tickling at his neck—Mr. Sikes fluttered at his ear.

"The spear!" squeaked the imp. "The magic spear will free the Book, Master McDaniels! The Demon is coming! Oh, you must be quick for all our sakes!"

Max swallowed and glanced again at the cavern entrance, half expecting to see Astaroth's smiling face peering from the darkness. Caillech shut her eyes, making a hasty sign against evil. David merely stared at the smoldering medallion.

"Now!" pleaded Mr. Sikes, his voice no louder than a tiny squeak. "With all your heart, strike swift and true!"

Max gripped the *gae bolga* tight and turned to eye the Book. With a sudden stride, Max raised the spearhead up and swung its razor edge straight down onto the glass. There was a sound like a thunderclap, a flash of pain, and Max was flung backward to the base of the brazier. Sitting up, Max clutched his arm, which had gone numb. He scrambled to his feet, glaring at the Book of Thoth, which remained suspended within the undamaged case. David and Caillech stared at him in silence, their eyes wide with shock. Turning to retrieve Cúchulain's spear, Max gasped.

The *gae bolga* had shattered into a hundred sharp fragments that were scattered across the cavern floor. Max stood and blinked at the glittering shards for several moments. Without a word, he walked across the room and tore a tapestry from the wall. Neither Caillech nor David dared to speak while Max crawled about on his knees, retrieving every last shard of metal and splinter of bone until they lay in a little pile on the tapestry. When all had been recovered, Max folded the cloth upon itself.

"Are you okay?" asked David.

"I'm fine," Max lied, walking to stow the bundled tapestry within David's pack. His voice was soft and calm. "I just wasn't strong enough—it was a stupid mistake."

Caillech said nothing.

"No," David said slowly. "I don't think it was a stupid mistake at all. You did the right thing. After all, *you're* not broken—the spear is. *It* wasn't strong enough."

Max looked at the other objects on the dais and came to a sudden, sinking conclusion. There were *two* spears in the cavern; he had chosen the wrong one.

Frowning, Max stepped decisively over to the cauldron and reached inside for the Spear of Lugh.

"No!" David cried, waving his arm. "Don't touch it! Use the sword—Caillech said that spear will kill you!"

Max paused a moment, remembering back to his brief audience in the throne room at Rodrubân. There was a calm, quiet truth to the words Lugh had spoken. Max now cast aside his misgivings; he was indeed the High King's son. As the realization washed over him, he was vaguely aware that David was pleading with him to back away from the half-submerged spear.

"It can't hurt me, David," muttered Max, closing his eyes as he pulled the heavy weapon from the water. The cauldron began to hiss and boil. A bloodcurdling wail issued from the spear as it was lifted above the water's surface. A slow trickle of blood bubbled from the spear's point to course down its length and stain Max's fingers. David shrieked and backed away from the terrifying thing as Max turned to face the Book. Once again, he brought a spearhead down against the glass. This time there was no pain.

A satisfying impact shivered up his arm as the Spear of Lugh pierced the case in a flash of white light. Glass rained down upon the cavern floor in thousands of tiny pieces. The Book of Thoth remained suspended in the air, while the spear writhed and screamed in Max's hands. Staggering back toward the cauldron, Max plunged the weapon back into the water. The cauldron steamed and frothed for several moments and then was still.

"You've done it," Caillech sighed, steadying her frail form against the dais before lowering herself to the ground. She leaned her bent back against the alabaster and breathed deeply. "Well done, my boy. I have waited a long time for this."

Wiping the blood from his hands, Max smiled at her. For the first time, Max saw the old woman smile, too. She turned to look at David, who plucked the Book from where it hovered in the air and cradled it against his chest.

"Now what?" asked Max.

"Now you must go home," croaked Caillech. "And take this Book from the Sidh, where it does not belong. It was not made here and cannot stay."

"How?" asked Max, remembering the *Kestrel*'s wreckage. "How do we get home?"

"With this," breathed David, running his hand over its golden cover. "The Book will show us."

Sitting cross-legged next to Caillech, David opened the Book of Thoth and touched his fingers to its thin sheets of papyrus. The only sound was that of the flickering torches as David pored over its many pages and strange, exquisite symbols.

Max paced the cavern, watching his shadow creep and glide along the walls and tapestries. Occasionally, he glanced at the medallion, which had been giving off a bright, pulsing glow. David would not be rushed, however, choosing to ignore Max's grumbles while he devoted all his attention to the Book. He dribbled the remaining vials of Maya's wondrous blood onto the Book's pages to decipher its contents. The blood beaded like droplets of quicksilver, skittering across the pages until the papyrus absorbed them. Turning a delicate page, David spoke, his eyes glistening with tears.

"It's so beautiful," he said. "So much simpler than I ever expected."

"You understand them, then?" asked Max. "The symbols and things?"

"It's not just the symbols," breathed David. "It's their sequence; it's their shape; it's everything! And I *do*! I do understand them!"

His face alight with wonder, David lifted his hand and spoke.

"Mllthias braga cibil fah."

Max blinked. David began to laugh; there upon his hand were a pair of birds. The birds were small and smooth, with long beaks and brilliant blue feathers flecked with yellow. They chirruped and hopped up David's arm to peer at his face.

"What kind of birds are those?" asked Max.

"I don't know," breathed David, smiling at them. "They don't have a name yet—at least not a common one. They didn't exist before, Max! These are the first two!"

Max walked over and bent close to look at them. They were beautiful and delicate, with shiny black eyes that peered up at him unafraid. Of course, they'd have no reason to be afraid, Max realized. They had no memories or evolved instincts to shape their view of the world or its inhabitants. All was new to them. They had simply sprung from David's words, shaped from

nothingness. Caillech was speechless, casting a wary eye upon the birds as one hopped into Max's hands.

"What should we call them?" asked David. "You choose a name, Max."

Max glanced at David and back to the brilliant blue bird in his hand. He felt like a naturalist stumbling upon the Galapagos, giddy with the possibility of naming so many things as yet unknown. Just as he was about to speak, however, there was an unexpected flash of light.

Bram's talisman had burst into a phosphorescent flame.

Black smoke guttered from the melting metal and Max's heart began to pound. Another voice sounded in the room.

"Why not call them Folly and Hubris and have done with it?"

Max turned and saw Astaroth standing upon the road's last cobblestones. The Demon smiled and extended his hand. The birds abruptly flew from Max and David, swift and darting as hummingbirds, to land upon his open palm. Astaroth's eyes crinkled into merry slits.

"Lovely work, David," he said, inspecting the birds closely. "But do not be greedy and keep such fragile beauties to yourself. You should share your creations with the Sidh! Its inhabitants will be most delighted."

Then Astaroth whispered to the birds and stroked each upon the head; they promptly hopped from his palm and sped from the cavern. Astaroth watched them go, their chirrups fading as they flew away. Turning back to David, Astaroth leaned out, over the last white cobbles, and extended his hands.

"Now be a good boy, David, and bring me the Book before you make any more mischief."

"No," said David, clutching the miraculous artifact to his chest.

"You are clever and can speak its secrets," warned Astaroth, "but you do not truly understand the Book of Thoth and its possibilities. No mortal can. Your life is but a flicker, David, while I burn bright and eternal. The Book of Thoth is not meant for one such as you. Its mastery is not in your nature. Even now, Elias Bram rails at your foolishness."

"Elias Bram is dead," said David.

"His body, but not his being," replied Astaroth with a slow shake of his head. "Beneath the halls of Solas, I spent my last breaths consuming him. Bram's spark—his soul—lives within me and bears witness to my victory. It must be torturous indeed for Bram to know that you have undone all his painstaking work and recovered for me what I could never have obtained on my own."

"But Bram's letter!" cried David. "The talisman! He *told* us to seek the Book and keep it from you! I—I verified them!"

"No, David," said Astaroth. "*I* told you to seek the Book and keep it from me. The letters and talisman are mine, planted by my servants, and you have danced to my tune, a merry little puppet indeed!"

Astaroth clapped his soft hands together, filling the cavern with an echoing applause. The Demon's eyes flicked at Max; he raised an eyebrow in amusement.

"You see, Max? There *are* fates worse than death. Now, convince your friend to surrender the Book, or I shall have to punish you."

Max's fear turned to anger. He stabbed a finger at Astaroth.

"You promised you wouldn't hurt us while we were in the Sidh, but you lied! You promised I'd see my mother beneath Brugh na Boinne and you lied again!"

"I've done no such thing," said the Demon, shaking his head with a sly smile. "Don't press false charges on me, Max McDaniels, hoping to invoke the Old Magic. I have not lied at all. While you are in the Sidh, I will not touch a hair upon your head. And your mother sits behind you, Max, though not so fair as once she was. It is *she* who will bear the brunt of my wrath and beg for a death denied her. And *that*, my boy, is a promise!"

Max whirled to gaze at Caillech, who looked old and broken as she leaned against the dais. Her eyes met Max's and she smiled, giving a gentle nod. Max rushed to her side.

"Why didn't you tell me?" he asked, only now gleaning a hint of his mother's features peeking out from within the seamed and ancient face.

"I was forbidden to," Bryn McDaniels replied, squeezing his hand and blinking away her tears.

"Do you wish more pain upon her, Max?" called the Demon. "I can sear the skin from her flesh and crack her shins to suck the marrow, and *still* she will not die."

Max stood and looked at David, who held the Book tight within his arms.

"Max," said David, "I can't! I *can't* give the Book to Astaroth!"

"David's right," said Max's mother. "Do not trouble over me. My life is spent."

"David would have her burn, Max!" hissed the Demon. "He cares nothing for flesh and blood or the bonds of family. Knowledge is his one true love!"

Turning, Max stared at David. His hands began to shake once more.

"Max . . . ," David whispered, taking a cautious step backward.

Max ignored his friend's plea and turned his attention to Dagda's Cauldron and the terrible spear sleeping within it. Gripping the spear, Max met David's eyes once again and made his decision.

The spear gave a shrill cry as it was wrenched from the water. Eyes widening with rage, Max took one hop at David before casting the weapon at Astaroth with all the strength in his body. The screaming spear crossed the cavern in a blur, impaling the Demon where he stood.

Astaroth howled with pain and clutched at the spear embedded in his belly. The surrounding cavern began to collapse, as though the magic that sustained it had been spent. Bits of rock fell from the cave's roof while its walls sagged and spilled inward.

Holding the Book open, David yelled more strange words. The burning brazier tipped over and crashed onto the floor, sending burning coals skittering across the cavern as though pulled by invisible strings. A tapestry promptly ignited, its pastoral image blackening quickly under sheets of bright flame.

"Into the tapestry!" shouted David, running forward to tug at Max and his mother. "Quickly, before it burns away!"

There was no time to argue. Max grabbed David's pack and hoisted his frail mother up off the cavern floor.

Astaroth's agony was deafening. Max turned and saw the Demon wrench the spear slowly from his belly. For a moment, their eyes met, and Max almost went mad with fear. The burning tapestry loomed ahead, yet through the smoke Max swore he could glimpse Old Tom's tower. Holding his mother tight, he held his breath and leapt through the flames.

~ 17 ~

THE TALE OF
DEIRDRE FALLOW

Max and David emerged through the burning tapestry into the sudden shock of cold air. They were standing on the hedged lawns before Old Tom, whose clock shone white and luminescent. Behind them, Max glimpsed a terrifying sight. Through the flame-wreathed portal back into the Sidh—through the smoke and rubble—Max could still see Astaroth. The Demon was clutching the awful wound in his stomach, peering intently at the burning gateway as though trying to gauge where they had gone. From the cavern came an inhuman cry that made Max want to fall to the ground and cover his ears. Flames consumed the opening, destroying the portal and leaving them in the dark and quiet of a winter night at Rowan.

Gasps and muffled voices sounded from the steps and walkways. Max set his mother gently on her feet while gawking students and faculty hurried over from the academic buildings to see what was happening. Bryn McDaniels clutched her son's arm and sank slowly to the ground, sitting on a crusted patch of snow. Max huddled next to her.

"Dad is here," he whispered, hugging her close to keep her warm. "You'll see him soon."

"I'm so glad," she said, peering out at the surrounding campus.

Shadows loomed, dark and jagged on the bright snow. Max looked up to see Commander Vilyak and several members of the Red Branch standing before them, looking grim. All were armed.

"You're back," muttered Vilyak, shining a lantern upon their faces.

"Yes, sir," said Max. "We have to get her inside."

Vilyak paused a moment, scanning the faint scars and taller boy before him. Visibly puzzled but apparently satisfied, he glanced at Mrs. McDaniels. "And who is she?"

"Bryn McDaniels, sir. My mother," explained Max, helping her to her feet. "She's a graduate of Rowan."

Mrs. McDaniels blinked at Commander Vilyak.

"It's Deirdre Fallow," she said. Max said nothing but stared at the snow upon hearing the unfamiliar name. Apparently, more surprises were in store.

"Deirdre Fallow?" gasped Commander Vilyak, stepping closer to shine the lantern on her face. "What *happened*? Where have you been all these years?"

"A long story," said Mrs. McDaniels. "And I cannot tell it now—I am so very tired."

"We're taking her to the healing ward," said Max, helping her past the Agents, who readily parted for them. "Please tell Ms. Richter that David needs to see her immediately."

"Whatever you need to tell Gabrielle, you can tell me," said Commander Vilyak. "The Director is very busy."

"I'd rather tell her myself," said David, coughing into his collar.

"And I'd rather hear it directly from David," said Ms. Richter, walking smoothly across the snow, wrapped in a white shawl. She acknowledged Commander Vilyak with a nod before stopping to look at Max and his mother. A kind, understanding smile passed over her face as she gazed at Mrs. McDaniels. "Hello, Deirdre," she said. "This is an unexpected but very pleasant surprise. I did not think we would see you again. I look forward to a long chat when you've rested."

Walking forward, Ms. Richter placed a protective arm around David. Together, the four of them walked past the assembling onlookers and onto the Manse's broad stone steps.

"Ms. Richter?" asked David while the Director shooed away a trio of gawking First Years. "How long have we been gone?"

"Over three weeks," replied the Director. "We were beginning to lose hope. I trust you were successful?"

"I'm not sure," said David, hugging the Book tightly to his chest and following Ms. Richter down the hallway to her office. Max escorted his mother to the ward, pausing every few steps so she could catch her breath.

When the Moomenhovens had tucked Mrs. McDaniels into a soft bed with a stitched quilt, Max made his way up the stairs and down the corridors to his father's door. Mr. McDaniels answered on the second knock, rubbing at his eyes and blinking groggily. He had not shaved for days and looked a mess. For several seconds, his father did not say anything; Max imagined it must be quite a strange thing to look upon a loved one last seen sailing off into the blue.

"Am I dreaming?" his father asked at length.

"No, Dad," said Max. "I'm here. I'm back."

Scott McDaniels reached out a hand and cupped Max's strong chin, his eyes wandering over the faint and fading scars.

"You look different, Max—older."

"I *am* older, Dad," said Max softly. "I've been away a lot longer than three weeks."

"How can that be?" said Mr. McDaniels with a hesitant smile. "Where were you, Max? Where have you been all this time?"

"Far away," said Max. "Under hills—in a different time. A strange place."

"I wanted to go with you," said Scott McDaniels hoarsely. "It's a terrible thing to watch your boy go off into the unknown."

"I know, Dad," said Max. "Let's step inside. There's something I need to tell you."

Inside Scott McDaniels's room, the two sat on the edge of a rumpled bed that was still warm. Max reached for a framed photograph of his family taken when he was eight. He stared at the image of his mother, confirming that the sleeping woman in the ward was really she. Any remaining doubts fell away and in a quiet, patient voice he explained to his father that his mother had been found and was indeed alive, resting within the Manse. Max's insides knotted into icy cords as he watched his father's face flicker and then ignite suddenly into joy.

"There's something you have to know," said Max firmly. "Mom's not how you remember her."

Mr. McDaniels glanced sharply at him; his smile began to fade.

"What do you mean?" he asked. "Is she hurt?"

"No," said Max. "She's not hurt exactly. I don't know how else to say this, but she's old now."

"What are you talking about?" chuckled Mr. McDaniels. "She's only forty-two!"

"Not anymore," said Max gently. "Time is different in the Sidh. Only three *weeks* have passed here since David and I left, but I've been gone for a long time. It's been three *years* since Mom disappeared, Dad. She's a very old woman now. . . ."

"I'm going to her," said Scott McDaniels abruptly, standing up from the bed. Fastening his robe, he walked quickly to a mirror and ran his hand over his stubble. "I don't want her to see me this way," he muttered, filling the sink with water and briskly lathering his face with foam.

Rosy-cheeked and freshly shaved, Scott McDaniels put on his best shirt and gave his shoes a second glance before he and Max made their way to the ward. As they walked, Max informed him that Bryn McDaniels had also attended Rowan and that people here knew her as Deirdre Fallow.

"Don't be ridiculous!" snapped Mr. McDaniels. "Your mother's maiden name is Bryn Branson Cabot, and she attended St. Mary's Preparatory School in New Hampshire. I've seen her birth certificate and yearbooks, for cryin' out loud!"

"I'm just telling you what I heard," said Max. "It's all a lot for me, too."

"I know it is," his father muttered. "I'm sorry."

Quiet as mice, they crept into the ward where the Moomenhovens had already laid out chairs and a sleeping cot. Max's mother did not stir. Scott McDaniels stood for a long time, his hands deep in his pockets. He finally eased into a seat to gaze thoughtfully at her tranquil face. There, in the low firelight, the two sat while the Moomenhovens knitted and frost patterned the glass.

* * *

At first light, Max's mother awoke. Mr. McDaniels smiled and patted her hand while her eyes wandered slowly over his face, from the watery blue of his eyes to the deep dimple in his chin.

"Not much to look at, am I?" she managed.

"You're the most beautiful woman in the world," replied her husband, leaning close to kiss her cheek. She sighed and gave him an amused if disbelieving smile. Reaching out a fragile hand, she clutched his finger.

"I have some explaining to do," she whispered. "You two must be very angry with me."

"What happened that day, Bryn?" asked Scott McDaniels. "Why did you go away?"

"I received a visitor," she murmured. "Someone from a life I thought I had left behind."

Scott McDaniels nodded slowly, his face grave. One of the Moomenhovens hurried over with hot tea while Max and Mr. McDaniels propped up his mother on some pillows. She took a few tentative sips, and her voice became stronger.

"My visitor was a prescient I had known when I was a student here," she continued. "He prophesied that my son would someday be lost—lost within the Sidh unless I was there to guide him home. The day was Midsummer and that very night a penumbral eclipse of the moon occurred. It is a most rare occurrence, my loves—a time when a gateway might be found to the Sidh. There was no time to lose! We made our way to Ireland, where he led me to a door on the banks of the river Boyne. For a time, I wavered—aware of the terrible pain I would cause. Dawn approached and the doorway began to fade. I went through. And there I have lived—within the Sidh, waiting for the day I would be needed. I have missed you more than I can say."

"And who is Deirdre Fallow?" asked Scott McDaniels.

"*I* was Deirdre Fallow," explained Mrs. McDaniels. "Until I left Rowan behind and would become your Bryn. Bryn was the life I chose, Scott—a life with you and away from all of this. I found happiness as Bryn McDaniels."

"So you never attended St. Mary's?" asked Mr. McDaniels, looking confused.

"No," she said. "My new life required a new identity. I'm sorry."

"Did you know William Cooper, Mom?" asked Max, suddenly remembering Cooper's strange reaction to the photograph.

"Yes," said his mother, sounding surprised. "He was a year ahead of me. We were sweethearts here, if you can believe it! He was a lovely person—serious, but lovely. They whisked him away to active service after graduation and we fell out of touch."

"He looked after us, you know," said Max. "Dad and me and David and the others on our journey."

"And where is he now?" asked Mrs. McDaniels, smiling. "I'd like to see him again. William could always make me laugh!"

"I don't know, Mom," said Max. "We lost him in Germany."

"Oh," she said quietly. "I'm so very sorry."

Throughout this drift in the conversation, Mr. McDaniels remained silent—a rounded block with a forward lean and a contemplative face. He abruptly stood up.

"You must be hungry," he said. "What can I get you?"

"Oh, I'm not so hungry," said Mrs. McDaniels. "Old age gobbles up the appetite."

She chuckled, but Max and his father did not.

"No, no," said Mr. McDaniels, wringing his hands. "How 'bout Belgian waffles? You used to love 'em and I'll bet they didn't have any in the Sheee—or whatever it's called. You can't say no to golden-brown waffles with fresh maple syrup!"

"Okay," said Mrs. McDaniels, smiling. "Breakfast in bed it is. I'll be spoiled before long!"

"Back in a jiffy," said Scott McDaniels, kissing her on the forehead. He walked briskly from the room, visibly pleased to be of service. Once he disappeared outside the door, Max's mother sighed.

"The sweetest soul I've ever known," she whispered. "How I've missed him." She turned a pair of penetrating eyes upon her son. "I know who rules at Rodrubân, Max," she said at last. "And I gather you now know his relationship to *you*?"

Max nodded and stared at the quilt's red stitching.

"It's awkward to discuss this, but I want you to know that I was never unfaithful to my husband," she said. "Before you were born, Lugh came to me in my sleep and told me I would give birth to a marvelous boy. The boy would be a son of the Sidh—Cúchulain reborn. Of course, I passed it off as a ridiculous dream." Her eyes brightened. "You were such a beautiful baby! The nurses cooed and my heart nearly burst with pride to have such a fine son. And Scott! He rocked you back and forth while you squeezed his finger so tight it turned blue!"

They laughed together and Max reached for the small, gnarled hand that lay atop the quilt. It was no more than a wedge of bone and gristle and papery skin. He patted the fragile thing as she spoke, aware that she had been weakening appreciably ever since they'd found the Book.

"As you grew older, I knew it was no dream," she continued. "It pained me to see you suffer so, always wrestling with that monstrous spark within you. You straddle two worlds, Max, mortal and immortal. I could feel the Old Magic growing—burning you from within and biding its time. Do you remember those terrible days?"

"I do," said Max quietly. "I could never sleep. And the headaches . . . I thought I would die."

"But you did not," she said, shaking her head. "You managed as best you could. And now I must ask you to manage one more thing, if you can."

"Of course," said Max, leaning forward. His mother's voice was hushed and urgent.

"*Never* tell Scott the circumstances behind your birth," she whispered. "You're all he has, Max! He has loved you as his son since before you were born. It would do no good to share such a secret."

Max hastily wiped away a tear.

"I already made up my mind on all of that," he said, summoning a smile. "My father lives at Rodrubân; my dad lives at Rowan."

His mother said nothing but squeezed his hand with all the strength she could muster.

"You're a fine young man," she whispered.

Several minutes later, Mr. McDaniels returned with a covered tray.

"Voilà!" he said, setting the tray upon the bed. Upon a plate were four steaming waffles, a small pitcher of syrup, and a glass of fresh juice.

"Dear me," said Mrs. McDaniels, "I might die of shock. These aren't, er . . ."

"Burnt!" said Scott McDaniels triumphantly. "Yes, I know—I've learned a thing or two as well, my dear. Bob's a heckuva teacher."

"How *is* Bob?" inquired Mrs. McDaniels. "I used to chat

with him in the kitchens until that awful hag arrived. I can't imagine *she's* still here—tricked a First Year into a cooking pot! Poor thing thought it was all a funny game until he was floating in chicken broth and sliced carrots. Thank god Kraken arrived to put an end to it! Oh, what was her name?"

"Her name is Mum and she can hear you!" bellowed the hag from just beyond the doors.

"I should have said something," said Mr. McDaniels, cutting his wife's waffles into small bites. "You have visitors—lots of them, whenever you're ready. Should I send them away?"

"Absolutely not," said Mrs. McDaniels. "I'd love to see them—Mum, too!"

In came Bob and a scowling Mum. Following behind were Miss Awolowo, Mr. Vincenti, and Nolan, who held a sleek black bundle in his arms. The Director came last.

"Deirdre Fallow," exclaimed Nolan, stooping to kiss the top of her head. "When I heard the news I couldn't believe it! Deirdre Fallow back after all these years and Max's mother to boot! Who knew?"

Everyone laughed and greeted her in a flurry of careful hugs and well-wishes. Nolan laid the dark bundle upon the quilt. It moved and Max saw it was a cat so black that tinges of midnight blue rippled through its fur. Luminous yellow eyes blinked as it stirred from sleep.

"Isis!" exclaimed Mrs. McDaniels, reaching out a hand to stroke the cat's fur. "I didn't know if she . . ."

"Was still kickin'?" asked Nolan with an amused twinkle in his eye. "Yes, indeed. Sleeps most days, though."

Isis turned her head and sniffed Max's mother. A deep, contented purring sounded as the cat pawed and patted her way up the quilt, nestling her head beneath Mrs. McDaniels's chin.

"Isis was my charge, Max," explained his mother, stroking the cat's glossy fur. "I wasn't sure if she was still alive, much less whether she'd remember me."

"Some things don't change," said Nolan, smiling.

"And some things *do*!" declared Mum, elbowing past Nolan to peer closely at Max's mother. "I'll have you know I'm now a reformed hag and utterly indispensable to this establishment!" Mum suddenly abandoned her rant and sniffed casually along Mrs. McDaniels's wrist. "Yes, yes, I remember you now," she mumbled to herself. "Skinny girl with black hair; very suspicious— always watching. Should be served with a starchy side. Yes, yes . . . hmmm," she said, sniffing again. She eyed Max and seized his wrist suddenly, inhaling deeply. "How I never put the two of you together is beyond me!" she exclaimed. "Mother and son, sure as Bel and me are sisters. I ought to have my sniffer examined. . . ."

With a massive hand, Bob gently tugged Mum away, reaching over her head to lay a bundle of roses on the bed.

"Welcome home, Deirdre," said Bob, patting the covered lump of her foot. "Bob has missed his little Fallow. Or should Bob call you Bryn?"

Mrs. McDaniels glanced at Max and her husband.

"Bryn," she said decisively. "I am Bryn McDaniels now."

Max listened in fascination as the visiting faculty pulled up chairs and began to share a history of his mother he had never known. Apparently, she'd been an excellent student—winning Macon's Quill for academic achievement with offers to join her pick of field offices. As proud as he was, it was strange for Max to imagine his mother walking the same paths, attending the same classes—even having some of the same instructors that he had.

"Has Sir Alistair retired?" she asked, referring to Rowan's expert on diplomacy and etiquette.

"No," said Miss Awolowo.

Mrs. McDaniels said nothing but rolled her eyes, to the amusement of all.

The conversation soon turned to questions of the Sidh. According to her account, Mrs. McDaniels had spent a good deal of time wandering about, learning the strange rules, laws, and customs of the place: which rivers were perilous, how to skirt the many marching armies, which kingdoms were to be avoided during certain months and moons. While sharing her stories, she perked up considerably, and Max felt a flutter of hope that perhaps the effects of the Sidh would fade and the accumulated years peel away like layers of paint to reveal the mother he remembered.

A slow, sharp rapping sound snapped his attention back.

Peter Varga stood in the doorway.

He was thinner than when Max had last seen him, but his prescient eye still stared white and ghostly within its dark, lidded socket. The rest of his face was handsome, if sallow. Since the previous spring, he had been spending his days rehabilitating after the dreadful injuries he suffered from Marley Augur. Peter limped into the room, leaning heavily on a sturdy cane and dragging his right foot.

Max bristled at the sight of him.

"What are *you* doing here?" he demanded, rising to his feet.

Peter glanced at Max's mother, his eyes wandering over her gray hair and wrinkled skin.

"I came to welcome Deirdre back," he said quietly.

"Her name is Bryn McDaniels," said Max, "and she's my mother and this is all because of you."

Peter winced at Max's words. He opened his mouth to say something before shutting it once again.

"Should I go?" he asked finally.

"No," said Mrs. McDaniels, beckoning him over. "You are not to blame, Peter. Your vision was correct—I *was* needed in the Sidh."

"What do you mean, he's not to blame?" seethed Max. "He's the reason you're old! He's the reason the witches want David! He's probably the one helping Astaroth to get the Book!"

"Max," warned Ms. Richter, shaking her head.

"But it's true," said Max, stabbing a finger at Peter. "Did David tell you, Director? We have another traitor! Someone with access to the Archives! A traitor planted that letter and talisman so we'd go fetch the Book for Astaroth!"

"Max!" said Ms. Richter, demanding silence with a curt gesture.

Max glanced at each of his parents. Then he shook off Nolan's restraining hand and dashed toward the exit, letting the doors swing wildly behind him. As he rushed down the hallway, he passed a bewildered Hannah and her goslings as they waddled toward the healing ward.

"Max, honey?" called Hannah, concerned. He did not stop to answer.

Out of the Manse and into the bright morning he ran, almost knocking over some older students and an elderly couple walking their dog. He raced through the orchard and down the path to the Smithy, punching in the codes that would take him down to the Course.

Once in the trophy room, Max glanced at Macon's Quill and hurried onto the second elevator that descended to the scenario chambers. Several Sixth Years widened their eyes as he hurried in to join them before the doors could close. Max leaned against the brass railing and closed his eyes; the elevator still had the familiar smell of wood polish, sweat, and machine oil.

"Er, what level do you want?" asked a tall South African boy.

"Nine," said Max quietly.

"Seriously now," said the boy with a nervous chuckle. Level Nine was never accessed; the button's Roman numeral gleamed perfectly crisp and sharp compared to its worn and rounded neighbors.

"Level Nine," Max repeated, staring at the floor.

"Be my guest," said the Sixth Year, backing away from the panel.

Max leaned over and pressed the button. A woman's voice sounded from a speaker above them.

"Voice authorization required."

"Max McDaniels," he growled, stepping back to his spot.

"Access granted."

The elevator rocketed straight down, accelerating to dizzying speeds until it stopped at Level Five. The Sixth Years hurried out, a jumble of whispers and sidelong glances.

"Bye," said Max, glancing up, but the older students just stared at him until the doors shut once again.

Down and down he went, lost in his thoughts, until the elevator finally came to a halt. When the doors opened, Max found himself staring at a very rumpled-looking analyst. The man coughed and straightened his glasses, patting down his hair in a futile attempt to pretend he had not been sleeping.

"Special Agent McDaniels?" the man said, nodding politely at Max.

"Yeah," said Max, blinking at the title. He glanced at the red mark on his wrist. "I guess so."

"I'm Jürgen Mosel," said the man. "The analyst assigned to Level Nine. I'm honored to finally meet you and I apologize that I'm not more prepared. It's just that . . . no one ever really comes down here."

Max glided past him, taking in a small octagonal room furnished with a desk, a computer monitor, and a couch whose cushions betrayed the fading imprint of the disheveled analyst.

"Where's the programming panel?" asked Max, gazing at the single silver door across from the elevator. There were none of the usual controls.

"Nothing to program," said Jürgen with a shrug. "Level Nine scenarios are randomly generated—you're not to have any idea what to expect. I'm told objectives are revealed as you go. Before you enter that chamber, however, I'm required to warn you that—"

Nodding dreamily through the unsettling disclaimers, Max focused instead on the rising tide of energy and emotions within him. When Jürgen had finished, Max opened the door a crack and gazed in silence upon a void. The emptiness before him was almost tangible, endless stretches of numbing blackness. He thrust his hand forward and watched it submerge in the abyss as though he'd plunged it into a tub of ink. Slipping inside, Max closed the door behind him. He felt his body pulled gently but irresistibly away until his fingers slipped from the doorknob and he drifted out into the void.

Two hours later, Max emerged from the chamber to find the monitoring room filled with people. Jürgen had been relegated to an irrelevant seat on the couch, while members of the Red Branch spoke quietly to one another. Commander Vilyak was at the desk, peering intently at the computer screen. He tapped it several times and scowled.

"You there," he said, beckoning at Jürgen. "Something's not working. The screen's gone white."

While Jürgen fiddled with the computer, Vilyak rounded the desk to grip Max's sweaty, shaking hand.

"We came as soon as we heard," he gushed. "Sneaking off to Level Nine without so much as an auxiliary? Ha! I knew you were worthy of the Red Branch."

Raising Max's brand high in the air for the others to see, Commander Vilyak quickly made introductions. Max tried to remember the nine names—six men, three women—but he was exhausted and mumbled through his hellos. Despite their different races and nationalities, they all shared a common calm demeanor. With one or two exceptions, most appeared to be middle-aged. All had lean, purposeful faces.

"Have you fixed it yet?" called Vilyak to the analyst.

"I don't think there's anything to fix, sir," replied Jürgen.

Vilyak frowned and rounded the desk to peer at the screen.

"Of course there is," he barked, jabbing a finger at the screen. "Before I could see, now I can't!"

"I understand, sir," said Jürgen. "But nothing indicates any sort of malfunction. What you see—or *don't* see—is what actually occurred in the scenario."

Max walked over and peered at the screen while Vilyak scrolled back impatiently. There was Max, in the center of a circular chamber. Within the scenario, he was blindfolded and his right arm had been bound behind him. He clutched a thick wooden baton while his final adversaries surrounded him. There were no monstrous or supernatural enemies in this scenario— Max's opponents were the other members of the Red Branch, including Cooper. Vilyak slowed the images to a crawl as the assailants closed like a noose.

Max blinked at the scene; even in slow motion, his image skipped across the screen. Knives flashed, but the baton smoothly parried them and then swung in a blur, cracking against ribs, knees, knuckles, and cheekbones with appalling accuracy. Weapons were knocked away and opponents crushed down to the floor, where they scrambled away to regroup and attack again. In the midst of all the activity was Max, a beautiful, harmonious whirl of motion and feints as he sensed his opponents' positions and anticipated their every move.

As the fight raged on, however, he had begun to tire. Max winced as he saw the replay of Cooper's pommel crashing into the base of his neck. In the split second that his legs buckled, the others were upon him. As he was being borne to the ground, the image was suddenly lost in a flash of white light. Text appeared on the screen:

SCENARIO COMPLETED
OVERALL SCORE: 92

"How can it be a ninety-two?" asked Vilyak. "He was overcome."

"Er . . . I beg your pardon, sir," said Jürgen, calling up another screen and directing the Commander's attention to the readout. "But Max is the only one who survived."

Vilyak blinked and read the report, his eyes darting rapidly across the screen.

"Extraordinary," he muttered, rewinding the recording to study the lethal patterns and arcs of Max's movements. "What style is that you're using? It's not ours."

"It doesn't have a name," said Max. Scathach had no use for such things.

"And what happened here?" Vilyak asked as the moment arrived when the screen went white.

"I don't remember," said Max truthfully.

Vilyak glanced sharply at him, his black eyes disbelieving.

"Well," he said, sighing and tapping the blank screen, "perhaps

in time you'll share your secrets, eh? But we have not come solely
to applaud your performance, Max. There is an important meeting you must attend. They are waiting for us to begin now."

Several hundred attendees had convened in Maggie, crowded
upon the many benches of a large Mystics classroom. Entering
behind Vilyak, Max saw many of the older faculty and scholars
seated, looking rather curious and uneasy as they chatted quietly
amongst one another. Among them were dozens of unfamiliar
Agents and Mystics, recent arrivals from Rowan's fallen field offices. Max spied Rasmussen sitting at the far end of the first
bench. The man's eyes widened in apparent surprise before offering Max a sly, knowing smile. Ignoring him, Max took a seat
among the other members of the Red Branch. Vilyak strode to
the lectern.

"Thank you for waiting," he said. "Before we begin, I must
ask that each of you sign this document that I will circulate. It is
a Binding Scroll. Upon signing it, you will be unable to share any
aspect of this meeting, its attendees, or its content to any exter-
nal party until the deed is done. It is for your protection as well
as my own. Are we agreed?"

"Agreed," said the other participants. Max watched a long
cream-colored scroll snake its way swiftly through the crowd,
passed from hand to hand as each attendee signed under the
watchful gaze of the Red Branch. When the scroll came to Max,
he hesitated a moment, wondering what sort of meeting could
possibly require such secrecy. He glanced about for the faculty
he knew well; none were in attendance. The supervising Agent
placed the pen in his hand and gazed at him impassively. Max
was about to sign when there was a knock on the door.

"It is the boy," said Vilyak. "Let him in."

Another Red Branch member strode to the door and opened it. Max could not see who was there, but heard an exclamation of surprise—of joy even. The attendees leaned forward to glimpse whoever had arrived. Footsteps sounded. Max gaped as Connor Lynch strode confidently into the room, giving a jaunty salute to Vilyak before taking a seat on the first bench.

Another figure walked into the room, accompanied by the Red Branch Agent.

It was Cooper.

Max scribbled his name and passed the scroll to the next person as Cooper walked forward and exchanged quiet words with Vilyak, who embraced him like a son. Making his way through the attendees, Cooper took a moment to scrawl his name on the scroll before taking a seat next to Max. The Agent turned his ruined face to look full upon him. Many scars, some very fresh, twisted into the hint of a smile.

"Cooper!" Max whispered, beaming. He was bursting with a hundred questions.

The Agent patted Max on the shoulder and put a finger to his lips as Vilyak began to speak.

"Well, this is a most auspicious beginning," said Vilyak, rolling up the scroll once the signatures were complete. His gaze flitted from face to face; his authoritative voice filled the lecture hall.

"I will speak plainly—I know no other way. I've asked each of you here to discuss the current crisis of leadership that plagues Rowan and is driving her toward ruin. While we all acknowledge that Gabrielle Richter is a fine woman with many excellent qualities, the fact remains that her policies and decisions as Director have thrust us to the brink of catastrophe. Since her mishandling of the witches, we operate under threat of a curse, have driven the witches to Astaroth's camp, abandoned the field offices, and failed the Workshop in their hour of need. We now stand alone—a crippled, hidden harbor for refugees—while all outside falls under Astaroth's sway. The one bit of recent hope is the acquisition of the Book of Origins, achieved through the heroic efforts of Agent McDaniels, who has replaced Antonio de Lorca among the Red Branch. With the addition of this bargaining chip, a moment of truth has arrived when those who love Rowan must act on her behalf. You are here because I know you to be patriots who recognize that our first loyalty must be to Rowan and not to any one individual. It is time for decisive action."

"Hear, hear," called several people.

An elderly Mystic raised her voice. "What do you have in mind?" she asked.

"Three things," replied Commander Vilyak. "The first and most immediate is the deposal of Gabrielle Richter as Director. We do not have time for the ordinary protocols, and thus I propose that the Founder's Ring be taken by whatever means necessary and that she be confined to the Hollows forthwith."

"That's treason!" gasped an elderly woman who taught in the Languages department.

Max glanced in shock at Cooper, but the Agent merely stared stonily ahead.

"Second," continued Vilyak, barreling through the woman's protests, which continued until her neighbors hushed her, "that I take possession of the Founder's Ring and resume leadership as Director, invested with all necessary authority to command and negotiate on Rowan's behalf.

"And finally," he concluded, "that we meet with the witches, the Workshop, and Astaroth's emissaries to negotiate an agreement that is satisfactory to all. Even before we had the Book in our possession, I have been assured that our proposal would meet with a favorable reception."

Max leaned forward to glimpse Rasmussen, who sat with his hands folded on his lap, nodding as Vilyak spoke. One of the other Agents, a bearded Scot with a fringe of red hair, spoke up.

"And what is this proposal?"

"It is simple," said Vilyak. "In exchange for its allegiance, Rowan shall be left alone, free to administer its own domain without interference from Astaroth. This domain will comprise all of New England and New York State. We will accept refugees from other regions as our capacity allows, giving strict preference to those with needed skills. Current inhabitants who do not meet our requirements will be deported."

"Deported *where*, exactly?" asked the Languages instructor.

"That is not yet determined," said Vilyak coolly, registering the questioner with a glance. "Rest assured, they will be looked after. Where was I? Oh yes—Jesper Rasmussen is to be re-instated in charge of the Frankfurt Workshop, and together we will pursue a policy of closer cooperation. Meanwhile, we will eliminate the threat of a curse by placating the witches and hon-oring a portion of their old agreement with Elias Bram. David Menlo will be given unto them, as he should have been last au-tumn."

Max had opened his mouth to protest when he felt Cooper's hard fingers dig into his hand. The Agent's jaw tightened and he gave a barely imperceptible shake of his head; Max was to keep silent.

"And what of the Book?" asked an anxious scholar.

"The Book will stay with Rowan," said Vilyak proudly. "The threat of its power will ensure that Astaroth honors our agree-ment. Its secrets will help us to rebuild our strength; we will not only persevere but, in time, achieve the might and glory of our forebears."

"Negotiating with Astaroth?" muttered a willowy Mystic. "This sounds like surrender! It goes against everything we stand for!"

"What we *stand for*, Miss Chen, is the continued survival of the human race," said Vilyak, tapping his finger against the lectern. "I am ensuring that survival. And I take issue with your use of the term *surrender*. Those who surrender neither expand their territory nor dictate the terms of their peace and autonomous rule. That is what I intend to do. Perhaps you would prefer that we continue with this foolish charade of fractured resistance until we have squandered all basis for meaningful negotiations? Is this what you are proposing, Miss Chen?"

The woman shook her head and glanced meekly at those around her. Vilyak sighed and rested his hands on the lectern.

"My friends, I do not pretend that we would choose this unhappy course of events. But each of us has been taught that effective decision making requires an objective assessment of the situation. This is not the time for heroic stands or idealistic posturing; this is a time for survival. I urge you to consider carefully what I have said. I require your answer by tomorrow morning."

An ancient-looking Mystic in navy robes spoke up.

"It seems to me that a very important detail is missing from your proposal," he said. "How do you intend to depose the Director? She is most formidable and has the support of many."

Commander Vilyak smiled at the question.

"Leave that to the Red Branch."

~ 18 ~
THE DAWN SKIFF

Max and Cooper walked out together, lingering behind the others and pausing on Maggie's cold stone steps to watch smoke trickling from the Manse's many chimneys.

"This is terrible, Cooper," said Max. "We have to warn Ms. Richter."

"You can't," said Cooper quietly. "The Binding Scroll won't permit it."

"There must be a way," insisted Max.

"You're to do nothing that endangers you or David," said Cooper coldly. "Never forget the order I gave you: you are to protect David Menlo and keep him alive at all costs."

"David and I got the Book," said Max. "The DarkMatter operation is over."

Cooper shook his head and pulled his coat closer about him. "The order stands."

Old Tom rang the noon chimes, startling a pair of crows into flight. People streamed toward the Manse, where lunch would be served in the dining hall. Max watched them go: parents, grandparents, students, and siblings filing toward the broad stone steps. He glanced hopelessly toward the sea, which was a hazy gray beyond David's veil where seagulls called like ghosts.

"What are we going to do, Cooper?"

"I don't know yet," said the Agent. "I'll know more when I get my instructions. In the meantime, you're to do nothing that suggests disloyalty to Vilyak. It could be very dangerous to you and your family."

"My mother's here, you know," said Max. "David and I found her in the Sidh. Actually, she found us."

"I heard," said Cooper, his voice softening.

"She said you two used to be sweethearts," said Max.

"That was a long time ago," said Cooper quietly.

"I'm going to see her now," said Max. "Will you come?"

The Agent hesitated, touching his fingertips to the many scars and patches of taut skin that marred his once-handsome face.

"I will."

Mrs. McDaniels and Isis were dozing when Max and Cooper entered the healing ward. The visitors had departed, leaving Peter Varga and Mr. McDaniels in quiet conversation. Upon seeing Cooper, Mr. McDaniels dropped his soup spoon. He stood quickly and crossed to the door to shake the Agent's hand.

"William Cooper!" he sputtered. "When did you . . . ? *How* did you . . . ?"

"Just now, and very carefully," replied the Agent. "It's good to see you again, Scott."

"Is that William?" called Bryn McDaniels from the bed. Max's spirits sank at the sound of her voice; it had weakened to little more than a sigh.

"It is," said Cooper, removing his cap and clutching it between his fingers. He approached tentatively, stopping several feet away.

"Come closer so I can see you," croaked Mrs. McDaniels, stroking Isis's sleek coat.

Cooper cleared his throat and kneeled by the bedside.

"There you are," she said, her eyes searching the ruins of Cooper's face. "I am so happy to see you, William. I want to thank you for protecting my boys."

"It was my honor, Deirdre," said Cooper, letting her touch his scars and the taut patches of shiny skin.

"Long time," said Bryn McDaniels.

"Twenty-five years," said Cooper.

"Much longer than that," said Mrs. McDaniels with a twinkle as she glanced at her frail hands. "Where is my son?"

"I'm here, Mom," said Max, walking round to take his father's seat.

"Good," she said, turning slowly to look at him. "Sit with me for a bit, Max. Your father was reading me my Tennyson before I dozed off like a silly girl. Maybe he'll read some more?"

"Of course," said Mr. McDaniels, sitting on the edge of a cot and plucking up a book covered with worn brown leather. He put on his reading glasses and thumbed through the yellowed pages, stopping at a sliver of green ribbon. As he read, his deep, soothing voice conjured images of myrrh thickets and Arabian nights and the sorrowful Lady of Shalott, while Max held his mother's hand and Cooper kneeled at her side. Peter Varga sat in silence, his fingers knitted atop his cane while the poems wove their magic. Max watched the black gloss of Isis's fur rise and fall in a steady rhythm while the hour passed, measured in faint ticks by the clock on the mantel.

> Old age hath yet his honour and his toil;
> Death closes all: but something ere the end,
> Some work of noble note, may yet be done,
> Not unbecoming men that strove with Gods.
> The lights begin to twinkle from the rocks:
> The long day wanes: the slow moon climbs: the deep
> Moans round with many voices. Come, my friends,
> 'Tis not too late to seek a newer world.
> Push off, and sitting well in order smite
> The sounding furrows; for my purpose holds
> To sail beyond the sunset, and the baths
> Of all the western stars, until I die.
> It may be that the gulfs will wash us down:
> It may be we shall touch the Happy Isles,
> And see the great Achilles, whom we knew.
> Tho' much is taken, much abides; and tho'
> We are not now that strength which in old days
> Moved earth and heaven; that which we are, we are;
> One equal temper of heroic hearts,
> Made weak by time and fate, but strong in will
> To strive, to seek, to find, and not to yield.

Max felt a tiny pressure, an infinitesimal squeeze from his mother's hand as the poem ended. He glanced at her face. Bryn McDaniels lay in tranquil repose, her eyes closed in a gentle smile while she clutched her charge to her breast. Isis had stopped breathing and Max knew, in an instant of agonizing clarity, that both had passed. Removing his mother's hand from his own, he kissed it and laid it gently on the quilt.

"She's gone," he said.

"Hmmm?" asked his father, licking his thumb and turning the page.

"She's gone, Dad," said Max.

Cooper stood and made way for Max's father. Scott McDaniels bent close, gently feeling for her pulse while he smoothed a few stray hairs from her forehead. Carefully sliding Tennyson's poems beneath her arm, he turned to them. His eyes were filled with tears, but he managed a smile.

"I—I want to thank you for being here at the end," he stammered. "I'm so happy that my Bryn was able to pass in a soft bed surrounded by people she loved. To even see her again . . . well, it's more than I'd hoped for these past few years."

Peter Varga and Cooper stood to pay their respects to Max and his father. Before leaving, Cooper paused in the doorway and looked upon Bryn McDaniels one last time. His eyes flicked to Max and the Agent touched two fingers to his forehead in a farewell salute.

Scott McDaniels hugged his son tight and whispered that Max should go. Max nodded and walked quietly to the door. His father sat heavily at the foot of the bed while the Moomenhovens busied themselves with bandages and bowls of camphor oil.

David was in their room when Max entered, sitting cross-legged on his bed with the Book of Origins.

"That man was just here looking for you," said David.

"Who?" asked Max, shutting the door.

"Vilyak," said David. "Where have you been?"

"With my mom," Max whispered. "She died just now."

David closed the Book and looked at Max, his small face

looking very adult as he studied Max with an expression of concern and sympathy.

"I'm so sorry, Max."

"Thank you."

"Do you want to talk about it?" asked David.

"No," said Max, making his way toward his end of the room, where his sleigh bed was waiting. On the comforter was the folded tapestry that held the shards of Cúchulain's spear. Max moved it to the foot of the bed and removed Lorca's shirt of nanomail. Climbing between the sheets, Max pulled the covers to his chin, gazed up at the constellations, and assured himself that one more star now flickered bright among them.

A knock woke Max from sleep. He glanced at his watch; it was almost dinnertime. He heard David's footsteps patter to the door.

"If it's Vilyak, tell him I'm not here," called Max, pulling his pillow over his head.

David opened the door and Max could hear him speaking quietly with someone in the hallway. His roommate closed it once again and walked softly to Max's side of the room.

"It's Connor and the others," he said. "They brought you dinner. Should I send them away?"

"No," said Max, sitting up. He climbed from his bed and padded downstairs to throw on a sweater. Splashing water on his face, he looked hard at himself in the mirror before walking back upstairs to open the door. Connor stood outside with Sarah, Cynthia, and Lucia.

"Hi," said Max.

"We came as soon as we heard," said Sarah, hugging Max tightly. The others followed suit and filed in, bringing plates and bags and silverware. Cynthia set the table downstairs while Connor got a fire going.

"How is your father doing?" asked Sarah, wiping a tear away with her palm.

"He'll be okay," said Max.

"It is beautiful that you saw her again," said Lucia decisively.

"It was," said Max, smiling.

David walked over and returned the necklace that Cynthia had given them before they had stolen Bram's Key from the Archives.

"Ha!" said Cynthia, kissing the necklace and clasping it around her neck. "I knew I would get this back! And where has she been on her travels?"

"And how long has she been traveling?" asked Sarah thoughtfully, looking at Max, who had gained several inches on the tall Nigerian girl. Max felt self-conscious as their attention turned to him and the fading scars that laced his older-looking features.

"Far away and a long time," said David, piping up on Max's behalf. "We might have been there forever if it hadn't been for Mrs. McDaniels."

"Is that true?" asked Sarah.

"It is," said Max quietly. "We never would have found the Book or made it home without her."

"I suppose Richter's got it?" asked Connor, glancing quickly at Max. "The precious book that's got everyone whispering?"

"No," said David. "She wanted me to keep it safe."

"You've got it *here*?" asked Connor incredulously.

David nodded and pointed to his bed, where its golden cover could be seen peeking from beneath a fold of his comforter. Connor whistled and shook his head.

"All the world's dirty little secrets and they're just a-lyin' on an unmade bed."

"There's nothing *dirty* about them," said David defensively. "They're beautiful."

"Figure of speech, Davie," quipped Connor with a wink. "Let's go eat, eh?"

The boys and girls went downstairs and had supper together by the fire. As they ate, Max and David shared tales of the Sidh with their friends and Max was happy to laugh along with the others at David's stories from his days in the cobbler's shop. One involved a customer who apparently suffered from a forgetfulness curse and arrived at the shop each morning, loudly protesting that he'd been swindled, having paid for shoes he never received. The problem, of course, was that he had received them already and was, in fact, wearing them. Connor chuckled between bites of mashed potato.

"And he showed up each day?"

"Every single day," said David wearily. "He was really punctual, actually. Each morning, the cobbler and I would wager on whether he'd use old insults or invent new ones."

"And what would you tell 'im when he came in?" asked Connor.

"That we sympathized with his frustration, but certainly the excellent gentleman was in error and had forgotten that he had already taken possession of the shoes for which he had paid. We had a signed receipt to that effect and further proof was on his feet."

"And what would he say to that?" asked Cynthia, passing a bowl of green beans.

"Oh, he'd start to laugh and ask us if we thought him such a fool as to believe a crafty urchin who was clearly in league with the Evil One, as I have only a left hand, you see. 'Downright sinister!' he'd declare, and make the sign against evil. . . . Ooh!" said David, suddenly scanning the goodies the other had brought. "You didn't happen to bring coffee, did you?"

Sarah produced a thermos with a grin of triumph.

"Ah!" said David, twiddling his fingers with glee as she poured him a cup. "May the sun shine upon your splendid bosom in all eight kingdoms, Sarah lass!"

"David!" cried Cynthia as Sarah's mouth gaped in shock. David blushed furiously.

"Sorry," he squeaked. "It's just my bad translation of an old Sidh expression."

"Hmmm," said Sarah, raising an eyebrow and flicking Connor, who practically slid off his chair with laughter.

"Aw, Davie," said Connor, shaking his head. "We're gonna miss ya."

Max glanced sharply at Connor.

"I'm right here, Connor," said David. "No need to miss me."

"I meant we *have* missed you," corrected Connor, sitting up straight and reaching for a cookie. "It's a good thing that spell of yours kept us all hidden while you and Max were off in the Sidh," he said, deftly changing the topic.

"It'll stay until I dispel it," said David, happily sipping his coffee. "Even if I'm elsewhere."

"Must be a complicated bit of work," said Connor, doodling on a napkin.

"To cast, yes," said David, "but not to dispel. When the time's right, I can do away with it with a word."

"You're kidding," said Connor, bringing his distracted scribbles to a halt. "*Abracadabra* and it all comes crashing down?"

"David," warned Max, suddenly fearful that his roommate might share the perilous word. Max did not like the drift of Connor's questions. He longed to tell them of Vilyak's meeting, but found that the impulse strangely dissipated as soon as he began to open his mouth.

"It's okay, Max," said David. "I could write it on the front door and it wouldn't make any difference. I'm the only one at Rowan these days who can spark that word into action."

"Still," said Max, "it's best to keep it to yourself."

"Oh, c'mon!" said Connor, laughing as he tore at his thick chestnut curls. "You both know curiosity will drive me batty! You *have* to tell me, Davie."

"You're already batty," sniffed Lucia.

"Ha!" said Connor, thumping the table. "Could Batty Boy be acing all his classes?"

"*Please,*" said Cynthia. "We all know the secrets of your success, Connor. There's no point in pretending otherwise."

"And what's that supposed to mean?" snapped Connor defensively.

"Mr. Sikes," said Sarah. "We know he's been helping you with your classes."

"All right," said Connor, raising his hands. "I'll admit I *used* to summon Mr. Sikes for a bit of help. But I haven't used him in months."

The girls crossed their arms and offered disbelieving stares.

"Honest," said Connor, raising his hand as though to take an oath. "I, Connor Lynch, solemnly swear that I have not summoned Mr. Sikes since last fall. If I'm lying, may lightning strike me where I sit."

Lucia and Sarah abruptly moved their chairs away from him.

"Very funny," moped Connor.

There was a knock on the door. David started to get up, but Max waved him off and climbed up the stairs. Standing in the hallway was not Commander Vilyak but Mr. McDaniels.

"Dad," said Max, standing aside to let him in.

"Are you having a party?" asked his father, hearing the voices down below.

"No," said Max quickly. "Nothing like that—my friends just brought dinner."

"Oh," said Scott McDaniels. "That's nice. Mind if I pop down and say hello?"

Max shook his head and followed him down the steps to the lower level, where the other children promptly stood and offered their condolences.

"Thank you," said Max's father, accepting a hug from Cynthia. "It's awfully good of you to come and comfort Max."

"It's the least we could do," said Sarah. "Do you need anything?"

"No, Sarah," he said with a weary smile. "I just came by to tell Max that we'll be having the service at dawn tomorrow down at the beach. It would be nice if you all could come."

"We will," said Cynthia. "Is it okay if I bring my mum and brother?"

"And my parents, too?" asked Lucia. "They arrived last week."

"We'll bring everyone if it's all right with you, Mr. McDaniels," offered Sarah.

"Of course," said Mr. McDaniels. "That would be very nice. I'd like to stay, but there's lots to do."

"We should be going, too," said Cynthia, glancing at the others and stacking the plates.

Minutes later they filed out the door with parting hugs and promises to see Max first thing the next morning. Max watched the girls accompany Mr. McDaniels down the hallway. Connor lingered outside the door, waiting until David had gone inside and was out of earshot.

"I've got a message from Vilyak," whispered Connor, his ruddy face becoming deadly serious. "He extends his condolences and wants you to know you're off the hook. No assignment for you."

"What is he planning, Connor?" asked Max.

"Wish I knew," said Connor. "I'm just a messenger boy doing my job."

"And how did you get to be Vilyak's messenger boy?"

"Needs a pair of eyes and ears among the students, don't he?" Connor said with a shrug. "Seems to appreciate my talents even if the girls don't."

"*Why* are you doing this?" asked Max, almost pleading with his friend.

"Everything Vilyak said at that meeting was true and you know it, Max," said Connor. "The Director might be a fine and dandy peacetime administrator, but she ain't up to the job right now. My family's here, too, you know. I'm just glad I can do my part to keep 'em safe."

Max stared at his friend a moment, searching his face. Connor's eyes flickered with amused curiosity.

"What?" he asked.

"Who's here?" asked Max.

"My family, mate," repeated Connor, blinking. "You lose your hearing in the Sidh?"

"What are their names?" asked Max.

"Excuse me?" asked Connor, coughing into his hand.

"Their names," said Max, grabbing Connor's wrist. "Now."

"Mum, Dad, little Katie, and Uncle Liam," said Connor, ticking them off on his fingers. "Me mum's name is Margaret and Dad is Robert." The Irish boy frowned and jerked his wrist from Max's grip. "What gives?"

"Since when are you left-handed?" asked Max.

"What are you talking about?"

"You were doodling with your left hand downstairs," said Max.

"So what?" replied Connor with an exasperated shrug.

"Renard said it helps build motor control in the off hand. Jesus, does the Sidh make a boy paranoid, too?"

Max said nothing, but Connor sighed.

"Get some rest, Max," he said at length. "Tomorrow's a big day."

Giving Max a farewell pat on the shoulder, Connor slipped into his own room across the hall.

When the door had closed, Max hurried down the hallway and out of the Manse. His footsteps crunched on the ground as he wound past the steam-belching Smithy and the dark wall of trees lining the way to the Sanctuary.

Nick came at his call, cleaning his short, broad muzzle in the grass and licking his bloodied claws clean. The Sanctuary was nearly empty, just a few distant students carrying lanterns as they visited their charges in the Warming Lodge or cared for the clearing's nocturnal denizens. The lymrill seemed to sense something was amiss. There was no hiss or reproach or rat innards flung because of Max's long absence. The creature waddled close and pressed its body against Max's legs, giving its tail a soft rattle. Max scooped Nick into his arms and strode off toward the very thicket where he had first found the playful lymrill. Climbing high up into the boughs, Max held his heavy charge close and concentrated on a blue face with yellow cat's eyes.

Nick hissed and squirmed for a better look at Mr. Sikes when the small imp appeared, standing at the bough's end like an attentive butler.

"Master McDaniels," purred Mr. Sikes. "I feared you had forgotten all about me. I understand both congratulations and condolences are in order. Please allow me to offer both."

"That's not why I called you," snapped Max, restraining the lymrill, which seemed to regard the imp as an exotic dessert. "Have you possessed Connor Lynch?"

"I beg pardon?" asked the imp, widening its eyes at both the question and the lymrill's unblinking attention.

"Answer the question," said Max.

"Of course not, child," said Mr. Sikes. "My modest kind is hardly capable of such a thing. Any book on summoning will confirm it."

"Are you working with the Enemy?" asked Max, staring hard at the perplexed face before him.

"No," replied Mr. Sikes coolly. "I am not. And I would humbly ask that you devote *both* hands to your charming pet."

Max clutched Nick closer and ran his hands along the lymrill's quills to calm it. Momentarily appeased, Nick ceased struggling but continued to eye the imp hungrily, giving periodic snorts.

"Where have you been?" asked Max after a moment's pause. "Why didn't you come to Rodrûban with me? I was all alone there."

"I could not," explained Mr. Sikes. "That place is wound with many spells—no stowaways permitted. You may rest assured that I tried many times to visit, but I was always found and sent back. They are prejudiced against my kind there, I'm afraid. My troubles are of little consequence, however. The real question is how *you* are doing, Master McDaniels. It is a terrible thing for a boy to lose someone so dear. . . ."

Max nodded but said nothing. Throughout the night, he sat in the treetops and silently wept while Mr. Sikes's soothing voice spoke of hope and healing on the eve of his mother's funeral.

Before dawn, Max crept back to the Manse and padded down the hall to the showers. When he returned, David was already dressed in his formal Rowan uniform, sitting by the downstairs fireplace. Max carefully combed his hair and buttoned up his shirt before tackling his tie with stiff, mechanical movements.

His father was waiting in the foyer, dressed in a black suit. He took Max's hand and the two walked outside into the still, gray morning.

Along the paths they went, their way lit by the gas lamps that still burned bright in the gloom. They walked past Old Tom and Maggie and crossed to the rocky bluff, where they climbed carefully down the carved stone steps that led to the sea. Bob was already present, placing the last of many folding chairs that were arranged in neat rows. The ogre was dressed in an enormous black suit, and his craggy face was downcast as he ambled over to shake their hands.

"Is everything as you would wish?" asked the ogre.

"It is," said Mr. McDaniels, looking over the seating and fiddling with a paper in his breast pocket. "Was it difficult bringing everything down?"

"Not for Bob," said the ogre with a gentle smile. He pointed to a stretch of sand near the empty dock where the departed *Kestrel* had once been moored. There, on the beach, was a slim gray boat. Max saw his mother lying within it, wrapped in white silk, with her arms folded upon her breast.

"Good, good," said Mr. McDaniels, unfolding his paper and glancing at it. He thrust it at the ogre. "When the time comes, would you read this for me, Bob? I don't think I'll be up to it."

The ogre took the paper and peered at it through his monocle.

"Bob would be honored," he said, folding the paper and putting it in his shirt pocket.

Max and his father took the seats nearest the little skiff while people arrived, walking down the stone steps in small clusters as Nolan played a plain but beautiful tune on his old, worn fiddle. Hundreds came: faculty and students and families, arriving in silence until they filled the many seats or stood in the cold

sand or along the lawns atop the bluff. Max saw Bellagrog and
Mum dabbing at their eyes, the pair stuffed into ridiculous
dresses of black velvet and green doilies. Hannah waddled down
with the goslings, which followed after their mother without so
much as a disruptive peep. Max saw Ms. Richter sitting across
the way, flanked by Miss Awolowo and Miss Kraken. The Director's face was grave; her gray eyes stared out at the sea. When
the sun rose, a faint yellow haze beyond the thin veil of mist,
Nolan brought his playing to a close and Miss Awolowo stood.

She was dressed in beautiful black robes, with clacking
necklaces of jet and cowrie shells. With her regal carriage, she
walked across the beach to stand by the skiff. While her rich
voice carried over the sound of the gulls, Max knitted his hands
together and stared at the pale gray boat and the small, lifeless
body within it. He was vaguely aware that others spoke, too: Ms.
Richter, Miss Kraken, and an elderly teacher whom Max did not
know. When Bob stood, Max tore his eyes away from the skiff
and watched the ogre carefully unfold the paper. His lumpy features crinkled with concentration; his words rolled in Max's
mind, deep and hopeful.

> *Do not stand at my grave and weep,*
> *I am not there, I do not sleep.*
> *I am in a thousand winds that blow,*
> *I am the softly falling snow.*
> *I am the gentle showers of rain,*
> *I am the fields of ripening grain.*
> *I am in the morning hush,*
> *I am in the graceful rush*
> *Of beautiful birds in circling flight,*
> *I am the starshine of the night.*
> *I am in the flowers that bloom,*

I am in a quiet room.
I am in the birds that sing,
I am in each lovely thing.
Do not stand at my grave and cry,
I am not there. I do not die.

At the poem's conclusion, the ogre refolded the paper and handed it to Mr. McDaniels, whose shoulders shook. Bob looked out over the mourners and gestured for all to stand, and Nolan began to fiddle once again. Taking hold of the skiff, Bob slid it into the water. The ogre walked into the ocean up to his waist, guiding the boat through the rolling swells until he gave it a gentle push and it floated out upon the sea. Max watched the skiff go, bobbing like a cork on the gray swells, until it passed beyond Brigit's Vigil and was lost in the morning mist.

Bob led the mourners away from the beach and back up the stone steps. Max and his father filed out last, while Nolan continued playing behind them on the sand.

As Max climbed, a member of the Red Branch glided past them down the stairs, scarcely pausing to give them a second glance. Max was puzzled and stopped to watch the man's progress.

A sudden bellow erupted above them, followed by the sound of people screaming.

Leaving his father's side, Max dashed up the steps just in time to see Bob toppled onto the ground while another member of the Red Branch swiftly bound the struggling ogre. Several nearby people were unconscious, sprawled about the snow like scattered tenpins. Max heard Ms. Richter's voice call above the din, and he glimpsed her standing next to Cooper.

There was a sudden, terrible blow to the back of Max's head, and all went black.

* * *

Max awoke in the very bed where his mother had passed away. His tongue felt thick; his stomach rose and fell with nausea as the room came slowly into focus. His father sat at his side, still wearing his suit from the funeral. Max felt something move behind his head and was dimly aware of a Moomenhoven adjusting an icepack.

"What happened?" he murmured, his voice sounding funny in his ears.

"A coup," croaked his father sadly. "Vilyak says he's in charge now. Ms. Richter was knocked unconscious, and he stripped a ring from her finger before she was carried away with the others."

"Who?" asked Max, shutting his eyes.

"Bob," said Mr. McDaniels, "and Nolan. Awolowo, Kraken, Vincenti, and a bunch of other teachers, too. Cooper tried to help, but I guess Vilyak had been expecting it. Hazel practically went crazy trying to help William, but they got her, too—dragged them all off somewhere."

"Where?" asked Max, gesturing in frustration when the words were slow in coming.

"I don't know," said his father. "Somewhere in the Manse."

"The Hollows," whispered Max.

"Yes," said his father, nodding. "I think I heard one of them saying that."

Despite the thunderous pounding in his head, Max tried to sit up. His father shook his head and pushed Max back down onto the bed.

"No," said his father. "You need to lie still, Max."

"David?" asked Max.

His father's face fell.

"They got him, too," he said. "Caught him in some sort of

rope that made him go limp as a fish. I don't think he was hurt, though. I saw Connor taking him back to your room."

"Oh God," moaned Max, forcing himself off the pillow. "I've got to go—they're going to surrender David to the witches!"

"You can check on David later," said his father, trying to ease Max back down.

"There's no time, Dad," Max said, forcing himself up from the bed and staggering toward the door. The Moomenhovens tried to bar his way, but Max slipped past them and through the doors.

Staggering down the hallway, Max made his way to the shallow stairwell, clinging to the banister until he arrived in the foyer. Dashing down the hall to Ms. Richter's office, Max saw members of the Red Branch barring his way. A tall man with steel-gray hair intercepted Max and held him upright on his wobbly legs.

"Let me in," panted Max, struggling weakly against the iron-strong grip. "I have to talk to Vilyak."

"Director Vilyak's busy right now, McDaniels," said the man. "Sorry about that little tap I gave you earlier. Orders, you know."

Max glared at the man, who returned his gaze with unflinching calm. Ignoring the pain and dizziness in his head, Max strained and kicked and thrashed against the Agent's hold until several others had to help restrain him. The door to Ms. Richter's office swung open; Vilyak's angry voice filled the hallway.

"What is the meaning of this noise? I specifically ordered . . ."

His voice trailed away as his eyes fell upon Max.

"Agent McDaniels," he said quietly. "I'm pleased to see you up and about."

"What are you *doing*?" seethed Max.

"Serving Rowan's interests," replied Vilyak coolly. "Yours and mine and everyone else's, although you may not yet appreciate it. Come see for yourself."

At Vilyak's command, the Agents loosened their hold on Max and marched him into the office. Seated in chairs before Ms. Richter's desk were two robed figures. The first Max recognized as the witch he had last seen in the company of Astaroth. The second figure was robed in white and hooded, its face hidden behind a black, beaked mask similar to those worn by medieval healers. Astaroth's symbol was carved into its forehead.

"Greetings, Hound," said the witch, inclining her head.

"Dame Mako," breathed Max.

"Indeed," said Vilyak, seating himself behind Ms. Richter's desk. "Here also, at my invitation, is Astaroth's emissary, Lord Aamon."

The evil that radiated from the white-robed figure was nearly tangible. It bowed its head to acknowledge Max; no eyes could be seen behind the mask. Max felt he was staring into the very same abyss that had confronted him in the Course.

"How can you invite that here?" rasped Max.

"Our business is nearly concluded," said Vilyak. "And then our guest will go, never to return. Isn't that so, Lord Aamon?"

"The Book," whispered the masked figure, raising a gloved finger.

"I'd hoped we'd settled that," said Vilyak gruffly. "The Book stays here to ensure that you honor our pact. Fair is fair."

Something that might have been a laugh sounded from behind the mask. The figure leaned forward, its voice little more than a hiss.

"Two choices lie before you. You may give the Book unto Lord Astaroth as a token of your allegiance and be richly rewarded. Or you may spurn my lord's friendship and our servant will simply deliver the Book himself while Rowan reaps our wrath." The figure shrugged. "The Book is already ours, Yuri Vilyak. We merely extend you the courtesy of giving it to us."

"An empty threat," said Vilyak.

"It's within our reach even now, fool!" laughed the figure.

A terrible realization dawned upon Max. He wrenched himself free from the others and dashed out of the room. Racing to the foyer, he hurtled up the stairs to the third floor of the boys' dormitories. He galloped past startled students and adults, skidding finally to a stop before his door and fumbling for his key. Throwing the door open, he stepped inside and nearly screamed.

There, slumped against the foot of his bed, was David. A Passive Fetter had been fitted around his neck, glowing dully, while its other end was fastened to one of the bed's sturdy wooden legs. A sharp blade was pressed against David's throat by an assailant who cradled the Book of Origins.

The assailant was Connor Lynch.

"Now, Max," chided the ruddy-faced boy. "You're supposed to be sleeping."

~ 19 ~

A MIDNIGHT TEMPEST

"Connor," said Max quietly. "What do you think you're doing?"

"Actually, Master Lynch isn't here right now," came the reply, Connor's voice changing to a sly, sophisticated tone that was chillingly familiar. "You'll have to deal with me."

"Mr. Sikes," said Max, stepping further into the room.

"Quite right," said Connor, bowing his head with a wry smile. "I just need a moment more and I'll be on my way. Stay where you are unless you wish a glimpse inside David's pretty little throat."

"*You* put the letter and talisman in the Archives," said Max.

"Right again," said Mr. Sikes. "I've had free run of this campus ever since this little cock-a-whoop invited me in. After all, isn't Mr. Sikes just a harmless imp who brings lemonade and makes one's essays pretty?" Connor's possessed body laughed and shook its head. "Ah, and poor Connor thought he'd just blundered upon me out of sheer dumb luck! Poor boy. I almost feel sorry for him."

"You lied to me," said Max.

"Guilty as charged," said Mr. Sikes. "I'd apologize, Max, but we can't resist our nature—scorpions and frogs and whatnot. Had to keep you up late, though, didn't I? Gabbing away about your poor dead mother so you wouldn't dash off . . ."

Max thought back to the previous night. He had poured out his heart to the comforting imp, confiding every fear and misgiving to Mr. Sikes, who merely had been keeping him occupied until the funeral. The betrayal was so devastating and complete, Max almost became sick. He eyed the knife in Connor's hand.

"Don't hurt David," pleaded Max. "Don't hurt *either* of them."

"That remains to be seen," said the imp, placing a pen in David's hand. "Once your friend writes the word that will break his spell, I'll be on my merry way."

"*You* can't make it work," scoffed Max.

"Too true," admitted Mr. Sikes. "As you know, Mr. Sikes is but a humble imp. But his master can speak through his most trusted familiar, and Mr. Sikes's true master is most capable."

"And who is that?" asked Max.

"Astaroth himself," replied the imp. "I am his familiar, you see. And, unlike my fickle brethren, I've stayed true for over two millennia—even throughout his long imprisonment! For all his unwavering service, Mr. Sikes shall reap a most handsome reward. Who knows? Perhaps I'll even keep young Lynch as *my* servant. . . ."

At this, Mr. Sikes whispered again in David's ear. David blinked dully as though he'd been drugged, and scrawled a single word on the sheet of paper. Connor's hand snatched it from David's fingers, and he glanced at it a moment before incinerating the paper in a flash of green flame.

"You've got what you want," said Max. "Take the knife away from David."

"But there you are, blocking my way," said Mr. Sikes, a note of reprimand in his voice. "I'm leaving with this Book, Max McDaniels, and if you're a wise boy, you'll let me pass."

"The Book stays here," said Max.

"Have it your way," shrugged the imp. He winked at Max and sank the knife into David's side.

"Oh!" whispered David, sounding little more than mildly surprised, as he slumped against the footboard and slid to the floor. Max blinked, thinking perhaps Mr. Sikes had played a trick. David's response had been so calm, so quiet. . . .

Max glanced at David's chest and held his breath.

This was no trick.

A small stain blossomed like a red rose on David's dress shirt. The rose seemed to bloom and spread its petals, expanding quickly to nearly blanket David's side, until the blood saturated the fabric and trickled down in little streams to stain his tie and pants. Mr. Sikes leapt away from David, clutching the Book.

"I'll kill you," snarled Max, closing the distance between them in two blinks. Before Mr. Sikes could move, Max had seized him by the throat.

"Who would you be killing? *Me,* Connor Lynch, or David Menlo?" wheezed the demon, while Connor's eyes blazed bright with amusement. Max hesitated a moment.

Pop!

Where Connor had been, there was only empty air. The

Book of Origins fell to the floor, and Max watched a gypsy moth flutter out the open door. Max was nearly tempted to chase after it, but then he looked down to see his friend lying in a thickening red pool.

"Help!" cried Max, crouching down and ripping off the fetter as he put pressure on the wound. "Somebody *help*!"

Doors opened in the hallway. Rolf Luger stuck his head in the room.

"What's go—whoa!" exclaimed the boy, gaping in horror at the bloody scene before him.

"Get the healers," panted Max. "Hurry!"

Rolf's shouts and pounding footsteps receded down the hallway. Glancing about, Max saw David's pack lying within arm's reach on the bed. Seizing its strap, he swung it onto the floor and began fishing wildly through its depths for a jar of leftover Moomenhoven balm.

"Look at me, David," he said, squeezing his friend, whose eyelids fluttered. "You'll be fine—help's coming."

His fingers closed on a glass jar. Max snatched his hand out from the bag and saw that there was a bit of balm left, caked along the jar's bottom rim.

"C'mon, c'mon," he muttered, wrestling with the jar's stubborn lid. A few hard twists and the top clattered off. Max dug his fingers inside and scrabbled for every last bit of medicine. Glancing at his hand, he saw he'd managed a smear of ointment little bigger than a squeeze of toothpaste. Seizing hold of David's sopping shirt, Max felt for the tear and thrust his fingers inside to search for the wound. He felt it almost immediately— a fleshy gash of torn skin and splintered bone pumping blood thick as syrup. David gave a sudden, sharp intake of breath as Max spread the ointment around and into the wound.

"I know it hurts," Max muttered. "I'm sorry."

David wheezed and shut his eyes tight.

The two lay side by side on the floor, Max's palm pressed against the wound. After several minutes, frantic hoofsteps sounded in the hallway and a half dozen Moomenhovens hurried into the room, accompanied by Rolf. The plump, efficient healers gently pulled Max away while they cut away David's shirt and worked quickly to stanch the bleeding. Max stood, panting, and gazed down at his body, which was covered with David's blood. He saw Rolf, utterly white-faced, gaping in the doorway while other students crowded in behind him.

"I can't explain now," said Max, ignoring their questions. He wiped his hands on David's comforter and retrieved the Book of Origins from the floor. Stowing it in David's pack, he slung the leather strap over his shoulder and glanced down at the Moomenhovens. "Do you need anything?" he asked them. "Can I help you?"

The Moomenhovens shook their heads impatiently and waved Max away. Turning, Max saw yet another horrified face. Mr. McDaniels stood next to Rolf in the doorway.

"My God," breathed Max's father, gazing at the blood that spattered Max's clothes.

"I'm fine," said Max, hurrying over. "Stay with David, Dad. I'll come back as soon as I can!"

Clutching David's pack, Max squeezed past his father and Rolf, ignoring the growing crowd and running down the hallway. Leaping down the flights of the dormitory steps, he raced back to Ms. Richter's office. The door was open and there were raised voices inside.

Max hurried into the room and saw Vilyak, red-faced, leaning on the desk opposite Dame Mako. On the floor were Lord Aamon's empty clothes; the demon's mask had been cleaved cleanly in two.

"What happened?" asked Max, panting.

Vilyak took in Max's condition at a glance.

"I might ask you the same," he said, staring at the blood that stained Max's sleeve.

"David Menlo's been stabbed," he said, catching his breath.

"Will he live?" asked Vilyak, glancing at the witch.

"I don't know," said Max. "The Moomenhovens are with him now. He's hurt really bad."

"This is all Rowan's fault!" snapped Dame Mako. "If the boy had been sent to us as promised, this never would have happened! Our agreement is off, Director. By the blood and sacred oath of Elias Bram, I declare that Rowan's sons and daughters will fall stricken at their hour of need. The witches' curse is invoked!"

Dame Mako gathered up her robes and strode toward the door.

"Restrain her," growled Vilyak.

The witch spun on her heel and stabbed a sharp finger at him.

"How dare you threaten me!" she hissed. "I came here at your invitation and under your personal guarantee of safety, Director Vilyak. Do you wish to violate *that* sacred oath, too?"

For several moments, Vilyak merely stood and simmered. Suddenly, he swore and smacked his hand on the desk.

"Let her go!" he roared with a disgusted wave of his hand. Dame Mako glanced at Max and hurried past in a sweep of black robes. Vilyak, Max, and the other members of the Red Branch followed her out the front door and watched as she climbed inside the carriage. The team of black horses pulled away, trotting proudly down the long, straight road toward the sea before curving to the right and disappearing into the woods that led to the great gates.

"A discouraging day," murmured Vilyak quietly. He turned to Max. "Tell me what has happened. And, most importantly, where is the Book?"

"I don't know where the Book is," lied Max. "I only know that David's hidden it someplace safe."

Vilyak said nothing but stared at Max with a disbelieving glower. Max met his gaze and did not blink. At length, the man sighed and gestured wearily at Max's bloody clothes.

"And what does all this mean?" he asked.

"You can see for yourself," said Max, pointing toward a sky of bright blue, where the sun shone unseasonably warm. Shielding his eyes, Vilyak squinted toward the horizon while ice melted from the Manse's roof in a steady patter of drips.

"What?" snapped Vilyak, gesturing impatiently. "I see nothing."

"That's the problem," replied Max. "David's veil is gone."

That very day, Rowan began safeguarding its critical supplies and equipment. Classes were cancelled as generators, greenhouses, common foodstuffs, and priceless artworks were painstakingly disassembled or packed and carted away in slow progression through the Orchard and woods into the Sanctuary. Max learned that the Sanctuary extended farther back than he'd ever imagined and that a narrow gorge traversed the low range of snow-capped mountains that he'd always believed to be the Sanctuary's limits. Beyond this gorge, there was a great valley bisected by a swift river before it concluded at another range of gray mountains. A labyrinthine network of caves had been tunneled into these mountains, carved by Old Magic when Rowan was founded centuries before.

For Max, the weeks that followed were torturous. David lay in the healing ward, alive but far too weak to conjure his veil anew while he recuperated under the watchful eyes of the Moomenhovens. There had been no sign of Connor. Some students had seen him dash into the woods as David's spell had dissipated, but no Agents had been able to find him.

Despite the turn of events, Vilyak had refused to release Ms. Richter, Bob, Cooper, or any of the other captives taken on the day of the coup. Instead, the new Director often locked himself inside Ms. Richter's office, commiserating with Rasmussen or those Strategy instructors who had not been imprisoned. Since Dame Mako's departure, there had been no sight of the Enemy and no hint of the witches' curse. Rowan was faced with a gnawing uncertainty and a mounting sense of dread as days turned to weeks and winter began to subside. Arriving refugees were thoroughly screened, and Max's association with the Red Branch became common knowledge. He was assigned to long watches, keeping quiet vigil upon Rowan's gates or the broad, dark expanse of sea.

It was on such an assignment, late one evening in early March, when he heard footsteps approaching his perch on the rocky bluff above the beach. He turned at the sound and saw a pretty girl walking toward him, holding a lantern.

"Hi, Max," she said tentatively. "They told me you were out here."

"Hi," he replied.

"Do you mind if I sit down?" she asked.

"No," he said, moving over a bit on the flat-topped rock.

She placed the lantern on the ground and sat down to face the ocean. For several moments, she did not speak but merely tapped her fingers against the cold rock, while a cool wet breeze whisked in off the water.

"Does it get boring out here?" she asked.

"Not really," said Max, his eyes drifting to the rocks of Brigit's Vigil. "I kind of like it. It's quiet."

"You're so different now," said the girl with a sad smile. "You seem so much older, so much more serious than when you got here."

It was a curious thing for a stranger to say. Max turned to her.

"I'm sorry," he said, "but I don't know who you are."

The girl said nothing for several seconds while a thick bank of clouds passed before the moon, plunging them deeper into darkness.

"It's one thing to ignore me," she said. "I understand that you're probably angry, and you have a right to be. But it's another to pretend that you don't even know who I am. That's just rude."

"I'm not trying to be," he said, turning to reexamine her face in the soft yellow light. "I've never met you before and I don't know who you are. I'd remember."

"I'm Julie Teller," said the girl incredulously. "From Melbourne? I took your photo last year for the paper? We, er . . . kissed?" Max merely blinked and shook his head. Exasperated, she fumbled in her jacket pocket and retrieved a handful of letters, which she thrust at him. "Do you remember *these*?"

Max took the letters and turned them over. They were addressed to this girl in Max's own handwriting, postmarked from the previous summer. Reaching inside one of the envelopes, he removed its letter and read it. Several seconds later, he was blushing and his ears burned hot.

"That was the nicest letter I've ever received," the girl sighed. "I miss the boy who wrote it."

Max folded the letter quickly and stuffed it back in its envelope.

"I don't understand," he said quietly. "I don't remember you and I don't remember writing that."

"Something strange has happened," said Julie. "Last summer, I started having the same dream over and over. A little blue-skinned man with cat's eyes would appear and tell me that terrible things would happen if I so much as spoke to you. He came so often, I started to believe him."

"His name is Mr. Sikes," said Max quietly. "Never listen to him, Julie. He's very evil."

"Why would he visit *my* dreams?" she asked. "Why would he want to keep me away from you?"

"I think he wanted me to be alone," said Max, glancing at the letters. "I think he wanted me to confide in him—depend on him. It worked. I'm sorry for not remembering you . . . I'm sorry for everything." Max handed the letters back to her.

"I remember the day I'd heard you and David disappeared," she said, her eyes filling with tears. "No one knew where you'd gone. There were so many rumors—that the witches had taken you, that Cooper had murdered you. Anna Lundgren even said you'd gone over to the Enemy—I didn't know what to believe. And then you came back, and before I could talk to you, off you went—sailing away in the *Kestrel*. I thought I'd never see you again."

Max thought of the fates that had befallen David, Connor, and his mother.

"Maybe that would have been a good thing," he said quietly. "I'm to blame for all our problems."

"What a terrible thing to say, Max McDaniels," said Julie, placing her hand over his. "You sound like Anna Lundgren and that's beneath you. There's greatness in you . . . I can feel it." She tapped his arm, her breath misting in the night air. "My family's in the Sanctuary—they've heard all about you. From all the stories and rumors, my little brother thinks you're Achilles reborn!"

Max raised an eyebrow at this and she smiled.

"If we have to start over, then that's what we'll do," she said. "I'm Julie Teller. Pleased to meet you."

She leaned forward and gave Max's arm a squeeze, resting her head against his shoulder. Max shut his eyes, listening as Old Tom's bell chimed midnight with its hollow, soothing notes. Questions flitted through his mind like phantoms. When the last chime sounded, Max opened his eyes and gazed upon the sea once again.

Far out on the ocean, almost lost among the thin bands of fog, Max spied a glimmering light. It almost looked like a distant beacon, but Max had never seen a beacon there before. He blinked and rubbed his eyes. Another tiny light appeared next to the first. And then another. More glimmers emerged from the blackening gloom until it seemed that hundreds of tiny stars had spilled from the heavens and scattered like diamonds across the horizon. Max watched them in silence, strangely fascinated, as they twinkled and grew. The moon emerged from behind the clouds and cast the sea in a milky radiance. What Max witnessed made his heart skip a beat. He climbed slowly to his feet.

"Julie," he muttered, pulling her up. "Hurry back to the Sanctuary."

She opened her mouth to protest, but stopped as she followed Max's gaze toward the sea.

Hundreds of ships were sailing toward the beach, torches blazing at every prow.

The siege of Rowan was beginning.

As Julie retraced her steps along the frosted paths, Max raced toward Old Tom. He flung open the doors, dashing up the empty stairwells until he reached the summit of the clock tower.

Gripping the thick rope, Max pulled it toward him, causing the heavy bronze bell to swing back and forth against its clapper. Dissatisfied, Max seized a heavy mallet that was propped near some workman's tools. He swung the mallet against the bronze, over and over, until his eardrums nearly ruptured from the deafening ring. There was a terrible crack and Old Tom's bell broke from its supporting beam in a spray of broken timbers to embed itself in the floor. Coughing through plumes of dust, Max peered out the observation window and saw the lawns filling with curious onlookers. Among them he saw Vilyak, accompanied by Rasmussen and several members of the Red Branch.

"They're coming!" shouted Max, pointing out toward the ocean.

Dropping down the broken staircase and squeezing past the wreckage of the bell, Max hurried downstairs and back out to the bluff, where he found Vilyak staring out at the approaching armada in stunned silence. Many more ships had appeared; hundreds—perhaps even thousands—of lights converged on Rowan like a volley of burning arrows. Those in the forefront could now be seen in detail: ships with tall masts and black sails and decks that teemed with malevolent life.

"You did well to raise the warning, McDaniels," Vilyak muttered. "The Promethean Scholars are coming to mount a defense—everyone else must proceed to the Sanctuary."

"Fine," panted Max. "But that should include Ms. Richter and the others—you can't leave them in the Hollows."

"We don't have time," said Vilyak, shaking his head. "Those ships will land within the hour. We can only do so much to delay the Enemy."

"I'll get them," said Max, holding out his hand. "Give me the keys and tell me where to go."

"I'm afraid not," said Vilyak, turning on his heel.

Max spied Rasmussen standing nearby and gazing out at the fleet, which approached with the eerie majesty of an oncoming hurricane. Seizing the engineer by the sleeve, Max spun him around.

"*You* tell him," Max seethed. "Tell him that we need Ms. Richter—we need Cooper and Miss Boon." Rasmussen opened his mouth but said nothing. Max shook him. "Cooper saved your neck back at the Workshop. You owe it to him! They'll be helpless if we leave them here!"

Rasmussen blinked and nodded.

"Yuri," he called. Vilyak stopped and looked at the two of them as they hurried over. "Max is right," said Dr. Rasmussen. "Besides, we will need every resource you can muster."

Vilyak's face darkened; his lips twisted into a scowl.

"Sentimental nonsense," he said, reaching into his pocket and procuring a ring of worn iron keys. He tossed them at Max. "I have no time to spare—you'll have to find your way."

"Where should I look?" asked Max.

"Ask the *domovoi*," muttered Vilyak. "He was once the jailer, if I recall."

"Who?" asked Max.

"The jabbering loon who tidies the bathrooms," replied Vilyak.

"Jimmy?" asked Max, thinking of the strange little man who mopped the third-floor bathroom and terrorized those who forgot to bring him presents. "You mean *Jimmy* used to be the jailer?"

"I don't know what he calls himself," said Vilyak over his shoulder before he trotted away, barking orders to the Agents and minor Mystics who were assembling.

Max turned back to Rasmussen.

"Make sure my dad and David are taken to the Sanctuary," Max said. "Can you do that?"

"Why are you asking me?" asked Rasmussen.

"Because you owe them, too," said Max pointedly.

"I will," said Rasmussen, looking strangely moved. "I will look after them."

Max thanked him and tightened the strap of David's pack on his shoulder. Clutching the ring of keys, he dashed across the lawns toward the Manse, which was in a state of bedlam as panicked families and students streamed out the doors and hurried toward the Sanctuary. From out of Maggie's doors came the Promethean Scholars, twelve wizened Mystics clutching ancient books against their chests. They were led by Amulya Jain, who looked pale and downcast as the group headed toward the ocean overlook.

Arriving in the Manse's foyer, Max swam against a surging tide of bodies, pushing his way up the stairs until he arrived at the luxurious third-floor bathroom. Jimmy was perched on the marble sink, humming while he polished the belly of his porcelain Buddha.

"Max!" he exclaimed, upon seeing him. "Come in for a haircut? You look like a hippie."

"No time, Jimmy," said Max, shaking the keys at him. "We're under attack. I need you to show me the way down to the Hollows. We need to free the prisoners."

"You mean it's an emergency?" asked Jimmy, massaging his muttonchops.

"Yes, Jimmy, it's an emergency!" bellowed Max.

"Hot diggety!" exclaimed the strange little man, snapping his fingers and scooting off the counter. He snatched the keys from Max and waddled out the door, whistling happily.

Max fought the urge to throttle Jimmy while the little man offered a running commentary on various elements of the Manse's history.

"Of course, no one ever thought to ask me," said Jimmy as they hurried through an empty drawing room, "but I think the scheme in this wing is all wrong—what it needs is a dash of peach and cream. That'll put a smile on the girls' faces! None of this dark wood and—"

"Jimmy, *please*," said Max, trying to think.

"Well, it's true," insisted the little man, sounding hurt.

When they came to the end of a long hallway, Jimmy snapped his fingers and a Persian rug rolled back to reveal a trapdoor set in the floor.

"Long time since I've been down here," he sniffed, seizing the ring and pulling it open.

The two descended a steep staircase, winding farther and farther down until stonework gave way to bare rock.

"*Hurry*, Jimmy," said Max as the man picked his way carefully down the stairs.

"I *am* hurrying!" Jimmy snapped. "I'm three foot two, you twit!"

The carved steps finally opened into a cold, moist grotto whose walls were covered in gray-green fungi. Set into the rock was a stout iron door. Waddling forward, Jimmy selected a key and stood on tiptoe to insert it in the lock. As soon as he heard a click, Max wrenched the door open, almost toppling Jimmy in the process. Grumbling, the little man hurried after Max into the Hollows.

On either side of the long, dark corridor, Max saw rough-hewn cells carved into the rock like primitive zoo exhibits. Each of the cells was secured with thick iron bars that appeared badly corroded with age. Max wondered how these would hold someone as powerful as Ms. Richter or an ogre, until he came upon the first prisoner.

There was Miss Boon, sitting upright in a chair, staring out at him with a dull, blank gaze. Her intelligent eyes were dim; no recognition flashed across her face as Max stood just beyond the bars.

"What's the matter with her?" asked Max.

"Don'tcha see the baka?" asked Jimmy. "There, at her shoulder."

Max looked again and saw a little creature, like a pale-skinned imp, naked and shriveled, that sat upon the back of her chair like a hideous gargoyle. It was hunched forward, its mouth moving ever so slightly as it whispered in the young teacher's ear.

"The prisoners are all bewitched by those miserable creatures," said Jimmy, shaking his head. "It's an old practice I never approved of. The baka keep 'em dreaming—horrible dreams, I'd guess. I don't even know why we bother with bars. I never saw a prisoner move as much as a finger."

The sight of the hideous thing clinging to his teacher like a parasite revolted Max. When Jimmy opened the door, Max hurried inside and flung the small creature away. It gave a squeal and spread its arms to flap like a heavy, crippled bat up toward a ledge some ten feet up the rock face. Once there, it settled onto its haunches and hissed at Max through small, sharp teeth. Max ignored it and shook Miss Boon gently. She blinked several times.

"Where am I?" she asked, gazing about the cell.

"The Hollows," said Max. "You have to help me—there's no time to lose."

With Jimmy's help, Max and Miss Boon went from cell to cell until Ms. Richter, Cooper, Bob, and a dozen other faculty members were released from their delusional state. While the released prisoners recovered their senses, Jimmy and Max continued to free the others. Coming upon one of the last cells, Max gasped as he looked upon Mr. Morrow.

The traitorous Humanities instructor sat unblinking in his

chair while a baka clung to the white, tangled beard that had grown during his imprisonment. Conflicting emotions surged through Max as he gazed at the man who was responsible for so many crimes the previous year. Arriving beside Max, Cooper took the keys from Max's hands and unlocked the cell.

"We should leave him," muttered Max, recognizing that Astaroth might still be imprisoned if not for the treachery of the broken man before him.

"No," said Cooper, stepping inside the cell. "That would be murder."

The Agent led the bent, confused Mr. Morrow from his cell. The old man clung to Cooper like a child. His eyes widened when he saw Max.

"Thank God," muttered Mr. Morrow. "Thank God no harm came to you. . . ."

Max ignored him and spoke to Bob instead.

"Can you take Mr. Morrow and the others to the Sanctuary?" asked Max, despite the murderous glint in Bob's eye as the ogre glared at Mr. Morrow. Upon hearing the request, Bob stood to his full height and looked down his chest at Max.

"Bob will fight."

"*No!*" pleaded Max. "We need Mystics, not muscle. If those ships land . . ."

Bob frowned as he considered Max's words. With a slow, reluctant nod, he herded the older, non-Mystic prisoners up the steps. Max turned to Jimmy.

"I need you to do one more thing," he said.

"Another quest?" asked Jimmy hopefully.

"Another quest," said Max, shouldering David's pack. "We need you to call out for Connor Lynch. He's hiding somewhere on campus, and we need to get him in the Sanctuary. He isn't safe out here."

"On the double!" said Jimmy with a snappy salute, waddling up the stairs after the others.

"We have to hurry," said Max, leading Ms. Richter, Miss Boon, and Agent Cooper up the stairs as fast as their wobbly legs could carry them.

As they reached the ground floor of the Manse, they could hear the keening wail of the spirit that lurked in the waters off Rowan's beach. The four hurried through the deserted Manse and out the front doors, which had been left open to the rising storm.

Outside, a cold rain fell in stinging fits while moaning gusts rushed in from the ocean. Max shouted to Ms. Richter, but his voice was lost in the howling wind and he merely pointed toward the sea. Together, the four ran over the lawns toward the bluff where the Promethean Scholars stood in a line against the horizon. As they arrived, Max heard the sound of distant drums, followed by a sudden roar that might have been the crashing sea or the call of a thousand voices.

Looking past the chanting Scholars, Max gazed in horror upon the tossing ocean. Hundreds of tall-masted galleons stretched as far as he could see, some whole, others wracked and broken as though summoned from a long slumber in the deep. They lay at anchor offshore, their torches sputtering in the wind, while deep drums boomed and a thousand landing boats were rowed toward shore by vyes and goblins, ogres and men. The Promethean Scholars cast their spells, raising great breakers from the waves and churning the sea in an effort to capsize the approaching boats.

"Don't interfere," warned Vilyak, eyeing Ms. Richter. He stopped and gave the Scholars a shout of encouragement as one of the Enemy's landing vessels was dashed against Brigit's Vigil by a great black wave.

Vilyak's enthusiasm moved others to cheers, but not Max. He watched in silence, noting that wherever a boat was sunk, three more arrived to take its place, cleaving the broken spars and rowing swiftly past those who flailed in the sea and sank beneath the water. Overhead, the sky rumbled, slow and ominous. Hints of lightning flashed from deep within the thick, pluming thunderheads, and Max felt the air grow still.

There was a sudden, searing flash of light, and the world seemed to go silent. Max was thrown backward, landing on the ground with a jarring thud. As the ringing in his ears subsided, the storm's Jovian roar returned.

Rising to his feet, Max stared mutely at the scorched remains of the Promethean Scholars. Their bodies had been broken and scattered like rag dolls about the perimeter of a smoldering crater. The power that had sent such a bolt was unimaginable. Speechless, Max wrenched his gaze away from the carnage and looked out over the sea.

Astaroth was there.

Even from the shore, Max could see the white face at the prow of the hulking black flagship. The Demon's hands were outstretched, beseeching a sky whose churning elements responded to his call. The maelstrom above gathered mass and energy, assuming enormous proportions until it seemed a colossus, capable of swallowing the world.

"My God," muttered a terror-stricken Mystic, gaping at the storm's slow majesty. "We can't possibly fight this. . . ."

Others apparently agreed. Max watched them go, hurrying away toward the Sanctuary like frightened creatures scurrying to their burrow. The Red Branch and several other senior Agents remained, however—Max saw one pass a blade to Cooper. Another movement caught Max's eye: Miss Boon was snatching up whatever remains of the Scholars' books she could find before

the wind whisked them from the bluff. Above the pandemonium, Max heard Ms. Richter and Vilyak locked in a heated argument.

"I won't!" screamed Commander Vilyak.

"But you can't use it," yelled Ms. Richter. "You've *never* been able to use it!"

"It belongs to the Director!" protested Vilyak, covering the Founder's Ring with his other hand.

"There won't *be* a Director, Yuri!"

The statement seemed to have a profound effect on Commander Vilyak. He looked out again at the approaching armada, its progress now steady and uncontested. Snatching the ring from his finger, he practically flung it at Ms. Richter, then fled through the cold rain toward the Sanctuary.

Cooper's face twisted into a derisive scowl and for a moment, Max thought the Red Branch might pursue their cowardly commander. Instead, they turned their backs on Vilyak, following Cooper to the stone stairs that led down to the beach, where they would meet the first of the attackers. Max went to follow, but Cooper stopped him.

"Remember your oath, Max. Leave this fight to us."

Ms. Richter hurried over.

"Cooper," she said. "Call them off those stairs this instant—it's suicide." She turned to Max, her voice taut with command. "Where is David Menlo?" she demanded. "We need him *here*."

"David's been badly hurt, Director," said Max. "He can't help us."

Ms. Richter blinked and gazed up at the monstrous storm. Max feared that she, too, would be consumed with terror, but instead the Director's features became very still. She slipped the Founder's Ring upon her finger and beckoned gently to Miss Boon.

"Hazel," she commanded, "leave those be and take my hand."

The young Mystics instructor abandoned the clutch of precious pages and did as she was told. Max watched the two women walk to the cliff's edge. The Founder's Ring burned as bright as a living jewel. Ms. Richter raised it against the advancing ships.

Max felt the earth shudder once, then again. Sea spray whipped against his face as he marveled at the scene below.

The ocean was surging toward the beach as though the craggy bluff itself had taken a slow, deep breath. The inrush of water built momentum quickly, obliterating the *Kestrel*'s dock against the stone steps. Crashing against the cliffs, the water rose in a churning, gurgling mass. When it reached the height of the cliffs, however, the water did not spill over but instead rose higher, solid as the very earth. Max watched it climb, a trembling wall of seawater in which rock and boats and corpses were eerily suspended, mortared into place by some unseen force.

The Founder's Ring blazed brighter, and Ms. Richter sent the lethal wall of water roaring back toward the Enemy.

Max watched, breathless, as the crashing seawall snapped boats and backs alike. Even the distant galleons pitched precariously on the waves, and Max found himself cheering wildly as several of the massive ships finally succumbed, toppling onto their sides and spilling hundreds into the murderous sea.

"You're doing it, Ms. Richter!" cried Max. "You're beating them!"

The Red Branch echoed Max's cheers and even the storm seemed to weaken, shedding some of its awful force and scale. Through the rain, Max squinted and searched the sea, hopeful that the white face had been swept clear from its deck.

But it was not to be.

Astaroth stood, unmoving, at the prow of the flagship. The

Demon's voice carried on the wind until it seemed he whispered in Max's ear.

"I see you. And I am coming."

A gale came howling in off the ocean, so abrupt and powerful that all gave way before it.

Max pressed himself flat and clung to the wet earth, scrabbling for a hold as the wind screamed above him. Ms. Richter and Miss Boon were blasted off their feet, their connection lost as the women were sent tumbling like scattered leaves.

The storm thundered again and unnatural flashes of light danced from cloud to cloud like witch fire. Max saw Ms. Richter regain her feet and march with grim determination back toward the cliff.

The Director had almost reached her destination when the air grew hushed once again. A sense of dread consumed Max. There was an incandescent flash and a crack of thunder so piercing it shattered Maggie's windows.

Opening his eyes, Max registered the outcome with dull shock: Ms. Richter lay motionless within a pit of earth and fire.

~ 20 ~

SOMETHING WICKED

Miss Boon was the first to reach Ms. Richter's body. The Mystics instructor wept as she struggled to pull the limp form from the smoking crater, straining with all her might until Cooper arrived to help. The Agent laid the Director on the wet grass and shielded her placid face from the rain. Max stood by them in stunned silence, his eyes fixed on the Founder's Ring, which faded like an ember.

"We must get to the Sanctuary, Hazel," said Cooper, gently pulling Miss Boon away. "There's nothing more to do here."

"We're not leaving her behind," protested Miss Boon. "She deserves a proper burial!"

A member of the Red Branch interrupted Cooper's reply.

"William," called the man, staring over the bluff. Cooper stood and strode toward the overlook.

Max hurried over and saw the beach crawling with vyes and goblins, whose bent backs dripped with seawater and glistened under the moonlight. Upon landing, the creatures set to assembling pontoon bridges that were anchored into bedrock like a dozen jetties, extending farther and farther through the chop toward the galleons, where Max could see the silhouettes of great siege engines being hooked onto heavy cranes.

There was a hoarse cry from the beach as Max and the others were seen. Goblin arrows flew at them in lethal arcs. Max felt one thud against his torso, snapping harmlessly on Señor Lorca's shirt. Following the volley of arrows, vyes began to swarm up the ruined remnants of stairs that led from the beach.

Cooper yanked Max away from the edge of the bluff.

"Run!" he shouted.

Cooper gathered up Miss Boon and dashed back toward the Manse, whose windows were all alight and looking strangely festive. Turning, Max saw the dark shapes of the first vyes rise above the windswept rim of the overlook. Several stooped over the body of Ms. Richter. Max stopped running as rage boiled in his chest.

A firm hand seized him.

"Don't you dare," growled Cooper, pulling him forward.

More vyes scrambled over the bluff and fanned across the lawns in pursuit, some running upright while others galloped through the rain on all fours. Miss Boon began falling behind, unable to keep pace with the Agents. Without breaking stride, Cooper swept the teacher up onto his shoulder. The group sprinted past the Manse, Max and the others practically flying down the worn paths that wound past the orchard and Smithy, until they neared the Sanctuary door.

Dozens of people were already clustered about it, chattering in the cold as they waited helplessly in the downpour. Max recognized Mr. Morrow among the crowd. Bob stood in the group's center, towering above them and doing his best to shield them from the storm.

"Why aren't you inside?" yelled Cooper. "They should know we're coming."

"Vilyak came first," replied Bob with a growl. "We can't get in."

Cooper set to pushing and tugging at the great ring in the door's center. The door did not budge.

"Bob has already tried," muttered the ogre, a hint of grim humor in his voice as he watched the far weaker human tremble with exertion.

"Hazel," said Cooper, his voice even, "can you open this?"

Miss Boon hurried forward, muttering several spells even as howls and cries echoed from the woods around them. Despite her efforts, the door remained fast.

Snapping branches and hoarse calls sounded from the woods. Cooper yelled a word of command and the closest tree ignited like a sparkler whose flames leapt from tree to tree until the whole forest seemed ablaze despite the rain. Hideous screams rang out, sending the freed prisoners and elderly refugees into a gibbering panic. Practically frantic, Miss Boon tried spell after spell with no success.

Something galloped into the clearing.

It was a jet-black vye, its fur badly singed and its face hideously half human as it leapt over the fence of the stable's riding ring and hurled itself at Mr. Morrow. Max saw a great hand surge forward; the vye gave a strangled yelp as Bob caught it by its throat.

With sudden uncharacteristic savagery, the ogre dashed the vye repeatedly against the rain-spattered earth, continuing to snap its bones well after the monster was dead.

Bob stood panting over the vye's misshapen carcass a moment, a primal, horrifying gleam consuming his once friendly features. Cooper began to approach, but a low rumble emanated from Bob's chest and the Agent stopped dead in his tracks. Max knew there was language in that rumble—a nearly subsonic warning to keep well away from an ogre that had just killed for the first time in decades. Cooper backed away slowly while Bob leaned heavily against the fence, taking slow gulps of air as his massive head scanned the forest.

Other wolfish silhouettes arrived at the fringe of the burning woods. They rose onto their hind legs and assessed the situation, considerably more cautious than their maddened comrade who lay broken behind the ogre. One of the vyes lifted its head and howled. The others followed suit and soon the whole forest was alive with terrifying calls that led yet more vyes to the clearing.

Bob reached for a rusted spade nearby, hefting the heavy tool as though it were a toy. Straightening, the ogre stalked toward the vyes and gave a roar.

Even within the Course, Max had never heard anything so awful.

Only a cornered creature could make such a sound. It was a booming, defiant bellow that mixed fear and rage and love in equal measure. The vyes shrank back initially, preferring the shelter of the forest, despite the falling embers. But their courage grew as their numbers swelled and they began to encircle the ogre, baring their jagged teeth and clawing at the muddy earth for purchase.

Several vyes leapt forward and Bob swung the shovel, shattering one's muzzle with a heavy clang. With another swing, the ogre flattened a second vye. But then the others were upon him, snarling and snapping as they crashed into his hulking form and scrabbled for his throat. Bob roared again and pushed them back with his free hand, swinging the dented shovel wildly about as other vyes rushed in like the tide.

Max went to Bob's aid, but Cooper yanked him backward by the shirt.

"He needs help!" screamed Max.

"I've got it," muttered Cooper, taking ahold of Max's wrist. "Protect the others."

"No!" yelled Max, pulling away his hand with such force that Cooper almost lost his footing.

Max hurried toward the fray, trying to reach Bob, who was now surrounded and straining under the weight of four vyes that clung to him, sinking their teeth into his flesh and wrenching their heads from side to side like feeding sharks. Seizing the first, Max yanked its head back and exposed its throat to the cold moon.

Vye after vye fell to Max's knives. Their matted forms collapsed into the mud as Max moved among them, a lethal blur against the backdrop of rain and burning trees. From the corner of his eye, Max spied a particularly thick vye, almost boar-like in its visage, sneak close to Bob to venture a nip at the wounded ogre. Furious, Max whirled and split its head in two. He kicked its body aside and turned, looking wildly about for another nearby adversary.

There were none. Hundreds of vyes had gathered by now, ringed about the burning forest and peering at him, but none would venture close.

Panting, Max turned and looked at Bob. The ogre had

collapsed into a bleeding mound, his hand blindly groping for the shovel that lay beyond his reach. Tears burned Max's cheeks as he crouched in the rain by the ogre amidst the dozens of fallen vyes that lay about them, their tongues lolling from lifeless jaws. It was several seconds before Max realized Cooper was calling to him.

"Max, come here."

The Agent's voice was calm, but there was a quiet urgency to it. Max glanced back and saw the Red Branch in a defensive ring around the refugees. Beyond the people huddled by the door, Max saw Nolan's concerned face peering out from the Sanctuary tunnel.

"Inside, Max!" cried Nolan, pushing the door wider. "Hurry now!"

Max looked back at the cowardly vyes slinking among the trees. Blood drummed in his temples and his fingers twitched while he fought to master the Old Magic that surged and strained against his will. Max heard footsteps behind him and whirled. It was Cooper.

"Help me bring Bob in," said the Agent, taking hold of Bob's wrist.

While the refugees streamed inside the open door, Max and Cooper dragged Bob's thousand-pound body swiftly through the mud. The vyes crept forward from the trees as they retreated. The Red Branch entered the tunnel last, backing sinuously through the doorway, their eyes never leaving the advancing vyes.

Once all were through, Nolan slammed the heavy door shut. Cooper left Bob's side and helped Nolan slide its heavy bolt into place.

"Will it hold them?" asked Cooper, looking dubiously at the door.

"For a while yet, I think," said Nolan. Even as he spoke, however, dirt rained from the door's hinges as heavy blows fell upon it from the other side. "She's stouter than she looks, anyway—been strengthened by a heap of spells."

"How did you know to come?" muttered Cooper, ushering the others away from the door and through the canopy of trees, whose warmer air was fragrant with pine. Max followed quietly after, listening to the men's conversation.

"Vilyak showed up alone," muttered Nolan. "All by his lonesome and full of stories. He should know better than to lie to YaYa. . . ."

YaYa was waiting where the tunnel met the clearing, huge and majestic against the starlit waters of the lagoon. Her black fur shimmered in the dark as she stood panting, having evidently come a great distance at a great pace. YaYa was the oldest living thing at Rowan, and Max feared the journey had taken a hard toll on the ancient ki-rin.

It was YaYa, however, who volunteered to transport Bob, insisting that the wounded ogre be draped across her back until Nolan could fashion a crude stretcher at the Warming Lodge. The once welcoming building was now silent and dark, its stalls empty, as all the young charges had been evacuated. While Nolan built the litter, Max saw the extent of Bob's injuries. Deep puncture wounds riddled his back and arms, like stitching. In some places, whole chunks of flesh had been ripped away. The ogre lay silent while Miss Boon and several others did their best to stanch the bleeding.

Max could not watch.

He walked back outside and stood at the edge of the lagoon, stirring the water with his hand and calling softly for Frigga and Helga. But the selkie sisters did not come; no winking seal's face or bawdy joke greeted Max from the cool water. The realization that the sisters had gone—fled, most likely, to whatever distant waters fed the lagoon—somehow infused Rowan's predicament with a reality and weight that Max had not yet had the opportunity to feel. He felt it now, however. The siege and its many implications washed over Max in numbing waves while he stirred the waters and hoped the selkies were safe.

By the time the stretcher had been built, Miss Boon's spells had managed to halt Bob's bleeding and put the injured ogre to sleep. Once Bob had been secured to the stretcher, the group began the long, slow march into the Sanctuary's depths. While they walked, Max's rage subdued into a simmer and he finally felt capable of speaking. He turned to Cooper, who walked beside him as they trailed behind the group.

"I'm sorry I didn't obey," said Max.

Cooper waved it off.

"I learned things," explained Max. "In the Sidh. I knew I could—"

"I understand," said Cooper quietly. "It was right for you to be the one."

"Are you angry with me?"

"No."

They walked in silence, Max surveying the landscape, until Nolan came back to check on them.

"Have you seen Nick?" asked Max hoarsely.

"Not to worry, son," drawled Nolan. "He's with your dad. Most of the charges are safely in the cliffs by now and the others can best look after themselves. The wild ones are out, though—seen a few lurking around. I think they know something's wrong."

Max thought of the wild charges that had tracked them the

previous year when he and his friends had visited Mr. Morrow's distant cottage. Bob had warned that wild charges could be dangerous, having long since forgotten that humans ever looked after them.

As Max reminisced on that fateful evening, he found himself glowering ahead at Mr. Morrow. The disgraced instructor seemed to sense he was being watched and halted to peer back at them. Upon meeting Max's gaze, he looked away and hobbled ahead to engage an elderly couple in quiet conversation. Max swallowed his disgust and walked in silence, thinking instead of the wild charges and how he belonged among them.

They made their way across the wide clearing, guided by starlight, until they arrived at the low, forested hills that rose toward the first snow-capped peaks. They hiked along a path that had now been traveled many times, the way worn smooth by recent traffic. As they walked, however, Cooper lingered behind, muttering spells that masked their progress. In their wake, grass, rock, and soil were scattered and rearranged until the land looked wild and untouched.

Climbing through stands of pine, the group wound its way along high ridges until they descended once again, funneled down into a hidden gorge that knifed between the mountains. The gorge was dark and at times grew so narrow they could scarcely walk four abreast. By the time they had passed through, the sky had turned a periwinkle blue and the sun's first rays tipped the tall grass with gold. Max heard the gurgle of water and saw a broad river shimmering across a gently sloping plain. Far away, across the grasslands, loomed a wall of cliffs, carved of some dark rock. These cliffs seemed the very edge of the world, their summit lost in a gray haze that obscured the sky beyond.

Footsore, the stragglers trudged toward the river, following

Nolan across a path of low stones that lay just beneath the swift, dark water. Max marveled as the ki-rin walked across the water unimpeded, her great paws making nary a ripple as she towed the injured ogre across. Once they crossed the river, it was over a mile of trudging progress until they reached the base of the cliffs. Gazing up, Max saw openings cut into the rock face, many so high that they appeared no larger than mouse holes.

Nolan cupped his hands and yelled up. A head peered out far above and soon a large fenced platform was lowered on a system of ropes and pulleys. They stepped onto the sturdy platform and were promptly whisked up the rock wall, climbing some two hundred feet until the pulleys ground to a halt and the platform was lowered onto a smooth rock ledge.

Looking about, Max saw sacks of grain and bushel baskets of apples stacked next to oil paintings and bronze statuary. The people and property of Rowan had been stuffed into every nook and cranny of an enormous series of connected chambers and tunnels. Stepping off the platform, Max shouldered David's pack and gazed in wonder at the high arches and smooth stone. Nolan departed with Mr. Morrow and the refugees, while Max, Miss Boon, and the Red Branch escorted YaYa and Bob toward the hospital.

As they walked, Max gazed about, watching hundreds of Rowan students, faculty, and families busy as bees as they organized the spaces into storage or living quarters. In one cave, they spied people busily reassembling greenhouses whose bulbs were powered by humming generators. Max saw a familiar face overseeing the work and trotted toward Dr. Rasmussen.

"Did you get them here?" asked Max. "My father and David?"

"I did," said Rasmussen, wiping a smudge of grease from his chin. "They're safe, but it was not an easy trip for David."

Max thanked him and hurried across the cavern where some First Years were helping Mum, Bellagrog, and the kitchen staff as they unpacked mountains of crates containing canned and jarred foods of every description. As the convoy approached, Mum sniffed and spun on her heel, dropping a can of tuna fish. The hag blinked at Bob, who might have been a bandaged pile of masonry. With a shriek, Mum skittered over.

"What happened to him?" she bawled, practically bowling over an Agent as she hurried to Bob's side. YaYa came to a halt as the hag climbed about the motionless ogre, sniffing into every nook and cranny while her beady eyes inspected the more serious wounds. Mum slowly dissolved into sobs, a pitiful series of gulping wheezes, until Bob gave an irritated grumble and managed a squeeze of the hag's finger. Mum wept with gratitude, clinging to the ogre's massive body like a stubby starfish.

A shadow fell across the pair as Bellagrog waddled over.

"Oi!" she said, looking the ogre up and down. "Seen better days, eh, Bob? Shoulda kept yer nose outta trouble, I reckon, like me Nan always said. Whatchoo thinking about, anyway, love? You ain't in no shape to be scrapping awa—"

Bellagrog never finished the sentence.

With a shriek, Mum launched herself at her sister, swinging wildly at the bloated hag's protuberant nose. The pair toppled over in a snarling, scratching tangle of flowered skirts and skittering beads. When the Agents separated them, Bellagrog was bleeding from a nasty gash in her lip and Mum's crocodile eye was swollen shut. Flushed at the apparent draw, Bellagrog shook a meaty fist at her sobbing sister.

"I'll *kill ya* for that, Bea!" she bellowed. "Sentimental gobbledygook done rotted yer brain, ye silly thing!" A fiendish hush came over her. "You just made the top of me list."

"Ha!" screeched Mum in a peal of mad laughter. "You been yapping away about 'the list' since I was a hagling. . . ."

The two shrieked and threatened each other with an impressive array of grisly deaths until several Agents managed to gently but forcibly escort the feuding hags down separate corridors.

Despite the ugly scene, Max felt his mind shift into an assessment of Rowan's situation. Looking about, he felt somewhat heartened. The caves seemed almost impregnable and with all their supplies and preparations he thought they might indeed hold off an army until David was strong enough to join the fight. Max harbored no illusions regarding Rowan's chances—*everything* hinged on David Menlo and the Book of Thoth. As YaYa dragged Bob's litter onward, Max hurried after, anxious to see his friend.

They passed several caves with many tents and resting families until they came upon a vast cavern that had been converted into a sort of hospital. Moomenhovens scurried about, hovering over patients who were arranged in neat rows of cots. Against the far wall, Max saw his father sitting by David's bedside. Max, Cooper, and Miss Boon crept up, so as not to disturb David. Mr. McDaniels turned at their approach and stood to greet them, practically engulfing Max in a bear hug.

"How are you?" whispered Max.

"Snug as a bug in a . . . cave, I suppose," replied his father.

Max looked at his roommate, who lay on the cot. A bit of color had returned to David's face in the weeks since he'd been stabbed, but he still did not look well. Max stood by his friend's side for several moments, but David did not stir.

"I'll check back," he said at last, his gaze lingering on the wrap that covered David's ugly wound. Miss Boon nodded and kissed Max on the forehead before pulling up a chair next to Mr. McDaniels. His Mystics instructor had held up well since Ms. Richter had fallen, but now Max saw the event etched in the young woman's face. Taking a seat by David, she stared off into space, murmuring thanks when Cooper draped a blanket over her shoulders.

"This is particularly hard on her," said Cooper once he'd ushered Max away. The pair continued on, walking past more tents and cooking fires in long strides. "She idolized the Director, as I'm sure you know. . . ."

Cooper trailed off, his hard eyes staring at Max's training knife.

"I'd meant to ask you earlier," grunted the Agent. "Where is the *gae bolga*?"

Max had been dreading the question and almost winced as he replied.

"Here," said Max, shaking David's pack. "In a hundred little pieces. It broke in the Sidh, Cooper. The training knives are all I've got."

"That won't do," said Cooper, frowning as they followed the sound of hushed voices. They arrived at a cave, dark but for a cluster of lanterns at its center. Max saw the senior faculty, including Miss Awolowo and Miss Kraken, in quiet conversation. Several members of the Red Branch had already arrived, but Max looked past them to a shadowy corner where Yuri Vilyak dabbed gingerly at a bandage on his scalp. He nodded in greeting, but Max did not acknowledge him.

"If you're here to finish this coward, you'll have to wait," said Miss Kraken, gesturing for Max and Cooper to sit. She narrowed her eyes and offered Vilyak a scornful look. "It's a pity YaYa isn't a bit younger."

Vilyak shifted uncomfortably and cleared his throat.

"I've already said I believed the others lost—there was nothing else I could do," he muttered.

"A leader does *not* leave his people behind, Commander Vilyak!" erupted Miss Awolowo. "A leader does *not* bolt the door and leave his comrades to the Enemy!"

"Any verdict regarding Yuri Vilyak will have to wait," said Miss Kraken decisively. "We have other matters to discuss. It is my view that we cannot simply hide," she said. "We must seek to distract and delay them however we can until better options present themselves. We must send the Red Branch out to meet them."

"We already sent the Promethean Scholars," muttered Vilyak, earning a furious glare from Miss Kraken. The man raised his hands in a supplicating gesture. "You did not see the invading force, Annika. I did. And I tell you it would be folly to meet them in the open. Better to defend a strong place until David Menlo heals and can spirit us away or hide us again using the Old Magic. Until then, the Red Branch is needed here."

"You don't speak for the Red Branch," said Cooper. "I do."

"Nonsense," said Vilyak. "I never relinquished command. It's mine unless I'm—"

Vilyak went silent as Cooper drew his knife, testing its weight in his hand.

"We can honor the ritual if you like," said Cooper. "But we both know the outcome."

For long seconds, silence filled the chamber. Finally Miss Kraken spoke.

"Cooper, we don't have time for this," she muttered.

"It'll be over quick, Miss Kraken," replied Cooper, his voice taut as wire. "I promise."

Miss Kraken turned to Vilyak, who fidgeted uncomfortably while he searched Cooper's unblinking face. With a sudden cough, he dismissed a potential duel, affecting a good-natured laugh.

"Annika is right," he said. "This is a time for decisions, not misunderstandings and infighting. You take command, Cooper. After all, I'm hardly fit with this unfortunate wound. We can re-visit that issue later. . . ."

"Fine," snapped Miss Kraken with brisk authority. The old woman's eyes turned toward Max and her voice softened. "Max, I think you know where our hopes lie. . . ."

Max nodded, feeling all the eyes turn to him as Miss Kraken continued.

"When he returned, David Menlo shared some of his ad-ventures in the Sidh. He said he could understand the Book; he claimed that he could use it. Is this true, Max?"

"Yes, ma'am."

"The gate cannot hold and we cannot hide forever," said Miss Kraken, her keen eyes searching his face. "The Enemy is coming. Our only hope lies with David and the Book of Thoth. We have David, and the Moomenhovens say he is healing. We must know whether we have the Book."

The question was pointed, and Max was aware that Miss Kraken already knew the answer. He glanced at Cooper and the tall Agent nodded. Slinging David's battered satchel off his shoulder, Max retrieved the golden Book and held it to his chest.

"It goes to David," said Max. "Only David. Do I have your word, Miss Kraken?"

"You do, my child," said the old Mystic, offering a solemn bow. "I understand your misgivings—you have seen Rowan betray her own. We must learn to trust again. Let it begin with me."

Max crossed the chamber and placed the Book of Thoth in

the old woman's hands. She did not even glance at its exquisite cover but promptly wrapped it in the folds of her shawl. Vilyak grunted.

"So we have it," he said. "But how will we keep the wolves from our door, Annika?"

"I will," said Max. "I'll keep them away until David is strong enough."

"And how do you intend to do that, my boy?" snapped Vilyak.

Pride quickened the Old Magic in Max's blood. His fingers twitched and the leviathan within him began to stir once again. He glanced at Vilyak and thought how small and weak the man looked, propped as he was against the wall, nursing his wound. Max controlled his impulse and swallowed.

"I'll do it with fear," he said quietly. "The Enemy will fear to venture beyond the clearing."

Vilyak laughed with disbelief.

"Ah, the exuberance of youth!" he said. "Where does it go?"

Several members of the Red Branch smiled, but Cooper did not. Miss Kraken turned to him.

"You have seen the army and you know this boy," said Miss Kraken. "What is your counsel?"

Cooper's taut, shiny face stared at the ground in patient repose. He closed his eyes and spoke only after long seconds had passed.

"Max and I will meet the Enemy in the Sanctuary and delay them as best we can."

"And why is that your counsel, William?" asked Miss Kraken, ignoring Vilyak's muttering.

"Because I've never seen anything like Max before," replied the Agent. "And neither have they."

* * *

Twenty minutes later, Max and Cooper stood among the treasures of the Red Branch vault. The vault's contents had been moved from their splendid chamber within the Archives to a small, dim alcove far removed from the caverns' main passages. While Max surveyed his options, Cooper reclaimed his gruesome-looking kris and took up a shirt of black nanomail from where it lay draped over an oaken chest.

Max found that many of the weapons were storied but ancient and unwieldy. He frowned as he hefted Joyeuse, Charlemagne's sword, and Durandel, which had been Roland's. The swords were indeed fearsome, but too slow and heavy for Max's purpose. Finally, he stopped at a gleaming gladius with a black-ridged hilt and a short, razor-edged blade. Max hefted the short sword, testing its weight and balance.

"That belonged to Flamma," grunted Cooper, pulling the nanomail over his torso and tucking his wisps of blond hair back into his cap. "He was Rome's greatest gladiator. That blade was the emperor's own, till it was given to Flamma to honor him after a string of victories."

"This will do," said Max, sheathing the sword in its black scabbard.

Max heard a shuffling sound behind them and turned to see Lucia, Cynthia, and Sarah peering at them from the dark corridor. Cooper shone his lantern upon the trio, and Lucia scowled.

"We heard you came back," offered Sarah, rubbing her arms for warmth as she ventured into the cool alcove. She gave Cooper a wary glance, but the Agent said nothing. Sarah looked long and hard at the gladius in Max's hand. "Are you going off, then?" she asked.

"Yes," said Max, looking down. "I am."

"I see," said Sarah. "Have you told your father?"

"I can't," said Max, refusing to meet her gaze. "He won't understand."

"Max," said Cooper, "we must go."

Max nodded but reached forward to give Sarah's hand a fierce squeeze.

"Will you tell him for me?" pleaded Max. "I'd rather he hear it from you."

Sarah hugged him close, her voice barely a whisper in his ear.

"I will," she said. "Nick, too. And we'll see you when you get back."

Max and Cooper left the alcove and quickly made their way to the platform, whose pulleys and ropes lowered them slowly to the ground. As they descended, Max gazed across the plain at the slender gorge carved within the mountains. Beyond those peaks, an oily smoke rose lazily into the sky before it broke apart and drifted on the wind. Cooper said nothing, but the Agent set a swift pace as soon as the platform touched ground.

~ 21 ~

BARK, BRANCH, AND STONE

Max scratched at his face and hands, which had been caked with a mash of mud and pine needles to camouflage him against the senses of his enemy. Cooper motioned for him to stop.

"I know it itches," the Agent said. "Leave it be."

"They didn't bring anything modern," said Max, scanning the assembled army. "No guns, no tanks . . ."

"The Demon needs no such toys for little Rowan," muttered Cooper.

"It's more than that," whispered Max, thinking aloud. "I spoke with him in the Sidh—he doesn't approve of the modern world. I think he wants to turn back time."

"Good for him," said Cooper. "Coming here without guns and tanks. Shows dash."

Max grinned at the Agent's black humor as he watched small groups of dark shapes creep from the warmth of the campfires to head off in all directions—just as Cooper had predicted.

"There are our scouts," muttered Cooper. "Remember, Max—absolute silence. And, whatever happens, do not lead them toward the gorge. Direct any pursuit toward the dunes or the western range."

Max nodded, and the two dropped silently from the tree. They padded off through the forest, a pair of twilight shadows that stole quickly toward their quarry. Twenty minutes later, they intercepted their first patrol—five vyes and a bottle-nosed imp that crept along an old path. Max slipped the blackened gladius from its sheath.

There was a soft thump, a choked-off gurgle, and then silence. Max had dispatched the Enemy so quickly that he had not even frightened a nearby nest of sparrows into flight. One peered at him curiously while Max wiped the gladius clean on the matted fur of a stiffening vye. Cooper crouched nearby and set to work on the unpleasant task before them.

Minutes later, Max surveyed the six grisly bodies piled near the edge of the clearing. Cooper had propped them against a tree, taking care that the shock and horror frozen on their faces was made apparent to any passersby. Cutting a thick branch from the tree, Max carved in the wood the ancient Ogam runes he had learned from Scathach. The runes were a series of cryptic slashes, and Max knew they would be taken directly to Astaroth.

Be wary, those who walk these woods. The Hound of Rowan walks them, too.

"What is this?" whispered Cooper, glancing at the stake.

"A message for Astaroth," said Max, examining his handiwork.

"This is not a game," said Cooper, disapproving. "The bodies are enough."

"But it *is* a game," said Max, thrusting the stake into the ground. "And *we* have to make the rules. I'm letting Astaroth know I'm here—that I'm here and I defy him. Astaroth is prideful, Cooper. He can't resist such a challenge. The Demon will hunt for me, and that'll buy us time."

Cooper nodded, peering closer at the Ogam runes before following Max into the wood.

By dawn, many such stakes ringed the clearing. Max and Cooper chose a different perch and listened alertly as howls and horns began to sound in the chill morning. Their message had been discovered. Black crows—witch familiars—flew high into the air and wheeled about the sky as they searched the open clearing and the forest roof below. When the birds dipped lower to scour the trees, they found naught but bark, branch, and stone.

The Enemy's patrols became larger, but it made no difference. For three nights, Max and Cooper terrorized Astaroth's army, which searched in vain for both them and the hidden gorge. During the days, Max and Cooper managed whatever sleep they could and lived off berries and roots and rabbits when they could get them. As March progressed, Max felt himself getting stronger, but he also knew that Cooper was growing fatigued.

When the sun set on the fourth evening, Max spoke as Cooper shook himself from sleep.

"I'll go alone tonight," he said. "You need to rest."

"I'll be fine," replied the stoic Agent. "And it is too dangerous to go alone. They'll increase the size of the patrols."

"It doesn't matter," replied Max, and he knew it to be true.

"The patrols could number a hundred, and it wouldn't help them."

"Don't get cocky," growled Cooper, applying balm to a superficial wound he'd sustained on his shoulder. "It's foolish to tempt a broader battle, Max. Stealth must be our way."

"It's foolish to hunt half asleep," replied Max. "You know you need rest."

Cooper gave a reluctant nod and sat in silence for several moments. "And where would you lead them?" he asked reluctantly.

"Back toward the dunes," said Max. "That's where the last patrols thought we were hiding."

"A good plan," said Cooper, closing his eyes with meditative calm.

Max saw that a thin sheen of sweat now covered the Agent's forehead, and it worried him.

"You'll feel better tomorrow," said Max, shooing a fly away from Cooper's chin.

"Of course I will," whispered Cooper before dozing off.

Max watched the Agent for a moment, but he seemed to be sleeping peacefully. Pushing up from the rough bark, Max dropped from the tree. He stalked through the woods feeling powerful and predatory, winding his way through the forest toward the flickering firelight of the clearing. He stopped there a moment and peered out at the many tents, siege engines, and witch carriages that littered the open space.

A twig snapped behind him.

Max whirled and unsheathed his gladius in a blink. Its lethal point quivered at a pair of luminescent eyes several feet away. A deep growl sounded in the darkness, but the creature was no vye. Lowering the gladius a fraction, Max peered closer at the creature, whose dark coat rippled like a bolt of silk.

At first, Max thought it was a larger version of his mother's charge, Isis. But on closer inspection, he saw it wasn't so. The creature before Max looked like a blue-black tiger except that its legs ended not in paws but human hands tipped with hard, curling claws. He had never seen such a thing in the Sanctuary before and knew it was a wild charge. Max saw there was blood on the creature's claws and could further smell it on the animal's breath, which came in slow pants from its wet muzzle.

"I'm on your side," whispered Max, gripping the gladius tightly.

"S-s-s-si-ide," said the creature, repeating the word and stretching out its syllable in a sibilant hiss as though rediscovering it had the power of speech. Cocking its sleek head at Max, the creature backed into the forest. Its yellow eyes narrowed to blinking slits and then it was gone. Taking a deep breath, Max continued on his way.

It was some time before he encountered his first patrol; the soft clink of metal was a giveaway amidst the natural surroundings. Leaping into a tree, Max waited as the first of a dozen dark shapes emerged from beyond a thicket. A thin shaft of moonlight showed the telltale ears of many vyes, bent and wolfish with their long jackal snouts pressed against the ground. Something else, however, stood in the midst of them, and Max felt an unnatural cold seep into his body. He peered curiously at the hidden figure. An unnerving thought entered Max's mind, but he dismissed it—revenants could not venture aboveground. When the figure spoke, however, its hollow voice erased all doubt.

"What does the earth tell?" demanded Marley Augur.

"Shhh," hissed a vye. "Begging pardon, but we must be quiet! The Hound may be about."

"You should hope he is," replied Augur, turning to reveal

cold pinpoints of light in his sunken sockets. "Our lord's pets would welcome a little Hound to fill their bellies."

"Do not tempt him here!" hissed another vye, licking its needle teeth. "He took Thera and Myxll near this very spot! As wicked as a wraith, he is—I stood within a stone's throw and heard not a thing! Let us find their secret place and hurry back to camp!"

There came a sudden, sickening sound.

Max watched as the vye staggered forward and collapsed against a nearby tree in an awkward splay of limbs. Its head had been bludgeoned from its body. There was another clinking of metal, and Augur emerged into a patch of moonlight. The undead blacksmith leaned upon the long handle of his hammer and gazed thoughtfully at the severed head. The other vyes backed away on all fours, their eyes gleaming white with terror.

"I fear nothing that runs and hides and preys upon the likes of you," said the voice. "Who else wishes to run back to camp?"

The vyes said nothing but whined deep in their throats and lowered themselves to the ground in a display of trembling subservience. Augur turned slowly about the moonlit clearing, looking at the vyes, who could not help but retreat on their bellies, slinking away from the undead creature. Max held his breath as one of the vyes came to a stop at the base of his tree. His throat was within arm's reach, and Max took full advantage.

"Astaroth grows tired of this game," said Augur, straightening. He beckoned at something large that had been camouflaged among a thicket of trees. The blacksmith's skeletal horse trotted forward, its metal barding clanking on bone. Swinging stiffly up into the saddle, Marley Augur stabbed a mailed finger at the vye slumped beneath Max's tree. "You there, take up point."

The vye did not respond, but lay motionless while a dark pool spread beneath him. Another vye loped forward and lapped once or twice at the pool with her long tongue before giving a whine of terror.

"He's dead, my lord!" she hissed, her eyes darting about the dark underbrush.

With a sudden twitch of her ears, the vye looked up, straight into Max's eyes. The gladius stabbed forward and the vye gave a surprised grunt, toppling onto her back.

Max sprang from the tree into the midst of the clearing. The vyes howled at the sight of him and seemed poised to flee until Augur's great voice rose above the din.

"Seize him!" roared the blacksmith, turning his mount and hefting up his murderous hammer.

Spurred by terror, the vyes converged on Max, who stood ready. Suddenly a dark shape darted from the woods and cut the vyes down in a blur. With a grimace, Cooper let the last vye fall from his grasp, its matted body sliding to his feet like a bearskin rug. The wavy-bladed kris leapt from the base of the vye's skull, flying to the Agent's hand as he turned to gaze upon the revenant.

"I see," intoned Augur, looking from Cooper to Max. "Lord Astaroth will be most disappointed. I can imagine what he'll say: 'The Hound is but a pup and needs others to do his business.' "

In one seamless motion, Max sprang at Augur's steed and swung the gladius down. The undead creature gave a dreadful cry as Flamma's weapon sheared through its ancient barding to split the bones beneath. With its forelegs severed, the horse collapsed as abruptly as a broken table. Augur was thrown from his saddle, landing heavily on the ground.

Before the revenant could stand, Max sprang again.

Sparks flew and Augur staggered back against a tree with great gashes in his armor. He grasped wildly about, but it was several seconds before the revenant realized Max was well out of reach, already crouched and waiting in the clearing's center. There was a grating sound as Augur's undying steed clacked its bones together and made a pitiful attempt to stand.

"And what will Astaroth say when he finds *you* at the clearing's edge?" said Max, wiping his blade on a nearby vye before rising once again.

The possibility seemed to weigh heavily on Augur. Instead of hefting his hammer, the revenant grasped unsteadily for a signal horn at his side.

"I already knew you were a traitor," hissed Max, "but you're a coward, too."

"A change in days is coming," said Augur coldly. "Rowan will not write my history, boy."

Laughing grimly, Max called to his comrade. "I don't think he likes our chances, Cooper."

But the Agent did not answer.

Max glanced where Cooper had been standing only moments earlier. Now, however, the Agent was slumped against the trunk of a nearby evergreen. Even in the dim light, Max could see sweat pouring off the man's face as he took slow, laboring breaths.

Augur laughed.

"Don't speak to me of shame and cowardice. Rowan brought this upon herself."

It was the witches' curse, coming home to roost at Rowan's hour of need. Raising a mailed hand toward Cooper's helpless body, Augur clenched his fingers shut. Roots and branches snaked about the Agent, pinning him to the trunk and binding him fast. Max darted to the Agent's side as stinging pine needles flew in his face. Several branches had already found their way about Cooper's neck, but the man could merely tug feebly at them while his eyelids fluttered with fever. Max sawed franti-cally at the branches with the gladius.

Behind them, Marley Augur sounded a great blast on his horn.

With a determined cut, Max severed the branches and wrenched Cooper from the tree. Hoisting the Agent upon his shoulder, he turned just in time to see the blur of Augur's ham-mer arcing toward him.

Max twisted away, but the blow still caught him beneath the ribs. The impact sent him crashing into a nearby tree and caused him to lose hold of Cooper. For a moment, Max lay stunned. Breathing was painful and he became dimly aware that, despite Señor Lorca's shirt, several of his ribs had been broken.

He heard sounds all about—birds calling through the air. There was a rustling, and Max felt something dragging along his foot.

Turning his head, Max saw Cooper being pulled away from him. Marley Augur held the Agent by the ankle even as he raised his hammer high for another blow at Max. Max rolled away as the hammer crashed down in a spray of bark and earth. Springing to his feet, Max ducked another blow and slashed the gladius across Augur's face.

The revenant released Cooper and toppled backward, clutching at its mouth, which had split from ear to ear. Gasping from pain, Max snatched up Cooper's kris and hoisted the Agent on his shoulder once again as he scanned the forest.

The surrounding trees were filled with crows—witch familiars—sitting perfectly still among the branches and watch-ing the scene with glittering eyes. One opened its sharp beak to issue a hoarse croak, followed by another and another until the forest erupted into a mocking chorus. Max knew only one op-tion remained.

He turned and ran.

Despite Cooper's earlier counsel, Max made straight for the gorge. He had no choice: Cooper was sick and the only help lay in that direction. Gritting his teeth, Max hurried through the woods, doing his best to keep the jostling Agent steady on his shoulder. Behind him, he heard the echoing call of horns and booming drums while the crows wheeled above, croaking with their sharp black beaks.

Pursuit came quickly.

Dark shapes flitted through the trees on either side—vyes. Some of the creatures ran on two legs, others on four; all were very swift. Max dashed over a narrow stream and ducked into the thick stand of fir trees that marked the entrance to the gorge. The vyes funneled in after.

Max had nearly made it through the dim gorge, his lungs afire, when he realized that he could no longer outrun his pursuers. Gasping for air, he stopped and turned. Some thirty feet behind him, their yellow eyes gleaming in the gloom, were hundreds of tall vyes, lanky as greyhounds and clearly bred for speed. One rose on two legs and beckoned at Max.

"Leave us the man and we'll let you run a little longer," it chided with a cunning smile.

Max did not reply, but caught his breath and backed away, running his hand along the sheer rock wall until he felt it begin to narrow once again. The vyes hissed and laughed and crept forward, some wholly wolfish in appearance, others displaying decidedly human noses and lips and ears in a hideous, slavering visage.

Where the canyon pinched to a breadth of less than ten feet, Max ventured a look behind him. Just ahead were the hidden plains, an open space of gloaming gray. Once there, he knew they would surround him. Keeping his eyes locked on the vyes,

Max slowly lowered Cooper to the ground. The Agent moaned and slumped against the rock while Max rose with a weapon in each hand.

"Nowhere to hide, little Hound," said the closest vye, baring its teeth and bringing up a short spear meant for stabbing. The other vyes rose on their hind legs and howled until the canyon walls shook and pebbles rained upon the hard-packed riverbed.

Despite the howls, Max's world became eerily silent. Standing to his full height, he walked forward to face his enemy and offer the curt soldier's salute that Scathach had taught him. The vyes hesitated, talons twitching as they squinted and balked at this unexpected turn. When Max's hands began to shake, his pursuers came into sharp focus—every hair, tooth, and glittering eye visible in the most marvelous detail. The lurking presence within him began to boil and rage and this time he did not fight it. The Old Magic gathered force and rose within Max like a spring flood, so swift and dreadful that all would be swept away before it. When it burst its banks, Max screamed and the canyon erupted in a sudden flash of blinding white light.

Max awoke to the sound of a crackling campfire. Something moaned beside him and he sat up to see Cooper lying on a bedroll, his face shiny with sweat.

"Ah, he wakes," said a soothing voice nearby.

Max turned to see Astaroth sitting by the fire. The Demon's face was luminescent in the dark, his eyes merry little slits. The composed Demon seemed utterly different from the wounded monstrosity Max had last seen in the Sidh.

Max laughed.

"I'm dreaming."

"No," said Astaroth, smiling serenely. "You are not. This is all very real, I'm afraid."

Max frowned and gazed about at his surroundings. It was night—some dark, damp hour well before dawn. He and Cooper were camped a stone's throw beyond the gorge's opening. Behind Max stretched the river and the broad expanse of plain before the cliffs. Behind Astaroth were hundreds—perhaps thousands—of vyes, ogres, and goblins assembled in stupefying silence before a series of wagons and carts.

"Why aren't they attacking?" asked Max, reaching for the gladius, which was thrust in the ground beside him.

Now it was Astaroth's turn to laugh.

"They *would* like that," he said with an acknowledging smile. "You see, you frighten them, Max McDaniels, and thus they very much want to kill you."

Max looked warily at the vyes—some lean trackers, others bloated and boar-like. Sharp-toothed goblins crouched on their haunches, looking no bigger than cats, reclining at the feet of hunched, brooding ogres. Every creature's eyes were fixed on Max, and they practically simmered with hatred.

"Don't think them savage," said Astaroth. "After all, most creatures respond to fear in such a way—humans most of all. The gorge was nearly choked with their fallen kin, and they're understandably angry and fearful. I daresay you'd blanch if you knew what they wished to do to you—Marley most of all. He's been demoted, you see."

Max heard a hoarse muttering and saw Marley Augur, the ugly gash in his mouth sewn shut with crude stitching. Without his mount, the blacksmith was forced to stand, leaning on his hammer amidst a troop of ogres.

"And why didn't you let him?" asked Max, flicking his attention from the revenant to Astaroth.

"Because I am *not* afraid of you," replied the Demon. "And thus I labor under no blind instinct to destroy you, but instead can admire you as a worthy adversary. Your greatness burned so bright the poor things could not even look upon you. A worthy adversary, indeed. It is not my nature to dishonor such a foe or permit such a thing in my presence."

The Demon's red lips curled in a sly, conspiratorial smile.

"I must confess a certain temptation to consume you, however. I have desired to do so ever since your foolish gesture 'neath Brugh na Boinne. Such pain I haven't felt for an age! I nearly indulged myself until Lord Aamon reminded me that you have not yet earned such an honor. Thus I have restrained myself and offer other gifts as befit your noble stand."

"And what have you to offer?" said Max, still half convinced it was a dream.

"Several things," said Astaroth, smiling. "But let's start simple. Should you surrender the Book, Rowan shall be spared and be allowed a little place beneath its own banner. Should you, Max McDaniels, also agree to become my champion, your reward and renown shall rival that of the kings of old. Should Rowan continue this futile resistance, all it holds dear will perish in agony."

Max glowered and he began to speak, but stopped as Astaroth raised a warning finger.

"Consider well, and let wisdom temper pride," said the Demon. "Like your handsome friend, all of Rowan lies helpless within those walls of rock, weak as women in the pangs of labor. And thus they shall lie for many a day. While a son of the Sidh might evade the witches' curse and make a valiant stand, even he cannot stand forever."

Max looked hard at Astaroth, whose face was grave and contemplative.

"Yes, you *will* fall, Max, and you will do so having sacrificed many innocents at the altar of your pride. This is the second time I have stayed my hand and made a handsome offer. I'm sure you can understand that there will not be a third."

Max climbed painfully to his feet, clutching his side. He gazed back at the river gurgling behind him and the dark walls of rock in the distance where his family and friends lay defenseless. *We need time,* Max thought. *Time to endure the witches' curse, time for David to heal and use the Book, time for something—any-thing—to turn the tide.* Max looked down at the grass and felt the cool air wash over him.

"I need time to think," he said at last.

Astaroth smiled and shook his head. His silky voice fell to a whisper.

> *Blow, blow, thou winter wind*
> *Thou art not so unkind,*
> *As man's ingratitude.*

"Very well," said the Demon, also rising to his feet. "You shall have your day and we shall hope it brings good counsel. As a token of faith, we will not cross the river till you have answered. You have until sunset, and I pray you will think carefully about all you have to lose."

At a gesture from the Demon, the armored ogres stood aside and made way for a horse-drawn cart pulled by two emaciated mares. A boy sat upon the driver's seat and offered a smile in greeting.

It was Alex Muñoz.

The older boy had changed considerably since Max had last seen him in Marley Augur's crypt. Alex's skin had assumed a deathly pallor, and his eyes were faintly luminous. Witch-like tattoos covered the hands that held the reins. He looked down from his perch, proud and disdainful.

"Hello, Max," said Alex. "Long time."

Max nodded, speechless at how his former schoolmate had been transformed. He looked hardly human.

"We're doing things," said Alex. "Great things—and you can be a part of it."

"Alex," said Max, "I tried my best to get you out of there. I'm sorry."

"I'm sure you did," said Alex with a disbelieving smile, "but don't be sorry. You did me a favor, Max, and I'm here to return it."

There was a triumphant, sadistic gleam in the boy's face, and Max felt a prick of nausea in his stomach. Alex reached for a leather satchel and unclasped it to reveal a row of medieval torture implements. He plucked a small, scalpel-like blade from the grisly kit and thumbed its edge.

"I'm not a fighter like you, Max, so I've been trying to make myself useful in other ways," said Alex thoughtfully. "We all need information, and I'd like to think I have a talent for getting it. I've gotten a lot, you know," he boasted, glancing from the knife to Max. "Generals . . . diplomats . . . I even convinced a prime minister to share the most amazing secrets before he died!"

"What's your point?" snapped Max.

Alex climbed into the back of the cart and dragged up two hooded figures so they were propped against the side.

"Well, as good as I am," huffed Alex, "I can always use more practice." He hefted up the limp, masked bundles so Max could see them better. "And right here, I've got two fine specimens to work on—that is, as soon as this little curse has passed and they can really appreciate my work."

Max braced himself as Alex yanked the hoods away.

For a moment, he stared dumbstruck at the pair of prisoners. Max was not surprised to see Connor Lynch.

But he had not expected Ms. Richter.

"That's impossible," breathed Max, gazing at the Director, whose blinking eyes stared blankly ahead. "It's an illusion."

"No," interjected Astaroth, "she is alive, Max. This little bauble protected her from me, you see. An unexpectedly powerful trinket."

Max glanced at the Founder's Ring on Astaroth's hand.

"Give them back," Max whispered, half pleading. "All of them."

"Sorry," said the Demon. "The ring is not for sale at any price—I've got rather skinny fingers and it adds a pleasing bit of heft. The prisoners, however, *are* available for purchase. We've already discussed the price. You have until sunset."

Max had never felt so alone. He nodded at Astaroth's words, but his eyes never left Connor and Ms. Richter, who lay feverish and helpless in the cart. Stepping wearily to Cooper, his broken ribs sent stabs of pain down his side as he slung the Agent onto his shoulder once more and marched off toward the cliffs. When he had crossed the river, Max turned to see Astaroth's army resume its flow from the dark gorge, as silent and steady as an oozing wound.

~ 22 ~

MIST AND SMOKE

Max listened to the sound of the ropes and pulleys as the platform was hauled up the smooth rock wall. He turned and gazed down at the plain below, where massive trebuchets and siege works were assembled just beyond the banks of the river. Turning away, Max shut his eyes and felt exhaustion sink into his bones like a stain. The pulleys ground to a halt.

"Are they dead, mama?" asked a voice—a boy's.

"I don't think so," replied a woman.

Max opened his eyes and gazed at several people—refugees—standing upon the rock ledge. Their faces were fraught with worry; they looked upon Max and Cooper as though the two were ghosts. Shaking off his weariness, Max stood and dragged Cooper off the platform and onto the open ledge.

"Where's Miss Kraken?" Max asked.

"With the others," the woman replied. "They're all very sick."

"Who's in charge?" asked Max.

"We thought it might be you," replied the woman.

"Where's Dr. Rasmussen, then?" asked Max, realizing that the former Workshop leader would not have fallen victim to the witches' curse. For all the man's flaws, Max knew he was very smart and should be consulted. The woman told Max that Rasmussen had been holed up in the generator room, working round the clock as the others fell sick.

Max thanked the woman and left Cooper in her care before trotting off down the dim corridors. He didn't need a map, but merely followed the faint vibrations in the rock walls until he found the generators once again. Rasmussen was there amidst a pile of schematics, his face looking garish as he sipped a thermos of coffee by the light of a fluorescent lantern. Mum and Bellagrog were there, too, their plump bottoms side by side as the sisters knelt at the base of a disconnected generator, shining a flashlight into the dark, tight space beneath it.

"Oh, it's right there!" exclaimed Mum. "But my arm's too short to reach it!"

"And mine's too fat," grumbled Bellagrog, hastily slipping her sister a butcher's knife. "Are you sure you can't just get it for us, love? That bracelet belonged to our Nan, you know. Won't take a moment with your nice long reach."

"In a minute," grumbled Rasmussen, rubbing his temples. The man shook his head and muttered something unintelligible before making several notations on the blueprint. Max cleared his throat.

"Dr. Rasmussen, I need your help."

The man's eyes shot up, and he surveyed Max from behind his thin spectacles.

"Max," he said. "I didn't think I'd be seeing you again. . . . How go things?"

"Not so good," said Max. "I'm calling a meeting. Come with me, and we'll round up the others."

Rasmussen glanced at the schematic and shook his head.

"Tell me when and where the meeting will be," said Rasmussen. "I'm busy at the moment."

Max glanced at Mum and Bellagrog, who were standing by the generator making furious gestures for Max to leave immediately.

"The meeting is right now, and I need your help rounding up the others," said Max, ignoring the hags. "I'm sorry to insist."

"Oh, very well," snapped Rasmussen, tossing his pencil aside. Max let Rasmussen exit first, and the engineer wandered down the corridor, clearly preoccupied with whatever problem he had been solving. The hags scurried over to Max, Bellagrog's whole being trembling with indignation.

"Go away!" hissed the hag.

"Why?" asked Max. "So you can murder him when he isn't looking?"

"Whatchoo talkin' 'bout?" muttered Bellagrog innocently, just as a pair of brass knuckles fell out from beneath her skirt. The hag grimaced and snatched up the weapon and brandished it at Max.

"You're interferin' with Shrope family business!" hissed the furious hag.

"Shrope family business will have to wait," muttered Max. "I need him."

Ignoring Bel's threats and Mum's pleas, Max caught up to the engineer and made his next inquiry.

Within the hour, Max had managed to gather a small council. No grim Agents or wise Mystics were assembled; instead Max sought the advice of a few trusted souls who had been unaffected by the curse. While a Moomenhoven dressed and bandaged his wounds, Max stroked Nick's quills and quietly explained the terms Astaroth had offered. Hannah spoke first.

"What would it mean if Astaroth got his hands on this Book?" she asked.

"The end of this age," said Bob heavily.

"Well, what would the next age be like?" asked Hannah before shifting her attention to one of her children who had dipped its beak in Max's bowl of chicken soup. "Honk, get away from that!" she cried. "That's practically *cannibalism*!" Honk waddled away, looking cross.

"I don't know what the next age would be like," said Max, steering Honk back toward his mother. "I think that would be for Astaroth to decide."

"Well, maybe the world's ready for a new age," said the goose. "Maybe it will be nice!"

"Maybe," conceded Max, cheered a bit by her optimism. "But I don't think we can count on that. For all we know, people will be slaves."

"Better to die free than live a slave," concluded Bob, the ogre's basso voice rumbling from beneath his bandaged face.

"Inspiring credo," muttered Rasmussen dryly, "but I'd rather live to fight another day."

"That is a coward's choice at the moment of truth," said Bob.

"I see," said Rasmussen, tapping his finger. "For one who values freedom, aren't you rather quick to dictate others' options? What if I don't want to die? Why should a teenage boy make such a choice for all of us?"

Bob said nothing, but Mr. McDaniels bristled and jabbed a thick finger at Rasmussen.

"Max isn't trying to make a decision for you," he seethed. "He's asking your advice! What if it were you out there instead of Connor and Ms. Richter?"

"It's not," said Rasmussen.

"Well, maybe it should be!" snapped Mr. McDaniels, fidgeting in his chair.

"Dad," said Max, glancing over, "it's okay. This is hard for everyone."

His red-faced father said nothing but merely scooped up one of the straying goslings and let it play on his lap. Rasmussen shrugged and continued.

"Unless I'm missing something, it seems that Astaroth can acquire the Book and we can continue to live with a sliver of land to call our own. Or Astaroth can inflict a most painful death upon us and acquire the Book anyway. I'll choose the former, thank you."

"But can't we *win*?" asked Max. "Does it have to be a choice between living with failure or dying with it?"

"Given that we're holed up in a cave, accursed, and surrounded by an army that holds a valuable hostage, I'd say winning is out of the question, wouldn't you?" muttered Rasmussen.

"Is there any chance David's well enough to use the Book?" asked Max. "Any chance at all?"

"I don't think so," said Max's father. "Poor David could barely sip that soup."

Max's head drooped.

"Then I've failed," he muttered. "Everything we've done has been for nothing."

A great black mound stirred in the corner. YaYa raised her head from the floor and turned her milky eyes on Max.

"You have *not* failed," said the ancient ki-rin, her voice soft and soothing. "You have fought and bled and nearly died to save your people. My master did the same and still Solas fell! There are powers greater than you, Max McDaniels. And there are powers greater than Astaroth—even he cannot see all ends. Perhaps Hannah is right—perhaps the world is ready for another age. Perhaps she needs it."

Max considered YaYa's words, which both surprised and comforted him.

"Rowan is not what she was," continued YaYa with a note of sorrow. "She has, perhaps, lost her way and become that which she fears. But for all her flaws, there is still love and friendship here. And where those exist, hope remains. Let the Book go. It is a wondrous thing, but it is perilous and has brought ruin upon all who have sought to possess it. Let it pass to the Enemy."

Max closed his eyes and nodded.

"Where is it?" he asked.

"Miss Kraken left it with David before she fell ill," said Mr. McDaniels. "Should I go get it?"

Max shook his head and climbed painfully to his feet. He wound quietly through the caverns, pausing to look in on the sick. On two cots, just past Nigel Bristow and his wife, lay Cooper and Miss Boon. The two were sleeping, their hands clasped together, while Moomenhovens scurried about with basins and cool washcloths to attend the many patients.

Walking along, Max saw Sarah, Lucia, and Cynthia being cared for by their families. Max introduced himself and shared a quiet moment with the group, asking after their needs and patting Cynthia, who merely blinked at him and drifted back to sleep. Where the cavern opened into another ward, Max saw Julie Teller. He stopped a moment and glimpsed his little stack of letters peeking from the pillow beneath her head. A woman approached with her little boy in tow. Max looked up; it was the same woman and child from the ledge.

"Her fever's going down," said the woman, stooping to place her palm on Julie's forehead.

"Are you Mrs. Teller?" asked Max.

"Yes indeed," said the woman, while her beaming son hid behind her. "And we know who you are and what you've risked to keep us safe. I was at your mother's funeral, Max. She would be proud."

Max smiled and embraced her.

"I hope so," he said, saying good-bye and crossing quickly to the ward where David lay.

David opened his eyes as Max came to stop at his cot.

"Have you come to take it away?" he asked.

"I have," said Max, gently prying the Book of Thoth from David's arms. "Are you angry?"

"No," said David, managing a faint smile. "Good riddance."

"I have this terrible feeling, David," said Max suddenly. "A terrible feeling that this is the end of the world." His eyes filled with tears; he ran his finger along the Book's golden cover. "I don't want it to be the end of the world. There are so many things I haven't seen yet."

He began to sob quietly, clutching the Book against his chest.

"Shhh," whispered David, shaking his head. "Don't be sad. When one thing ends, another begins and the powerful play goes on. You are not ending. The world is not ending. Whatever comes, we will face it together. You and I."

Max exhaled and sat still for a moment, his eyes falling on David's night table. In the center of the table was a washbasin and, next to it, an old-fashioned clock. Dipping his hands in the basin's cool water, Max rinsed them clean of the dirt that still caked them. As he scrubbed the mud from his fingers, it formed clouds in the water. Max watched them expand and settle into layers of silt while the seconds ticked and David drifted back to sleep. When the water was still once more, Max rose and left the room.

Many faces crowded together, peering from the rock ledge, while Max sat astride YaYa and the two made their way toward the river. On the far banks waited an army ten thousand strong. At its head was Astaroth, sitting astride a great black wolf with eyes the size of yolks.

YaYa crossed the river and clambered up its shallow banks.

"Have you brought it?" asked the Demon.

"I have," said Max. "You'll take it, release the hostages, and leave as promised."

"Of course," said Astaroth. "And will you be joining us?"

"No," said Max.

"Pity."

Max did not respond. Reaching in David's pack, he removed the Book of Thoth and handed it to the Demon, who held it lightly by his fingertips. The army made not a sound.

Astaroth's expression was almost reverent as he slid a nail beneath the Book's cover, opening it delicately to peer at the very first sheets of papyrus. Max watched in silence as the Demon scoured one page after another. Astaroth suddenly glanced at Max, as though he'd forgotten he was there.

"This is very good, Max," said the Demon. "You have fulfilled our bargain."

At a gesture from Astaroth, Alex Muñoz whipped the thin mares forward and unhitched them from the cart. Within the cart lay Ms. Richter and Connor, bound and gagged and staring at the sky. Ms. Richter looked weak; Connor looked near death. The boy's ruddy cheeks had sunk into sallow hollows, while his unblinking eyes were devoid of their characteristic spark and humor. Max did not know much about possession, but he feared it had taken an irreparable toll on his friend.

"Will Connor live?" asked Max coldly.

"Yes," said Astaroth, "but he has learned that little boys should not meddle in such big affairs. Have you learned your lesson, too?"

"We'll see," said Max.

"That we shall."

Astaroth gazed fondly at the Book as though it were a favorite bedtime story. After several moments, he glanced back at Max. A smile crept across the Demon's face, and he whispered a single word. The syllable rolled off the Demon's tongue, and the wind rose in a gentle sigh. As Max watched, Astaroth and his army began to fade. A moment later, they were gone—vanished like so much mist and smoke.

Several days later, Max sat by the lagoon and watched the slow procession of people and equipment making its way back across the Sanctuary. Before him, glittering in the sun, were the pieces of the *gae bolga*, arranged upon the tapestry Max had taken from the Sidh. As Max reached for one of the larger shards, something broke the surface of the water.

It was Frigga.

The selkie exhaled and then drew a long, slow breath while her eyes adjusted to the light.

"Long swim," she managed at last, blinking at Max while she sputtered for air and bobbed like an enormous cork. A second later, Helga's sleek head appeared next to her sister's and she, too, made the adjustment to light and air. Their adjustment to the ruined Sanctuary took longer.

All the forest had been burned. The cattle herds were dead, their carcasses picked clean and bleaching on the scorched earth. Behind Max, the Warming Lodge lay in a heap of blackened timbers. Other than the creak of the procession, the Sanctuary was eerily silent. No birds chirped, no wind bent the grass, no creatures called or bellowed from the hills.

Helga was speechless, but Frigga seemed philosophical.

"It is bad," she concluded, gliding closer to Max.

"It's terrible," muttered Max. "I can't even bring myself to look at the rest of the campus. I heard the Manse is gone—torn down to its foundation."

"Oh," said Frigga, turning her bewhiskered head to gaze at the Sanctuary tunnel, which was no longer a proper tunnel but merely a broken wall. To Max, the opening looked naked—stripped of its majesty now that the surrounding trees had been hacked and burned away.

Frigga made a sound that might have been a sigh before turning her attention back to him.

"Where you go this year?" she demanded. "Our Max so big and important now, he don't visit Frigga and Helga anymore?"

"No," said Max quickly. "No, it's not that at all. It's just I haven't been here much this year." He thought back to the *Erasmus* and the Lorcas' warm kitchen and the *Kestrel*'s flight to the far-off Sidh. He glanced at the red mark on his wrist. "I've traveled and seen more than I wanted to, Frigga. I'm not really sure I'm your Max anymore. . . . "

The gargantuan selkies promptly shimmied out of the water and basked in the sun on either side of him, as they had when he first arrived at Rowan. Max waxed nostalgic for a moment until an enormous flipper smacked him in the back of his head.

"That no excuse," growled Frigga. "And you will *always* be our Max."

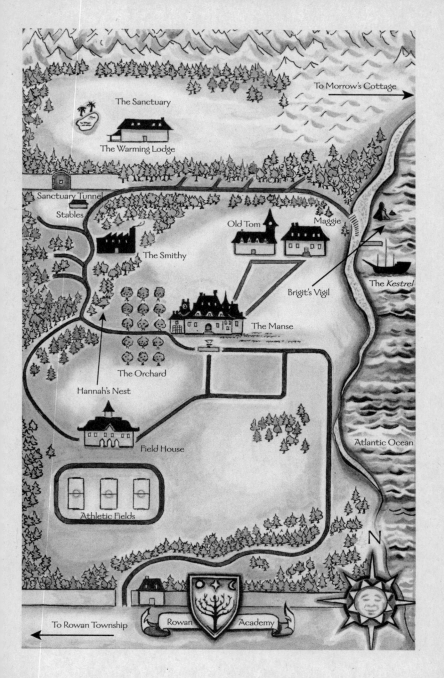

The Sanctuary

To Morrow's Cottage

The Warming Lodge

Sanctuary Tunnel

Stables

The Smithy

Old Tom

Maggie

Brigit's Vigil

The Kestrel

The Manse

The Orchard

Hannah's Nest

Atlantic Ocean

Field House

N

Athletic Fields

To Rowan Township

Rowan   Academy

ACKNOWLEDGMENTS

As a second book, *The Second Siege* posed a number of distinct challenges. Chief among these were developing existing characters, introducing new ones, and accelerating The Tapestry's pace while increasing its scale. To write and illustrate this book on a deadline while teaching has been the greatest challenge of my life. Without the support of family, friends, students, and colleagues, my sanity would have undoubtedly taken an ugly turn. I have many people to thank: Sean Carroll and Lisa Tarter, Christopher and Kirstin Casgar, Scott and Loretta Dahnke, Lesley Dalton, Jacquie Duncan, Michael and Catherine Farello, Heidi Hankins, Scott Kemper, Matt and Maya Markovich, Michael Markovich, Marilyn Mawn, Ed and Betsy McDermott, John and Jennifer Neff, Victoria Neff, Travis Nelson, Jill Paganelli, Brian and Elizabeth Payne, Doug and Sarah Reed, Josh and Ryn Richards, Gordon and Krista Rubenstein, Orestes Tarajano, Gavin Turner, and all of my colleagues, my students, and their families at Stuart Hall High School in San Francisco.

Special mention and my deepest gratitude go to my editor at Random House, Nicholas Eliopulos, whose brilliant feedback and patient prodding were essential to shaping up the second book and bringing it into being. That Nick always manages to do so with grace and good humor is both impressive and humbling.

My final thanks go to my mother, Terry Neff Zimmerman, whose tireless encouragement and timely feedback helped propel Max McDaniels and David Menlo across the Atlantic, deep within the Frankfurt Workshop, and, literally, out of this world. . . .

ABOUT THE AUTHOR

Henry H. Neff is a former consultant and history teacher from the Chicago area. Today he lives in Montclair, New Jersey, with his wife and young son. You can visit Henry at henryhneff.com.

Want to find out what fate has in store for
Max McDaniels?

Turn the page for a sneak peek
at the third book
of The Tapestry.

THE FIEND AND THE FORGE

~ 1 ~

THE MOON HAS A FACE

It was not the warm sun or the bleating lambs that woke Max McDaniels. Rather, it was the soft patter of little feet—sly, terribly eager feet—that converged upon him as he lay amidst the ripening corn. Max kept still while the first of his visitors hopped onto his chest. He did not stir at the second or third. But once the twelfth clambered up with an exasperated peep, Max cracked an eye and smiled.

Twelve goslings stood upon him. Downy heads bobbed; inscrutable eyes glistened like wet pebbles. With a sudden, triumphant honk, the boldest stepped forward and tapped its hard little beak on Max's breastbone. The others followed suit, and soon Max writhed and chuckled beneath the Lilliputian assault.

"Ouch!" he exclaimed, shooing halfheartedly. "I'm awake!"

The pecking continued.

"MAX!" bellowed a shrill female voice from nearby.

Several crows took flight as a plump white goose crashed through the cornstalks and into Max's row, looking frantically from side to side.

"There you are!" exclaimed the goose. "Sleeping away like a lazy bottom!"

"Bottoms can't be lazy, Hannah," murmured Max. He plucked the last of the marauding goslings off his stomach and placed it on the ground, where it promptly resumed its indiscriminate pecking.

"Like a lazy bottom!" sang the goose, aspiring to an operatic tremolo.

"Bravo," said Max, rising to his feet.

"Thank you," replied Hannah, curtsying. She waddled forward and gave him a motherly once-over. "Max, there's a gazillion things to do, and you should know better than to sneak off for a handful of winks."

"I've been working late every day for a month," protested Max, emphasizing the point with a bleary yawn.

"Excuses, excuses," retorted Hannah. "Stoop down a bit, dear." Max stood in silent resignation while the goose flicked bits of dirt and hay from his shirt and smoothed his dark hair into a respectable shape. She sighed. "You of all people should know how special tomorrow is. . . ."

"I do," said Max. "I'll do my part."

"You'll do your part *now*," she said pointedly. "On the double!"

The matronly goose buffeted Max forward with her powerful wing and whistled for the goslings to fall in line. They did so dutifully, and the group now formed an orderly column as they marched through the cornfield. When they arrived at the Sanctuary's main clearing, Hannah flapped her wings excitedly.

"Nearly all back to normal and pretty as a picture," she crowed, gesturing toward the rebuilt Warming Lodge. The long, low building seemed almost to bask next to its small lagoon. Its timbered walls were clean and smooth. There was no trace of splintered wood or blackened stone, nothing to suggest that this very building had been recently reduced to embers.

"Hmmm," said Max, privately thinking that Rowan Academy, while largely rebuilt, would never be "back to normal." Only six months ago, the demon Astaroth's armies had rampaged across the school's sprawling campus, burning its forests, razing its structures, and slaughtering its flocks as they marched upon Rowan's final refuge in the far cliffs of the Sanctuary. Many lives had been lost. It had been Max who ultimately withstood the enemy, fighting on alone until the only remaining option was to surrender the Book of Thoth to the demon that coveted it. It had been a wrenching decision, but Astaroth had seemingly kept his word and fulfilled their bargain. The monstrous armies were spirited away, and Rowan had been left in peace—battered and broken, but free to rebuild at its own pace.

By any standard, that pace had been remarkable. Using magic and muscle, crops were planted, stone was quarried, forests were raised, and herds were restocked. The Sanctuary's broad plain was now thick with grain fields, lush orchards, and grazing herds that were hemmed by a broad forest that sloped up into the mountains. Max inhaled the September air and spied a family of shimmering pixies as they skimmed toward a yellowing oak.

Recent glimpses of such notoriously shy creatures had roused Max's curiosity. There were other changes, too. Since Astaroth had claimed the Book, Max had felt the world *thawing*—as though the earth had clomped in from the cold, stamped snow from her boots, and settled by a comfortable fire. To his sharp senses it was unmistakable: a mild sweetness on the wind, an unprecedented richness to colors, a whispering chorus of new life emerging, growing, straining to claim a corner of its own. Max could almost hear roots spreading eagerly through soil, fragile flower petals unfolding, and ancient things stirring in their burrows.

"A new age is beginning," he muttered.

"It sure is, honey," remarked Hannah brightly, herding her goslings toward the Sanctuary gate. "And just like I predicted, Mother Nature was due for one."

"Can you feel it, too?" he asked. At times he wondered

if he was uniquely sensitive to such things. Max McDaniels was a son of the Sidh, a hidden land where gods and monsters slumbered amidst the hills. As the child of an earthly mother and an Irish deity, Max straddled a tenuous line between mortal and immortal. Within his blood coursed rare sparks of the Old Magic: primal forces that could make Max as wild and powerful as a storm. Hundreds of enemies had given way before Max during the Siege of Rowan. Not even Cooper, scarred commander of Rowan's elite Red Branch, would train with him anymore.

"Of course I can feel it," replied Hannah, her head bobbing in time with her step. "Things growing, the air brimming and crackling with magic. It's like a ray of sunshine on my beak! You'd have to be a ninny not to feel it!"

"Do you believe Astaroth's behind it all?" asked Max.

"Who knows?" The goose shrugged. "But once he got his hands on that book, I'd wager he's been changing a thing or two. Can't say it's ruffling my feathers, either."

"So you think things are better?" asked Max, feeling somewhat defensive. He had been expecting fire and brimstone following Astaroth's victory, not a peaceful, bountiful summer. The quiet was unsettling.

"Around here they are," Hannah concluded. She spread her wings and puffed out her chest to absorb the autumn sunshine. The goslings imitated their mother.

"But what about the cities?" Max mused. "What about everything else outside Rowan?" His mind raced from nearby Boston to New York and other cities around the world. Since the Siege, travel beyond Rowan's battered gates had been forbidden.

"Not my concern." Hannah shrugged again. "As long as I've got twelve mouths to feed and a nest to mind, I've got enough on my plate. Besides, honey, humans can look after themselves. They always have," she said. "Anyway, I've done what I was supposed to do: find *you* and direct your lazy bottom back toward the Manse. So you go mow lawns or weed gardens while this goose goes and gets her *groom* on!"

"Excuse me?" asked Max.

"Deluxe feather tufting, Swedish beak massage, and a pedicure," explained Hannah. "The dryads owe me big-time. Big-time! So be a dear and watch the goslings while you do your chores. You know they just love it when you babysit. Mind you that Li'l Baby Ray's been wheezy, so don't let Honk play too rough. And Millie's not allowed any sweets since she's been a *very* naughty gosling, and . . ."

Max's eyes glazed over while Hannah recited a litany of special instructions for each of her children—her fidgeting, utterly indistinguishable children. Once Millie's pesky skin irritation had been addressed, Hannah waddled away, greeting a nearby work crew with the amiable ease of a big-city mayor. As soon as she disappeared into a grove of olive trees, Max felt a sharp peck on his shin. The goslings were jostling at his feet. Implacable stares met his own.

"Mind your beaks," said Max, and with that he led them

toward a mossy wall and the stout wooden door that separated the Sanctuary from the rest of Rowan Academy.

A symphony of sounds greeted them as they made their
way through the tunnel-like arch of interlacing trees. Ham-
mers, saws, shouts, laughter, and innumerable other noises
blended together in a happy hum of endeavor. Emerging into
daylight, Max saw hundreds of chattering students and adults
touching up the stables' trim and fitting the last planks for
a riding pen where palominos pranced and whinnied. The
invigorating air smelled of fresh paint, autumn leaves, and
the sea. Max felt a rumbling in his stomach and toyed with
the notion of stealing into the kitchens for a bite. . . .

But duty called. Max led his little charges to the broad
expanse of grass and gardens that served as Rowan's central
quad. On one sizable square of lawn, clusters of children
were polishing colossal seashells with rags they had dipped
in tubs of yellow goop. Some of the seashells were no bigger than a beach ball, while other ancient specimens loomed
large as mail trucks. The yellow goop was a thickened form
of phosphoroil—as the waxy, pungent substance was ap-
plied to the shells, they began to give off a soft glow, like
gargantuan fireflies. The effect was diminished by daylight,
but even so a golden haze hovered above the lawns as
though El Dorado lay beneath. Max stepped past a giggling
group of children and sized up an imposing nautilus.

For the better part of two hours, Max polished the shell.
It was monotonous but satisfying work as each smooth,

curved section was burnished to a natural gleam until the oil saturated its surface and it began to emit a phosphorescent glow. While Max worked, the goslings were reasonably well behaved. They seemed content to gaze at their ghostly, distorted reflections in the shell, until Honk managed to roll—or plunge—himself into a tub of phosphoroil. While Max scrubbed the indignant, struggling bird, a shadow fell over him.

"Well, what have we here?" chuckled a familiar voice.

Turning, Max saw Dr. Rasmussen, the deposed Director of the Frankfurt Workshop. The hairless, nearly skeletal scientist grinned at Max from behind his thin spectacles. Some dozen adults accompanied him.

"Ladies and gentlemen," said the engineer, "please allow me to introduce Max McDaniels. This young man visited the Workshop last year, but given the circumstances, I fear that many of you did not get to meet him. Let's amend that now. . . ."

Max nodded at the strangers as they were named. They did not return his greeting, but merely stared at him with expressions of cold curiosity. Putting aside their rudeness, Max was surprised to see members of the Workshop at Rowan, much less in the company of Dr. Rasmussen. The Workshop was a techno-centric society—a scientific faction that had splintered off from Rowan long ago and now lived within a network of self-sufficient subterranean cities. Until the previous year, Jesper Rasmussen had been the

Workshop's Director, but his colleagues had driven him out on Astaroth's orders.

Since that day, Rasmussen had taken refuge at Rowan, offering his technical expertise. Unfortunately, his expertise was invariably peppered with arrogant asides, and requests for his input had dwindled away. He was now Rowan's most sullen dignitary.

"When did they arrive?" asked Max, looking past Rasmussen at the visitors.

"This morning," replied Dr. Rasmussen. "They're here to . . . make amends."

"With you or with us?" asked Max, keenly aware that the Workshop had done nothing to resist Astaroth's assault on Rowan or the world at large. For all Max knew, they had by now sworn allegiance to the Demon.

Rasmussen ignored the pointed question.

"Does Cooper know they're here?" asked Max.

"Yes, yes," muttered Rasmussen. "Everyone here has the requisite authorization. Thank you for making sure, however." He offered a prim smile to his colleagues. "Wherever would we be without the endearing insolence of teenagers?" He gleaned one halfhearted laugh, but no more. Shooting Max a peevish glance, Rasmussen beckoned his colleagues along. They began to follow until one of them—an angular, humorless-looking man—abruptly stopped.

"What is that mark, Jesper?" asked the man, pointing at Max's wrist.

Dr. Rasmussen frowned and peered closely at the crimson tattoo of an upraised hand.

"Hmmm," mused Dr. Rasmussen. "Agent Cooper has the same one, I believe."

"You did not mention anything about a mark," said the man, sounding aggrieved.

"What is he talking about?" asked Max, snatching his arm away from Rasmussen.

Rasmussen offered no response, but merely scrutinized the tattoo for a few more seconds before waving his colleagues on. The group departed with the exception of the man who had first observed the mark. He stood rooted to his spot, allowing his pale, watery eyes to wander over Max's face and body without a hint of hurry or embarrassment. Max might have been a laboratory rat.

"Why don't you just take a picture?" Max snapped.

The man blinked, as though Max's question had jolted him from deep contemplation. Strolling closer, he rested his hands upon his knees and leaned forward until his thin, impassive face hovered only inches away.

"And why would I do that?" the man whispered. "I can see you whenever I want. . . ."

Straightening, the man offered a curious smile, and walked briskly away to rejoin his colleagues. Max felt a surge of anger as he watched them go; he despised the Workshop and its smug representatives. Still, it suddenly dawned on him that these very representatives were from *outside.* The Workshop was based in Europe. Surely they would know the status of various governments and cities; they would know what was happening in the wide world beyond.

"Hey!" called Max, running after them. "Hold up."

He caught up to them as they were climbing the Manse's broad steps. Rasmussen tried to hurry them inside, but they stopped and turned in response to Max's breathless question.

"How is the rest of the world?" Max asked. "What's going on in Beijing? Or Berlin? Or Paris!"

He was met with silence. Clearing his throat, Rasmussen glanced at his colleagues. An olive-skinned woman in a pale gray suit shook her head, and Rasmussen's thin lips tightened.

"Max, do yourself a favor and forget about Paris," he said softly. "It's forgetting about you. . . ."